Honey Bunches of Oats

One day you will be mine, oh yes you will be mine

SYN

Davern Ramone — DAVERN RAMONE

authorHOUSE®

AuthorHouse™
1663 Liberty Drive
Bloomington, IN 47403
www.authorhouse.com
Phone: 1-800-839-8640

© 2010 Davern Ramone. All rights reserved.

No part of this book may be reproduced, stored in a retrieval system, or transmitted by any means without the written permission of the author.

First published by AuthorHouse   8/11/2010

ISBN: 978-1-4520-6716-2 (e)
ISBN: 978-1-4520-6715-5 (sc)

Library of Congress Control Number: 2010911981

Printed in the United States of America

This book is printed on acid-free paper.

Because of the dynamic nature of the Internet, any Web addresses or links contained in this book may have changed since publication and may no longer be valid. The views expressed in this work are solely those of the author and do not necessarily reflect the views of the publisher, and the publisher hereby disclaims any responsibility for them.

To Kirby H for all your help and support over the years.

Special thanks to:
Krissy VanAlstyne,
Kiki Von Waou,
Amy Louis of Organic Chaos for all your patience and beautiful artwork,
and all my friends for your kind words that helped keep me writing.

1

"Hello?"

"Hey man, it's Pete, you up?"

Looking down the bed at his nicely formed tent, Holden said to himself with a snicker, 'hello there, you're up early.' Answering Pete, he said, "Yeah, some of me is" laughing at his own inside joke. "What do you want?"

"Jeff and Andrew are coming into town around three. We're going for a bite to eat then planning a late night, you in?"

"Uh…Ya, what time is it," Holden asked looking over to his nightstand to see the flashing 12:00. "Fuck." he said to himself annoyed at the power outage and the fact he was to lazy to get a battery backup. He didn't wait for Pete to answer. "Yeah, call me when they get there"

"Will do." Pete agreed.

After hanging up the phone, Holden rolled over a couple of times but couldn't fall back asleep. "FUCK!" He got out of bed and walked into the living room still in his boxers and sat on the couch. He turned on the TV and opened the lid to his laptop to check what happened in the world while he was asleep. Messages received 0, emails 0. 'Oh to be popular,' he thought. Checking the clock on his laptop it said nine o'clock and he decided to lie down on the couch to watch TV and take his morning nap. The phone rang again. "Hello?"

"Hey man, you ready? We're going out in half an hour."

"HALF AN HOUR?? I thought you said threeish," Holden said in horror.

"Dude, it is three."

"What? Fuck, alright. The boys in town? I need a shower; I'll stop by when I'm done."

"Sounds good," Pete acknowledged. Holden was amazed he slept so long, he had to verify the time on his laptop. The TV was now showing some cooking show, the chef was explaining how to make the perfect Chicken Kiev. Yeah right, Holden said to himself as he clicked off the TV. He leaned over to the laptop once again, plugged in the speakers located in the bathroom; he stared at the screen for a moment trying to decide what to listen too off his extensive play list. He decided on some rock to shake off his late morning, early afternoon nap. Zeppelin was the obvious choice. "I has got to get the led out" he said with to himself with a horrible British accent. The speakers came alive with the lyrics "Hey hey momma said the way you move, gonna make you sweat, gonna make you groove". Ahh, *Black Dog*, almost perfect, his fingers slid across the volume control to the max. 'Now it's perfect.' He mused.

After the shower he quickly dressed, threw on the first things out of his dresser and after sliding on his favourite Chuck Taylor's he ran out the door. Pete's house was only five blocks away, but Holden still felt the need for his MP3 player. He used Billy Talent as his walking music.

Ding dong. Ding dong. Holden pressed the doorbell over and over again. He let out a chuckle as the song *Why Do Birds Suddenly Appear* popped into his head. As he was pushing the doorbell he heard his friend shout to him from an open upstairs window. Holden slowly opened the door and saw his buddy Andrew standing at the top of the stairs. Before Holden could even say hello, Andrew yelled, "Heads up asshole!" and Holden saw a can of beer come flying down the stairs at him. Instinctively he caught the beverage, cracked it open and had his first sip of beer before he could even take off his shoes. He knew it was going to be a very long night. "Damn nice to see you Andrew." Holden said sincerely.

He walked up the stairs and saw the boys wrapped up in an intense game of Guitar Hero. Holden sat down and took another drink of beer. "So, what brings you guys into town?"

"Jeff has a job interview at some law firm and I thought I'd come for the road trip." Andrew said.

"Law firm eh? Look at you growing up so fast." Holden said with a laugh.

The four had been friends since elementary school and they had just finished their last year of college. Upon graduation Jeff and Andrew went back to their home in Muskoka for the summer while Holden moved from his school in Oshawa to Toronto. Pete, who went to college with Andrew and Jeff in Toronto, elected to find work in the city. It was their first weekend they hung out since graduation. Holden was happy to finally be living in Toronto. He spent the last two years alone in Oshawa taking the Sports Administration course while his childhood friends all elected to go the same college in Toronto. Holden now had an entry level job with a local roller hockey team. Pete took Law Enforcement and was recruited by the Metro Toronto Police and was going to leave in a couple of weeks for his training. Jeff with his legal assistant course under his belt was hoping to get a job with the prestigious law firm he had an interview with the next day. Andrew had taken Office Administration and had a job lined up at a resort in Muskoka starting Labour Day weekend. It was possibly one of the last times the four would be able to get together for the foreseeable future.

"Damn nice to see you guys." Holden randomly said.

"Awe, do you need a hug?" Pete asked sarcastically as he continued to kick Jeff's ass at Guitar Hero. The other two guys gave him a courtesy chuckle.

Several beers went down range when Pete finally decided he was hungry. They finished up their drinks and headed out the door. Although it was supper time, the restaurant they picked was fairly empty and they got their seats right away. Their waitress was a beautiful young blonde; her shirt was at least one size to small, accentuating her rather large tits. The boys couldn't have been happier with their server. They ordered their first round of drinks and then looked through the menu. Holden hoped to order Chicken Kiev, he didn't understand why but he was craving it. Finding it under entrees, Holden threw the menu on the table just as the first round showed up. He looked around the restaurant; every waitress was blonde and very ample. He began to wonder if they had walked into Hooters by accident. Nope, they hadn't he determined. Apparently the restaurant just had a fantastic recruiting program. The waitress flirted with the table as she took their order. Jeff was obviously in love with their waitress so Andrew, being the friend that he was, made small talk with her. He casually mentioned the fact that they were from out of town and only in Toronto for a few days. She took the bait, asking them where they were from and what the special occasion was that brought them to the city. Andrew threw his arm around Jeff and loudly exclaimed that they were there because Jeff had an interview at a law firm to become a lawyer. Jeff, the shiest of the bunch, started to blush and quietly began to correct his friend saying that he wasn't actually a lawyer. Andrew cut him off, making him take the promotion and all the attention that comes with such a job, whether he liked it or not. Obviously impressed, the waitress focused most of her flirting on Jeff for the rest of the night.

The meals came and went, as did several more beers. Jeff was slowly coming out of his shell with a boost in confidence from the waitress' flirting and, of course, the liquid courage didn't hurt. Before the bill showed up they started coming up with a plan for the rest of the night. Andrew, the ladies man of the group, at least in his own mind, said that he heard a new "ballet" opened up in town and said he would like to stop in and say hi to the ladies. All the guys knew that he was referring to a new strip club. It was like teasing kids with candy; once the seed of naked women was planted in their brain there was no stopping them. They jumped at the idea and they were off. Jeff was still obviously worked up from the waitress, Misty or Mimi or whatever the hell her name was. He almost ran to the strip club. As the boys rounded a corner they saw the big flashing pink neon sign. "Fantasia." Pete opened the door and Jeff almost plowed him over to get inside. The doorman stopped them; despite the fact they were college graduates, the doorman still had the nerve to ask them for their ID. Pete huffed in mock discontent at their inconvenience, getting a laugh out of the group. They quickly took their seats on pervert's row so they wouldn't miss a thing. Girl after girl came on stage, all shapes and sizes. The odd girl came up and as sexily as she could and asked each one of them if they would like a dance. They decided their beers and the floor show were good enough for the time being. It was now 8 pm; the evening crew was starting to filter in. After becoming bored with the generic girls on stage with their thump, thump, thump generic hip hop music, Holden began to look around at the girls walking in. He always found the girls in their street clothes much sexier than the scantily clad "stripper outfits."

"HOLY SHIT!" Holden yelled, turning around slapping Jeff across the chest, almost knocking him out of his chair.

"What the fuck..." Jeff asked confused.

"LOOK!" Holden said with enthusiasm.

"Oh my god." was all Jeff said.

The other two guys started to cheer when they noticed the waitress from the restaurant walking in carrying a bag. "You think she dances here?" Jeff finally muttered.

They all agreed it wasn't out of the realm of possibility, but also said there was a chance she was only waitressing there as well.

Only a minute later, out popped the waitress wearing big plastic high heels, white knee highs, a very short plaid skirt with slits to the waist band on both sides, and a tiny white blouse with only one button done up. Her red lace bra shone through her blouse under the black lights. Holden turned to Jeff, "I think the chances of her dancing here greatly improved." Jeff just nodded in agreement. Andrew leaned forward shouting for the group to give him money. Pete and Holden knew what he was up to, so they freely coughed up some dough. After collecting all the cash, Andrew frantically waved the money into the air. The waitress recognized them and a big smile lit up her face. She pranced over to them, her tits bouncing freely with every step. Definitely hot. She leaned into Andrew; he whispered something into her ear. She looked at Jeff and gave him a wink. Jeff, now speechless, started to blush and he gave her a wave back. She slowly, seductively walked over to Jeff, gently grabbed his hand and led him to the back room. Jeff was only too happy to follow her. Holden slid over into Jeff's chair. "One down and three to go." He said with a laugh. Andrew was the next to go when a beautiful French girl wearing a corset and thigh highs approached him, leaving only Pete and Holden on "the row".

Even with the crew change, the girls all looked the same; the music was the same generic dance club music. Holden definitely liked the odd beat but thought it was too much. He wondered why they didn't break it up with different genres of music. His train of thought was interrupted as HEY HEY MOMMA SAID THE WAY YOU MOVE, GONNA MAKE YOU SWEAT, GONNA MAKE YOU GROOVE came blaring over the clubs sound system. The D.J. paused the song after the opening line and said "Ladies and gentlemen, get ready to beg for forgiveness because taking the stage next is Syn." The rock started again the second the D.J. stopped talking. Holden's attention was fully on the stage when the most gorgeous woman he had ever seen walked up the stairs. Holden first saw her very long curly black hair. Her big brown eyes looked as sweet and innocent as the best girl next door. Her devilish smile told a different tale though. She had a well tanned complexion and it was accented by her dark hair. She had on a black mesh shirt, the holes were big enough to reveal her black plastic bra. The bra had a white trim and a skull half covering a broken heart and cross bones on her left breast. She had her thumbs through holes in the sleeves of her shirt, somewhat hiding her hands except for the very tips of her fingers which had black painted fingernails. She was also wearing black cotton boy cut panties, complete with white trim and the skull with broken heart cross bone design on her left cheek. Syn was written in the heart. Black knee high fish net socks and a pair of converse Chuck Taylor high tops with the tops turned down completed the outfit. She walked around the stage making eye contact with every guy in the place. Her movements were very graceful and in perfect rhythm to the music. Holden couldn't take his eyes off her. Pete elbowed Holden, acknowledging Holden's lifelong weakness for punk rock girls. Holden ignored him; he was in a trance watching Syn's every move. Besides the look, he wondered what made her different, what made her amazing. Holden tried to convince himself that he was being silly; she was a dancer like all the others. Only the music was different. That was it. He tried to convince himself that he didn't fall instantly in love with her, that he only loved the song, he thought back to his shower earlier in the day. Despite his objections he still couldn't stop watching her. Her dancing, her crowd interaction was like no other. She obviously really enjoyed what she did. As she worked her way visually through the crowd, she finally met Holden's steel grey eyes. She stumbled and stopped dead. Their eyes locked on each other. She instantly picked Holden out of a crowd. She had many admirers, guys that came back night after night to see her. She flirted with each and everyone knowing she needed them to make a living but once she saw Holden she knew he was different. Not only were his eyes glued to her watching every movement but she saw something deeper. He had wavy blonde hair and was wearing a button up short sleeve plaid shirt that clung to his muscular chest. What made him different she thought was his smile. His jaw was defined and strong looking but he had an innocent, sheepish look about him. She knew he was waiting to see her naked but she also knew he wasn't like the other perverts in the place. She regained her composure once she realized she was still on stage, she began getting back into the groove of the music but she continued to look towards Holden giving him her sexiest, baddest smile. The first song ended, the familiar guitar intro of Marilyn Manson's "I put a spell on you" started up. 'Fuck, she has style; I'll give her that.' Holden thought. The second song is when the dancer typically begins to shed clothing. Holden was nervous; it was the first time he ever felt like that in a strip club. Pete noticed Holden's anxiety and tried to make fun of him but Holden just blocked him out. As a matter of fact Holden managed to block out the entire crowd making it feel like she was dancing only for him. She did a spin around the famous brass pole and continued to twirl to center stage, her right foot kicked her ass then slammed to the stage bringing her twirl to a halt. She was now standing directly in front of Holden, her feet apart, she stared down at Holden with an intensity like no other. Her smile faded, her eyes were now burning into him, she reached down, grabbed the bottom of her mesh shirt and slowly pulled it over her head. Holden was so fucking hard, he was worried if he had to stand up too fast there wouldn't be enough blood flow to his brain to keep him stable. With a toss, her shirt went sliding towards the stairs of the stage. Her eyes kept an eye on the garment ensuring it landed a safe distance away from her. Her body remained still; she snapped her head back towards Holden. She reached back to unclasp her bikini top, forcing her elbows as far back as possible showing off her perfectly formed tits. The top loosely fell open as she bent at her waist, her head almost touched the floor as she looked at the table behind her. She reached back and ran her hand up her leg and over her pussy. She then put both her hands on the floor, her head tilted up so their eyes met again, giving Holden a quick smile. She realized she broke character and then forced herself to be the hard punk rock girl again. The intensity was back as she began to very slowly rise. Her top fell to the ground and her hands reached behind her neck, her forearms buried themselves into her tits showing off a star tattoo on her right elbow. Syn looked at Holden, Holden thought her bare stomach looked very hot, she wasn't as skinny as the other girls but she was also nowhere near chubby. She had more mass giving her some very sexy curves as well as a unique softness if you were to touch her. Holden wanted her so badly. He tried to convince himself not to be stupid, she was a professional, he knew he couldn't fall for her. He then realized she must have saw his puppy dog eyes and she was playing him up because he was mostly likely going to pay for dances after. She spun around, showing Holden her perfect ass; she then dropped her arms to the cheers of the crowd on the other side of the stage. She reached her hands back, digging her fingers deep into her ass cheeks and she began to squeeze. With a flip of her hair, she looked back at Holden and gave him a wink. She moved around the stage again, walked to the pole, climbed to the top and in a show of true athleticism she used her arms to extend her body out fully parallel to the floor. Everyone's jaw dropped. Then, even more amazingly she just let go of the pole dropping to the ground. Everyone thought she fell; Holden began to stand to help her until he saw her twist in the air and she landed in a push up position. With one pump she pushed herself up so she was standing. Everyone applauded her exceptional dancing skills; she ignored the accolades and carried on with her routine. Putting one foot behind her, resting on her toes, she used that foot as a pivot and she began to spin several times as she slowly spiraled on to the floor, ending up on her side, once again with her back to Holden. He found it very frustrating, he wanted to see her face and her tits but he appreciated the game she was playing. It added some excitement to the night and having a hot, naked girl flirt with him, regardless of the reason was always an ego boost. The guys across from Holden appeared to be getting a good show as they cheered. All Holden could see were her hands moving over her body. He recognized the last verse in the song; her second set was almost over. Holden didn't want to see it end but he knew the third set was for all the marbles, he would hopefully have the opportunity to finally see his goddess naked. She collected her things, left the stage and disappeared into the changing room. "Syn will be right back for her last dance shortly" the DJ announced. *Fuck, I don't' want to wait that long,* Holden thought to himself. On the upside Holden had time to finish his beer and order another. Andrew and Pete were still gone. Holden looking at the two vacant chairs turned to Jeff. "They must be having a good time" he shouted. Pete nodded in agreement, he elected not to try and speak over the blasting music.

As the filler song ended, the lights went out, except for 2 red spotlights. The music started, the DJ came across the speakers once again "Syn is back for her last song of the set, but don't get to close there is no absolution for this Syn." She looked back at him giving the DJ a mock glare of discontent. She changed during her off song. She was now wearing a long elegant black dress with the slit up to the side of her waist and fishnet gloves that went to her elbow but she was still wearing her Chuck Taylor's and fishnet knee highs. Holden laughed to himself, "yup" he though, "I never go anywhere without mine either," as she stood in center stage, the two spot lights went to black. The sound of a church bell rang, with the first ring the red spot lights flashed, with the next ring white spot lights flashed, it continued for 4 more rings of the bell, during the flashes Holden could tell Syn was focused back on him. He could feel her passion, her intensity burning into him. Fuck, he thought, he wanted her so badly. As the instruments joined the bells for "Hells Bells", the full set of lights came on matching the beat of the music. She again walked slowly around the stage, every movement in rhythm with the music; she made it look so effortless but so intense. She was like no other dancer he had ever seen before. She dropped to her knees and crawled over to him, her long black curly hair hanging down off her shoulders. Holden wanted to reach out and grab it, pull her to the ground and fuck her right there on stage. He tried to control himself as she moved his beer out of the way, grabbed him by his short blonde hair and pulled him towards her. She slid her cheek down his, bit his ear and whispered "Hi, I'm Syn." and then she pushed Holden back in his chair and said something else. Holden couldn't quite make it out and then she continued on with her routine. "What did she just say?" Holden frantically asked Pete.

"Dunno" was all he replied. "FUCK," what did she say Holden asked himself.

Holden tried to let it go, he grabbed his beer and sat back trying to look relaxed as she slowly slipped out of her dress; she was looking right at him as the gown fell to the stage floor. During the break she didn't put her bikini top back on so her tits were now fully exposed to Holden. She could see the lust in his eyes as she slid her hands behind her neck playing with her hair. He knew she was intentionally letting him get a good look at her. Holden continued to look into her eyes as she gave her own hair a pull forcing her eyes to the ceiling as if she could read Holden's mind. Holden took the opportunity to stare; her tits were perfect. Natural and they were no bigger than a B cup which coincidently was just slightly bigger than Holden's preference but he was quiet alright with it. She looked back down at him giving him a knowing look like she just caught the kid in the cookie jar. She turned away; she was still wearing her boy cut panties that accentuated her ass perfectly. She turned her side to Holden and dropped to her knees, she then laid back onto her elbows, leaning her head back until it touched the stage. Her toned legs showed great definition under the stage lights. Her stomach was very hard and flat and her tits were firm and perky. The way she was positioned was by far the sexiest pose a woman could do in any circumstance, Holden was definitely hooked. She slid her legs out straight then pulled her knees to her chest. She moved her arms to her waist and hooked her thumbs into the waist band of her panties. The crowd anticipating her getting naked erupted once again. Holden could tell that she really thrived on the crowd's cheers. Her intensity level increased and with a quick move she ripped her panties off her ass, past her knees and over her shoes and gave them a toss towards the stairs. She gently opened her legs giving some guys at a table by the stairs a nice show. Her hand moved to her breast, momentarily covering them then she slid it down her ribs, her stomach to her pussy. Holden couldn't exactly see what she was doing but the guys at the table seemed to be enjoying the show. Her hand slowly made its way back up her body to her lips; her finger disappeared into her mouth as she licked the finger that was just inside her pussy. She tilted her head so she was staring right at Holden as she ever so slowly stuck out her tongue to give her finger a long lick. Then she slid it back into her mouth sucking off all the flavour. She leaned over onto her side; her knees were slightly bent, like she just rolled over in bed. Their eyes were locked onto each other. She rested her head on her hand as they had a stare down. Neither of them wanted to be the first to look away, the music continued to play in the background but neither of them were paying attention to it. Holden wasn't sure how long she was laying there but before they knew it the song was over and without hesitation she just stood up and walked off the stage. Another song played meaning another girl would soon be on stage but Holden knew none of the others would compare to Syn. Holden fell back into his chair as some other top 40 piece of crap started on the speakers and some other bubble gum teenager took the stage. Holden felt abandoned. 'What in god's name was I thinking, getting worked up like that over a stripper.' He thought to himself. Just as he was about to turn to Pete to comment on the absence of their other two friends, Holden heard a door slam over the clubs loud music. He looked up and saw Syn. She looked pissed off as she stormed through the crowd, her head down, she was very focused. Holden wondered what happened and he began to hope she wasn't in trouble or leaving when he saw what the problem was. It was him; she charged over to him, picked him up by his collar. Not giving him a chance to get to his feet she dragged him to an arm chair that lined the walls of Fantasia. All he heard from Pete as he was being dragged away to what he thought was his sure death, or at least a pretty hefty ass kicking was "bye." She threw Holden into the chair, put her arms on the arm rests and slammed her knees between his legs and the chair. She pulled the back of Holden's hair so his neck was exposed and he was looking up at her.

"What the fuck is your story?" she asked him.

"What?" Holden questioned

"You, asshole. You know what I mean, what's with you."

"I uh, don't know what you mean."

"Yes you do, the way you looked at me; you threw me off my routine."

"Sorry?" Holden said with confusion in his voice.

"No you're not!" she said very aggressively "and honestly neither am I. Come on, you're buying a dance, you owe me." She said, the aggression turned to a gentle sweetness he wasn't expecting.

"Alright, but I should warn you, I have two left feet." Holden said as he was dragged into the VIP rooms. They walked by some open rooms, Holden saw Jeff and Andrew with their dancers. They were obviously enjoying themselves. Andrew gave Holden a thumbs up as he saw him walk by. Syn picked the room she liked and told Holden to have a seat. She sat on his lap. "Hi, I'm Syn." she said with a smile.

"Ya I think I heard that before." Holden said playfully "I'm Holden."

"Holden?" she questioned to make sure she heard him right.

"Ya, you know, from …." She interrupted him

"Catcher in the Rye." She said finishing his sentence. "I loved that book in high school"

"Ya, apparently so did my parents." Holden said, laughing.

She extended her hand and said she was very pleased to meet him; happily Holden accepted her hand and shared her sentiments.

"Sorry I'm sitting on your lap, I just find it so hard to talk in here over the music."

"Oh, its okay, I guess." Holden said as if he was put off. She laughed and slapped his arm. "Poor guy, I'm sure you'll live."

After several songs of casual conversation she said it was time for her to dance for him. Holden said "It was lucky they were in the right place then." Trying in vain to make a joke. Syn added that she found it hard dancing in the booths because she couldn't pick the music and that she hated most of the music the other girls selected.

The next song started, never breaking eye contact she slowly started taking off her clothes, getting as close to Holden as possible. Her bra fell to the ground from the bottom of her mesh shirt which she kept on. The next and last to go was her panties, as she reached for them Holden commented on how awesome they were and she jokingly said she could leave them on if he wanted. Holden said he could live without them and told her to continue. She smiled and stood up, bending over at the waist as far as she could, her ass tightened.

'It was so beautiful he thought.'" It was so close he wanted to lean in and bite it but he refrained. She slowly pulled the panties down over her perfectly shaped cheeks and dropped them to the floor; she paused momentarily letting Holden see her pussy. It was perfectly shaved and by the looks of it, it was very wet. She turned around seeking acknowledgment. All Holden said was it looked like she enjoyed her job; he had a sexy smirk as he said it. With an equally sexy smirk of her own she replied "Some days more than others." Turning her back to Holden she fell into his lap pushing her back into Holden's strong chest. Holden left his arms on the arm rest, she reached down and pulled them to her stomach. As he reached around she cuddled deeper into him, resting her head onto his shoulder, her shampoo and perfume filled the air and he thought she smelt fantastic.

He pressed his cheek against hers. She let out a very sexy sound, a small moan of satisfaction. Holden hugged her tighter, he thought if they weren't in a strip club it would be a very romantic embrace. She leaned back further, breathing deeply into his ear. She felt the same as Holden, and she felt less like a girl dancing for a customer and more like a woman in her lover's arms. Leaning further into Holden's chest, she breathed deep into his ear, gently kissing his ear lobe. She was straddling his leg and he knew she had to of felt his hard cock through his jeans. A fact he became aware of when she started slowly moving her hips, grinding into his leg. Holden squeezed her stomach; she started breathing heavier into his ear, his hand wandered all over her midsection. She began grinding into him harder, he could feel her thigh against his hard cock and she could feel his large member against her. She wanted to reach in and pull it out; she wanted to feel him inside her. She was amazed at how carried away this stranger was making her. She knew this wasn't an average night for her and by no means was Holden an average costumer. She clamped her hands down onto his legs and squeezing tightly. Holden's fingernails dug into her stomach as he dragged his fingers to her sides. A loud moan emitted from her, the sound snapped her back to reality. Worried one of the staff might see her getting carried away she stood up, composed herself and continued with a more traditional dance. She turned to Holden looked up and down his tall well toned body. She could tell as he watched her during her stage show that he was in good shape but it took the private dance and her being so close to him for her to feel his muscles under his clothing. What got her attention was the bulge in his pants, she smiled and put her fore finger to her mouth, biting it giving Holden an oh so innocent look. Holden looked at her and he melted, she looked so hot with her sweet innocent façade and he just wanted to throw her into the chair and fuck her hard. Again he resisted and decided to just enjoy the rest of the show. Her hands slid over her tits, down her stomach and she started massaging her pubic area. She put one leg up on the chair between Holden's legs. Her one hand continued to work over her clit; the other extended to his face and traced his jaw line to his open mouth. Holden barely opened his lips to accept her fingers and she just tapped his nose and waggled her finger saying "no, no, no." Rejected, Holden fell back into his chair giving her a sad look. She smiled and spun around to put her back to him yet again. She bent at her knees, leaned back and tipped her head back into his crotch, her hair draped over his lap. Her hands were resting on her knees as she began to shake her head back and forth like she was continuing to tell him no. Leaving her head in place, she turned her body around so she was now kneeling before him; her mouth was inches away from his throbbing cock. Holden wasn't sure how much more he could take. He looked down at her and caught a light glimmering off her cheek. Holden looking for ways to ease the pressure looked hard at the sparkling light. He noticed it was a piercing, surprised he didn't notice it before he asked her if she had any others that might be taken out for work. She showed him the keeper she had in her eyebrow. Holden confessed that piercings and tattoos were his weakness. He told her that he had four himself. "Where?" she asked.

"Well, I have one nipple and three elsewhere." With the elsewhere, she looked down at Holden's bulge; she bit her lip and nodded towards it as if to ask "There?"

"Ya." Holden confirmed

"Can I see it?" Syn asked.

"Well, ya, I guess. I could send you a picture or something to your email if you want."

"NO, NOW! I want to see it now." she demanded.

"Well, I don't mind showing you but I know enough about strip clubs to know that whipping your cock out would get me one hell of a beating." Holden said with a laugh.

Syn agreeing with the predicament, she got up and looked out the door of the booth. "Okay, coast clear, hurry." She once again demanded.

"Seriously?" Holden asked looking for confirmation.

"Yes, now hurry." she said impatiently.

"Um, okay but remember you asked, if the cops come." Holden said chuckling, he then proceeded to unzip and pull out his cock, it was very hard. Holden was happy that she was seeing it in its best possible condition, erect. Once it was out he looked at Syn, he couldn't believe he was pulling his cock out in a strip joint. Her eyes widen. "Wow." She whispered, "I want to suck that so bad."

Holden laughed and he could feel his cheeks get warm with embarrassment. "Stop it, you're making me blush."

"No, seriously, that is very impressive." she added "the piercings are cool too." They both laughed at her comment.

"Well, if it was big I wouldn't have had to decorate it; did you see the top bead is the superman logo? I call it my little man of steel."

"Don't sell yourself…ahem, short. It's not that small at all."

"Um, well thanks, can I put it away now?"

Laughing, she said "of course."

Zipping up quickly, Holden blurted out "so…wanna get married?" "Sure, but the minister has to be Elvis and the bridesmaid Marilyn Monroe." she shot back

"Elvis? Marilyn? Where do you think we are? Vegas? Seriously though, I do have two tickets to the theatre tomorrow night, my friend cancelled at the last minute and I was wondering if you would like to come with me? That is, if you're not working."

"You're in luck, I have tomorrow off. What show?"

"The Phantom of the Opera at the Pantages Theatre."

"I have always wanted to see that, sure, but I don't have anything to wear though."

"No problem, I was going to go pick something up for myself tomorrow, we can go shopping together, dinner then to the show. What time do you want me to pick you up?"

"Meet me at my favourite coffee shop, the corner of Younge and College at say, two? Where were you going to go shopping?" she asked.

"It's a surprise, I'll see you at two, if you don't stand me up." Holden joked.

"I wouldn't dream of it, call me Paige by the way, you can text me if you get lost." She said as she whispered her number into his ear. "Don't stand me up Holden, It was nice meeting you."

She gathered up her clothes and disappeared out the door. Holden had no idea what time it was or how long he was in the booth with Syn. He wasn't even sure if his friends were still around; he questioned himself, thinking he was just setting himself up to get hurt. He paused at the entrance to the VIP rooms, he realized he didn't pay her, he began to wonder if she forgot. That couldn't be it he thought, she was a professional she wouldn't just forget. He then wondered if she stole his wallet. Nope, still in his back pocket, he figured he would see her before he left and he could pay her then. He looked around, he saw his friends as he walked across the bar. His cock was still fully erect; he assumed it was painfully obvious to all that was paying attention. He took his seat; everyone else was already back and ready to go. "So, how was it?" Pete asked, knowing Holden was twitterpaited with Syn prior to leaving with her to the VIP room.

"Great thanks." Holden said, the others laughed at his response. Holden ignored their remarks as he frantically punched her number into his cell phone; he looked up from his phone to Pete, with a cocky smile he said "save contact."

"And you Jeff? How was your night?" Jeff turned to the group with a beaming smile.

"You're not the only one with a date." He boasted.

"That a boy." Andrew said. After they finished up their beers they headed for the door. Holden paused and told the boys he had to say goodbye to Syn. He finally found her and he went up to her, "I think I forgot to pay you for your hard work."

She smiled "First ones free, you want any more you have to come back to me." she winked turned and walked away.

Holden left the bar, joined up with his friends and climbed in the cab. They all sat in silence thinking all in all it was a great night out with the boys.

2

As Holden got off the subway he looked at his watch. 1:45. Fifteen minutes to spare and College Avenue was just two blocks away; he figured he would get to the coffee shop in plenty of time. All Holden could think about was his upcoming date with Paige but he also tried to remain guarded so he wouldn't be too disappointed when he got there and saw that she wasn't there. He tried to shake the negativity from his head but it persisted. "She was just being nice, in her line of work she must have hundreds of guys hit on her. It's her job to make each one feel special." He decided once he got to the coffee shop he would wait until 2:30, that was respectable. He also knew he had her phone number, that is, if it was indeed her real number. As Holden reached the corner he looked around. Just as he feared, no coffee shop. He looked up and down the block, thinking maybe he had missed it. Just when he was about to give up, he saw a sign on a door; it was small and easily overlooked. The doorway was above a short set of stairs that led down into a basement. Holden followed the stairs and hesitantly opened the door. 'Yup, it was a coffee shop alright.' Holden strolled up to the counter and ordered a coffee. He didn't spend a lot of time looking around; he was 15 minutes early and assumed he arrived first. His plan was to grab his coffee, sit and read the newspaper patiently waiting for his date. After getting his order he turned and looked for a suitable seat, instead what caught his eye was a very beautiful woman. He tried to look away but he was unable to do so; he was mesmerized by her. The woman was sitting alone with a backpack resting up against her chair. She was wearing a white tank top with her black bra straps exposed on her soft shoulders. She was also wearing ¾ length cargo pants, ankle socks and a pair of black puma shoes with white trimming and a pair of dark rimmed glasses. After looking at this woman for several seconds, he paused, "Is that Syn?" He wondered. The woman at the table didn't notice him watching her, her head was buried in a book and she was listening to some music on her MP3 Player. Holden took a closer look, trying to not get caught staring. "It can't be her," he told himself; he remembered Syn being beautiful, but this girl was breathtaking. He thought about walking by a little closer to see for sure. Then he had a brainwave. He decided to send her a text to tell her that he was there. Just as he hit send, the girl reached into her backpack and pulled out a beeping cell phone. With a tilt of her head her long curly hair fell down over her shoulder. When she reached into the bag he saw the familiar star tattoo on her elbow. He knew without doubt that this goddess was Syn, and she was there to meet him. As Holden approached the table, Paige read the text. She smiled; her legs became tingly with nerves because she had shown up to the coffee shop an hour early to wait for Holden. She didn't want to risk missing the man that had made her emotions run wild the night before. She had been thinking about him all night and now that he was close her nerves began to overwhelm her. Before she could panic, Holden was standing at the table. "Excuse me; I can't seem to find a seat, mind if I share your table?" Holden asked. Paige looked around the near empty shop; she chuckled at his weak pick up line and invited him to take a seat. She was trying her best to hide her giddiness; she fought back her smile that was already starting to form on her beautiful lips. She was scared she would look like a crazy high school girl. As Holden put down his drink he grabbed a chair and began to take a seat, Paige gathered up her things to make room for him. "Whatcha readin'?" Holden asked. Paige looked up at him over the top of her dark rimmed glasses and blushed ever so slightly. She showed him the cover of the book, "*Catcher in the Rye*, for some reason I was inspired to reread it." Paige felt embarrassed at her confession, "What must he think, I know, he thinks I'm a psycho stalker that's what he thinks," she thought to herself. Holden was very flattered that he influenced her like that. "Ya, I hear that's a good book," he said and they both laughed.

"Ya, some freak last night made me think of it so I thought I'd pick up a copy for old times sake," she said, taking a sip of her coffee to try and hide her embarrassment.

"Some freak, eh? He sounds like a very smart guy to me." Holden joked. "I wasn't sure if you were going to be able to make it, you were up late last night." he added. She leaned forward grabbed his collar and pulled him towards her, she put her lips to his ear. "I couldn't wait to see you today, I woke up at 9 to get ready," she confessed.

"Well, it was worth it, you look fantastic," he said, not knowing what else to say, he was still trying to process her words.

"Thanks," she replied with a smirk.

They quietly continued their coffees as they made small talk for roughly the next hour. Holden felt like he could have sat there talking to her all afternoon, but he subtly suggested that they should get going. "Oh goodness yes," she agreed, "Sorry, I didn't realize how long we were here." They gathered their things, in unison they stood and slung their backpacks over their shoulders causing them both to smile at one another. When they left the shop Holden made a right turn and had them heading towards Kensington Market. He thought to himself that it was a lucky coincidence that her favourite coffee shop and his favourite place to buy clothes were within only a few blocks of each other. The walk passed by quickly. The market was a great little area hidden in the heart of Toronto; it had everything from groceries to vintage clothing which was why it was one of Holden's favourite shopping places. It was the clothing that drew them there that day. "You're looking for theatre clothing here?" Paige asked. Holden smiled at her, gave her a wink and diverted into the first shop. The counter was at the right of the entrance where a young Goth girl looked up and welcomed the couple as they passed through the door before she went back to reading her magazine. The shop had all kinds of old clothes; 70s style tuxedos, old band uniforms, suits, Victorian dresses and so much more. Paige left Holden's side and wandered around the girl's section while Holden took his time looking at the men's wear. He occasionally pulled out fun clothes to show Paige. She was doing the same thing with her findings. There were great things in the shop but nothing stood out, so they left and continued down the street. They went through three or four more shops before Holden found his perfect outfit. He grabbed Paige's hand and pulled her towards his finding. The piece de resistance was a maroon 70s style tux with tails; highlighted in pink trim; a matching ruffled shirt, bow tie and cummerbund. He loved it. Paige whole heartedly agreed with the awesomeness of the tux. Holden went to try it on; when he exited the change room both the clerk and Paige were waiting for him. Paige couldn't control her laughter. "That's awesome, you HAVE to get it," she exclaimed excitedly. "Oh, I found this while you were changing," she said as she threw him a black cane with a silver skull handle. It was the perfect accessory for a suit so fine and was just the right height for Holden; he took it as a sign.

"So ladies, what do you think?" Holden leaned on the cane, folding one leg over the other in a classic Charlie Chaplin pose. Paige, still laughing, thought the cane was the perfect touch, and the clerk agreed. "So…I don't look stupid?" he asked, looking for confirmation.

"Very" Paige said "but in the best possible way ever"

"Sold, how much?" Holden asked turning to the clerk.

The clerk looked over the items as Holden handed them to her over the change room door. "Okay, the tux and the cane will be $30.00." Paige and Holden both commented on the remarkable price. "Okay, one down. Now let's go get you something equally as awesome," Holden remarked to Paige.

"Agreed!" Paige said, giving her head a big nod. They both thanked the clerk for her work on their way out. Holden grabbed his bags and they left to continue their hunt. Passing on a few more shops and potential dresses, they kept looking for perfection while keeping in mind which shops had the best plan B. The second to last shop on the block had Paige's newest wardrobe addition. The dress was low cut, full length Victorian style with maroon coloring and pink lace trim, which complimented Holden's tux perfectly. It was as though the two garments were made together. She went to try it on and like Holden's tux, her dress was a perfect fit, except she looked much better in hers than Holden felt he did in his. As she exited the change room Paige felt very elegant, like she was in a fairytale. She was a bit self conscious though, that was until she saw Holden's expression. He looked at her like a princess. Her heart melted as she looked back at him, she never felt more beautiful. Paige did a twirl for Holden's benefit. Holden walked over to her and wanted to hug her, however he forced himself to remember that it was their first date and they weren't that familiar yet, so he held back. She noticed his intent and reached out putting her arms around his shoulders. Holden responded by putting his arms around her waist. They pulled each other close; the smell of her perfume reminded him of the intensity of the night before. She whispered "So…I look good?" "Ya, you look amazing."

"I think so too," she replied with a smile, "I'll take it." She leaned in and kissed his cheek. After the transaction was complete, they left the store. Paige suggested that they go to her place to change, since her apartment wasn't too far from the coffee shop they first met at. As time was becoming a factor Holden agreed and Paige led him by his hand down the maze of streets to her place.

Located over a restaurant her apartment was small. "Must be easy to get take-out," Holden joked.

"Ya, that place is going to make me fat," she replied. They climbed the stairs and got to her apartment door; she fumbled with her keys until she finally managed to get the door unlocked. Over her shoulder she said, "Ignore the mess; I think my roommate is at work so make yourself at home."

"No problem, you should see my place," He said in an attempt to comfort her.

The door swung open and he realized she wasn't kidding about the mess. Her place was a very small older two bedroom apartment. It had all the look and feel of a typical college student's room. As Holden walked in, he noticed the living room area to his left; the couch was old and torn with jackets and clothes thrown over the back. The table wasn't much different accept instead of clothes it had dirty dishes and papers covering the top. Immediately to the right was a bedroom. Paige threw her backpack on the ground behind the couch, she then turned and headed into the bedroom, she stopped in the doorway, turned around and said, "You can change in here, my roommate won't be home for hours, I'll be out in a minute." With that she started to take off her tank top, showing Holden her bareback. "Tease," Holden yelled as she used the heel of her foot to close the door. "Whatever do you mean?" she yelled back through the closed door. Her question had a playful tone and Holden knew it was definitely rhetorical.

Holden looked further into the apartment; just on the other side of Paige's bedroom was their tiny kitchen. The countertop had more papers, some dirty plates and cookware. Hanging over the counter top was some wine glasses dangling upside down by their stems. The small fridge and stove were retro style golden colour. The stove had a now cold pot of something that was still on the element. Holden took a peak through a small window on the opposing kitchen wall. There was a small rickety table and a lone chair. The table was another throw back from the 70's and could have definitely been bought from the market they were at earlier. The table had a white top with brown swirls subtly mixed in the pattern and long steel legs, the chairs had green upholstery and the same steel legs. The table set reminded him of a similar one his parents had in his childhood home. On the table was a small laptop with a half a bottle of water beside it and nothing else. The floor was covered in a very old and worn carpet. It had shoes and clothes tossed everywhere making it as difficult to negotiate as a minefield. At the very back of the apartment was the second bedroom and on the right of the bedroom door was another door which Holden assumed was the bathroom. He took a peak in through the open door, the room was a disaster. The mess made Holden smile a bit. Overall the apartment had a nice smell and a very comfortable feel about it. Holden took some time to look at the pictures on the wall. Most of them were collages of Paige and what he assumed was her roommate with different friends from various parties and landmarks around the city. Holden heard a bang and a thump from Paige's room. He turned to see what was going on. "I'm alright," Paige yelled while she was laughing. Holden couldn't help but laugh as well.

Holden found a spot by the dining room table to put his bags. He started to undress; it felt so weird to him to be getting undressed in a relative stranger's house, especially fearing her roommate could be home at anytime. Holden reached into the bag and pulled out his new tux. He was beginning to get excited for the evening. As he was getting dressed all was going well until he got to the bow tie. "Damn, it's not a clip on," he cursed to himself. He had no idea how to tie a bow tie. Holden threw his old clothes into the shopping bag, slipped on his black leather Chuck Taylor's and he was ready to go. He looked at the computer on the table and wondered if she had internet, maybe he could search 'how to tie a bow tie.' Not overly worried about it, he made himself comfortable on her couch and turned on the television. Paige heard the noise and yelled out, "Are you ready?"

"Sort of, don't suppose you know how to tie a bow tie do you?" he asked with a chuckle. "I'll be ready in a minute; I'll see what I can do."

Holden found a game show on TV and thought he'd watch that while he was waiting. His feeble attempt at answering the trivia questions made him feel pretty stupid as he knew only a few of the answers. He thought to himself, "definitely not smarter than a 5th grader." He heard a rustling at her door and turned in time to see it swing open. His jaw dropped. Paige stood in the doorway, doing various mock modeling poses. "What do you think?"

Holden was speechless; he thought she looked amazing. The long pink dress clung to her perfect body. It was low cut which highlighted her cleavage; the waist was cinched tight like she was wearing a corset and the bottom of the dress had a white lace trim and a subtle maroon strip. It had a small train trailing behind her. The sleeves and collar were trimmed with maroon lace as well. What pulled the entire outfit together and made her look gorgeous, was her long black curly hair hanging off her shoulders. She had accessorized her hair with two white diamond hair clips that sparkled in the dim light of the room. Paige had also added a pair of black elbow length fishnet gloves that only had a loop for her middle finger, keeping her cute fingers exposed. Holden once again had the urge to jump over the couch, push her back into the bedroom, pull the dress up over her ass and fuck her. She was still doing her modeling poses, she paused and waited for his response, then she pulled up her dress to show him her legs. She had changed into a pair of fishnet nylons and the same black Chuck Taylor's she was wearing the night before. "I think I love you," Holden said, in awe of her beauty.

"Um, thanks? So you approve then?"

"Oh, very much so. Hey! We have matching shoes," he said, positioning his leg so she could see his footwear.

"Nice, now come over here and let's see what I can do about that bow tie."

Doubting her skills, he walked over to her anyway. She turned him around, reached her arms around his neck and moved in nice and close to him. He felt her tits pressing into his back and could once again smell her hair. Between her smell and her touch he was getting hard. Wearing tight polyester pants was not an ideal time to get an erection. It took her only a minute and she had him tied up. She left her arms on his shoulders and told him to turn around; their faces were only an inch apart. Paige was feeling swept up in the moment, she loved the power of her dress. Holding Holden as close as she was, she wanted to take him on the back of the couch but like Holden, she knew it was their first date and she didn't want to come on to strong. She gathered her emotions and settled for staring endlessly into his eyes. Her beauty and the sweet scents filling the air was sensory overload for Holden. He wanted to kiss her. She read his eyes and throwing her inhibitions aside she leaned in slightly, Holden met her halfway. Their lips touched, it was their first real kiss. Holden didn't want to rush things but he certainly wasn't going to stop. Their lips spread ever so slightly, the kiss became deeper and more passionate, it was a kiss neither were willing to end. They finally pulled apart, Paige said she had to go fix her lipstick; Holden followed her into the bedroom and sat on her bed. Her bed was covered in the clothes she was wearing earlier; her dresser was cluttered with various make ups and perfumes. On the floor were more old clothes and shoes in separate distinct piles, there were also two piles of panties and socks. Holden assumed it was piles for clean and dirty. However it was all broken up, it made the small room appear very full. Holden took a peak at her clothes and shoes to get a better idea of her style. Messy as it was, she still had style. "I'll keep her," he thought to himself. At the head of the bed was a window. The window ledge had various knickknacks. At the foot of the bed was a wardrobe closet with more stuff covering the top of it. The walls were covered in band posters, a shelf with a radio and a stack of CDs. The wall had a big nail with some medals, necklaces and bracelets hanging from it. All in all, it was typical of all the other college girls' rooms he had seen. After Paige finished her make up she smiled at Holden and said, "Let's go."

As they ran down the stairs, Holden had his back pack in tow and Paige was careful not to trip over her train so she didn't hurt or embarrass herself. She asked him "So, where we going for dinner?" Holden looked at his watch, it was already 6. They only had an hour until they had to be at the theatre. "Nothing fancy," Holden said. "Sorry."

"Oh, all dressed up with no where to go," she said. Holden glanced at her and smiled. They walked down the street until they arrived at a fast food place; Holden reached for the door and held it open for Paige. "After you ma'am," Holden said putting his hand on her back to escort her through the door. Not having much time or money, it was pretty much the only choice for them. As they got to the counter they were being met with some very different stares, some impressed, some pointing and laughing. Holden was happy to be noticed, mostly because of the gorgeous girl on his arm. Paige seemed a little more uncomfortable, despite being used to the stares of strangers. At work she was in control, at the restaurant she felt vulnerable. Holden, seeing the unease in her eyes, moved closer to her, put his arm around her waist and reassured her how incredible she looked and that it was him that looked out of place. She laughed, and with her confidence back she approached the counter and ordered. Grabbing their tray, Holden led Paige to a table in a far back corner, away from gawkers and so they could have some privacy. Before Paige sat down she told Holden she had to go 'powder her nose' trying to be as prim and proper as the style of the dressed was intended for. Holden happily excused her. "It's all coming together," he thought to himself. She was no sooner out of sight when he went to work. He knew she would be awhile by the time she sorted her dress out. He put his back pack on the vacant table next to theirs, along with their food trays. Reaching into his bag Holden pulled out a white tablecloth, two candles with holders and a lighter, along with a plastic flower arrangement, two paper plates and plastic glasses. Holden removed the food from its packaging and spread it out on the plates; he also disposed of the empty cartons before Paige had a chance to get back.

As she turned the corner, she paused and let out a gasp at Holden's efforts to 'class the place up'. She looked hard at the table arrangement and then turned to Holden. Her smile beamed, her eyes lit up wide and her hands covered her mouth. "Oh my God, that is the sweetest thing anyone has ever done for me!" she exclaimed. Holden walked towards her, took her by the hand and escorted her to her seat. As she sat, Holden held on to her hand, looked into her eyes and kissed her fingers. He finally let go of her hand and took his seat, Paige reached for a fry. "STOP!!" She jumped, dropping the fry; she looked at him quizzically wondering what she did wrong. Holden reached into his backpack and pulled out two cloth napkins. He handed her one and placed the other onto his lap. "I wouldn't want anything to get on that pretty dress of yours," he said.

"Oh yes, we can't have that now can we." The rest of dinner consisted of small talk and constant looks from passers-by. Holden heard an elderly couple, the woman turning to the man "Oh honey, isn't that sweet." The sentiment made the young couple smile.

When dinner was finished, Holden looked at his watch. "Shit, we have to get going." He blew out the candles, tossed the garbage and stashed the rest back into his backpack. As they walked through the door, Paige reached down taking Holden's hand in hers. She was nervous, but he was so good to her all day, she couldn't resist feeling his warm skin against hers. Holden, when he felt her hand grabbing his, became nervous as well. The calm cool demeanour he was trying to maintain all day was about to go out the window. His legs became weak and the butterflies in his stomach were in an uproar. "Relax, play it cool," he thought to himself. Looking at his watch when they exited the restaurant, he knew they didn't have time to walk so he hailed a cab and, in true Toronto fashion, a cab wasn't too far away. Assisting Paige into the car, he made sure her long dress wouldn't get caught in the door as he closed it. He then walked around and took the seat next to her.

The cab pulled up in front of the theatre, it barely had time to stop when a young kid with black spiked hair wearing a red suit jacket opened Paige's door. They were both overwhelmed by the bright lights of the theatre that over hung the side walk. Paige, feeding into the atmosphere extended her hand to the valet. He gladly accepted it and assisted her out of the car. Holden got out and walked around the back of the cab and met up with Paige. The valet was obviously quite taken with Paige. He couldn't keep his eyes off her and he blushed when she gave him her hand. As Holden joined Paige, the valet looked at the pair and commented on their 'retro' attire. Holden, pretending he was accustomed to such treatment, nonchalantly reached into his pocket and casually tipped the young valet. The couple turned towards the theatre and noticed two large oak doors which were carved with intricate detail. As they approached, the doorman, who was also dressed in a tuxedo, smiled and swung open the seemingly heavy door so they could easily pass through. Holden held out his elbow and Paige gladly slid her arm into his. He knew everyone's eyes would be on them and he couldn't have been prouder to walk in with someone so beautiful. Paige's hesitancy at the restaurant had all but vanished with the lavished treatment they were receiving. Holden whispered to Paige that he was going to go check his bag. Paige looked at her watch and mentioned that they had 10 minutes before they had to be seated and that she was going to go stand in the line up for the bar. Once his bag was checked, Holden found Paige in the line. Getting swept up in the atmosphere of it all, they each got a glass of wine in lieu of the bottles of beer, which, under normal circumstances, they would have preferred. They sat quietly drinking their wine, commenting on the theatre and the other patrons. They truly were overwhelmed with all the glitz and glamour and were also impressed that all of the employees dressed in black tie, as were most of the other patrons. The lobby lights dimmed twice indicating it was time for everyone to find their seats. Holden jumped off his stool, grabbed Paige by the hand and helped her jump down from hers. Tickets in hand, they found the doors closest to their seats and showed the ushers their stubs. They got a smile of approval from the usher as she showed them their seats. The seats were well situated, first section, middle of the row. In order to get to their seats they had to pass by several already seated theatre goers. On the walk past they could tell their outfits were again being met with very mixed reactions. Neither Holden nor Paige really cared either way what the others thought. They were happy and they were together, no one else in the theatre mattered to them. Holden felt like the King of the world and Paige definitely felt like his Queen.

The curtain opened to the auction scene. Paige didn't know much about the Phantom of the Opera so she was caught off guard when it came to lot 667, the chandelier. She almost jumped out of her seat when the orchestra played the overture. Holden too was getting goose bumps, especially when an over excited Paige tightly gripped his hand.

The time went past very quickly and before they knew it, it was intermission. They headed back into the lobby for another glass of wine. As they talked about the performance, Paige had a very distinct glitter in her eye as she spoke about what they just saw. Holden's adrenaline had him all pumped up as well. They took their last sips of their wine and as if on cue, the lights flashed once again and the couple headed back to their seats.

After the final curtain they quickly grabbed their things and headed into the cool Toronto night. A string of yellow cabs lined the sidewalk in front of the theatre. It was almost midnight when Paige asked Holden what he wanted to. Holden suggested a night cap at a local pub then asked her what she had in mind. Paige looked at her watch and said it was getting late and she didn't have much money but she had some beer at her place if he wanted to go there for a drink. Holden, taking less than two seconds to think about her offer, had a cab hailed and they were en route to her apartment. As Paige gave the cabbie the address; he picked up the radio and told the dispatcher his destination. Paige snuggled up to Holden, grabbed his hand and looked up at him; her big brown eyes melted Holden as she spoke. "Thank you for such a great day; I've had so much fun."

"It's not over yet, or is it?" Holden said with a sly smile and a wink.

"We'll see," Paige said coyly, "I just wanted you to know how much fun I had."

"Ya, I've had a great day too, even if it does end now," Holden said squeezing his arm tighter around her. The cab finally pulled up in front of Paige's door. Holden paid the cabbie by throwing a fist full of cash at him as he scrambled out of the car to catch up to Paige, who was already through the front door and up the stairs to her apartment. As she got to her door, she once again slowly and quietly fumbled with the lock. "Shhh, I don't know if Melissa is sleeping." Once they got through the door they took a look around. They saw no evident signs that her roommate was home. Paige told Holden she was going to go change and for him to make himself comfortable. Holden took a seat on their old yet comfortable couch, flipped on the TV to try and find something on to watch, which, if he wasn't interested in infomercials, was going to prove to be a challenging task. Holden ended up flipping past endless channels of paid programming before he finally found a rerun of *Family Guy*. Holden did his best to ignore some rustling in Paige's room until he heard the door open. He turned to look at her. She had changed into an older, slightly worn, tight white T shirt that clung to her perfect tits and a pair of old, baggy, grey sweat pants. She flashed Holden a smile as she made her way to the kitchen.

Holden kept his eyes on her the entire way. The track pants had some faded writing on the ass, which of course was designed to draw your attention to that particular feature. In Holden's mind it was perfect because the cotton pants definitely accentuated her magnificent ass. Holden felt himself getting hard as he watched her walk into the kitchen. "Not yet, I don't want to get ahead of myself, it was a beautiful night with a beautiful girl; I'll have a couple of drinks and call it a night, nothing else," he thought to himself as he fought the direction of the blood flow. He didn't want to move too fast, since he didn't want to ruin any chance of seeing her again. Holden soon heard the familiar sound of bottles being opened and Paige quickly reappeared holding a couple of beers. Holden was sitting on the corner of the couch; Paige nestled up into the other corner. As she sat down, she handed Holden his drink and looked at him; she couldn't believe that one guy could be so great. She wanted to rip his tux off him with her teeth but she was hesitant, if he was indeed genuine she wanted to take her time and do things right. On the other hand she also wanted to maintain her guard in case he was just playing her along to get into her pants. Getting her mind off of all the possible scenarios she decided to just relax and see how the night progressed. "Oh, Family Guy, I love this show." They sat quietly drinking and watching TV, after a short time Paige finally broke the silence. "I can't believe you're still wearing that, it has to be uncomfortable." Holden smiled at her concern, he reached down and untied his bowtie. "There, that better?" he asked.

"I think you could do better," she replied with a coy smile. They then went back to sipping their beer and watching TV. At half past the hour, Holden flipped to the TV guide channel. Paige saw a movie she liked and encouraged Holden to flip over to it. After Holden found the channel, Paige suggested popcorn and without waiting for his response she jumped up and made her way to the kitchen. Holden stood up and walked over to his bag. He told her that he was going to go into her room to change while the popcorn was popping. As he changed, the smell of popcorn filled the tiny apartment.

Holden joined Paige back into the living room; he was wearing the same clothes he was when they first met up in the coffee shop. He was surprised to see that Paige turned off all the lights in the apartment, the only light now was from the TV and what had to be 20 candles throughout the apartment. The glow cast shadows on the ceiling and in the corners that made her apartment look a bit eerie. Holden took his spot back on the couch just as the introduction to the movie was beginning, neither of them missed much. After putting the bowl of popcorn on the table she laid down on the couch with her head in Holden's lap and stretched the rest of her body out on the remaining length of the couch. Holden, looking to get comfortable put his feet on the coffee table and placed his hand around her shoulder then they snuggled in to watch the movie.

Halfway through the movie they both began yawning like crazy. She finally said "Well, it's getting late." Taking her remark as a hint, Holden shifted around and looked at his watch. "Ya, you're right, I guess I should be going. Thanks for the…"

"Not so fast," she said cutting him off. She too shifted around; her head was still in his lap, she put her hand on the back of his neck and pulled him in so they could kiss. Holden didn't hesitate, taking the opportunity while he could. Holden put his hand on her head and began playing with her hair, gently pulling it as he stroked it. Her kiss tasted so sweet, Holden thought. Wrapped up in the moment he accidentally pulled her hair harder than he intended. The extra force caused her to let out a soft moan and her hand squeezed tight on his thigh. The positive reaction made Holden pull a bit harder, this time in more control of the force. Her mouth broke its lock on Holden's as she opened her lips slightly. Her head leaned back and her eyes rolled back into her head as she let out a louder moan and a very soft "fuck." Holden kept pulling as he repositioned himself so he was lying beside her. He finally let go of her hair and began kissing her again. Paige was now getting worked up, the fatigue she was feeling earlier had disappeared, her body was alive and Holden was moving too slow. She appreciated the restraint he was showing but she decided he now needed some encouragement. Paige put her hands around his back and pulled him on top of her. Very ungracefully, he lost his balance and instead of a smooth transition he fell on top of her, landing only an inch away from her face. He was worried his body was crushing her, he looked deep into her beautiful eyes and the light from the candles lit up her face. To Holden he felt like he was looking at a porcelain doll, he paused taking in her beauty. "Hi," he said.

"Hi," she said with a big smile. "Thank you for tonight, it was the best I've had in awhile." "It's not over yet," he whispered with a devilish grin of his own. He then shyly bit his bottom lip after he said the words. She looked up at him; her hand moved off his back to his head and pulled him towards her. Holden met her kiss and returned her tight embrace. He could feel her tits against his chest and this time he wasn't able to keep his erection under control. Which didn't go unnoticed by Paige, she slid her hand down his side, past his waist to his cock. She grabbed it hard through his shorts and gave it a gentle squeeze. The unexpected squeeze made Holden moan. "I love your cock," she said matter of factly. Holden fought back a laugh as he thought, "Well, he's awfully fond of you too," but he remained in control and didn't say anything. After her squeeze, he decided that she too was fair game. His hands began to tremble as his brain told them his intent. He didn't understand why he was getting so nervous now; he had been with a lot of girls before and never felt this nervous, well not since his first time. He was concerned that she had such an emotional grip on him so fast and he was setting himself up for heartbreak. Paige too, throwing caution to the wind, was concerned that she was setting herself up to get hurt but every ounce of her being told her that what she was doing was right so she decided to take the chance. Holden, no longer thinking about the possible heartbreak, was only thinking about the beautiful girl that lay beneath him with her hand on his cock. He decided it wasn't his brain making the decisions at this point anyways, so he continued. He moved his hand down her chest, over her tank top slightly grazing her tit as it made its way down to the waistband of her pants. He paused when he felt flesh. Her legs opened slightly as she interlocked them with his. Her hand moved to his back and she dug her nails deep into his flesh. Holden felt her hips move slightly as she positioned herself so his cock was pushed up against her pussy. Holden, who was already hard, only got harder with the sensation and the thought that he was soon going to be inside her. "Can this really be happening? Is she really going to let me fuck her?" he thought to himself. His hand slid under her soft cotton tank top and up her body. He felt her soft stomach and her ribs. He slowed down to take his time so he could feel every inch of her but more importantly so she could feel his hands on her making the anticipation build. The touch of Holden's hand on her skin sent shivers up her body, as his hand moved slowly against her skin, it tickled her. She wanted him to grab her, touch her, to feel her, the anticipation was killing her. She wanted to grab his hands and pull them to her chest. She knew it was only a matter of time before she felt his strong soft hands on her breasts, so she decided to enjoy the moment as it was. She just wished he would hurry things up a bit. Holden was hoping his slow deliberate movements would drive her to the point of begging for him to touch her. Her kisses moved to his neck and ear, her breath caressed his skin; it was too much for him to take. His plan of making her beg was beginning to backfire. He unsuccessfully tried to refocus on what he was doing. His hips began to move in unison with hers as his cock ached to penetrate her. His hand gently traced each rib. Her hand roughly groped him, scratching his back and grabbing his ass to push his cock harder into her. Holden reached his left hand up to caress her face; he played with her ear lobe trying further build the anticipation. His right hand slowly continued its journey up her body, rib by rib; he was so close to her tits now he wanted to pounce on her with both hands. He wanted to grab her spectacular tits and go to town, but he fought every urge that was coursing through his body. Sensing Paige wanted him just as badly, he knew the fight was futile. To keep her off guard he ran his finger down her ribs with an unexpected force. As he did, she let out a gasp and jolted forward into him. Trying to overload her senses, his left hand grabbed a handful of her gorgeous curly locks and pulled her back down to the couch. Her head tilted far back, her neck was fully exposed. Holden quickly slid his hand to her breast and cupped it; it felt so soft in his hand. He could feel her longer than average nipple erect in the palm of his hand.

Paige's heart raced as Holden forced her head back into the couch, the tenderness he was displaying disappeared in that brief moment. The pain caught her off guard so much so she didn't feel his hand on her tit right away. As she caught her breath, she felt his fingers kneading into her; she felt his heart beating through her own chest as his breathing increasing. She never wanted anyone more than she wanted him at that moment. They both began moving their hips faster and faster, Holden was becoming concerned he would become too stimulated and end things too quickly. He continued to caress her breast which fit perfectly in his hand, he applied pressure onto his finger tips and around to the heel of his palm trying not to get into a rhythm. He wanted her to guess where and how she was going to be touched next. All in one fluid motion Holden leaned into her using his chest to put pressure on her other breast and he gently bit her neck. Her legs squeezed even harder around his as she tried to force his cock into her through their pants. Holden moved his hand all around her tit and her nipple, which was still very erect. He took a moment to play with it and to tease it. He then slid the same finger around her soft flesh doing his best to not be predictable. Playing Holden's games, Paige, in an act of unpredictability rolled over, throwing Holden to the floor. "I'm going to bed now." She proclaimed. "DAMN, did I do something wrong? Did I go too far?" Holden wondered as she stepped over him and walked into her bedroom. Just prior to reaching the door she reached down, pulled her tank top off and threw it to the floor. She looked back at Holden and used her left hand to cover her bare breasts so she didn't expose herself to him but it gave him a great view of her side boob. She said "You coming or what?" Holden thought he felt like a cartoon action figure, in his mind he was up so fast he almost knocked her down as he passed her and jumped onto her bed. In actuality, he stood up quietly, composed himself after his trip to the floor and he walked over to her. She turned and started walking into her bedroom with her arms hanging by her side. Making it only about three steps, he caught up to her and as his fingers touched her back she turned to him. The only light they had to navigate by was that of the TV and the still flickering candles. Paige reached around his waist as Holden's arms went around her bare shoulders; with her free hand she slammed the door. Her room suddenly became very dark, Holden couldn't see a thing. Confident the door was secure, she started walking forward pushing Holden back. He cautiously walked backwards blindly trusting her to guide him through the maze of clutter on the floor. Holden almost lost his balance as the back of his legs hit the bed. Paige quickly caught him and kept him standing. Unsure of where she was, he felt her hands tugging at the bottom of his t-shirt and with a quick movement she had it up over his head. Happy with her success she put her hands on his hips and turned him around so he had his back to her. Paige pressed her body against his so her tits rubbed up against his muscular back. Her hands ran all over his chest, finding his nipple rings. She let out an 'oooh' and started fondling them, gently pulling on them simultaneously. Holden reached back and put his hands on her waist. Her arms wrapped around his as she continued to rub his chest. Holden could feel her cheek press against his back, her hot breath warming his cooling skin. Holden wanted her so badly but she was definitely in control now. Her hands got lower and lower. She snuck her arms under his and started patting him as if she was frisking him. When her hands finally found his erection, she patted it a couple of times. "Oh, what do we have here?" She asked, trying to sound like a cop that just found a weapon on a suspect. Before she gave him a chance to reply her hands busily worked away at his belt and button on his shorts. Once she unfastened and unzipped him, with her thumbs in the waistband of his boxers she pulled them to the floor, bending at the knees as she guided them down. She held them in place allowing Holden to step out of the clothing. She then dropped to her knees; she bit his ass then kissed it better. Her hand worked up his legs, Holden felt a shiver, he didn't know if it was from the coolness of the room or the fact that her hands were slowly approaching his cock. Holden just stood there letting her do her thing. Paige's fingers worked inside his thighs and around his hips until they found his waist. He could feel her trying to reach for his cock with her fingers while keeping her hands firmly on his waist. She was so close, just millimetres from his shaft. He wanted to reach down and pull them onto him until she had a handful of cock, but he didn't. He couldn't believe how horny he was, he was truly becoming concerned that he was about to cum before anything had a chance to happen. Paige's hands grabbed his waist; her thumbs buried themselves deep into his ass cheeks as she forced him to spin around. As he spun, his cock accidentally slapped her across the face. As Holden apologized, she put her hand on the side of his cock and playfully slapped it back. "Bad," she said giggling. She then grabbed a hold of it with a more serious look on her face. "Mmm, this is what I've been waiting for," she breathed as she leaned forward. Her breath that had been tantalizing various other parts of his body throughout the evening was now teasing his cock. Her grip was firm but pleasant; her lips touched the head of his cock as she kissed him. She kissed further down his shaft, her hand wandered up and down his length, stopping at each piercing, gently pulling, poking and prodding them. Her kisses became faster and harder before she moved her hand to his bag, gently giving it a squeeze. Her kisses stopped, she opened her mouth and slid her soft lips around his cock. Paige tasted the precum that was already oozing out of him. She cleaned it all off with a flicker of her tongue. "Oh god, don't cum now," Holden chanted to himself over and over again, knowing he only had one chance to make a good first impression. Her hand squeezed and fondled his balls as her lips and tongue continued to work their way up his shaft. Just when he was about to reach the point of no return, she suddenly stopped everything. She stood up on her tippy toes and kissed him. Holden was all too eager to kiss her back. She stopped and then he could feel both her hands thrust against his chest knocking him onto the bed. "Get comfortable, I'm going to get some light in here." Holden could hear some rustling and then several seconds later the room came alive with a flickering candle. It cast shadows over her body accentuating her breasts and belly button. Holden had failed to notice that she took off her pants in the darkness. She was standing before him wearing only her panties. He couldn't tell exactly what colour they were because of the glowing yellow flame but he did know that she was wearing a G string. He couldn't help but stare at her perfect body. Although he had seen it before, it wasn't her alter ego Syn he was looking at. It was Paige and as sexy as Syn was, she wasn't nearly as beautiful, intense or passionate as Paige. Paige slowly walked towards Holden; she couldn't keep her eyes off his sculpted naked body. Despite being cold the cotton sheets of her unmade bed felt very comfortable and inviting. He was confident they were about to get much warmer. She got a couple of steps from the bed when she stopped to look at him. She watched as Holden slowly lowered his hand to his own cock and gently touched it, stroking it up and down, waiting for her to take over. She wanted to wait and watch him finish himself. As she watched, she began running her hands over her own body, over her tits and sliding down to her pussy. As one last tease, she turned around letting him get a look at her round ass; the string of the G string was hidden perfectly in the crack of her ass. She turned around again and took the last two steps to the bed. She crawled her way up to him starting low by his feet and slowly worked her way up, over his body. Her tits rubbed against his legs and her face slid against his cock. As she moved up she slid her tits over his cock, her nipple tickled his head making him jump slightly. She finally made her way up so they were face to face. She was straddling him, his cock was rubbing against her soaked pussy. He could feel the heat and moisture radiating through the thin layer of cotton, which was the only thing preventing him from penetrating her. She pressed her chest against his as she continued to kiss him and run her hands through his hair. Her hips began grinding into him again. He could feel her pussy rub up and down the entire length of his cock; her smooth bare legs squeezed his hips. Holden ran his nails down her back; she arched her back in defence of the sensation. She pushed her hands against his chest and in two short bounces she was sitting up right. She bit her lower lip like Holden often did, her eyes widened like a kid at Christmas and with a big smile, she looked into Holden's eyes. "Fuck me." Being one to follow orders Holden rolled over forcing her onto the bed. A soft moan was all that came out of her. "Now it's pay back," Holden said to her. Having her pinned on her back, Holden was now in control. Paige ate up the submissive roll; she reached up for the wire headboard of her bed, giving Holden complete access to every part of her. His heart was racing faster than before, he was no longer worried about premature ejaculation he was more worried about a heart attack. "What a way to go though," he thought. Holden kissed her lips and her cheek. He rested his body against hers, pressing her tits into him like she was doing to him earlier. He bit her neck and ear and whispered how beautiful she was, how hot she was and that he was going to fuck her like no one ever has before. After getting a positive response from Paige, Holden kept moving, using his left hand for support, he leaned to one side so he could get a better look at her. His right hand explored her body, first caressing both tits, lightly grazing every part of her gorgeous breasts, then pressing firmer in spots; he leaned in to bite one of her erect nipples. She closed her eyes so she didn't see what he was about to do. Firmly holding the wire headboard, she bucked a bit, her legs moved around as they searched for something to wrap around. Her moans and her movements told Holden that she was enjoying his touch. He slid his hands down her hard stomach, past the waistband on her panties until he ever so lightly brought the tips of his fingers over her panties so his hand was cupping her pussy. His fingers were very gently grazing her cotton panties. He could feel that her panties were not only getting hot but they were also very wet and sticky, he couldn't believe that he got her so horny. Holden was normally very confident sexually but with Paige it was different; she had him nervous and feeling very much like a virgin. He knew that being a dancer she got a lot of advances from a lot of different men each night. She was definitely no stranger to sex and he was worried he wouldn't be able to please her. Her panties told a different story, with his heart racing and renewed confidence he continued on. Using the same technique as he did earlier with her tits, he applied different pressures to his hand slowly moving it around teasing her very sensitive pussy in an attempt to keep her guessing. His left hand started playing with her hair and her ear; her hips were trying to get him to press harder onto her eager cunt. Holden resisted, making her want him even more. As her hips moved faster and faster, he knew she was ready. He positioned himself between her legs, reached down and gently removed her G string like he was unwrapping a fragile present. As her foot slid through the floss like string, he held her foot. He began to kiss her toes and he stared at her glistening pussy. Her free foot moved up her other leg, bending at the knee; she spread as wide as she could. Holden kissed her ankle, her calf, her knee pit, her inner thigh until he got to her freshly shaved mound. Unable to get over the pure lust he was feeling for her he continued, hoping to give her the best orgasm of her life, or at least hoping to give her an orgasm at all. He reached in and flicked her clit with his tongue. Paige's body tightened. "Fuck yes, lick me hard," she moaned as her hips thrust around. "So far so good." He took one long deep lick of her entire pussy, her juices splashed on his cheeks and dripped off his tongue. She was so wet and she tasted so good, he wanted to spend hours licking her. In an effort to get deeper inside her, he put both his hands on the back of her knees and pushed them towards her chest. She let go of the headboard and started rubbing her tits, violently squeezing them and pulling them as his tongue worked its way inside her. He looked up at her.

"Oh, she likes it rough," he noted. He extended his tongue as far as possible getting as deep as he could. "Oh to be Gene Simmons right now," he thought. He could feel her orgasm building; her entire body began to shake. She almost poked his eye out when she quickly moved her hand from her breast to her clit. She frantically rubbed herself as fast and as hard as she could while he continued to eat her out. In vain, Holden tried to match his tongue with the pace of her hand but she was moving to fast for any human to keep up with."FUUUUUUUUUUCCCCCCCKKKK KKKK" she screamed. Her body continued to tighten and convulse with every lick of his tongue. Her pussy felt like a tsunami as she ejaculated. Holden swallowed as much as he could, what he couldn't, covered his face and her sheets. He was feeling proud of his accomplishments, he lapped up every drop until she begged him to stop and she requested his presence up top. Requesting him really meant she grabbed a handful of his hair and pulled him up to her. He tried to reach down to play with her in hopes of keeping her orgasm going but she stopped him. "OH no, no, no too sensitive," she said in broken English. Holden laid beside her, she started to kiss him, she could taste herself on his face. She licked up as much of it as she possible could. "Sorry for the mess," she said sarcastically.

"Ya, be more careful next time will ya," Holden said with a snicker.

"Oh, you think there'll be a next time do ya?" Paige said toying with a now silent Holden, she continued talking. "I guess it's my turn now you bad boy," she said sliding down his body. Without hesitation or delay, she took his cock in her mouth. Her tongue again was flickering his piercings as his cock disappeared in and out of her mouth. Happy with his oral performance, he laid back and enjoyed her head. Taking her example, he reached over his head and grabbed the headboard behind him. Her firm lips felt great on his cock as she took the entire length in her mouth. Holden froze as he heard the door unlock and people enter the apartment. Paige stopped sucking his cock to listen and she heard her roommate yell. "Hey Hun, you home?"

"Ya, I'm in here," Paige yelled back.

"You left the TV on and the candles lit again."

"Oh. Sorry about that, I was in a bit of a hurry," Paige said laughing.

"You're going to burn the damn place down some day. How was the date?"

"Still going good, I'll talk to you in the morning," Paige said trying to end the conversation.

"Wait, I have something to tell you," she said as she burst through the door. Paige was still holding Holden's cock inches away from her freshly fucked mouth. She rolled over on her other side so she could see her roommate. She used her fingers to wipe the saliva and precum from the corners of her lips. Her roommate was unfazed as she sat on the bed.

"Oh my god, you'll never believe what happened to me tonight."
"MEL, can't you see I'm busy?" Paige asked her.

"Oh right, sorry," Mel said as she turned to Holden, "Hi, nice cock," and then refocused back to Paige.

"Isn't it though," Paige agreed. "Look it is pierced," she said showing off Holden's cock. Holden, not sure how to feel about the situation, just let Paige do her thing.

"Get out!!" Mel said excitedly as she leaned in to look. Paige moved his cock around giving her roommate a better view of his hardware. Not sure if it was the beer or the extreme comfort level he was beginning to share with Paige but he didn't mind the interruption and he even thought that maybe Paige would invite her to stay. "That is awesome," the roommate said as she reached out and poked them and then she ran her fingers down the middle of the three barbells. "Here we go," Holden thought with the anticipation of the manage et trios. Like a giddy high school girl Paige squeaked, "Awesome eh?"

"Very weird, what do they feel like?" the roommate asked as if Holden wasn't even there.

"I don't know, but I'll let you know in the morning," Paige said hopefully.

"Well, just keep it down, OH; I came in to tell you I picked up too, that's what I wanted to say before I got distracted." She said and as quickly as she appeared, she left the room pausing at the door to issue Holden the standard don't hurt my friend speech and then told them to have fun. As the door closed Paige looked up at Holden. "Sorry about that. Now, where we?"
"I believe you were seconds from making me cum"
"Well, don't want to miss that do we?" She said as his cock disappeared into her warm mouth. In the background they heard her roommate's bedroom door slam. One of Paige's hands ran up and down Holden's chest, the other groped his balls. She felt his cock twitch, his body stiffened, he reached down and grabbed a handful of her hair making sure she had the ability to move when the big event happened. She took him deep in her mouth, squeezed his balls, her tongue ring flicked the base of his cock and that was it. "I'm going to…" was all he was able to get out before he exploded in her mouth. She didn't move an inch, Holden's intense orgasm lasted

for what seemed like a minute and Paige took all of his cum letting it slide down her throat, her lips massaged the base of his cock making sure she got every last drop. Confident that he was finished, she slid her lips up his shaft, squeezing out the last of his cum. Letting his cock fall out of her mouth, she leaned forward to give his head a lick. Collapsing on his chest her eyes still fixated on his now flaccid cock. "Wow that was a lot of cum." Embarrassed Holden said, "Sorry, I tried to warn you."

She turned around, her hair fell onto his cock, it felt very soft against his skin as she slid up to him. She reached her hand down to his penis, pushing her finger into the tip then pulling it away. There was a long string of cum hanging from her finger. Keeping an eye on him, she moved her finger to her tongue, dropping the string on her outstretched tongue, she then licked her fingers saying with a smile, "It's ok, I love cum."

"Yup, you really are the perfect woman aren't you," Holden said with a wink.

Paige laid her head on Holden's chest as they both caught their breath. They started to laugh at the same time as they could hear the faint sounds of screaming coming from the back bedroom. "Sounds like your roommate is having fun."

"Yup, she's a screamer alright."

"For Christmas last year my dad got me a sweater," Holden said randomly.

"Oh ya?" Paige said quizzically.

"Ya, this year I hope he gets me a screamer," Holden said with a laugh.

"Oh that's bad," she said gently slapping Holden's leg. Several minutes pass as they lay holding each other. Paige, getting cold reached for one of her blankets and covered them. Holden adjusted himself so they were facing each other. Paige rested her head on Holden's arm, he started to fondle her ear and neck, her body moved around as she was still sensitive from her last orgasm. He knew it wouldn't take much to get her heated up again. He kissed her, casually played with her tits then slid his hand down to her wet pussy. Not much encouragement was needed, as she opened her legs. Holden gently ran circles around her clit applying more and more pressure until he was pressing hard on her magic button. He started vibrating his fingers slowly at first than faster and faster with more pressure. Her second orgasm built quickly but Holden decided he wasn't going to be that nice. He stopped dead; it took her a couple of seconds to regain some of her senses. "Don't stop," she begged.

"Oh, I won't, just warming up." She let out a noise of acceptance. Holden repositioned himself between her legs; he was craving the taste of her again. His tongue worked around her already sensitive clit, he slowly slid a finger inside her. She was so soaked the first one slid easily inside so he decided to add another finger. He let them work around inside her, moving them independently to touch as much of her as he could. Her hips moved around as she tried to fuck his fingers, her hips and his tongue began to work in unison. She was obviously enjoying it; he occasionally stopped licking her to blow on her pussy, the shock of the cold air on her hot cunt kept her senses guessing. Again, he could feel her orgasm mounting, he stopped. He heard a disgruntled snort emit from Paige, he smiled and reassured her that her time was coming. Now that she was good and warmed up and so sensitive that every touch made her jump, Holden thought back to a video he once saw, a training video. In the video the guy claimed he could make any girl squirt by following his simple instructions. The technique he used was he got the girl worked up, like Holden had just done with Paige. The guy in the video said kneeling or standing beside the girl was the best position. He went on to tell the viewers to insert two fingers inside the girl with the pointer and pinkie finger fully extended pointing down her ass. The end position was supposed to look like the horns of rock seen at concerts, but in this case they were pointing down and inside someone. The heel of the palm was pressed on her clit; the pressure would be gauged by the girl, adjusting as necessary. Holden had tried the technique before and although he didn't successfully get the girl to squirt, her orgasms were definitely intense. Looking for a memorable closing move Holden decided to try this move on Paige. He started off slowly at first, and immediately she responded. Reaching back grabbing the headboard, her body was flailing around. Holden used his spare hand to massage her tits and chest, occasionally rubbed her nipples between his forefinger and thumb. He started rubbing her pussy harder and faster. Paige closed her eyes; she knew she was losing control. As Holden worked around inside her, she felt her body spasm, the urge to piss was overwhelming and she was scared she was going pee all over Holden. She wanted to tell him to stop but she couldn't formulate a coherent sentence. She felt her hands let go of the head board as she lost muscle control in her hands, her legs began to twitch violently. Never has she experienced such a sensation before. Paige felt herself making strange noises and screams but she was unable to stop herself.

Holden felt her body react; he knew her orgasm was imminent.

Reading her body he knew she was going to release her orgasm soon, he reached up with his spare hand and put it to her throat and lightly chocked her, as he did, he moved his other hand faster and harder. Just as she tried to reach down to the hand on her throat he knew she couldn't take any more. He let her go and quickly pulled his fingers out of her. Immediately following his fingers was a long stream of water shooting a couple of feet down the bed. Paige let out a very long loud scream of pleasure; Holden watched the water stream he wished he could have drank ever drop of it, like she did for him. She started convulsing violent like she was having a grand mal; Holden watched her, her eyes rolled back into her head. She tried to reach out for Holden but she didn't have control of her body yet. She began giggling uncontrollably as she squirmed into the fetal position while continuing to convulse. Holden reached down and put his hand on her shoulder, his touch set off another series of convulsions. She rolled over onto her back, her legs flailed everywhere. She tried to reach up to him but again she couldn't get the dexterity required, she barely got out a long "ffffuuuuuuuuccccccccckkkkkkkkkkkk…….meeeeeee." Holden laid down beside her; she was still giggling and shaking violently. Every touch from Holden made her start convulsing all over again. "What….the….. fuck," she tried to say while using broken English. Not being able to think straight, she was barely able to utter the odd syllable. Holden began laughing, he was very proud of himself, "Thank you video instructor guy; you're the best," he thought to himself. Holden grabbed the blanket that was covering them earlier and pulled it back over them. He laid down beside her taking her in his strong arms. He held her tightly in hopes to get her shaking under control but having his naked body next to hers only seemed to exasperate the situation. He held her for what seemed like hours, she slowly regained her mental faculties. She rolled over towards Holden, putting her arms around him and gave him a kiss and was able to squeak out a 'good night.'

    Morning came. Holden woke up with a huge hard on. Not again he thought, but he couldn't blame it, he looked over at Paige's naked body, half covered by the sheets. Holden wanted to wake her up to fuck her but he decided she had a busy night and he knew there would be other opportunities in the future. Quietly he got out of bed, found his boxers and T shirt and decided to go watch some TV so she could sleep in. He strolled out of the bedroom to the kitchen and grabbed himself a glass of orange juice and sat on the couch. With the remote in hand he flipped through the channels before settling on a sports highlight show. Paige's roommate's door swung open quickly, startling Holden. Her roommate stumbled over, wearing only an open white bathrobe, her hair was a sure sign of the rough night she just had. Holden wasn't sure she saw him because she left her robe open. He whispered a hello to her so he didn't scare her and wake Paige or the other guest. The roommate had the same idea Holden had except she added two aspirins' to her orange juice breakfast. With her robe still open she sat on the chair beside the couch but she didn't sit in the traditional fashion. She squatted on the chair opening the robe further, revealing a small strip of hair on her pussy. Holden figured they were implants, not that he was about to complain. Trying not to stare, he met her eyes and said hello again. As she looked up at Holden, he was amazed to see it was the waitress/stripper Jeff was lusting after. He couldn't wait to tell him, then he wondered if maybe Jeff was her date and he was asleep in the next room. She took a sip of her juice.

"Mornin'" Holden said to her. Making as little movements as possible she replied, "Sounded like you two had fun last night."

"Ya, it was okay," Holden said with a big smile. "Your night sounded pretty good as well."

"It better have been great, I'd hate to feel this shitty for nothing." Her eyes widened as random flashbacks from the night before started to come back to her. "Oh my God, I came in on you two last night didn't I?"

"Yup, you did," Holden said holding back his laughs.

"Your cock is pierced isn't it?"

"Yup" Holden said nodding.

She put her hand in her head and gave it a shake. "I touched it didn't I?"

"Yup."

"I'm SO sorry," she said, obviously embarrassed.

"Think nothing of it," Holden said casually still trying to hold back his laughs.

As if to save her from the awkwardness Paige emerged from her bedroom wearing the same sweat pants and tank top as the night before. She threw Holden his pants then floated into the kitchen and grabbed herself a glass of orange juice before sitting on the armrest next to her roommate. "Nice to see you dear, all off you," she said trying to adjust her roommate's housecoat in a vain attempt to cover her up. Although Paige and Holden didn't drink that much the night before, there was no excuse for Paige being as mobile and alert as she was. Holden felt like hell and he knew Paige didn't have much more sleep than he did. "Holden, have you formally met my roommate Mel?"

"Sort of, from the restaurant and the club," he said responding to Paige. "Hi," he said to Mel, extending his hand, Mel painfully reached out and gave his hand a shake.

"Don't be rude," Paige said slapping Mel on the back of the head causing her great pain. Mel just made a disgruntled sound. Holden thought back to the first night they all met, he tried to remember Mel's stage name. "Sunshine? Yup, Sunshine, that's it." Mel left her bedroom door open and her company started moving around in the room. Mel's date climbed out of bed and with his back to the living room, he bent over to put on his pants. Holden was concerned that he couldn't look away, he just kept thinking about what a great ass that guy had. He was more concerned that Paige was sitting there in his field of view, another beautiful naked girl sitting in front of him, but yet he kept looking at the guy's ass.

Mel's guest didn't bother putting on a shirt when he came into the living room. Holden was more than relieved when he realized the guest was a girl. "Thank God," he thought. She was startled to see Holden, but not enough to cover up. Holden thought to himself that that day was starting out to be the best day of his life. Mel's date leaned in and gave Mel a good morning kiss, then she started kissing Mel's neck while whispering something to her. Mel slammed down her glass, stood up grabbing the other girl by the hand and they headed for her bedroom. "Nice meeting you," Mel yelled over her shoulder and then she slammed the door, not waiting for a response from Holden. Witnessing the brief lesbian encounter, Holden realized he was rock hard. Paige joined Holden on the couch, he put his arm around her and she snuggled into him. The moans and screams began from Mel's room. Paige turned up the TV to mask the sound to no avail; Mel was just way into her new friend.

Together Paige and Holden watched TV for a couple of hours before she looked at her watch and said, "I'm sorry Holden but I have to start getting ready for work."

"Ya, I should get going too," and as if on cue his cell started to ring. The call display read "Pete" and a picture of him passed out on a lawn flashed to the screen. "Dude, I have something awesome to tell you, I'll call you later," Holden said skipping the traditional phone etiquette. Paige stared at Holden disapprovingly, Holden tried to figure out what was wrong when he recalled the conversation he JUST had with Pete. "NO, NO, NO, the awesome news was that your roommate is the girl my friend has a HUGE crush on from the restaurant."

"Sure, sure," she said laughing. "You go brag to all your friends about your conquest; I'm going to go get ready for work."

"Will I see you again?" Holden asked hopefully.

With a look of focus and purpose she walked over to him, she grabbed him by the collar slammed him against the wall. "You're fucking right you will."

Smiling and feeling reassured Holden bit her neck. One of the symptoms of "the move" is that the feelings can be recalled hours later. Her knees went weak and Holden had to catch her before she fell to the floor. "Damn you," she said. "GO, we'll get together next weekend if that's okay with you," she said pushing him out the door so he wouldn't distract her from getting ready.

Holden bounced down the stairs without a care in the world. His heart and mind were racing with possibilities. "Don't get too far ahead of yourself, it was only one date, one amazing date," he thought. He opened the door to the street; the sunshine hit him in the face. "Yup, a beautiful day."

3

Shortly after Holden rang the buzzer to Paige's apartment, he heard a loud thump, thump, thump down the stairs. Holden thought that the steps sounded like they were coming from a person twice her weight. When she swung open the door; Holden was once again stunned by her beauty. She was wearing her hair in a pony tail which was tied up with elastic bands, complete with bright red bobbles. She was also wearing a white low cut cherry printed summer dress that hung to her mid thigh. To complete her outfit she wore big Doc Martin boots that came up to mid calf with white knee high socks underneath. As he fantasized about spinning her around, pressing her face against the rigid red bricks of her building, lifting up her skirt and fucking her against the wall, he realized he was getting hard. To avoid the potential embarrassment of getting caught with a hard on, Holden began making small talk on the way to the subway station. They talked about the weather and what she had done over the last week since they last saw each other. He had a decent idea since they had spoken to each other often on the phone. During a recent conversation they decided that if the weather was good on the weekend they would take advantage of it and go for a walk in the park along side Lake Ontario. The park was only a couple of subway stops away but it was too far to walk and since Paige had to work that night they figured they would rather spend their time in the park than on the busy city streets. Holden loved taking the subway, they were both people watchers and the TTC definitely gave them ample opportunity to see some strange people. As they made their way down the tunnel, they passed the usual people begging for change or sleeping in corners and other dark spots. They walked around a corner and saw a guy playing the saxophone; they stopped and listened to him for a minute.

Both agreeing he was quite good, Holden tossed him some change before moving to the platform to wait for their train.

Holden and Paige were met with a gust of wind that indicated that their train would soon be there. The familiar sound of chimes filled the nearly empty platform as the doors of the subway slid open. The pair climbed aboard and found their seats. During the ride, Paige entertained Holden with funny stories from her work, stories about the patrons and her coworkers. Holden listened intently; he could have listened to her all day because she was very upbeat and positive. As she talked, Holden casually looked around the train. He noticed the stares Paige was getting from pretty much everyone else on the train. It filled Holden with a sense of pride knowing everyone wanted her, yet she chose to spend her time with him. Station after station flew by when the P.A. finally announced that their stop was coming up next. They stood up and huddled by the doors waiting for the train to come to a stop. Once it was safe, the chimes sounded again, the doors opened and Paige and Holden jumped out and headed for the surface.

The park was not very far from the subway station, so the walk did not take that long. Once they got to the park they found a series of paved trails. After taking a look at the map they decided on the route they wanted to take to the lake. Holden cautiously reached for Paige's hand. He was nervous; even though they had held hands at the theatre, this was a whole new date. He didn't want to rush things but after his hand touched hers, she clenched tightly onto him and asked him what took him so long. Holden was starting to feel really comfortable with her, he was still hesitant, not wanting to throw his heart out too soon only to have Paige stomp all over it, but she was making it very hard for him not to fall madly in love with her.

The warm summer sun kissed their skin, the gentle breeze brought the smell of the surrounding trees, the lake and Paige's perfume ever so slightly to Holden's nose. He inhaled, eagerly taking in the scents. Along the trail they had to dodge inline skaters, joggers and dog walkers but even with all of that, the park wasn't as busy as they thought it was going to be on such a beautiful day. Paige spotted a swing set; her big brown eyes lit up as she ran over to it, dragging Holden behind her. They were all alone on the set as they sat down and casually dangled in the wind. They had an amazing view of the lake and were happy that no one else was around. They continued to sit on the swings, not really talking, just absorbing the moment and the view. Finally, they started some very casual conversation which quickly turned to more substantial talk about family and childhood memories. Paige told Holden how her parents divorced at a young age and her mom remarried shortly after the divorce. She went on to say how her real dad wasn't in the picture, but her step dad was very supportive and filled the role of male figurehead. She told him how her step dad always put an emphasis on schooling, which is why he pushed her into going to university. She also said that she took 2 years of a business degree before leaving to dance full time. Her relationship with her step dad had been rocky ever since because he couldn't understand the lifestyle. He told her that she was going to be living a life of sin and was throwing her life away. She explained to Holden that she wanted to go back to school after she figured out what she really wanted to do with her life. In the mean time she said she really enjoyed dancing and she was making excellent money doing so. There was a brief pause in the conversation, they got off the swings and continued walking to a more secluded patch of grass that still had a view of the lake. They laid down on the soft grass together. She rested her head on his stomach and looked up at him. He got lost in her eyes; he was starting to feel really comfortable with her and since she already opened up about her family, he asked her some more personal questions, about life and previous relationships. Eventually the topic of conversation turned to first loves and first times. Holden asked Paige when and how she lost her virginity. "Well, there isn't much of a story. I was 18, we were just about to finish our last semester of school. My boyfriend and I had been together for almost a year. We were both heading off to separate schools and he said the long distance relationship probably wouldn't work out. I agreed. We were both lying in bed knowing that that night might be our last time together. We were both virgins and after some time, lying there talking, I worked up the nerve to ask him to have sex with me. I told him that since we loved each other and I didn't want to go away to school only to get drunk and lose my virginity to a complete stranger, I asked if we could be together before he left. Since I was always the one telling him to wait, he was all for it. He said that he agreed that the first time was important to be with someone you love, because you always remember the first time. He said he wasn't going to forget me anyway so it only made sense. We started kissing and touching each other…don't get me wrong, we had fooled around a lot together, but that night it all seemed new. He appeared more awkward than normal. He stood up and took his clothes off, he had a beautiful cock that was very hard…, and I got nervous knowing it was soon going to penetrate me. He leaned over and undressed me, then stood at the side of the bed looking at me. I didn't know what to do so I just spread my legs, he fumbled over to me, reached down to his cock and after a few attempts he finally got inside me. It hurt at first. I wasn't sure if he was doing it right but I couldn't ask, it was his first time too so he didn't know if he was doing it right either. He was only inside me for what seemed like seconds when I saw that familiar look on his face. We weren't kissing and he wasn't touching me. I think he was too focused on fucking me to think about the other stuff, so I was just watching him. I was trying not to think about the uncomfortable feeling inside my pussy. He tensed up and pulled out of me so fast. As he did I could feel his cum shooting all over me like a fire hose. He stopped, looked at me uncomfortably then he got dressed, came over to me then gave me a big kiss and walked out. I didn't see him again for a very long time. It was so odd. Even though we had been together for so long, the way he left, it made me feel a bit dirty."

"Wow that was awful. At least it was with someone you loved."

"Ya, at least we had that...but when I saw him again, he made me feel so bad."

"How so?" Holden asked.

"Well, when he came back from school, he had a new girlfriend. She was beautiful, she looked like a Barbie doll. Back then I was such a tomboy, it made me feel awkward seeing them together, I was already very self conscious. Then to top it off he looked at me, well, through me, and said it was nice to be dating a real girl for a change. You have no idea how much it hurt. I didn't know why he would be so mean, we left under good terms, the only thing I could think of was that he was embarrassed about his performance and he was trying to make me feel bad for it. But whatever, I got over it."

"I'd say, you're gorgeous, has he seen you lately?"

"No, fuck him, he's an asshole. Ok, you, tell me about your first time," Paige asked.

"Mine? Well, it's not as dramatic, it was my 16th birthday. I was talking to a girl on the phone; she asked what I was doing for my birthday. When I told her nothing, she said she was sad that I was alone for my birthday and had her dad drive her to my place. Once she was over, I jokingly asked her what she brought me. I was kidding of course, but she said nothing, then quickly the conversation turned to sex. She asked if I had ever done it before. I told her I fooled around before, but never actually had sex. She walked over, grabbed my hand and led me to my bedroom. My parents were both away at work for a few hours; her dad wasn't coming to pick her up for awhile, so we had lots of time. We went into the bedroom; she pushed me onto the bed and stripped for me. She obviously knew what she was doing. I had no clue, it was the first time I had ever see a girl completely naked, I almost cam in my clothes." Paige laughed with the comment. "She asked if I was going to get naked, so I stood up and ungracefully undressed. As I did she took my spot on the bed, put her hands between her legs and started playing with herself, it was beautiful. I was excited to think I was about to fuck her. I was also nervous. Of course I had fantasized about sex, but it was about to become a reality. I got naked, laid on top of her and didn't bother with foreplay because, well, I had NO clue where anything was or how to work any of it. I tried getting my cock inside her; I couldn't find the hole anywhere. She got frustrated but she still giggled a bit trying to put me at ease. I'm sure she could tell I was REALLY nervous. She guided me inside her and well, like your first time, I only lasted about 2 seconds. I wasn't wearing a condom but I cam inside her anyway. I didn't think to pull out and I didn't want the feeling to stop. She understandably got mad at me for cumming inside her, and all I could think of was to say sorry. I rolled off of her, got dressed and laid beside her again. I tried kissing her, but I had no idea what post sex protocol was. Satisfied my present was delivered, she got dressed, called her dad, then we kissed when he got there and well, we never really talked about it again. It was a mess, but well, I was happy to finally get the first time over with. However, I assure you, I've gotten much better since then," Holden said with a wink

"Sure, sure, that's what they all say," Paige said. They sat quietly for a bit before Holden finally asked her "So, besides the money, what made you get into dancing?"

"Do you really want to hear the story?"

"If you want to tell me, I'm definitely interested," Holden said.

"Well...okay, but remember, you asked."

"Oh, this has to be good," Holden said with an air of curiosity in his voice.

Paige smiled as she continued, "It was the summer after my second and last semester of university. Like I said, I was a tomboy all through school, yes me. I honestly was," she said after seeing Holden's doubtful look. He couldn't imagine such a beautiful, feminine woman as being a tomboy, but he didn't say anything so she continued. "All my friends were guys; I just never got along with girls growing up. One of our friends had just turned 19; he was the last one of our group to become 'legal' so we took him to a strip club. We started off in the afternoon at my best friend's apartment.

We had a lot of beer, smoked a joint and headed out to the bar. I thought the dancers were hot and was amazed at the attention they got, not only from the guys in the audience but by all my friends. The way they looked at the dancers, I was jealous; no guy ever looked at me like that. We thought it would be a nice idea to get the birthday boy a lap dance. After picking out what we all agreed was the hottest girl in the bar, she came over, led him by the hand and disappeared into a backroom. I was curious about what happened back there. My best friend took my questions as a cue to get me a dancer of my own. I objected at first until this beautiful young girl came over and ran her fingers through my hair, just grazing my ear as she leaned in and whispered

'Hi, I'm Sunshine. I hear you'd like to go for a dance.' I couldn't refuse, she wasn't what I expected strippers to be and I actually found myself getting aroused by her. She led me by the hand to the back room. She paraded me past the open booths and past my friend who was stunned to see me back there. My friends that bought me the dance were disappointed she wasn't going to dance at the table so they could watch. Sucked to be them I thought. I sat down in the chair, not sure how to act; she sat on my lap, we chatted about why I was there and she totally put me at ease. I started to relax and the next song started to play, I watched her get naked. It was the first time I really looked at another girl naked before. Sure, I've seen other girls in the shower at the gym and in sports but I have never really looked at them; and here was this girl, her vagina was inches from my face. She told me I could touch her anywhere I wanted. I was hesitant at first; she grabbed my hands and put them to her tits as she sat in my lap. I started to feel them and compared them to my own, hers were definitely bigger and they felt so great, her back was pressed into mine as she asked me if I liked them. I of course told her I did and she asked if she could feel mine. I didn't have time to answer her when she spun around and she was now straddling me. I looked down I could see her legs spread, her clit was just about pressed against my jeans, I could feel her hands all over my chest. I was getting really turned on, she told me how much she liked my tits, how firm they were and before I knew it she reached up my shirt and started feeling me. I only had a couple of guys touch me like that; I was surprised to have a girl feel me up but I was even more surprised how gentle she was. She was definitely much more gentle and tender than any of the guys I was with. I really liked her. I started asking her about her life story, how she started to dance, etc. She told me it was to put herself through school because the money was great. I asked her about drugs and drinking and all the stereotypical things you hear about strippers. She said that those things definitely exist in the profession, but they aren't as rampant as everyone thought. Most of the girls were shy, quiet girls when they weren't at work. They were just there trying to make some money. I asked her how taking off her clothes and being worshipped by so many guys made her feel. She said it was hard to get over at first, she was nervous and uncomfortable but the other dancers made her feel comfortable and the guys cheering definitely helped motivate her. I asked her what it was like dancing for some gross guy and letting him touch her. She said that she tried to find a happy place and go through the motions to get it over with as fast as possible, and standing just out of reach didn't hurt either. But she also said most guys were respectful and not that bad to dance for. In no time our song was over. She started to get dressed and casually mentioned that I should become a dancer. I laughed and said that there was no way I could do something like that; I wasn't in the same league as the girls working there. She said she thought I was hot. I didn't think much of it, I went back to my friends table and they applauded as Sunshine and I emerged from the back room. After asking all my friends if they'd like a dance too, she leaned in and gave me a kiss on the cheek. I was surprised how hot she made me. The guys of course wanted a play by play recount of my dance. I told them to mind their own business and grabbed my beer. After several hours and several beers, we decided to continue drinking back at the apartment. On my way out, I heard 'WAIT!' We all turned around and saw Sunshine running towards us. She grabbed me and slid her hand in my front pocket, not so discretely copping a feel, as she whispered in my ear, 'In case you have anymore questions.' After we were in the cab, I looked at what was in my pocket; she slipped me her phone number. My friends were impressed and it was their turn to be jealous.

When we got home, I took my normal spot on the couch next to my best friend, one of the guys sat in an old arm chair at the end of the couch, and the other in a love seat across the room. Trying to be funny, one of the guys put on a porn flick and in a moment of drunken weakness, I told the guys that Sunshine said I should become a stripper. They roared with laughter saying I was too much of a tomboy and that I could never pull it off. I told them that I thought I could; my best friend told me to prove it. He turned off the porn and put on some music. 'Strip for us if you think you're so good,' he said as a dare, thinking I would never take him up on it. Well, I don't know if it was the pot or the beer but I stood up, started moving my hips to the beat and looked around. The four guys had their eyes glued on me. It was a sensation I had never felt before. It was very empowering. I first thought all I would do was tease them and chicken out; but as I kept going, the more I wanted to keep going. I put my hands under my shirt and lifted it up showing them my stomach and ribs. The guys were dead silent; all four were on the edge of their seats with their jaws dropped. I lowered my shirt just long enough to undo the top button of my jeans; I pulled them down just below my panty line and then raised my shirt up higher this time, giving them a peak of the bottom of my bra. I tried to dance like the dancers I saw that night but it wasn't working. The guys seemed to appreciate my effort anyway." Paige said with a laugh, she continued, "I turned around and bent over, letting them look at my ass. They still sat quietly, all wondering how far I would go, but none of them said anything in case the interruption made me change my mind. I was starting to get really worked up and before I knew it, I had my shirt up over my head. I heard a gasp from one of the guys as he saw my muscular back. We were all friends since childhood, but I don't think any of them saw me as a girl. I was just one of the guys and in less than two minutes they all saw me as a sexy woman. The gasp from one of the guys was all I needed to push me over the edge; still with my back to them I stood up, unzipped my fly and pulled off my jeans. I turned around, stepped one foot out and kicked the jeans up at my friend. He didn't move; they hit him in the face then fell to the floor. I kept trying to move to the music but it was harder the more worked up I got. I started to let my hands run all over my body until I slipped them under my bra and pushed it up over my tits, the only thing covering them now was my hands. I wanted them to see me, oh God how badly I wanted them to see me. I moved my hands to my back and unfastened my bra. I heard one of the guys say 'oh God', I could tell they were all getting hard, hard for me, it was an incredible feeling having four guys attention knowing at that point I could make them do anything. I continued to play with my tits and I rubbed my hands over my waist and pussy. I turned around again and pulled my panties up into the crack of my ass, giving myself a camel toe. I was positive that my white cotton panties were so wet they were see-through. With the panties up my ass like a thong, I played with my ass cheeks, spreading them apart, bending over and looking at my friends through my legs. Over the last 15 years I have known these guys, none of them looked at me before, and now I certainly had the attention of all four. I was getting hot. I turned around and started rubbing my tits again; I ran my hands through my hair which was blonde at the time. As my arms reached above my head, it pulled my already perky tits up. I caught a glimpse of myself in a mirror on the wall, they looked fantastic and I looked fantastic. Seeing myself gave me even more confidence and I took my fingers out of my hair and slid them down my body to my panties. I pulled the waist band down, forcing them out of my ass and off my soaked pussy. I dropped them to the ground, picked them up and gave them a long sniff, copying a move I saw a girl do on stage. That was it for the guys, I could see their smiles and I imagined their hard cocks growing as they watched me. I kept dancing, completely naked. I tried to move around so they could see all of my body. Apparently it was too much for my best friend to take. Out of the corner of my eye I saw him fidgeting with his jeans. I thought I knew what he was going to do and I could no longer focus on dancing, I just wanted to see his cock. Well, that's exactly what I saw, he pulled out his cock, it was so big and hard, he started rubbing it while he looked at me. I started to touch myself; that was all the motivation the other three needed. In seconds all the guys had their cocks in their hand. I had to touch them all; I dropped to my knees and crawled over to my friend. I reached out and took his cock in my hand; I started to gently rub it, making eye contact with the other guys. I eventually leaned in and took his cock in my mouth. I started sucking him like it was the last cock on the planet, like a porn star. It of course wasn't the last cock as I found out when I felt some pressure on my hips and before I could look around I felt a dick slide into me. I didn't notice that the guys had all moved around me. One of the remaining guys was on his back; he slid underneath me until I felt his tongue working over my clit. I reached out and grabbed the cock of the guy that was now licking me, his mouth felt great on my pussy so it was the least I could do for him. The last guy crawled over to me and was kneeling patiently waiting for one of my holes to fuck. I started rubbing his cock too. Then it dawned on me, I was taking four cocks all at once; I felt so very dirty yet so alive. My pussy was aching with pleasure, which they all noticed because of my moans that were getting louder and louder. The guys all reacted to my moans, the cock in my pussy was fucking me harder and faster, the guy licking me was now in rhythm to the cock fucking me and the vibrations of my moans on the cock in my mouth was driving that rod nuts. I almost ripped off the two erections in my hand as my orgasm grew to the point of release. At the same time I started to orgasm, I felt the cock in my mouth explode. I had never tasted cum before, but I swallowed ever last drop and now I associate the taste of cum with that night, the smell of it almost makes me orgasm retroactively. I just can't get enough of it." Holden sat silently, he reflected on what her last sentence possibly meant for him and without saying anything he let her continue. "As my friend finished cumming in my mouth, he graciously got out of the way making room for the guy under me to move in so I could start sucking him off. I still gave the other guy a hand job. I had the taste of cum in my mouth and I wanted more, I sucked the cock with renewed vigor and I was jerking off the other one with an intense purpose. I felt the guy in my pussy tremble, the cock thrusted deep inside me and I could feel his cum explode. The tongue was still licking my now very sensitive clit and I felt like I was going to orgasm again. I had never had multiple orgasms before, not even by myself. The guy finally pulled out of me, he was still cumming. I felt it land all over my back and ass, then I felt his hand rub it into my skin. I couldn't do anything but continue sucking the cock in front of me. The guy barely had time to stop cumming and the guy getting the hand job took his place. I heard someone say something about sloppy seconds and then I felt his cock plunge deep inside my pussy then slide completely out. I wanted to be fucked, I was about to look back to encourage him to fuck me but then I felt the tip of his cock putting pressure on my ass. I had NEVER had anything in my ass before, I wasn't sure what to expect but since it was a night of new experiences I didn't stop him. I felt his cock, the largest of the four, slide into my ass, inch by inch. I tensed at first, but I quickly realized that tensing wasn't helping so I tried to relax by focusing my attention on the cock in my mouth. The cock slid all the way in my ass and slowly started to work in and out of me. It felt great. Seeing that I was comfortable with him fucking my ass he started fucking me faster and faster, I finally orgasmed again, an orgasm more intense then I have ever felt before. The cock in my mouth blew. Since I was already gasping for air from my own orgasm, I couldn't take his cum, instead I let it fall out of my mouth and I began jerking him off, milking out all the jiz. It sprayed hard against my face, so much cum, I was almost drowning in it, I was glad I didn't let him shoot it all in my mouth. I think the sight of me being glazed like a whore in the videos we were watching and the knowing he was the first in my tight virgin ass, the guy fucking me release inside me, I felt his large cock twitch and the cum filling me up. After his cock slipped free of me, I rolled over onto my back, my legs still spread, and the guys were all lying on the floor next to me. I was spent. 'So, you guys still don't think I could become a dancer?' I asked them. 'You have our vote,' was the unanimous decision. I woke up naked in the middle of the floor, one of the guys moved to the couch, one to the loveseat. The two remaining guys were on the floor next to me. I looked around, all four were also still naked. Sobering up I could feel that the cum had dried hard on my face, making it hard to see. I thought I would really regret what I did, but seeing all those cocks and remembering not long ago they were all hard for me, it turned me on. My friends and I have never talked about that day, and we all have gone our separate ways, only talking once a year or so. I called Sunshine the next day and well, the rest is history. Oh my God, you must think I'm the biggest slut."

"Oh, quite the contrary," Holden said, trying to reassure her. He was now lying on his stomach like she was, she was completely oblivious to the fact Holden had a raging hard on from her story. "Sunshine, as in your roommate Sunshine?" He asked.

"Yup, one in the same. Coincidently that day was the same day I saw my ex, he already put my femininity into question so I thought I had something to prove before the night even started."

"That is crazy, I want to hear more Syn and Sunshine stories another time, but seriously I thought that story was SO hot. It's too bad your ex was such an ass, but at least something good came out of it. You became who you are now, and I think you are amazing."

"Awww, thank you. But seriously though, what could you be thinking about me except I'm some slutty stripper?"

Laughing Holden replied, "Trust me, I don't think that at all. I think it is awesome you're so open sexually and I'm very flattered you're willing to tell me such a personal story and well, I'd be lying if it didn't turn me on."

"You're just saying that, but thank you and I'm sure I'll never hear from you again," she said reluctantly.

"Oh, you're going to hear from me again. Trust me, I would rather be with a girl that's been with a thousand guys than a virgin."

"What?"

"Ya, really, I figure if you date a virgin one of two things will happen. Either she isn't ever going to like it or feel comfortable during sex, so it will always be the same boring thing over and over OR, she will LOVE it and wonder what she has been missing and eventually she will cheat on you or leave you. If you date a girl that is sexually free and has had many partners and experiences by the time she settles down with you, she knows exactly what she wants and that she wants you."

"I never thought of it that way before, but I haven't been with THAT many guys," Paige said laughing.

"No, no, I wasn't saying that you were with a lot of guys. I just like that you're willing to try new and different experiences, I have experimented myself."

"Oh ya? Like what?"

"I have never told another living soul this story; you have to promise me you won't judge me or repeat it to anyone"

"After what I told you, how could I judge you?" Paige said.

"Wait for it, promise me."

"Ok, I promise."

"Okay, it happened one night in college. The boys and I went out to a strip club, unfortunately, it wasn't the one you were working at or maybe we could have met months ago. Anyway, after several lap dances we all got horned up and headed home. I got back to residence; I thought I was being all sneaky and quiet when I stumbled through the door. I was sure I didn't wake up my roomy. I turned on the TV and there was soft-core porn on. I took it was a sign and in my state of liquid courage I decided to take the time to masturbate. I stripped right down to nothing, I took my now rock hard cock in my hand and started stroking it. I'm not sure if I passed out for a minute or if I was too drunk to realize it but next thing I knew my roommate was now sitting on the edge of my bed watching me jerk off. Startled I tried to cover up, he said 'No no it's okay,' as he interlocked his fingers with the ones on my cock. I threw my hands in the in air and let out a startled scream. Then I realized his hand was still on my cock, his grip was much tighter and he was stroking me. He could see the anxiety in my face, he just told me to watch the TV and imagine that the girl on the screen was the one jerking me off. In my drunken haze, I turned my head and I hesitantly let him continue. I kept denying it to myself but it felt amazing, so firm, so hard, yet so wrong. I was caught up in the TV and the sensation I didn't realize he changed his position and his mouth was now wrapped firmly around my cock. He sucked me off like no girl has. His mouth expertly slid up and down my hard shaft, his tongue was toying every inch of me. He positioned his hand so he held my balls in his palm. He rolled them around, never missing a beat while he continued to suck me. I fought the urge to release in his mouth. I stopped watching the TV and focused completely on not cumming and the fact that another man had his lips on my cock. As he continued to fondle my sack, his fingers grazed my asshole a couple of times, it felt odd, a good kind of odd. I guess since I didn't jump or push his hand away, that gave him a green light. As he continued to take me deep into his mouth, his hand slowly left my balls and he had a finger making small circles around my asshole, slowly getting deeper and deeper with ever circle until he penetrated me. I jumped, like your story; nothing has ever been inside me like that before. I'm embarrassed to admit it, but it felt GREAT. I let him finger me for about 10 seconds and that was all I could take. I could only let out a OH MY G…when his mouth slide off my cock, his free hand grabbed firmly onto my shaft and gave me a couple of very firm tugs, his finger slammed deep into ass, as deep inside as they could possibly go. I began to cum, so hard with so much pressure, I even managed to hit myself in the face. I have never made so much cum before. He didn't stop, his hand jerked me off hard until every last twitch and ounce of cum was out of me. I laid there breathless and motionless. Random thoughts started running through my head about what just happened, I questioned my sexuality, I wondered if I was gay or bi, I wasn't sure, but what I did know was that I wasn't attracted to him. I didn't find his body sexy or anything but I did love the way he touched me. He was still kneeling beside me looking at his handy work that was still splashed across my stomach, chest and face. 'My, my what a mess, let's get you cleaned up,' he said, I went to stand up to grab a towel and he forced me down then started to lick my cum off of me. I was still drunk and paralyzed with ecstasy, I didn't know if I liked what he was doing but I let him continue, everything was great so far. His tongue slowly worked its way up my neck; his hot breath started the blood flowing again, he noticed I was getting hard. 'Wow, so soon?' he said with a smile, he then went back to licking the cum off of my face. He stood up and walked beside me, his cock, which was longer and thicker than mine was inches away from my face. I knew what he wanted but I wasn't sure if I was ready for it yet. I wasn't sure if I wanted to even feel it in my hand let alone my mouth. He finally got tired of waiting for me, he grabbed my hand and guided it to his cock. I didn't fight him; instead I reached out and wrapped my fingers around it. I was definitely shy at first until he gave me the advice to do the same as I would do to my own cock while I was masturbating, do to him what I like done to me. I started to slowly stroke his cock, it didn't feel weird at all and he was definitely starting to get into it. I started beating him off just as hard and as fast as he did to me. I wanted to make him cum, it was my personal goal. I saw the tip of his long cock starting to glisten with precum, he felt it too, he took the tip of his finger and cleaned off his cock. The cum formed a string to the tip of his finger which he extended to my mouth. I amazed myself, I didn't fight or say no, I just went with the flow leaning my head back, I opened my mouth and stuck out my tongue and his fingers slid across it. I was very hard again, I was no longer questioning my sexuality; I just went with it, and I knew I loved women but this was too great to pass up. I finally worked up the courage; I leaned forward and took his beautiful cock in my mouth. I sucked him, clumsily at first, I had never even thought about sucking a guy off before let alone proper technique. I just remember his advice of doing it the way I like it to be done to me. I took him as deep as I could without gagging. He moaned with pleasure and then started thrusting his hips as he fucked my mouth. His hand slid down and grazed past my cock. That slight touch almost made me cum again. He went straight for my asshole. He started fingering me deep and fast. I started moving my hips to fuck his finger as his cocked worked away inside my mouth. Unexpectedly he pulled out and moved my hand. I was wondering if I did something wrong, I didn't think he was about to cum. He soon answered my question with an action; he pulled his finger out of me and put it behind my knee. He started shuffling down the bed, I let out a faint no and he just kept saying it was ok and to trust him. I let out another less convincing no; all I heard from him was shhhh. He was now between my legs as he leaned his body onto mine. I thought he was going to reassure me, which he started too, but while he was talking to me, he positioned his cock so the tip was already starting to ease into me. I didn't fight him or resist, I just clenched my fingers into the bed as he slid his large cock slowly inside me, and I could feel it getting deeper and deeper. I was amazed my ass could take a cock let alone stretch big enough for his. It didn't even hurt; he was so slow and careful, very gentle. He slid back down my body and was kneeling erect between my legs as he continued to inch his way further inside me. As much as I was embarrassed by the fact I had a cock inside me, it felt SO good, I was getting harder. Once he was fully inside me and gave my ass enough time to expand to fit his girth, he began fucking me. Slowly then working up harder and deeper, he wouldn't let me touch myself telling me it wasn't time. Precum was oozing from me; he occasionally took a taste of it using his finger as a spoon. He was fucking me harder and harder, the girl on the TV began to moan as she satisfied her own cock. I couldn't believe that the simple act of getting my ass fucked was about to make me cum. He started to moan heavily. I told him to fuck me harder, then I heard him tell me he was going to cum. He grabbed my cock and almost ripped it off as his body tensed, his cock slammed deep inside me and with that mighty thrust I could feel his cum shoot inside me, the pressure was enough for me and I cam in his hand. He reached his cum soaked hand to my mouth,

I couldn't believe it, was he really going to feed me my own cum? He was serious and as I ate it all off of him, I could still feel his cock twitching inside me. He eventually pulled out, I cam again, this time it was like a fountain. I didn't think I would have had any left in me but yet, I was cumming and I couldn't stop. I almost went into convulsions, I lost ALL control. It was amazing. Then suddenly he was out of me and started to walk away. I asked him what would happen the next day, he just looked back at me and asked what I was talking about, told me I was drunk and it was all in my imagination. We never mentioned that night again, nor have I been with another man but I have gained a whole new respect for anal sex."

Paige looked at Holden for several seconds before she grabbed his shirt and pulled him to her, she started kissing him then stopped. "Sorry, and wow, did that really happen?"

"I swear to God."

"That is so hot, thank you for telling me."

"So you don't think less of me?"

"Not at all, I just would never have imagined. Despite the tattoos and piercings, no offense, but you look pretty conservative."

"Well, ya, that's just the tip of the iceberg, I am open for almost anything."

"Sounds like we might have a lot in common," Paige said.

"Ya, but the worst part is, the more adventurous I get the more adventurous I have to be the next time."

"Me too, that's why I keep dancing. The intensity and sexuality from the night with my friends, I was hoping dancing would duplicate it and sometimes it comes close when the bar is full and the crowd is cheering me but really, it just hasn't been the same."

"Have you ever escorted?"

"No, I have thought about it and even though I know there can be a distance between love and sex, I think that's even a boundary I'm not willing to push. I do fantasize about being paid for sex and being used but I think that is something that will just have to remain a fantasy."

"Cool, for the record, I haven't escorted either. Not because I think it's morally wrong but well, I have a hard enough time giving sex away for free let alone trying to get someone to pay for it." They both laughed at Holden's joke. "So, why Syn?"

"Well, I got the idea from my step dad, that argument we had, he said I was off to live a life of sin. That word stuck in my head; to me it means so many things. It symbolizes everything that is wrong if you're religious but being an atheist, I use it as an anti-statement. Meaning you can live a life as a dancer, let strangers enjoy seeing your naked body, profit from it even, be sexually explorative and still be a good person. That's why I spell it with a Y instead of an I"

"Wow, all that in a name and up until now I just thought it was a cool name."

"See, you learn something new every day," she said with an adorable laugh.

Holden stopped and looked at Paige. "Is it just me, or have we learned way more about each other than we should have on a second date?" "I know, I don't know why I got into all that, I normally gloss over details but Holden, excuse the pun, you have a hold on me. You better not hurt me." She shimmied up his body and started to kiss him with a very deep and passionate kiss. Her hand found the back of his head as they continued to kiss. Holden put his arms around her waist and squeezed. Having her in his arms felt very familiar, like they have been together for years. It was a feeling he didn't want to let go of easily as he squeezed her even tighter. Their embrace must have lasted for an hour, before they knew it the sun was starting to set over the lake. She took a quick look at her watch. "We don't have much time; I have to be at work in a couple of hours," she said with genuine disappointment. "Let go sit on the swings again." As they got up, Holden tried to hide his erection.

The park had no one else in sight. They took their seats and swung hand in hand until Paige jumped off her swing and used some of her dancing talents to grab the chains of Holden's swing and pulled herself up face to face with him. She put her legs through the chains beside him and lowered herself onto him until she was sitting on Holden's lap. As he hugged her, they kissed again and it was so pure and raw. The fact that her relatively short skirt was over his lap, leaving nothing between them except possibly some panties, didn't escape Holden. Their hands ran all over each other, while the swing gently swung in no particular direction. Finally, she spoke and Holden could tell she was thinking about what she was going to say for awhile before finally working up the nerve. "Your story made me fucking hot, I want to fuck you, I want to feel your piercings inside me." Holden didn't need much more incentive; he reached down to his shorts. As he was trying to unzip, he had Paige look around for any unsuspecting voyeurs. Satisfied they were alone, she once again used her dancing prowess to pull herself up the chains high enough so that her waist was above his head. Her skirt blew up enough for him to see that she wasn't wearing any panties. That had him even more excited. He quickly got his fly unzipped and pulled out his cock. She leaned over to take a look, confident neither of them would get caught in the jagged metal of Holden's zipper she slowly lowered herself down positioning his cock to match her wet pussy. She slid down taking all of him inside her. At the last inch she let go of the chain and slammed down on him. Holden was startled and thought he must have let out a strange sound, because Paige asked him if he was okay. Holden quickly reassured her and they hugged tightly. They didn't immediately start fucking, instead they just started swinging back and forth, feeling each other with each pump of their legs. It was slow at first but amazing. Paige thought about what she was doing, what it meant. She rarely, if ever, gave herself to a guy on the second date but she knew there was something special about Holden. She was happy to have such a memorable first time with such an amazing guy. The experience was like everything else to this point in their relationship. Perfect. Their eyes locked onto each other as they swung back and forth, her dress was covering his waist. If anyone was to walk by, they would look just like any other young couple in love sharing a ride on a swing; they wouldn't expect the naughty event that was taking place. Holden's cock gently worked away inside her, easing in and out as they swung back and forth. "So, do you like the piercings or do they hurt?"

"Ummm hmmmm I like them, they don't hurt at all," she said in her best cute little girl voice.

Their swinging got faster and faster until they were both pumping very hard. Her pussy slid up and down his cock, their eyes were still locked on each others. They were so fixated on each other they missed the strain that they were putting on the children's swing. They heard a loud BANG as the chains broke sending them crashing to the ground. They never separated in the fall; their embrace was just as tight after they landed. When they landed, she came crashing down hard onto his cock forcing him to penetrate her deep, tearing into her. He was scared he ruptured something inside of her and she was concerned that she hurt him in the fall. After a quick assessment of each other they decided they were both okay and they kept on fucking. Since they landed in the sand, she stayed on top; she fucked him fast and hard. The adrenaline from the fall was making their hearts race. She leaned down in such a way he could see down her dress, her tits freely jiggled around with the momentum. He thought it was so hot when she leaned into his ear and whispered, "Cum for me,

I want to feel you cum." Holden wanted to wait for her to orgasm, but it was soon out of his hands, she was fucking him harder and harder, her breathing was getting deeper and more sporadic. He knew she was about to cum too, waiting till he was certain she could finish without him, he squeezed her hand and shouted "I'm going to cum!"

"FUCK ME!!" she screamed even louder. Not as a direction to Holden but more of a scream of ultimate satisfaction as she felt his cum fill her pussy. Holden felt her hot liquid rushing against his cock fighting against the juices of his own orgasm. She collapsed onto him, her boots were digging into his legs as she squeezed her legs closed holding his cock in place. They both looked at each other knowing that if his cock was to slide out of her, their fluids were going to gush out of her all over his shorts. Since he didn't have a change of clothes or a jacket or something to cover up the mess, having it leak out of her at that point would be a very bad thing. With her thighs firmly against his, they rolled over with him now on top of her. He used his powerful arms to push them up so they were kneeling, her arms and legs were tightly secured around him, he managed to stand up with her holding onto him. Like a gentleman, he lifted her skirt as she eased her grasp and parted from him. As expected, once the cork was free the combination of their collective cum rushed out of her. She let out a pleasurable moan with the unusual sensation. Holden had to catch her as her knees buckled momentarily. They looked each other over for evidence of their act, Holden had a small wet stain on his shorts but it wasn't that obvious against the camouflaged pattern. Paige adjusted her dress that had become all twisted. They looked down at the wet spot between her feet; she looked back up at Holden with a look of pure satisfaction on her face and a devilish smile. Holden wanted to jump her again but instead he extended his hand. She reached for it and Holden pulled her into him. She looked at him after the unexpected collision of bodies. "Hi," Holden said to her. Paige looked at him and as she bit her bottom lip she managed to get a 'hi' out. Holden leaned in and gave her a kiss. Again they wrapped their arms around each other, running them wildly all over, their kiss was long and passionate. At least Holden thought it was passionate, right up until he caught Paige looking at her watch. "Fuck, I really have to go get ready for work and thanks to you I need a shower," she said with a wink. Grabbing his hand they started walking towards the subway station. The entire train ride Holden was paranoid everyone could see the sex stain on his shorts. She fidgeted around in her seat as she felt their cum drip out of her. They finally got to her place. Holden stopped at the door as she eventually got her keys into the lock. "I'll see you later?" she said with an air of anticipation in her voice.

"You better believe it," he replied. Satisfied with his answer, she spun around and ran up the stairs. Her quick departure made Holden smile; he smiled even bigger when he overheard her singing as she ran up the stairs. Holden turned around towards the street, looked up at the beautiful night sky.

4

A couple of weeks had past since Holden and Paige last saw each other. They did however; talk on the phone and online regularly. They found it difficult to find time to hang out as they were both working a lot, especially since Holden had a day job and Paige having a night job.

Holden's phone rang. "Hello?"

"Holden its Paige, how are you doing?"

"Good thanks, what's up?"

"I got an offer to go dance in North Bay this weekend. I've never been there before and I really don't want to go alone."

"Oh ya?"

Paige started to laugh at Holden's attempt to make her spell it out. "Ya, what are you doing this weekend?"

"Let me check my schedule." Not even letting a second past he remarked, "Yup, I seem to be free."

"Well, would you like to go with me? The club will pay for gas and a motel."

"What kind of a club is it? Will you be safe? What will be expected of you?"

"I talked to one of the girls that has been up there. It's about the same as here as far as their touching policy. She said its clean safe place and the owner/manager is a good girl to work for. I would just feel more comfortable with you there. That is, if you're up for it."

"Sure, what time do you have to be there?"

"I have to start around eight on Friday night. It's about a four hour drive and I would like to get there in time to see where the club is, get dinner and settled into the motel. Would it be possible to leave by 2ish?"

"I work Friday, but I'm sure I can duck out early. I think they'll understand."

"Thanks Holden. You're a lifesaver."

"Anything for you pretty lady. See you Friday."

Since Paige's call on Wednesday all Holden could think about was their weekend away together. He was getting excited and nervous. He knew she'd be working and he didn't know his way around North Bay at all. He didn't know what he was going to do to kill time but he did know he couldn't afford to hang out at the club all weekend.

Friday finally arrived. Holden snuck out of work at noon, went home, packed and got ready. He drove over to Paige's apartment and, as luck would have it, he managed to find a parking spot right in front of her building. Holden just chalked his luck up to the fact that it was a Friday afternoon and most of the city seemed to evacuate up to their cottages in Muskoka on Friday afternoons.

Holden walked up to Paige's door and rang the door bell. He soon heard the familiar thump, thump, thump, thump down the stairs, the door swung open and Paige clumsily fell through the doorway with her luggage in tow. Holden grabbed her bags and helped her to the car. "You know it's only a couple of days, eh?" He said poking fun at her.

"Well, I do have to look my best," was her answer.

"Fair enough, ready?"

"Yup. This your car?"

Holden forgot that she had never seen his car before because he rarely drove it in the city, the public transit system and his inline skates were definitely more convenient. "Ya, that's her."

"It's awesome."

"Thanks" Holden said glowing with pride. His car was a 'classic' 1984 BMW 633 csi. It was his pride and joy. Holden walked over to the car, popped the trunk and packed her things away. After asking Paige if she had everything and her confirming that she did, they jumped in the car and began heading out of the city.

The drive was going to be long, but Holden looked forward to having the opportunity to spend all that time with Paige. The weather was a perfect summer day; a great day for a road trip. As expected, the traffic heading north was crazy. Holden anticipated stop and go for the first little bit. They had the CD player cranked to some good rockin' tunes as they tried to make the best of the situation. They were both singing and playing air guitar. Paige looked gorgeous; she was wearing fishnet thigh highs,

Chuck Taylor's, a plaid skirt and a white blouse. She didn't do anything special with her hair, it was just washed and still a bit wet. Her natural curls hung freely over her shoulders. Holden tried his best to keep his eyes off her and on the road. As she was busy rocking out in the passenger seat he found it that much harder not to watch her. She was so fun and full of life. He was happy just being near her. At one point she started looking out the window, holding his hand and taking in the scenery. As they got stuck in yet another traffic jam, Holden glanced over at her and knew it was going to be impossible to keep his eyes on the road. Her hands started running all over her body. She then undid a couple of buttons on her blouse, exposing the red lace bra that just a moment ago was only hinted at beneath her white top. Her hands caressed her tits; she put her left foot up on the dashboard and the other out the open window. Her skirt rode up exposing the tops of her fish nets and almost far enough to show off her pussy. The unexpected show got Holden hard. He was going to ask her what she was doing, but decided to just enjoy her antics. She stopped holding his hand and wasn't paying attention to him at all now. Both of her hands were running all over her body until they found her knees. They slowly slid up her legs to play with the bows on the top of her thigh highs for a minute before continuing up to her inner thighs. She pulled her skirt up giving Holden a peek of her sheer black panties. As she was still looking out the window and it became clear to Holden that the show wasn't for him. Holden didn't care why she was doing it, he was just happy that she was. Her hands caressed her thighs, one hand started rubbing her pussy, and the other reached up to her tits. Both hands were rubbing frantically, her hips started moving as she got more and more into her show. By this time Holden's cock was hard. His jeans were tight and they created a lot of resistance to his little man of steel causing him some discomfort. Luckily the traffic wasn't going anywhere because he didn't want to stop watching the show going on in the seat next to him. She started firmly rub her clit. The soft moans that came from her lips were almost unbearable to Holden. Her hand reached under her bra to caress her bare breast. Holden couldn't see what was going on past her open shirt, but the knowing was good enough for him. Unfortunately the traffic started to move and he now had to split his attention between Paige and the road. As the car started to move she stopped what she was doing and randomly flipped the bird out of the window. She brought her feet back down to the mat and started to laugh. Holden looked at her with a very confused look. "What was all that about?" He asked her.

Paige, laughing almost uncontrollably, "That trucker beside me was staring at me for the last hour so I thought I would fuck with him."

"All that was for a trucker just so you could fuck with him?"

"Ya, my bad," she said with a devilish smile.

"Wow, if that's how you fuck with people, you can fuck with me anytime," Holden said with a chuckle.

"Oh, sorry, I hope I didn't bother you," she said biting her lip holding back her smile. Her eyes ever so slowly lowered down to Holden's jeans, she could see the bulge that was now very prominent. Reaching over, she gave it a pat like someone would pat the top of a pet's head. "Sorry about that, I'll make it up to you. I promise." Holden just gave her a smile and continued to drive. His hard on wasn't as easy to pacify; it stayed attentive for the next hour.

The miles passed with more casual conversation, rocking out and comfortable silence. Finally, the traffic opened up a bit. Holden's car was running perfectly at 150 km/h, making up some good time as they past Barrie. Paige looked at her watch, which had a skull and cross bones covering the face and a band that had the same print. To see the time she simply flipped up the skull. "I'm hungry." Holden said they were almost half an hour out of Muskoka and that he was going to need gas around that time so he asked her if she could hold off until then. Confirming that she could, Holden then enticed her further by telling her he had the perfect surprise for her. "Oh, I like surprises," she said.

"It's not a big one so don't get too excited." He said trying not to get her hopes up. The minutes continued to pass; there was now a nice mix of city and country scenery. The traffic was thinning as they passed more and more exits. The sun was still shining with not a cloud in the sky. More songs played, more conversations passed. Finally, Holden saw what he was looking for, a big green exit sign that said 'Severn Bridge.' Holden decelerated and took the exit. Paige was surprised by the sudden turn. "Where are we going?"

"Just for a side trip, trust me." Holden said. They continued down the road, past some twists and turns, until Holden finally let Paige in on his little secret. He was going to take her for a tour of his hometown. He pointed out his old house, other family members' houses and neighbours that they didn't like. He showed her everything. Paige took in the sites, she didn't say much but he was happy to share his hometown with her while he had the opportunity. Eventually she broke the silence. "I knew you were from Muskoka, but I just assumed you were from a town."

"Nope, I'm as backwoods as they come. Still love me?" Holden said with a laugh. He took the back roads to the highway and headed north to find something to eat in the nearest city, which was only 15 minutes away. Instead of driving into the town they found a small restaurant on the highway. Holden knew Paige, in her sexy little outfit, wasn't going to stand out because the community was used to all the vacationers in the summer. Holden down shifted the powerful BMW engine and guided the car off the main highway onto the gravel driveway. The gravel crunched under the tires as he pulled into a parking spot. Paige took a minute to gather her things, so Holden took the opportunity to walk around the car to open the door for his beautiful girl. Like a lady, she swung both her legs out so that she didn't give the locals the same view a lucky trucker got earlier. Holden extended his hand making her smile as she and reached for it. Grabbing Holden's hand she pulled herself out of the car. As they walked into the diner, Holden placed his arm around her waist opening the door to the sound of a 'bing bong', which alerted the staff to the arrival of their new patrons. They barely got a glance from others as they found their seat. The waitress came over and took their drink order while dropping off the menu. They perused the limited menu and eventually both decided on burgers. While they were waiting for their food, they looked around at the other diners, mostly locals with the odd tourist thrown into the mix. Like Holden, they didn't want to drive off the main highway to find some generic fast food place. The radio was playing some horrible elevator type music. It was hard to tell exactly what song they were ruining, but they did know that whatever it was, they succeeded. Holden and Paige shared knowing glances and nods towards some particularly strange customers. Their attention snapped to each other as they both acknowledged the song that was playing. It was a very poor cover of a song they were listening to in the car. Smiling, Holden stood up, walked over to Paige and once again extended his hand. She just sat and looked at him confused. "Care to dance m'lady?" Paige looked at him like he was crazy. Holden stayed by her with his hand extended, not willing to take no for an answer. "You are crazy," Paige confirmed as she grabbed his hand and stood up. He pressed his body against hers and put his hands around her waist. She put her arms around his broad shoulders. They slowly started moving to the music, ignoring the disapproving stares of the other diners and staff members. Paige giggled through the entire dance; Holden fought back his urge to laugh as well. Time seemed to stand still as they shuffled back and forth in that dirty old diner on the side of the highway. Neither of them was sure if the song they originally started to dance to ended and a new one began, however they did know their dance was over when the food arrived. They parted and retook their seats to the applause of one or two of the spectators. Holden wasn't sure if they were applauding their dancing or them stopping, either way, the only person Holden cared about was sitting across the table from him sinking her teeth into her hamburger.

Dinner was over rather quickly and they got back onto the road, North Bay was just over an hour away and they were both anxious to get there. The BMW sparked to life. Holden hit the gas and all 6 cylinders threw them back into their seats as Holden accelerated to match the flow of traffic whizzing past them. Paige flipped up the skull on her watch, it read five P.M. The sunny skies were misleading, the sun was burning brightly like it was only early afternoon. Paige relaxed, happy in the knowledge that even with their stops they were making good time. As they got closer Paige became more and more nervous about dancing in a strange town but felt better having Holden there with her. As they traveled further north, the cities stopped and the sites turned into the rare small town surrounded by wilderness. They both remarked how beautiful it was but it made Holden a bit home sick. Paige unfastened the seat belt and snuggled up next to him, putting her head on his shoulder and wrapping her arm around his. He could smell her hair which reminded him of their walk in the park and that began to arouse him. Her hand started rubbing his leg until it crept further and further up his thigh. Her head started moving around on his shoulder as she pressed her breast into his arm. Holden took his right arm off the steering wheel and put it around her shoulders, her body slid down so her head was now in his lap. Holden gently caressed her hip as he continued to rocket them down the highway. With her head snuggled in his lap it didn't take her long to notice his erection under his jeans. She pressed her cheek into the bulge and moved her head around a bit. "My, my, what are we going to do about this?" "I can't do anything, I'm driving so I guess it's on its own."

"Good, safety first, you drive. Don't mind me." She repositioned herself so that she could undo his belt and zipper. Once she had them completely open she slid her cold hand into his boxers and with a firm grasp she pulled out his cock. Her hand gently slid up and down his entire length a couple of times before she opened her sensual lips and took his cock into her mouth. The warmth of her saliva was a nice change from her cold hands which were still wrapped around the base of his cock. Her finger tips reached down to gently tease his testicles. Her head bobbed up and down sliding the full length of his cock in and out of her wanting mouth. Holden took the opportunity to reach down to her ass and pull up her skirt. Between trying to keep his eyes on the road, sneaking peaks at her perfect body and watching her give him head, he had his hands full. Holden slid a hand under her panties and his fingers carefully teased her ass and pussy. He could feel she was wet as she sucked his cock. Because of the positioning Holden couldn't get his fingers very deep inside her; she was just out of reach. Paige didn't seem to mind, she was too focused on his cock. They passed car after car, Holden occasionally looked out the window at the vacationers. "If only they knew," he thought to himself. He was sure at least some of them could tell. Paige's tongue danced around the tip of his cock, lapping up some precum. Her fingers were more aggressive as they dug into his balls. Paige occasionally let out slight moans that he felt vibrate through his cock. The feeling, he thought, was incredible; she had his entire cock in her mouth. His fingers were barely in her ass when he felt that oh so familiar feeling. "Oh fuck Paige, I'm going to cum," he said warning her. He didn't hear her response, but he did feel the vibrations on his cock that sent trembles through his piercings. That was all he needed, his fingers slid out of her ass and quickly grabbed the steering wheel as he unloaded in her mouth. She swallowed a couple of times trying to keep up with the large load. After he was done, she continued to suck his cock, squeezing out all of his cum. Happy that he was finished she moved around again, this time she pulled up his boxers and jeans. She tried in vain to zip him up and buckle his belt but she just gave up, leaving him to deal with it later. She readjusted her skirt and cuddled up next to him to kiss his neck and bite his ear, and after several minutes she whispered, "Thanks for not killing us and don't worry, it's all gone," she said referring to the semen that just filled her mouth.

"That's the last thing I was worried about."

"Thanks for coming," Paige said

"Um, it was my pleasure?" Holden said as if he was asking a question.

Paige began to laugh, "NO, not that, I meant to North Bay with me."

"Oh, I was confused because, well, I could do that anytime you wanted." Holden said as they both laughed.

"No doubt," she said, slapping Holden's leg.

The rest of the drive went by rather quickly. Before they knew it they saw a sign that read 'Welcome to North Bay'. She looked around and pulled out some directions she had written out on a napkin. "Okay, it's on this highway, not too far into town. The place is called Bottom's Up."

"Bottom's Up?" Holden asked

"Hey, I didn't name the place," she said defensively.

"Fair enough."

"OH, I think we're coming up on it. Yup, there it is and there's our motel right across the street," Paige said excitedly.

"Convenient," was all Holden said.

"Ain't it though?"

"So, what do you want to do first?" Holden asked.

"Well, I think we should go in and take a look around, find out about the motel and what time they want me."

"Good enough." He turned off the highway and into the clubs parking lot. The time was about 6:30pm and, if they still wanted her for 8, they had plenty of time to settle into the motel.

Holden walked up to the door of the bar and held it open for Paige, following her in as she passed through the open doors. The place had all of the look, feel and smell of a typical strip joint. Only the odd florescent light from beer advertisements and the black light that lined the stage lit the dark bar. Paige approached the bar and asked to see the manager. The manger was an older yet very attractive woman, she flashed Paige a warm smile as she shook her hand. Paige introduced her to Holden. The manager shook Holden's hand and gave him a stern warning. "I don't care if boyfriends come in to watch, especially if they're from out of town like yourself, but I tell you Syn is single while she is working in my establishment. If you have a problem with that, stay out, I won't tolerate any trouble."

"Yes ma'am, I promise I won't cause any trouble."

"Ya, I've heard that before, but for now it was nice to meet you," she said with a cordial snarl.

"Like wise," Holden responded. Paige went with the manager to sort out the last of the details, as well as getting the key to their motel room. She reappeared and the two left the club to go check into their accommodations.

The room wasn't anything special, but it was much better than Holden expected. Paige quickly unpacked, undressed and jumped in the shower. Holden loved watching her take off her clothes, knowing that in just a couple of hours she would be doing it in front of so many strangers got his blood flowing. She comfortably walked around the room naked. Holden couldn't keep his eyes off her. While she was in the shower, Holden unpacked the last of her things, spreading out the outfit she planned to wear that evening onto the bed. Holden heard her turn off the faucet and after several minutes the bathroom door opened. Paige was standing in the doorway wearing only her towel. In a mock disgruntled voice she said, "I can't believe I had to be in there all by myself, who knows what could have happened to me, I thought you were supposed to protect me."

"Ah, yes, but who's going to protect you from me?" He said. Before he had a chance to move, she came charging over and jumped onto him. Her force knocked them both onto the bed, her towel fell to the floor during the short run. Her pussy was just above his belt buckle, her tits hung down against his shirt and in between kisses she said, "Next time eh? You owe me!" As she kissed him, she caught a glimpse at the alarm clock, "FUCK, I have to get ready!"

Changing gears quickly from the idea of a potential quickie Holden flipped on the TV. Paige grabbed her makeup bag and outfit and once again disappeared back into the bathroom. Holden flipped through the few channels that were available, finally settling on some sitcom. It didn't take Paige long to change and leave the bathroom. She made an amazing transformation from Paige to Syn. It was the first time he had seen Syn since the night they first met and he forgot how completely different she looked. Holden thought he must have been staring a bit too hard because she asked him if everything was ok. "Oh ya, everything is fine, it's just that you look so beautiful."

"Don't I normally?" she asked trying to trap him.

"You know what I mean," he said, not falling for her game. She gave him a smile with a subtle wink as a reply.

"Okay, I'm ready to go, you going to come in for a beer tonight?"

"I don't know. Would you want me too?" He asked hesitantly.

"Of course, I would love to see you tonight," she said excitedly.

"Well, in that case, I might have a beer when I drop you off, but I won't stay long. Feel free to text me whenever you get time."

Pouting she said, "Oh, you're not staying?"

"No, I don't want to cramp your style, do your thing and I'll be waiting for you when the place closes."

"FINE! I'll text you lots, but for the record I wouldn't mind if you wanted to stay longer, but I understand." She then crawled onto the bed and gave him a kiss on the cheek. "We should go."

"FINE!" Holden said mimicking her. The bar was only across the street but the street was a main four lane highway and he didn't feel comfortable letting her walk there by herself dressed the way she was. They jumped in the car and did the two second drive. Paige disappeared into the girls changing room once they got inside, taking all her stuff with her. Holden found the darkest corner and took a seat all by himself. Before he had a chance to get comfortable the waitress was there to take his drink order, and on the waitress's heels was a dancer. "Care for a dance?" she asked. Holden used a line he loved to use at strip clubs. "No, sorry, I can't dance, I have 2 left feet." More often than not it got a laugh, but sometimes it got no response having the dancer just walk away. The girl gave a polite chuckle at Holden's feeble attempts to be funny and then just stood there looking at him. "No, thank you. I'm just going to have a drink, watch the floor show then take off." He said politely rejecting the mostly naked lady's offer. "Suit yourself, have a good night," the dancer said obviously very offended.

"Ya, you too," Holden shouted after her. His beer finally showed up, taking a sip he leaned back in his chair and watched the girl on stage start her show. Normally Holden wouldn't have been caught dead in a strip club alone, but he kept reminding himself that he was there for Paige. He also felt comfort in the fact that he was in a strange city and no one would possibly know him. The bar was relatively slow with only a few old guys scattered around. Paige emerged from the change room and she walked up to the bar and ordered herself a drink. After she got it, she took a look around until she spotted Holden sitting in the dank corner. Drink in hand, she confidently strutted over to him and sat down in the seat closest to him. She told him all about what the change room looked like and the couple of girls she had met in the short time she was there. She told Holden the girls weren't too talkative, but they rarely warm up to the new girl right away. It was like that in all the clubs. Holden asked her if she was going to be okay and she reassured him that she would be fine. He reminded her that if she needed anything or if she got into trouble to call him. She patted him on the head and told him she was a big girl and that she could take care of herself. Holden downed the last sip of his beer and told her he was going to get going. She asked him what he was going to do the rest of the night, he said her he was going to go sightseeing, check out the city, grab some food and beer and possibly head back to the motel to watch some TV. Before he left, he asked Paige if she wanted anything when she got off work. "Only you," was her perfect answer.

"How about food or drinks?"

"No, I'll be okay, I'll get something to eat here and I know I'll have enough to drink," she said with a laugh.

"Ok, be careful, have a good night." "You too."

Holden left the bar and headed for his car. He felt bad for leaving her there alone, but he knew she was a professional and she'd be fine. Holden no sooner got the car started when he felt a vibration coming from his pocket. He pulled out his cell and the screen read 'new message'. He clicked on the envelope icon and it came up with a picture of Paige with the words 'I miss you already, thanks for coming here with me.' He texted her back, 'It's my pleasure, thanks for inviting me, see you at two.' He hit send and went on with his drive.

The town was bigger than he expected and it was situated along side a beautiful lake. He took some time driving around the city to look at the sites. He also took a walk along the boardwalk, eventually stopping at a lakeside pub to have dinner and a pint. The town was actually quite pleasant and he was enjoying his evening, even thought he was alone. His waitress was beautiful and quick witted, which made his dinner that much more enjoyable. He was willing to sit by the lake drinking beer, chatting with the waitress all night but he wasn't sure how to get back to the motel. He also couldn't forget he was driving, so he decided to pay the tab and find his way back. Taking a different route back to the motel, he wanted to see if he could find his way. This way, so he planned, he could see more of the town. He also tried to remember where the restaurant was, so that he could take Paige there for lunch. He passed a liquor store and figured that a couple of drinks in the room probably weren't a bad idea. He bought a 12 pack and a bottle of wine for Paige and him to share before bed. He didn't notice on the way into the liquor store that there was a flower shop next door but saw it on the way out. An urge warmed over Holden causing him to stop and buy Paige some flowers. Holden laughed to himself at the proximity of the two stores, "definitely cuts down on travel time to say you're sorry for a night of drinking." Purchases complete, he finally managed to find his way back to the motel. He parked and strolled up to their room. The only thing left to do was wait until 2 am. To make sure he didn't fall asleep on Paige, he set the room's alarm clock and his cell phone alarm for 1:30 am. Just as he hit set, his phone came alive again, vibrating in his hand. It was a new message from Paige that simply said "Thinking of you." He replied with "Me too, I hope you're having fun." Her reply was "gtg back to work." Feeling happy she was thinking about him, he cracked a beer and leaned back in the bed to watch whatever cheesy movie was on.

He woke up a short time later to BEEP, BEEP, BEEP emitting from his cell phone. He couldn't believe he dozed off. Just as he was getting his bearings the room alarm clock started to scream a very loud piercing sound. "Guess no one will sleep through that." He turned off both alarms and looked at the screen of his cell phone. '3 new messages.' "Damn," he hoped she wasn't mad at him for not writing her back. He read the messages; he had 2 more "thinking of you" texts but the 3rd text really caught his attention. "I love you." Holden smiled at the thought of her being in love with him, but he figured she was just drunk. He grabbed his car keys and flowers and made the very short trek to the bar next door. Holden discretely walked in, trying not to attract any attention, but Paige saw him immediately. "HOLDEN!" Paige yelled across the room. She ran over and jumped into his arms, she wrapped her legs around his waist. "I missed you baby," she said giving him a kiss on the cheek. "You want a dance big boy," she asked smiling.

"Maybe later," Holden said, Paige knew what he meant.

"Deal," She said with an exaggerated nod.

Holden put her down and they walked up to the bar. Paige was behind Holden with her hands around his waist, she leaned in and whispered, "Go sit down, this one is on me for being so nice to me." Holden resisted at first but she insisted, so as not to offend her he turned and found the same table he was at earlier. After getting the drinks she walked as sexy as she could over to Holden, her eyes stayed focused on his. When she got to the chair she didn't sit in the one beside him, she instead knelt on his chair, pressing her tits into his face, placing their drinks on the small table beside them. "I missed you so much, did you get my texts?"

"Ya, sorry, I dozed off," Holden admitted embarrassedly

"Oh ya, what did you think of them?"

"They were very sweet"

"and…?" Paige asked getting frustrated with Holden avoiding her real question.

"You love me?" Holden asked making sure that's what she was talking about.

"Yes I do," she said just before she leaned in to give Holden a kiss.

"Oh you, you have to be drunk," Holden joked.

"Nope, except for the drink we had when we first got here and this one, I've been drinking water all night. I don't like to get drunk in strange places around people I don't know."

"Sounds reasonable, so you're completely sober?"

"Yup," she said looking down at him with her big brown eyes, biting her lip in that very sexy way that she did. He could tell she was waiting for him to say the words back to her. He looked up at her, happily holding her in his arms. His eyes glued to hers confidently, he told her he loved her too. She let out a little shriek of joy, clapped her hands, gave him another kiss and walked away. She approached another dancer and he watched them talk. Paige pointed in Holden's direction and then they both clapped their hands and laughed. Holden wondered what he had gotten himself into, but he was happy to now have the attention of almost all the dancers in the place. He knew they had only been together for a few weeks, but those few weeks had been awesome. He really did believe that he loved her. Holden thought about Paige, what he just said and how much more difficult the news he was saving for the drive home was going to be.

His beer wasn't even finished when the lights came on and the doormen began ushering people out the door. Paige told the doorman that Holden was her ride, so he allowed him to stay with the other boyfriends while they waited for the girls to change. The guys made idle chit chat and cracked a few jokes as they finished their drinks. Paige came out wearing jeans and a t-shirt; one Holden recognized immediately, it was his retro space invaders shirt. She saw the look on his face when he recognized it. "I didn't think you'd mind, I love this shirt and besides, I look much better in it than you do."

Paige was looking forward to getting out of the bar. Holden could see that she really wanted to go so he took a final sip of his beer, put the bottle on the counter and escorted her to the door. She told him he could have finished his beer if he wanted. Sympathizing with her working a long shift and knowing she wanted to get back to the room for some sleep it was no loss for him to abandon his beer. Paige was happy that Holden had made her a priority, rarely had any guy ever done that for her. As they left the bar, Paige looked at the other girls that had slowly made their way out of the dressing room. She proudly grabbed Holden's hand and led him outside. Once they got to the car, Holden went to open her door when she stopped him. Paige grabbed him and pushed him against the car. "Fuck, I have wanted to do this all night." She started kissing him, the most intense powerful kiss of their young relationship. She was groping at him, hugging him and pulling at his clothes. "Gear down there big rig," Holden said to her. He unlocked the car and opened her door; she was about to sit but she saw the flowers at the last minute. "FOR ME?!?" she exclaimed. Holden nodded. She picked them up and tore into the paper wrapping. "They're beautiful!" She dropped them back into the front seat and started kissing him again. She finally stopped and told him she wanted to get back to the room; she was exhausted and she needed a shower. Holden asked her if she was hungry. She said that a pizza wasn't a bad idea, but her focus was on having a long hot shower to rinse the grime of the place off of her. Holden agreed to the plan.

They made it back to their room. Holden swiped the magnetic card to get access to their room, as he turned on the lights she gasped. "Oh my God Holden, you're amazing."

"I promise one day I'll do it up right for you, but for now this will have to do." While she was working he had gone to the dollar store, bought a couple of candles and some flower petals. Taking the risk of burning down the place, he had lit the candles before he left to pick her up. He had spread the flower petals all over the bed and had a full assortment of Chinese food containers on the table. She almost began to cry looking at all the effort Holden had gone through for her. "Thank you," was all she was able to say.

"Don't worry about it, it was the least I could do. After all, you worked hard all night and I just sat on my ass. I would have had a hot bath waiting for you but well, I personally wouldn't bath in a motel tub," he said with a laugh.

"Ya, that would have been gross," she agreed. "Okay, I'm going to go shower if that's alright, and then we'll eat?"

"Works for me." Like earlier, she got undressed by the bed before walking to the bathroom that was only a few feet away. Holden listened for the sound of the faucets being turned on, he could hear the shower curtain open and close and finally the sound of water splashing against the tub. Confident that she was now in the shower and couldn't hear the bathroom door being opened he decided to take her up on her offer from earlier. He undressed, walked into the bathroom and pulled back the curtain. She let out a scream, obviously startled by Holden's other surprise. She regained her composure and invited him in. Her body was already lathered in soap, her tits were glistening from the water and soap bubbles and her normally curly hair laid flat against her back. Her bare pussy had goose bumps from the cool air as her back was to the running water so she could talk to Holden. She smiled as she looked up and down his body. Holden was freezing but he felt lucky his cock maintained its erection and didn't shrivel up to become an inny, like its first instinct told it to do. Her hands were soapy from the shampoo which she first intended to rinse the smell of smoke and bar out of her hair. Instead it found his member;

she started moving her hands around like she was washing his hair. She then slowly started stroking his cock, the lubrication from the soap and water that was splashing over her shoulder felt great against his skin. His head was already very sensitive, he almost jumped through the roof as her hands grazed it. Holden grabbed the bar of soap and lathered his hands to get them really soapy. He started running them all over her body. He began with her neck and back. Once he was confident they were clean, he refocused his attention to her tits, rubbing them, ensuring they too were nice and squeaky clean. She continued rubbing his cock as he lathered up her chest. He skipped her stomach and pretty much the rest of her body and went directly to cleaning her vagina and ass. He had to pull her closer to him so that he could reach around her. They were close, he could feel his cock against her skin as she continued to clean it. It must have been very dirty, he thought, because she started working harder and faster making sure his shaft was exceptionally clean. Matching her momentum with his hand, he cleaned her clit. She put one of her feet on the edge of the tub letting Holden get in nice and deep. His fingers disappeared inside of her; his palm was firm against her swollen clit. Their hands brushed against each other as they frantically continued to clean the other. Their bodies were so close, only their hands separated them. He thought about how close he was to being inside her, yet so far away. They kissed, he could feel her hips moving against the palm of his hand. He applied more resistance and moved his fingers around inside of her. The grip she had on his cock got firmer, Holden moaned as they continued to kiss. He moved his fingers in a 'come here' motion tickling her g-spot. "I'm cumming," she screamed; her body tightened and moved involuntarily, almost ripping off Holden's cock in the process. The unexpected force on his cock set him off, he pressed up against her body as he squirted all over her pussy. When they were both done their orgasms they held each other; their soapy wet bodies pressed together as one. He grabbed her ass and pulled her tighter into him, they could feel his cum smearing between their bodies. She finally slid her hand off his cock, she could see his cum covering it. He expected her to rinse it off in the water flow, but instead she looked into his eyes and brought the cum to her lips and used her tongue to clean her hand. After several minutes of holding each other, their chins resting on each other's shoulders, no words were spoken. They finally spread apart and quickly cleaned themselves properly and left the shower. Holden only needed one towel to dry himself off. Paige used about three: one for her hair, one to dry her body and the other to wrap around herself. Together they went to the table, Holden pulled out Paige's chair for her. "Not going to eat?" she asked.

"In a second, I just have to get something first." He walked over to the bar fridge and pulled out two chilled wine glasses and a bottle of wine. Holden popped the cork and poured them both a glass before he finally sat down with her to enjoy their late night dinner. As she brought her glass to her lips, the towel fell of her head and onto the floor. She barely gave it a thought as she continued to drink. Holden watched her as she drank. Her wet locks now freely hung off her bare shoulders; she didn't have any make up on and was wearing only a towel. She looked more vulnerable than he had ever seen her before. Once they were both done eating it was time for bed. He got up and crawled into bed first. Paige blew out all the candles and turned off all the lights except for the one on the bedside table. She stood at the end of the bed, picked up the towel that had fallen off of her head and tossed it into the bathroom. With the throwing motion, the towel she was wearing became undone and almost fell open. Quickly, she saved it. "Uh oh," she said, teasing Holden as she opened and closed the towel, giving Holden peeks of her naked body. She was careful not to show off any of her naughty bits. Her lips formed a very evil grin that was amplified by the shadows cast by the dim light. She kept opening the towel wider and wider, each time pretending it was about to fall off, with her saving it just in the nick of time. Holden was enjoying her show; she looked very cute. He couldn't help but laugh at her antics. Finally the look on her face turned from happy and playful to very focused. She opened the towel and let it fall to the floor. She stood at the foot of the bed letting him examine her body. Holden was immediately hard. She started rubbing her hands all over her body. She turned around and bent over to pick up her towel, letting Holden get a good look at her bare ass and pussy. She picked up the towel, spun around like a ballerina and gracefully tossed the towel into the bathroom. Standing there naked, she started running her fingers through her hair. "Well, it's late, we should get some sleep." She slid her hands down her body again, this time they found her pussy. Her fingers gently ran all over herself, her eyes glued on Holden's. He didn't want her to have all the fun so he reached down to his cock and slowly started stroking himself. Their gaze never broke from each other. No words were spoken as they mutually masturbated. Just as Holden was about to get up and grab her so he could throw her to the bed, she put her knees on the bed and crawled up to him. Her face made it as far as his waist, her hands left her pussy and went for his cock. She started stroking him and without any hesitation her mouth found its mark. He could feel her tongue flickering away in her mouth as she took him deep. Eager to start satisfying her, he reached down and grabbed her leg and pulled it towards him. Getting the hint she let his cock fall out of her mouth as she shuffled over. He used his hand to guide her leg over his head. Once her knee was over his face she shuffled down, moving her cunt into position, inches away from his face. Confident she was in the proper position, she went back to sucking his dick. Holden didn't wait long before dipping his tongue deep inside Paige. It was hard for him to concentrate on licking her as her mouth moved masterfully over his cock. Holden's pride kicked in; there was no way he was going to let her get him off without him first giving her an orgasm. She had one earlier, so it shouldn't be that hard for him to get her back in the mood. His hands reached around on the outside of her legs, grabbing her ass and pulling her cheeks apart allowing his tongue to get just a little bit deeper inside her. He kept his eyes open so that he could see all of her. He tried to read her body to see if she was enjoying what he was doing, but it was hard. His cock was twitching, her tongue moved up and down his shaft, playing with each bead on all three piercings. Her hand massaged his balls. Eager to take his mind off his own mounting orgasm, he tried something new. His tongue left her pussy and moved up to start teasing her ass. At first he just gave her button light flickers then progressed to small circles, he tried to read her reaction as he licked her. He wanted to know if she liked it. She responded better than he expected, she moved her hips lowering her ass closer to his mouth giving him a very clear sign that she enjoyed Holden's new game. He used his hands that were already on her cheeks and pulled them further apart allowing his tongue to get deeper inside her. Her ass was so tight, although he couldn't penetrate her further, he was in deep enough to stimulate her. He tried moving his hands around her cheeks. His tongue danced between long strokes of her pussy and teasing her asshole. She used his cue and slid a finger in her mouth which was sharing space with his cock. The sensation was new to Holden and it only lasted a second before she slid her finger out of her mouth and into Holden's ass. The second he felt the pressure on his own ass he grabbed hers and squeezed hard making her emit a moan. He wasn't sure if the moan was pain or pleasure but either way, Holden was sure she was ok and honestly at the time he didn't really care what the sound meant. He moved his mouth to just beside her pussy lips and gave her a small bite on her thigh as her finger disappeared into his ass. Holden moved awkwardly around so he could get a finger inside her. Her mouth went back to his cock violently taking it in and out as his finger worked inside her. With the violent motions of her mouth, her finger began jerking sporadically inside him. He wanted to cum so bad; he tried his best to hold out as long as he could. He tried to get her off faster by getting his tongue deep inside her pussy. Her hips started grinding hard into his face and his finger. He didn't want to cum yet, in her violent movements he felt her teeth accidentally digging into his cock. He let out a small ouch and a flinch. She gave him an apology, which was muffled by his cock. He felt her hand slide up his body; she started rubbing her clit knowing he couldn't reach it himself. She was now fingering him as well as herself while sucking him off. All three body parts moving simultaneously got them both off. Holden tried hard to do his part, his fingers reached as deep inside her ass as he could get, his tongue applied more pressure to her pussy. Rubbing her own pussy got her to the point of orgasm faster than Holden would have been able to do on his own. He appreciated the extra assistance because he knew he wasn't going to be able last much longer and he didn't want to make her wait for her release. He knew if she was almost to the point of orgasm, his cumming would break her flow and they would have to start all over again. That was something he wasn't opposed to but he felt it would be better for both of them if they could orgasm close to the same time. Her finger thrust hard inside his ass causing him to orgasm without warning. What he didn't realize until his own orgasm subsided was that she got over excited by her own orgasm, which was what caused her to thrust her finger in him as hard as she did. His face was soaked with her juices; he tried to lick as much out of her as he could before she had to move. "Oh my god, it's so sensitive," she said as she rolled over and collapsed. Holden was lying beside her knees as her head was still on his waist inches from his now flaccid cock. Her finger scooped up his cum, which was continuing to leak from him and brought it to her sensual lips. "Wow," she said, "It's been a long time since I have had so many orgasms in one day." Feeling proud of himself, he tried to remain realistic and remember his own limitations. "That last one was all you; I was just along for the ride," he said giving her, her due credit.

"We both cam and that's all that matters," she said out of breath.

"Indeed," Holden agreed.

They both fell asleep in that position. At some point in the night Paige moved, making Holden jump. She crawled out of bed and went into the bathroom leaving the door open and the light on. Holden was now awake, his heart still racing from the late night scare, he decided to watch Paige brush her teeth through the open bathroom door. He was still naked lying above the covers. After spitting and rinsing she joined Holden back in the bed, she patted his cock which was resting on his hip bone. "Good Boy," she said and snuggled up next to him, pulling the blankets over them. She gave his cheek a kiss. "Thanks again for coming with me." Holden laughed, "I believe you've said that already."

"I know but this time I meant the other way," she said making Holden laugh, she continued, "No seriously, I know I said it but I'm really happy you're here."

"I'm happy I'm here too, I couldn't imagine being anywhere else."

"Me too."

Holden reached up and turned off the lights. Within seconds they were both asleep, naked, intertwined in each other's arms and legs.

Not sure of the time, Holden woke up to the sound of running water. He rolled over to say good morning to Paige but she was gone, the water running was her in the shower. "Damn early risers," he thought to himself, as he looked at the alarm clock which read 11:45. "Up at the crack of noon, still too damn early." He rolled over and tried to go back to sleep. The thought of joining her in the shower crossed his mind, but he was still tired and his cock hurt from the sex the night before. He no sooner rolled over and closed his eyes, when Paige dove on the bed waking him up. "Get up lazy bones," she said, he thought she was way to chipper considering the night before. "Why are you in such a good mood?" He asked as he tried to bury his head under the covers. "Like you don't know," was her reply. She pulled the blankets off Holden and gave him a big kiss. He was wide awake now, but wasn't going to make it easy for her. "Get up, let's go to lunch."

"FINE, let's do everything YOU want to do," he said mocking her.

"Damn right," she said. "Oh, nice, shake it baby," she commented, as she watched him crawl out of the bed, naked and walk to the shower.

Once they were both ready, they jumped in the car. Paige asked where they were going. He told her about the restaurant he found the night before. They pulled up and, even though it was lunch hour, the restaurant was fairly empty. They had no problem finding a seat on the deck. They had an amazing view, the sky was a clear blue, and the sun was shining down making them nice and warm. There was no wind so the lake was as smooth as glass. Paige was in awe as she looked around at the restaurant and the view. The waitress came right over to take their order, it was the same girl as the night before. "Oh, it's you again," she said with fake disappointment. Holden smiled, he was flattered she remembered him.

"Well, you know, I just can't stay away." Paige starred disapprovingly at Holden for his innocent exchange with the waitress. Her jealousy made Holden smile. After they ordered, Paige gave Holden shit for flirting. He told her it wasn't a big deal; she was just being friendly because he was sitting there all alone the night before waiting for her. "You told her about me?" Paige asked doubtfully.

"Of course I did, why wouldn't I?" Paige let it go, she was content with the fact that he told the pretty waitress about her when she wasn't there. The next time she came around Paige relaxed and started joking with her as well. After their great lunch they realized that the time passed to fast and since Paige was working the supper hour to close shift they soon had to get her to work. She had her work clothes in a bag so she could change at work, making the stop at the motel unnecessary. They paid the bill and generously tipped the waitress. She even told Paige she might go see her dance later that night. Holden got lost in a fantasy of Paige lap dancing for her, but he tried to hide his thoughts as best he could.

The traffic was light, so Holden was able to get Paige to the bar in plenty of time to change, have a drink, and then start her shift. Holden didn't go in with her; he knew she was safe and that she knew some of the other girls there now. He told her he was just going to catch a movie. She gave him a kiss and cheerfully bounced out of the car and into work. Holden turned around and started to pull away when his cell phone vibrated again, 'Miss you already,' was the text. It made Holden smile, 'I'm really lucky,' he thought as he sent her a text back 'Miss you too.' By the time the text was sent, he was in the motel room. He laid on the bed and watched TV and flipped through the paper to see what was playing at the theatre. After finding something worth watching, he located the theatre on a map and set his cell alarm so he that wouldn't forget about it.

Paige started her shift by looking around the crowd, she found some guys she recognized from the night before, but one customer stood out. It was a smiling, warm and very friendly face. It was the waitress from the restaurant they had their lunch at. Paige joined her on "pervert's row." "Hi, I'm Amy."

"Hi Amy, I'm Syn." Amy then asked her when she was going to dance on stage. Syn looked at her watch and said she wasn't up to dance for about an hour or so because the day crew was still cycling through their last sets. "So, you have time for a drink and a dance?" Amy nervously asked.

"With you? Definitely," Syn said in a flirty tone. Amy caught the tone and gave her a smile as they got up to go to the bar to get some drinks.

When they got back to the table they talked for a long time, casually sipping their drinks. Finally Amy asked when Syn was going to take her into the backroom. "Oh, I thought you were kidding," Syn said.

"Not at all," Amy said with a very serious tone.

Syn stood up and led her new friend into the backroom. Since a song had just started as they walked to the private rooms they used the couple of extra minutes to talk. Syn treated her just like every other customer. She placed a small towel down on Amy's knee then she sat on her lap as they talked. The DJ announced the next dancer and the song started. That was Syn's cue to start dancing. She stood up, started moving her body to the music, receiving ooo's and awes from Amy. After several seconds, Syn slowly undressed much to the joy of her customer. After losing her very short dress, she leaned back into Amy. She pretended she was having trouble with her bra. With her head back so her mouth was pressed against Amy's ear, she whispered, "Can you help me out? I seem to be having a problem." Amy slowly slid her hands up Syn's bare back. Because she had her back pressed up against Amy's chest, Amy found it hard to find the clasp. After a couple of attempts, she finally got it open. "Thank you," Syn whispered into her ear. She stood up and turned around so that Amy could see her bra slowly fall to the ground. Amy stared at Syn's perky tits. Finally it was time for the last article of clothing to come off. Syn hooked her thumbs into the waist band of her thong. She turned her back on Amy as she bent over to slide her thong down her ass, ever so slowly, past her legs and finally dropping to the floor. Syn again took a seat on Amy's lap, this time between her legs pressing her naked body into Amy's body. She could feel Amy's much larger tits pressing against her back. "Nice tits," she said to Amy, much like Sunshine had said to her a long time ago.

"I was just thinking the same about yours," Amy said as she reached around and started massaging Syn's breast like she had done to her own several times before. Syn spun around in the chair, "May I?" she asked, looking hopefully at Amy.

"Absolutely," Amy eagerly responded. Syn slid her hands under Amy's shirt, under her bra and she started playing with Amy's ample breasts, while Amy did the same to her. They both started moving around in their seats; Syn started grinding her pussy into her towel that was still resting on Amy's leg. Amy was obviously getting into the act. She slid her hand down Syn's ribs to her stomach. Before Syn realized it, Amy had her hand between her legs and a finger slipped inside her. Stunned at first, she was also more than a little turned on so she let the fingering continue longer than she should have before she jumped up and grabbed her clothes. "Oh no, that's a no, no. Sorry Honey," Syn said trying to hide her obvious pleasure. Amy just looked at her, and then brought the finger that had just penetrated Syn to her lips. "Sorry," she said feigning remorse as she licked it. Syn had gotten her money for one dance, grabbed her drink and told Amy she'd see her around. Syn was anxious to get away from Amy because she was worried she would do something very inappropriate with her that might get her fired or hurt Holden. She ran into the girls change room to regroup in hopes that she wouldn't let her newly acquired sexual frustrations get her into further trouble. After texting Holden with what just happened, she took a drink of water and went back into the bar. Waiting for her was Amy, standing right outside the door. "I hope I didn't do anything wrong," she asked.

"No, no, it was just well, unexpected and against the rules here." "But you were okay with it?"

Syn formed her trademark mischievous smile. "I won't say anything this time, just don't let it happen again," she said, scolding Amy in a very unconvincing manor.

"Okay, I was worried after you took off like you did. Here, this is for you," Amy said as she handed Syn a small piece of paper. She turned around and left without giving her a chance to read it. Syn unfolded the note and read it. It was Amy's phone number and a short note, 'Syn it was nice meeting you. I know you're leaving town tomorrow, but I really want to fuck you. I know you have a boyfriend and if that's what it would take to get with you, I would gladly let him join us. Love Amy, xoxox.' Paige was very flattered and was definitely going to show the note to Holden later, but for now she had to put her mind back on work. She put the note in her purse and continued to look for potential business.

After the movie, Holden decided to stop in and see Paige. The late show got out at one am and there was only an hour before Paige was off work anyways. He walked up to the bar and the bartender recognized him and got him his beer. The bartender and Holden were having a conversation when he felt fingers run down the back of his neck. The sensation sent shivers down his spine. Excitedly, he turned around to see Paige. She looked at him and she went through introductions, pretending she was a stranger picking up the hot guy at the bar. Holden thought it was a fun game, so he played along with it. Paige and Holden continued their banter; he wasn't sure where it was heading but he was hoping it would end up with him getting a lap dance. Paige violently spun around and stumbled, almost falling over. Holden wasn't sure what happened until he heard another female voice. "You that whore Syn?" Holden looked around Paige to see a tall brunette wearing khaki pants and a grey hoodie. Her hair was messy and she had a look of pure hatred in her eyes. Paige didn't have a chance to answer when Holden stood between the two girls. He knew Paige would be pissed at his interference and it may get them in trouble with the manager because of Holden's promise to the manager, but he certainly wasn't going to let his girlfriend get hurt. "What the fuck?" Holden shouted at the stranger.

"This whore was fucking around with my girlfriend, that's what the fuck."

"What?" Holden asked again

"Tonight, that slut was fucking around with my girlfriend. She felt Amy up and she let her stick her finger in her cunt. WHORE!" she shouted at Syn. Holden turned to Paige, who was now being held back by a staff member. She looked at Holden with a glimmer of acknowledgement in her eyes. Holden started to piece the story together from Paige's text; he turned to the angry woman and told her to relax. He then said that she should keep her girlfriend out of strip clubs and tell her to stop assaulting the girls if she was that jealous. The last words barely escaped his lips when he felt a burning sensation on his cheek. It caused him to take a step backwards but he managed to maintain his balance. It took both Paige and Holden a minute to realize the angry woman had just hit him. Holden turned and grabbed Paige, who was rushing in the girl's direction. He grabbed her and told her he was fine and to not make it worse. Paige settled down, taking her cue from Holden as she remained calm and decided to talk out the disagreement instead of compounding it with a fight. Holden fought back the urge to hit the angry woman, but he knew that would be the worst possible thing he could do. He then focused on not giving her another opportunity to hit him again. Before Holden had to decide what his next move was going to be, two burly bouncers grabbed the angry woman and dragged her out of the bar kicking and screaming. Holden again turned to Paige to make sure she was ok. Of course they had the full attention of the packed bar. The owner/manager came running over to them. Paige took one look at Holden's swollen face and her own face went flush and she started to cry. "Oh my God Holden, you ok?"

"Ya, I'm fine why?"

"You're bleeding." "Nah, It was just a punch to the face, not a big deal."

"Ya you are, badly, let me look at you." As Paige got closer, he could feel the warm liquid running down his face, the adrenaline caused him to not notice it before. 'Son of a bitch, she cut me,' he thought to himself. Paige started looking at it. "It's deep, you should really have it looked at."

"Ya, you're right, get me that hot little nurse I saw running around here. No, seriously I'm fine, how are you?"

"Ya, I just got pushed, you didn't have to do that for me you know."

"I know you can take care of yourself, but I wasn't about to sit back and watch you fight."

By the time they were done the conversation the manager was standing next to him. "What did I tell you the first night you were here," she asked, directing the question towards Holden.

"I'm sorry ma'am but I didn't do anything. I was just running interference to try and stop something from happening between Paige and that bitch," Holden said pleading his case.

"I don't care, you have to get out, both of you, and go get yourself looked at." "I'm fine," he said not directing the comment to anyone in particular. He was upset that he might have caused Paige the job.

"Look, these things happen. I know what happened and I know you weren't the aggressor, but I can't have this shit go on in my bar." The bartender handed Holden a clean rag to put it on his cheek to stop the bleeding, he then felt the sting of his injury.

"Go home, come back in at noon tomorrow to get paid and we'll talk about you staying to finish your shift tomorrow afternoon," the manager said with a smile.

"Thank you and sorry," Paige said to the manager sheepishly. She then turned her attention to Holden and started fussing over him again. He assured her he was fine. "Do you want to go to emerg?" She asked him.

"Hell no, it's not that bad, lets just get back to our room." Before they left, Holden had the bouncers take a look around the parking lot to ensure that the psycho bitch wasn't waiting for them. Confident they were safe, they got in their car and went back to the motel. Once inside, they took a long hot shower together. Paige carefully inspected his injury. When they were out of the shower Paige went down to the receptionist and got some gauze and medical tape from a first aid kit. Fixing Holden up, they crawled into bed. Paige was still visibly upset that she had gotten Holden hurt. He tried to tell her it wasn't a big deal, but she kept cursing her job and the fact that he had gone out of his way to help her this weekend and to pay him back she got him hurt. Again, Holden tried to reassure her but nothing was helping. He finally asked her what exactly happened. She told him the entire story about Amy the waitress, the lap dance, their momentary encounter and the note, which she produced for Holden. He tried to make Paige feel better with a joke. "HEY, wait a minute. Does this mean the threesome is out of the question?"

"I'm sorry," she said again as she started to cry, still upset from the situation, not from his joke.

"Paige, honey, it's okay, really. I play roller hockey and I box, I've been punched in the face before and I survived. I'll be fine, I promise." He put his arms around her to comfort his girlfriend.

"Ya, but this time it's my fault, it's just not worth it." Holden didn't say anything, he just held onto her tightly, hugging her and letting her cry on his shoulder. They fell asleep in their tight embrace. Holden didn't sleep well that night, the throbbing in his face kept him awake but he wasn't about to tell Paige that.

The alarm woke them up at 11 o'clock. Paige was still upset, thinking about what happened the night before. She was so impressed with Holden that despite everything that was going on, even after a punch to a face, he remained calm electing to try and verbally resolve the situation as opposed to flying off the handle.

At noon they went over to the bar. Paige told the manager she couldn't dance that day. The manager agreed that it probably was for the best and she told Paige she should take Holden to the hospital for stitches or a tetanus shot or something. She graciously paid Paige for three days even though she had only worked for two. It was easy to tell the manager liked both Paige and Holden. They could also tell she was sincere when she invited Paige back to work, she even said Holden was more than welcome back in the club anytime. Paige took the money and politely thanked her for the opportunity to work there. She then said her goodbyes and after giving hugs to a couple of the other dancers they were out the door. The car was already packed, so all they had to do was get in and start the long drive home.

The drive home was much more subdued than the drive up north. The radio was playing the same rock that they were listening to on the way up, but this time they weren't singing along or dancing. They were both tired and just wanted to get home. Paige occasionally asked if everything was ok, Holden was happy to reassure her as often as she needed. He told her he was fine but tired. Holden started playing with her hair and smiled at her just so she knew he wasn't mad at her. When he looked over at her, she got a horrific look on her face which turned to a smile. "Oh my god, that is so bad, I'm sorry," she said reaching out for his bandage. Holden laughed at the expression on her face. "Trust me, it's all good, no worries honey." Paige snuggled up against his arm. He put his arm around her and continued driving; he had a lot on his mind.

Halfway home they stopped at a very popular hamburger place for a bite to eat. It was so popular they had to install a pedestrian walkway going over the highway. He told Paige how great the place was. While they ate, they sat in relative silence, only speaking to make witty remarks about the other diners. As they walked back to the car, she could tell Holden was distant, she was nervous, thinking that that incident ruined their relationship. She didn't want to say anything again but it was eating away at her. Holden had thoughts of his own that were weighing heavy on his mind as well and he wasn't sure how he was going to bring up the inevitable unpleasant conversation. He finally got his break when Paige broke the uncomfortable silence. "Holden, I can't stand it anymore, what's going on? I can tell something is bothering you."

"Paige, we need to talk, I have something I have to tell you." "Oh God," Paige said as she crawled up into a ball in her seat making herself as small as possible, fighting back her urge to cry.

"You know I'm falling in love with you, I love spending time with you, and this weekend was great but…."

"But what? I'm sorry Holden, please don't," she said starting to cry harder. His heart was breaking but he knew he had to tell her. "This is so hard for me, but well, I got another job offer. I will become the director of operations for the Vancouver Witch Doctors…I have to move to B.C."

"What? When do you move?"

"At the end of this season, I have to be there just after Christmas to get things ready for the new season."

"So, you being distant has nothing to do with last night and you're not breaking up with me?" She asked hopefully.

"No, I told you last night was nothing, I'd take a punch to the head for you any day. As far as the breaking up goes, a long distance relationship would be almost impossible," he said the sadness radiating in his voice. Paige was happy she didn't blow things with them that weekend; she stopped crying and almost began to smile. The news that he would be leaving really hadn't sunk in for her yet. She gave him a kiss on the cheek. "I love you."

"I love you too," he said with confidence, knowing that he really did and that weekend proved it. Finally, a look of realization warmed over her. "Wait, you have to move to B.C. in just over 2 months?" She said, sadness in her voice, the tears were almost back. "Yes," he said reluctantly.

"What about us?

5

The gravel crumbled under the tires as they pulled into Paige's parent's house. Holden's legs went numb with nerves. She could tell he was a bit anxious and gave him a reassuring smile. "It will be okay. I promise they won't bite."

"It's not them biting that I'm worried about." He opened the car door and went to get their things out of the trunk. He was hesitant because of the circumstances in which he was meeting her parents. He would have preferred to have met them for dinner on a casual evening, not show up at their house for an entire weekend. Especially after the bombshell he had dropped on Paige only a couple of weeks before.

Holden was very busy at work and it was the worst possible time for him to go away, but he knew it was important to Paige for him to meet her parents before he had to move. Since it was important to her it was important to him. They approached the door and he took a deep breath as Paige turned the knob. "Hi, I'm home," she yelled, as she barged through the door. Holden fumbled with the bags as he followed her into the house. Her mom came running down the hallway. "Honey!" she screamed, as she embraced Paige in a big hug and gave her a kiss on the cheek. Paige's stepfather wasn't too far behind his wife. After seeing Holden, her dad extended his hand to him. Holden gladly shook it. "Hello sir, I'm Holden."

"Come in boy, don't just stand there. Here, let me give you a hand with those bags." Holden gladly handed him a suitcase, then they both remarked at how much Paige packed for just a weekend. Holden followed her dad into Paige's room; they dropped off the bulk of the luggage before her dad showed Holden to his room. Paige warned Holden on the drive over that they would be sleeping in separate rooms. Her parents were more traditional and wouldn't feel comfortable with them sharing a room, not because they weren't married, but because their relationship was only a couple of months old and they had never met him before. Holden completely understood. He felt that it was a very natural parental concern and thought his parents would have done the same thing. Holden looked around the room that he would be occupying for the next two nights. It was a small room, but the single bed looked very comfortable and he had plenty of space on the floor to put his things. After dropping off the bags, he joined Paige and her mom in the living room. Paige was sitting on the couch talking a mile a minute, filling her in on everything that went on since the last time they talked.

Paige's father came out of the kitchen with two beers. He handed Holden one while looking at the girls on the couch. "I think we'll need these," he said, laughing at his own joke. He sat at the dining room table; Holden joined him and they got into their own conversation.

Holden and Paige had arrived after dinner and the nightly ritual in that household was to go for a long after dinner walk. Holden was anxious to see Paige's hometown and hear stories of a young Paige. They started off in a group, but her parents quickly picked up the pace. Paige and Holden struggled to keep up at first; however they soon found their rhythm. Her parents told him stories about her growing up, some embarrassing while others made them swell with pride as they spoke. They also told him about their other daughter and a bit about what they did for a living. They surprised Paige with the news that her sister was also coming home for the weekend causing Paige to get giddy with excitement. She grabbed Holden's hand and started telling him about her sister; it was obvious that she loved her very much. Her parents also mentioned that her Aunt and Uncle were coming for supper the next day. When all the stories were done, the sun had begun to set. Paige and Holden dropped back slightly; she grabbed onto his arm. Once they were alone she pointed out sites and other childhood memories as they walked. Her parents started to hold hands as well. Holden and Paige thought it was cute and just as the last of the sun disappeared over the horizon; they rounded the corner and were back at the house.

After cleaning up, they gathered downstairs in the TV room. Her parents had a beautiful set up which included a big screen TV, surround sound, blu ray player and 3 large leather sofas arranged perfectly so they all had the best possible view of the screen. Holden was in love with the set up and knew he wanted a room like that in his house, when he could afford it. He wasn't sure of the movie they were going to watch, but he and Paige staked out the best of the 3 couches, grabbed a blanket and laid down together in anticipation. Her mom brought down a big bowl of popcorn and some drinks for the four of them. Her dad sparked up the theatre system by pushing one button on the remote. The lights dimmed and the TV came to life, as did the seven speakers that were optimally arranged around the room. The opening credits began to roll and the bass shook the room. Holden made a very quiet comment to Paige about how great the vibrations of the bass would be during sex. She agreed. Halfway through the movie they had a couple of drinks put away, the popcorn was gone and her parents were fading fast. Holden discretely started kissing Paige's neck and whispered naughty things in her ear. Holden could feel her ass press against him and slowly start to move around, grinding up against him. Holden squeezed Paige tightly, and she fidgeted around a bit. He was worried she would draw to much attention to them, but those thoughts faded fast when he realized her hand was going for his crotch. He whispered to her that it was a bad idea, as her parents were right next to them. She didn't seem to care as her hand slid down his pants and wrapped tightly around his member. With very gentle movements she started rubbing him. He wanted to reciprocate, but he was too nervous thinking that her parents would see them. Her cold hands felt great against his warm skin as she stroked him. Since her dad as eager to show off the capabilities of the system he picked an action flick because the only true way to have a good demonstration was with lots of explosions. The sound from the TV was enough to mask his involuntary moans. He tried to pull away as Paige had him on the brink of orgasm. She refused to let him go, she thought it would be funnier if she kept tugging on him. His cock twitched, he gave her a big squeeze and she could feel his hot cum soak her hand. He trembled with pleasure and closed his eyes to take in the moment. He reopened them when her dad started clearing his throat. Holden's eyes were huge as they saw him sitting on the edge of the couch. His daughter's hand was covered in cum and still firmly holding Holden's penis. Holden froze; he stared long and hard at him. Paige too was frozen. He just looked at the two of them. "Well, I guess we're off to bed, can we get you guys anything before we hit the sack?"

"Um, no, I think we're good," Paige replied. Holden kept his eyes glued to her father's; he looked back at Holden with a 'caught you' look before giving him an angry glance. He ushered his wife out of the room and before he left he turned and said, "Just hit off on the remote, it will take care of everything." Then he gave Holden a smirk and a wink before disappearing out the door. "Whew," Holden sighed. Paige laughed as she pulled her hand out of his pants. "Oh ya, Dad's cool. He knows what's what." "Cool," Holden said, relieved. After Paige got her hand out of his pants she brought it up to examine the mess. There was a lot of gooeyness dripping from her hand. As a reflex she brought it to her mouth and licked the string off before it had a chance to drip on to the carpet. She stopped and realized what she had just done out of habit and looked at Holden, then she seductively finished cleaning off the mess with her tongue. Holden wanted to pay her back by fucking her into an orgasm of her own, but he knew as cool as her dad was, that would be pushing their luck.

The movie ended, they tidied up the basement and headed upstairs. Holden stopped at Paige's room and gave her a kiss before he made his way down to his own room. Holden laid in bed thinking about the next day, he was nervous about meeting the entire family but since meeting her parents went well he was cautiously optimistic.

Holden woke to the smell of bacon and the sound of voices talking. He put on his jeans and a T-shirt and strolled into the kitchen. "Good morning sleepy head," Paige's mom said to him. "Good morning," he replied, realizing the voices he had heard were actually the TV tuned to a talk show.

"Would you like a coffee?"

"Oh, very much so, please." She handed Holden a coffee as Paige walked through the front door. She was already awake and gone for a jog. "About time you woke up," she said, laughing at him. "I hope my parents were hospitable while I was out."

"Well, what can I say, the bed was insanely comfortable and ya, you're parents were terrific in the 5 minutes I've been up."

"I was going to wake you up to go for a run but I figured you needed your sleep."

"You saying I need my beauty sleep?" Holden said defensively.

"Damn, these potatoes are bad," Paige's mom interrupted. Paige and Holden looked at her. "I'm going to have to run to the store to get some more."

"No, no Mom, if they're not a big hurry, I'll shower then Holden and I will run to the store and pick up some things for you. Make a list of everything you need."

"Thanks dear, Holden, you don't mind?"

"Of course not, Paige offered to give me a grand tour of the town today anyway." Paige started walking down the hallway. Once she was hidden from her mother's view she coughed to get Holden's attention. He looked at her and watched her take off her sweat soaked T-shirt and running shorts. She wasn't wearing any panties underneath. Holden smiled and shook his head as she ran her fingers up her leg, over her pussy and to her lips where she then blew him a kiss and went into the bathroom to shower. She locked the door behind her.

Her dad came in just as Paige locked herself in the bathroom. He was apparently outside mowing the lawn. Holden hadn't heard the mower running. Holden was amazed at all the activity he missed out on in the morning. He blamed it on the soft bed and the great sleep he got because of it. Holden sipped his coffee and they all made casual conversation about current events, which TV programs they liked and a bit about what his family did for a living. Paige quickly showered and dressed; before he knew it, she was ready to go. She looked great wearing only a pair of old gray sweat pants, a plain white T-shirt, a black ball cap and minimal make up. Holden had never seen her go out 'casual' before, but it was a look she could really pull off. Holden laughed when she put on her black Chuck Taylor's that didn't go with her ensemble, but matched the ones he was wearing. She grabbed the list from her mom, gave her a kiss on the cheek while Holden drank the last drops of his coffee. He quickly put the mug in dishwasher and followed Paige out the front door.

Holden started the car, Paige slipped in a CD she found in her room and gave Holden the directions to where they were going. The music on her CD was good, very retro. Some of the songs made her embarrassed but Holden was a gentleman, he only teased her for, well, the entire drive. Holden asked Paige where the grocery store was but she told him she had other things she wanted to show him first. He saw her elementary school, her high school, the place she first smoked up, some friend's places, ex's house's and some of her other favourite sites. Finally, she said she had a very special spot to show him. They took a winding dirt road up a hill. He wasn't sure if his car was going to make it up the trail or not. Paige reassured him that it wasn't much further and then out of nowhere the trees parted, and they were in an opening overlooking the town and lake. Holden thought it truly was an amazing spot. Paige told him stories of drunken parties and make out sessions she had there. He parked the car and got out to walk around. The clearing was small, only enough room to park about five cars and a small camp fire area. Judging by the empty beer bottles and condom wrappers laying around, it was still a popular spot with the local teens. They sat down on a log that was beside the fire pit. They didn't say much; they were busy taking in the scenery. Holden didn't want to talk; he could tell Paige was reminiscing internally. He was happy that she had shared her spot with him. Finally she stood up, and without saying anything she reached out for his hand and they started walking toward the car. He thought she had had enough and that they were going to head back down the hill into town. Just as they got to the front of the car, Paige pulled his hand spinning Holden around and pushed him onto the hood of his car. She started grabbing at him, pulling his shirt up and running her hands over his hard stomach. The angle he was sitting at had his abs flexing; she remarked how tight they felt and how beautiful they looked, but she had her sights on something much grander. She pulled at his belt buckle and after successfully unbuckling him she didn't bother to unzip the fly; very quickly and aggressively she pulled down his pants. She giggled as his cock flapped around after being violently freed from its confines. Holden thought it was never a compliment to have a girl laugh at the sight of your junk, however he didn't mind because after the giggling stopped when she took it in her mouth. Holden loved the view of the lake, the forest, the town far down below and the hottest girl he had ever dated working over his knob. Her hands caressed his stomach as her mouth moved around his shaft and head. She was sucking him as though she hadn't seen a penis in a year. He didn't know what had gotten into her, if it was memories of an old boyfriend or the fact that being home made her feel like a high school girl again and "making out" in that spot made it dangerous and forbidden. As if she was getting away with something. He didn't care why but he did know it felt amazing. Holden just leaned back on the hood. The engine was still hot but he ignored the heat as he soaked in the sun and the fantastic oral he was receiving. Not being satisfied with having him in her mouth, she wanted him elsewhere. She pushed him further back on the car. "Pull your pants down," she commanded. Holden obliged by pulling his pants the rest of the way off as she did the same. She crawled up the car, took his member in her hand and held it in place as she lowered herself onto it. She didn't kiss him, talk to him or even look at him. Her hands pressed against his six pack and he laid back using his own hands to support his head off the steel of the car. Paige grinded her body onto his cock harder and faster than she ever had before. Confident that no one was within ear shot, she let out sounds, again, like nothing he's heard before. The trip home was apparently good for her. She was screaming and moaning as she fucked him. She bounced up and down, using the flex of the thin metal of the car hood as a springboard. She made her pussy contract tightly around his length as she moved her hips forward and backwards and up and down. She was all over the place, like a woman possessed. Holden knew he was nothing more than a tool for her output, something he was very alright with. He did his best to move around to help her, but she had him pinned down so hard that he could barely move. He could feel how wet she was, her juices were dripping down his balls and hips onto the hood of his car. He wanted to know what got into her head that inspired the passion. He hoped to figure it out later so he could try and replicate it. Her cunt tightened, her hips thrusted forward as she slammed down hard onto him, letting out one incredibly loud scream. Holden felt the fluids pouring out of her. "CUM NOW!" She ordered. Holden was always one to follow a simple command. He released his sperm deep inside her. She moaned as she felt the pressure squirting into her. She finally leaned forward and kissed him. The change in position released everything that was inside her into one sudden flow all over Holden's waist and car. She kissed him passionately. "I love you."

"I love you too," Holden said back to her.

"Come on, they'll be waiting for us and we still have to hit the grocery store."

She rolled off of him and did a ballerina dismount as she cleared the fender of the car and landed on her feet. Just like that the switch was off, and whatever had been possessing Paige seconds ago was gone. They got dressed and started the drive back down the hill to complete their task in time to save supper.

Paige and Holden walked into the house, the smell of turkey filled the air. He was impressed that they were going through so much trouble. Paige's sister was already home and her aunt and uncle were expected any minute. Paige quickly disappeared into the bathroom, undoubtedly to tidy herself up a bit. Holden introduced himself to her sister. She was just as pretty as Paige, but she seemed a bit more timid and introverted than her older sister. Holden could still see the familiar mischievous sparkle in her eye like the one Paige had. She and Holden clicked right away, even though he did most of the talking because of her shyness. Her mom and dad teased her a bit, which made her want to talk even less. Holden thought it was cute. In the middle of a sentence, he could see her eyes widen and a smile grow across her lips. "PAIGE!!" She screamed. Although her sister had been there when they got home, Paige missed her when she headed to the bathroom. They ran towards each other and hugged. Paige was obviously excited to see her baby sister. As the three women started chatting, Paige's dad reappeared and without speaking handed Holden another beer and shook his head in the direction of the women. The girls finally broke up their little pow wow. Paige grabbed Holden and they went to the kitchen to get the place settings to set the dining room table for supper. Paige began hinting that she had a surprise for Holden later on. He was curious, but played it off at first. However, the more she hinted the more he wanted to know. He asked her several times but she didn't budge. As they set up the table, the doorbell rang and her aunt and uncle walked in. Paige ran over to see them, Holden followed close behind. Introductions were made and Holden slipped away to finish setting up the table as Paige's family reunited. Paige soon joined Holden and gave him a kiss on the cheek saying it was sweet of him to help out. Judging by the smell in the house, the turkey was just about ready. The family slowly made their way to the table. Paige's mom began pouring the wine. Holden took his seat next to Paige, her sister sat on the other side of Holden, her parents on each end and the aunt and uncle sat across the table. Holden didn't know what their family traditions were, so he waited to see if someone was going to say grace or if they just started eating. He was relieved to see that they just dug in. Paige's mom told Holden not to be shy, as she splattered some mashed potatoes on his plate giving everyone at the table a good laugh. Everyone took their portions and began eating and drinking. With every sip of wine the conversation loosened up, turning from superficial conversations to things more substantial. Paige's little sister kept staring at Holden the entire dinner; he thought the attention was cute. Holden was involved in conversation with Paige's family so he didn't notice Paige excuse herself from the table. He was surprised when she snuck up behind him and put her arms around him. She said loudly, "Isn't he the best?" She reached out for his hands, he put them behind his back as she talked, then she put her hands in his. She discretely placed something in his palm and whispered in his ear. "A little something just for you." Holden took the gift and tried to maintain the same discretion she displayed. Although he was curious as to what he now held in his lap, he had to wait for the perfect time to look. The opportunity came quicker than he anticipated when Paige's aunt knocked over her wine glass. Everyone scurried around to clean it up, so Holden took a peak at the object in his hand. It was a tiny silver object with two apparent settings, an on/off switch and a small slide that read min/max. Holden was very curious as to what the tiny remote controlled. He hit the on button and was very surprised to see Paige's reaction. She was bent over the table helping with the cleanup effort and almost jumped through the roof as she let out a little screech. She turned to Holden and gave him a dirty look followed by a big smile. He gave her a quizzical glance. He still had no idea what he was holding nor did he know what was up with Paige's unusual reaction. Her mom asked Paige if she was alright and Paige brushed off the incident. No one was paying Holden any attention as he started playing with the min/max setting sliding it up to max. Paige fell into her seat. He watched her eyes roll back in to her had, her hands clamped firmly onto the table. Everyone stopped and watched her. Holden laughed as he hit the off button. Holden's outburst drew attention away from Paige. He excused himself from the table. Paige gave him another evil look mixed with her mischievous smile. It took him awhile, but he finally realized what it was she had given him. It was a device for some sort of sex toy Paige was wearing. He smiled knowing the power he held in his hand. He slid it safely into his front pocket to keep it for later use.

As they finished up dinner, Paige's dad went into the kitchen to get dessert. Holden took the break to put his hand in his pocket, slid the setting to low and flipped on the on button. Paige jumped again and looked at him, her hands clenched the table, her movements were better controlled than the last time but her eyes still said it all. They flickered and started to roll back in her head as she fidgeted in her seat. She was trying to be as discrete as possible but after a couple of minutes her movements became more pronounced. It was obvious to Holden that the harder she tried to hold back her pleasure the closer to orgasm she got. Just when he thought she couldn't take it anymore, he hit the off button. She let out a sigh of relief. Her dad brought out a chocolate cake, which drew comments from everyone at the table. Just as they were about to cut the first slice Paige stood up. "Mom, Dad, everyone I have something to tell you." Her family all glared at Holden. "NOOO, I'm not pregnant," she said with a laugh. A collective sigh could be heard from everyone. Her dad, who was still holding a knife said, "Oh good, I guess I don't have to kill you." Everyone laughed, Holden's laugh was more nervous than the others. He wasn't completely sure her dad was kidding. Paige continued, "Holden got a job with a professional roller hockey team, it's definitely a promotion from what he does now." Everyone began congratulating him and asking him questions. Paige interrupted them. "He will be Director of Operations for the team, which means he'll be in charge of running the team administratively and he will be the youngest in the league." Again, everyone began shaking his hand, and Paige once again interrupted. "The bad news is, the team is in Vancouver BC." The table fell silent, cautiously exchanging glances. Paige jumped again; Holden decided to break the awkward silence by hitting the on button and quickly turned it off again. Paige shot him a quick look. "So, what does this mean Paige?" Her mom asked.

"Well Mom, Holden asked me to move with him and I said I would." They paused for the family's reaction. "Where are you going to work? What are you going to do out there?" Her dad asked.

"I'm going to go back to school. I applied to the university there, and Holden called his boss and asked him to make some calls. They pulled some strings and got me in the winter semester, and to top it off they are accepting all my other credits. For work, I'll be working in Holden's office part time to help out with the bills."

"How are you going to afford school and rent only working part time?" Her dad asked in a very somber tone. Paige began to answer when Holden interrupted. "Sir, Paige has some money saved up from dancing, the team is paying me very well and she only has a year left to get her degree. I don't mind helping her out, and then once she graduates she can support me." Holden said with a laugh, getting laughs from the family as well. "Will you still dance?" Her sister asked. Everyone, especially her dad sat up to hear the answer. "This is the part you're going to love Dad. I'm going to start a new life out there, a new me. I have retired from dancing. I mean, it's still a possibility should we need some extra cash…." Paige was saying until Holden cut her off again. "But, it's a very last resort; we want her to be able to concentrate on getting her degree."

"When do you leave?" Paige's mom asked.

"At the end of the season, we'll be driving out in October, after Thanksgiving. The team doesn't need him until after Christmas but we're excited to get settled before school and work start." The table fell silent. Paige and Holden looked at each other as the news slowly sunk into everyone. Holden reached into his pocket but Paige shot him the dirtiest look. He smiled as he brought his hands back up onto the table. Paige's sister was the first to break the silence. "That's cool, can I come visit?"

"Of course you can, you all can. The team arranged for us to get a two bedroom condo with a view of the ocean," Paige said. They all started talking amongst themselves, trying to see how everyone else felt about the news before they shared their own feelings. Her dad was the first to express his opinion. "Well Paige, Holden, you two haven't known each other that long, it's a very big move but you two definitely sound like you've done your homework. Your mother and I are very proud that you're going back to school and I've never liked you stripping. I guess all I can say is best of luck to both of you, but Paige, if you need anything you call us. Your room will always be yours, and if you need money call us. And you young man, treat my little girl right. Vancouver is only a quick plane ride away."

The subtle thread wasn't lost on Holden as he said, "Yes sir, I will and it isn't too far at all, I hope you all come and visit often. Especially when I have to go away for work, I don't want her to be alone."

The rest of the family started to share in their excitement. They drank more wine and ate their dessert. As everyone was starting to calm down Holden reached his hand into his pocket and hit the on button while using his thumb to fluctuate the speed. Paige quietly ate her cake as the vibrator strapped to her clit revved higher and lower. She started gently moving her hips around again, subtly, trying not to get caught. Holden gave her three quick bursts on high speed; she put her head down and then very quickly pushed herself away from the table and grabbed her plate. "You guys go watch TV, Holden and I will clear the table."

"We can't ask you to do that, Holden's our guest." Her mom objected.

"It's no problem, really," he said.

"I'll help," Paige's little sister volunteered.

"NO!" Paige and Holden exclaimed at once. "We'll be fine, go watch TV with everyone else," Paige finished. Holden grabbed a stack of plates and Paige grabbed a handful of glasses. Holden left the remote setting on low as they tidied up. Paige awkwardly walked into the kitchen with Holden following her. The kitchen was completely closed off, except for a window to the dining room that looked like it had never been opened. Paige peaked through to see if the coast was clear and Holden assumed it was, because Paige turned around fast, grabbed him by the shirt and pulled him in close. "I love you," she said before she started kissing him, with all the intensity of the kiss they shared up on the hill. Holden slowly turned up the rpms' on the remote. Paige reacted positively as she began groping at his fly. "No, we can't, not with everyone in the next room," Holden objected.

"Fuck me NOW!" She demanded. Paige turned around to peak out the window again; he took her up on her offer. She didn't see him pull his cock out of his jeans and he surprised her when he grabbed her waist and pulled down her pants just far enough to give him all the access he needed. As Paige maintained watch, Holden slid his throbbing cock into her soaked pussy. He could feel the toy that was attached to her panties still vibrating away, and with every thrust he could feel it vibrate on his balls. The relief of telling her parents their plans, the fact they could be caught at any second and the three hour long build up over dinner all combined into one passionate act. Paige reached one hand between her legs and started rubbing her clit as he pounded away behind her. She grabbed a clean dish towel off the counter and stuffed it into her own mouth to muffle her screams as she began to lose control. Holden was pretty close to cumming hard inside her. He just wanted to wait; he knew she was close because her movements became more jerky and her muscles spasmed as she masturbated. Holden heard her screams as they soaked into the dish towel. He couldn't control himself as he shot a hot load deep into her as he thrusted his shaft as far up into her as he possibly could. He felt her pussy contract around him; it was so tight he couldn't pull his penis out of her. The vibrator kept humming along as Paige fought to remain standing as her knees buckled from under her. They stayed in that position for a minute or two. Paige finally spit the towel out and Holden slid his now flaccid cock out of her. She pulled up her pants as he put his man of steel away and zipped up. Paige turned around, put her arms around him and they started kissing again. "Oh gross!" They heard. They spun around to see her sister standing in the doorway. "Um, how long have you been there?" Paige asked.   "Just got here. Why?"

"No reason," Holden said laughing; they were both relieved to know they weren't busted. Paige and Holden left the kitchen to go gather more dishes. After everything was either in the dishwasher or soaking in the sink, they joined her family to watch another movie.

The next day they woke up early and packed the car. Her parents were obviously sad to see her go and even though he had just met them, Holden felt a bit empty leaving their warm and inviting house. Her family wished Holden luck with his new career, he thanked them for their hospitality and then they were off.

Paige and Holden shared their excitement and relief during the drive home. He was excited for the move and the prospect of a new life with Paige and the Vancouver Witch Doctors.

6

After the dinner with Paige's family, the rest of the summer seemed to be a blur to them, passing by quicker than expected. The couple had their respective farewell parties and the professional movers had their lives packed up and in the back of a truck ready to accompany them on their trek to start new lives in British Columbia.

Neither Paige nor Holden had ever driven across the country before. They were both very excited for the opportunity to see new things and explore as much of the country-side as possible. Before they left, the movers told them not to expect their furniture for at least two weeks. Since Holden had a very loose check in time with his new employers, and the organization was going to pay for accommodations anyway, the two decided to take their time and go on side trips whenever the mood struck them.

The drive through Northern Ontario seemed to go on forever, but it was very beautiful with lots of windy roads, hills and, of course, Lake Superior shadowing them for most of the drive. The first night they decided to stay in Thunder Bay. Holden was very tired after the lengthy drive. He felt okay at the time and elected to drive the entire length himself, even though Paige offered to alternate several times. Holden was enjoying the challenging drive. When they finally pulled into the parking lot of what seemed like the only hotel with a vacancy sign, they grabbed their bags and went in to the lobby to secure their lodgings. The room was small, but more than adequate for their intended use. They threw their bags on one of the two double beds in the room and quickly turned around to head out for a bite to eat.

With their bellies full and the long drive to Winnipeg on the horizon, they crawled into their warm bed, acknowledging the fact it was their first night together. As excited as they were, they cuddled up closely and embraced each other as tightly as possible then quickly fell asleep. They woke to the ringing of their wake up call Holden requested when they checked in. They showered together and got dressed, paid the bill, packed the car and were off for their next journey.

The drive started off like the other had ended, in thick woods on either side of the hilly road and Lake Superior peaking through the trees at every opportunity. As they pair drove on, they passed several local touristy stores and Paige wanted to stop in them all. Although Holden wanted to get to the next destination, he was happy to take a break to stretch his legs. Seeing how excited Paige was, it made him interested to see what each shop had to offer. Wandering around store to store, they both pointed out interesting knick-knacks but bought nothing. They were growing weary of the drive and anxiously looked forward to their stop in Winnipeg. The road started to level out and become straighter; they were finally clearing the Canadian Shield and were heading into the Prairies. They knew that Winnipeg couldn't be much further. The sky opened up as the trees and rocks all stopped in what seemed like one very distinct line marking the border between Ontario and Manitoba. The lights of Winnipeg were on the horizon and the two let out a sigh of relief. Easily finding a room in Winnipeg they elected to splurge for one with a Jacuzzi. Too tired to think about going out again, they ordered room service and a movie. The room was grander than they expected and Paige wasted no time in running water for the tub as Holden waited for room service. Just as the tub filled and Paige was out of her last stitch of clothing, there was a knock at the door followed by a meek voice, "Room Service." Paige dove into the tub, sinking as low as possible. Holden looked back at her to see if she was ready for him to open the door, giving him a quick nod, he let in the hotel worker, he signed the bill and locked up after they were alone in the room. Holden brought Paige's meal over to her, grabbed his own, poured them both a glass of white wine then slowly removed all his clothes. Paige, sipping her wine, made catcalls to the stripping Holden and playfully splashed water at him. Holden jumped into the water and let out a shriek as his naked body made contact with the unexpectedly hot water. "How can you stand that?" Holden asked Paige.

"It's great once you're in, you big baby."

Holden, now ready for the heat, very slowly lowered his body into the 'Syn soup', Paige couldn't help but laugh. After Holden was finally in the boiling broth, he reached for his glass of wine and his meal. Paige had already begun to eat her dinner. Holden held up his wine glass, "To us and our second night". Paige smiled widely as she raised her glass and then they went back to enjoying their dinner as Holden hit play on the remote to start the movie. After they were done eating, Paige moved around so she was sitting between Holden's legs. He put his strong arms around her and held her tightly as they soaked in the Jacuzzi watching their movie.

Half way through the movie the water started to cool and their fingers began to shrivel so they elected to move to the bed. Holden jumped out of the tub and grabbed two towels. Holden wrapped the over sized towel around Paige's delicate frame as she stepped out of the tub. Shivering, she was happy to have the warmth of the towel around her. After drying themselves off they decided not to put on any clothes as they found warmth and comfort under the blankets, they took every opportunity to sneak a touch of each other's body.

They both fell asleep to the movie, letting it play over and over again as they slept. Once again, the phone's ringing woke them up and they quickly gathered their things and hit the road. There plan was to push on to Banff, where they had reservations.

The dew was still on the car as they started that day's journey. Leaving Winnipeg, Paige and Holden quickly realized where the prairies reputation came from. The horizon stretched on forever, the golden wheat danced in the wind and the blue sky was only tarnished by the sporadic whisper of a cloud. Paige and Holden were both amazed at how flat the prairies really were. The lack of towns and highway stands made the trip go by faster than the previous days. As they hit the rare city, they took the opportunity to tour around and see what each province had to offer. Manitoba was soon in their rear view mirror and the "Land of Living Skies" was filling their windshield. After touring Regina for an hour, they elected to move on so they could still make their reservations in Banff.

Before long, the foothills of the Rockies made an appearance on the horizon. The Calgary skyline was impressive, especially after endless hours of nothingness. Paige asked Holden if they could stop in Calgary for supper. Holden was only too happy to oblige, he too was looking forward to seeing the city.

Finally reaching the city limits, they began looking for signs to indicate the downtown core. After following the bulk of the traffic towards the CN tower looking thing, they made it downtown. As Holden negotiated traffic, Paige kept a keen eye out for a restaurant that they might be interested in trying. She finally spotted one and Holden steered the car into a spot fairly close to the entrance. The hostess seated them in what she described as the best seat in the house. They were placed in a booth next to a picture window that had a view of the mountains and the ski jump from the 1988 Olympics. After learning they were from out of town and on their way to Banff for the night, the waitress warned them that driving through the Rockies the first time can be intimidating, especially at night.

The pair enjoyed their dinner as a fire crackled in the background. The view of the sun setting over the mountains made the scene even more impressive. The peaks cast shadows over the city just before the sun disappeared into the Pacific Ocean. The lights of the ski hill illuminated the side of the mountain.

The bill finally came. Holden threw down his credit card and wasn't looking forward to crawling back into the car. It had already had been a very long trip, but fortunately he knew it was going to be their last night of traveling. However, he also realized that because their place would not be ready for several more days, Banff wasn't going to be the last hotel they slept in before they were in their new home.

The drive from Calgary to Banff was short, and at night it seemed pretty unadventurous. The hotel they had reserved was very nice but not nearly as grand as the one they had stayed in the night before. The room was on the 2nd floor and the entrance was on the outside of the building. They immediately crawled into bed but neither had a good sleep. They were as excited as kids the night before Christmas because they knew the next day they would be home. Like every morning of the trip, the phone rang telling them it was time to wake up and like every other morning on the trip they woke up, showered packed and prepared to leave the room. Unlike mornings prior though, they were left awe struck when they opened the door. The view that was missed in the darkness of the night before was incredible. The door over looked the heart of the Rockies. Snow peaked mountains engulfed the tiny hotel hidden away amongst the majestic mountains. They were unreal; pictures and descriptions could not do this wonder justice. They felt so small, so lost. Everywhere they looked there were towering mountains and some of the tallest trees the pair had ever seen. They stopped on the walkway and took in the view for as long as possible. They didn't realize they climbed as high in altitude as they had, but with altitude came dropping temperatures. Before too long Paige was starting to feel the effect of the cold weather and urged Holden to keep moving. Taking one last look around, Holden grabbed the bags and they were walking towards their car.

They barely turned out of the parking lot when they stopped at the first of many spectacular sites. There was a very large elk eating out of a flowerpot that lined the sidewalk. Paige was trying her hardest to take pictures as Holden maneuvered the car as close as he dared so Paige could get the best possible shot. Satisfied, Paige told Holden the picture was taken, cuing Holden to start driving. They looked for signs that pointed them west. They found the sign they were looking for, and before long, they were off for the last leg of their journey. Around every corner and over every hill was a new, more spectacular view. Holden was finding it difficult to concentrate; he wanted to stop every kilometer to take in the sites, but they knew that wasn't possible. The traffic on the narrow highway was heavy and with the R.V.s and transport trucks sharing the road, it made some of the passageways treacherous. Paige got really excited and yelled for Holden to stop, unfortunately the roadway wouldn't permit a vehicle stopping so he couldn't. Paige told Holden as she leaned out the window that there was a grizzly bear walking alongside the road. He knew something had to be going on, as all the cars were bottlenecking in that area. Paige struggled to get a shot but managed to only get something that resembled a bear, regardless she was proud of her picture. She kept trying to show Holden her prize photo but he could only laugh at her attempts to distract him. She leaned over and gave him a kiss on the cheek. She was obviously getting more and more excited as they went deeper into the mountains. Every few kilometers there was a new animal on the road, from mountain goats to more elk, moose and bears. Neither had ever seen so much wildlife in one place in their lives. Holden thought back to the warning the waitress had given them and he was very thankful they didn't venture too much further into the Rockies at night, than they already had.

Road signs counted down the distance to Vancouver. The sky began to open again as the towering mountain range appeared to shrink into the ocean. The houses and buildings became more frequent and the road improved greatly. They knew they were starting to hit the outskirts of a city. The next sign read, "Vancouver 10 km." They both felt the anticipation grow as they continued to take in the sites. Although the beautiful natural sites had been replaced by city structures, they were just as excited. Paige was pointing out unique buildings and possible stores she'd like to shop in. As traffic began to congest, Holden had to concentrate more on the road ahead and missed many of the areas of interest Paige was so excited about.

Even though their furniture wouldn't arrive for a few more days they couldn't wait that long to see their new home. From the pictures they had seen, it was a beautiful place with a view of the mountains and the ocean. It was a condo on the 10th floor of a 12 story building. They both loved city life and looked forward to having a place that over looked so much of their new surroundings. Paige connected the GPS Holden had bought for the trip. To this point the navigation had been easy, just point the car west, but finding their place in a new city was going to prove to be much harder so Holden thought the electronic help was needed. Paige quickly typed in the address as the GPS acquired the satellites and began giving the appropriate turns to take and the distance to each turn. The default voice was an English woman with an ever so slight accent. Paige had never used a GPS before so she began playing with the settings. The one that caught most of her interest was the voice settings. She began cycling through the voices making them laugh at some of the bizarre options. It had a well spoken male voice and different languages, but the funniest to them was the Yoda setting. "Turn right ahead you must not," was one of the directions Yoda issued. This confused both of them. Holden scrambled to read signs to see if he should be turning right or if he should continue straight. He eventually elected for straight, mostly because he passed the road and it was too late to turn. Holden asked Paige to change the voice to something that gave clearer instructions. She began to mock him in her own Yoda voice, Holden just looked over at her, and he couldn't help but laugh.

Their apartment wasn't that hard to find, especially with the aid of a GPS. They parked the car and looked around the outside of the building. It was very nice, in what seemed like a good neighbourhood and the mountains appeared to be right in their backyard. They couldn't wait to see inside but they knew that there were going to have to. They typed 'hotels' into the GPS and one showed up just a few blocks away. They decided that would be the best one since they could tour around the neighbourhood more and see what it was like at night.

After they got settled in their temporary home, Holden made some phone calls letting his bosses know he was in town and made dinner plans with them. They were happy to hear from him, one of the guys he would be working with was a course mate of his from college and was the main reason Holden landed such a key position. Although they stayed in close touch after school, they hadn't seen each other since graduation and Holden was looking forward to reuniting with his friend. Paige was nervous to meet all the new people and wanted to look good for Holden. He reassured her that his friend was laid back, maybe even more so than his friends in Toronto, and he would love her no matter what. As for the other two guys going, Holden wasn't sure what to expect. Mike said they would meet them at a restaurant up the block from the hotel at six. Because the drive from Banff to Vancouver was less than six hours, Holden and Paige had made it into town around mid afternoon, which gave them a few hours to sleep and shower before their night on the town.

Watching Paige undress down to her boy cut panties and sports bra made Holden wish that they hadn't vowed to not have sex again until they actually moved into their new place. The vow was hard enough to keep on the trip, the missed opportunities to fuck in some new places was okay because they were both so tired from the drive, but now that they were in Vancouver, Holden was feeling particularly horny. Paige kept glancing over at Holden as he stripped to his boxers. She could see the outline of his cock beneath the thin cotton, how badly she wanted to crawl over to him and plead for him to use it on her. She wanted to reach into the elastic waistband and pull out his thick member, feel it in her fingers as she jerked it off inches from her face. She wanted to make him nice and hard then lean back on the bed allowing him to feed his "man of steel" into her willing pussy. She yearned for the piercings to hit her just right, as they often had before, but she resisted. 'Damn vow.' But it was her idea after all, she wanted their first night as a real couple to be something special. She laid in bed with her hands very gently caressing her panties, making sure she touched her clit, she began to touch herself harder and a little bit more carelessly. Scared she would set Holden off she sprang out of bed. "I need a shower, I feel gross."

"Okay honey," Holden said, as he watched her climb out of bed and pull her sports bra over her head, carelessly throwing it on the floor near their suitcase. Holden could see her thumbs hook into her panties and begin to pull them down as she used her foot to close the bathroom door. Holden couldn't hold back, once he heard the water running he reached into his boxers and grabbed his thick cock. His fingers firmly gripped the shaft and he began pulling on himself. He was more aggressive than normal because the trip had him very worked up from not being able to fuck his beautiful girlfriend and not having any privacy to take care of himself. He knew his time was limited and he was going to take full advantage of it. He pictured Paige just as she was moments before she went to the shower. He closed his eyes and imagined her hand gripping him, her scent was still alive in the room, making a visual that much easier. He had her kneeling beside him, his arms behind his head as she told him to relax and let her take care of it. Her fingers caressed him just as he liked, she wasn't trying to take it slow, she had one thing on her mind and that was to get him off. She began jerking him faster and faster and before he knew it he was cumming with so much force he felt some cum splash up on his own chin. When he opened his eyes, she was gone and the shower still running. A huge puddle of cum oozed from his hand and stomach, with the odd drop across his chest. As happy as he was to have relieved himself, he now had the tedious task of cleaning up. He stood up, trying not to drip anywhere. He made it to the sink outside the bathroom door and used a wet face cloth to clean himself. Satisfied there was no evidence remaining, he put his boxers back on and crawled into bed.

 Paige closed the door behind her; she couldn't wait to get her clothes off. Paige turned on the water and was almost giddy to see the shower head was the massage wand style. She turned up the hot water and crawled in. She rinsed herself off for a minute or two but couldn't wait any longer. Her pussy ached for attention; she too, was feeling the effects of the vow and lack of privacy. She began to let the water cascade off her shoulders, splashing onto her very sensitive breasts. She leaned her shoulder into the shower wall to stabilize herself so she didn't run the risk of having a slip and fall accident in the tub. Her hand began to move towards her crotch, she ran her fingers over her pubic area and took note it was time for another waxing. She quickly put that thought out of her mind as her fingers continued to ever so gently graze down her mound, teasing herself. Almost to the point of losing control she began to rub her clit, her forefinger pressed hard up against the magic button and she began to rub it back and forth as fast and hard as possible. It built the urge for an orgasm quickly, but wasn't enough to finish the job. She knew what would. She reached up to the shower head and adjusted the flow until it hit a high pressure pulsating setting. She spread her legs as wide as she possibly could without slipping, then positioned the water flow so that it hit her clitoris just right. Her free hand started groping at her breasts. She elected to skip the flickering of her nipples that she liked so much and went right to sinking her fingers into her tender flesh, squeezing them as hard as she could. The hot pulsating water proved to be too much for her in that position, she had to lie down. She put one leg on the edge of the tub and the heel of her other foot on the opposite corner. She pushed the nozzle hard against herself. The water hurt at first, but in her mind the sensation it gave her made the temporary pain worth it. The shower head was big enough that some of the water was forcing itself inside her. The weird sensation of hot water penetrating her combined with the amount of unpredictable force riddling her pussy and the already pent up sexual frustration made her quickly reach the point of orgasm. To fully finish herself off she knew she was going to need more penetration. She adjusted the water to the maximum focused stream and positioned the wand so all the hot water filled her pussy. Having the water touch every part of her insides and then flow out of her was foreign too her. She reminded herself to buy the same style shower head for their new home. She began to feel herself up as the water worked its magic, within minutes she was erupting in a full body orgasm. She found it difficult to hold the shower head, and even more difficult not to let out an earth-shattering scream. She finally lost control of her body; she lay convulsing in the tub with water spraying everywhere. After the convulsions stopped and she regained control, she found herself lying freezing in the bottom of the tub with water all over the bathroom. She stood up, lathered herself with soap, readjusted the water flow to something gentler and rinsed herself off. She exited the bathroom wrapped in a towel and decided to sleep naked worried that even the cotton between her legs would set her off again. She crawled into bed and snuggled up to an already sleeping Holden.

Just as Paige closed her eyes, Holden's cell phone rang waking them up. It was the alarm he had set just before their nap. She looked at the alarm clock and couldn't believe she had been asleep for three hours. He said he was going to have a shower as he crawled out of bed. She watched him walk by, paying particular attention his muscular calves flex as he walked. Then she moved her eyes upward to catch a glimpse of his ass before he disappeared into the bathroom. She loved how the boxer/briefs cupped his firm ass cheeks, she also loved that the cotton was starting to separate from the elastic band. Paige thought it was cute that she was going to have to buy him new underwear and take care of him. It made the seemingly independent and strong Holden appear just a little vulnerable and that made her feel needed. When Holden finally got out of the shower he was amazed at the speed with which Paige had gotten ready. He was also amazed at how good she looked. She had her hair in pig tails that made her curly hair look very thicker than normal. She also applied a thin trace of black eyeliner and had brushed on several layers of eye shadow, having it come to a point in the corner of her eyes like cats eyes. It was very discretely applied, so it didn't jump right out. She was also wearing a black blouse buttoned up not to show off much cleavage, but still managing to accentuated her breasts. She had on a red plaid skirt that was cut just above her knees and a thick black belt with big silver buckles on the front of it. On her feet she was wearing white knee high socks and black boots that came up mid calf which had the same buckles on them as her belt. "No fair," Holden said looking at her, referencing their vow of celibacy. She glanced down at him and nodded at his growing penis. "Same to you."

He didn't notice his towel slipped off, and seeing Paige in that outfit had given him an erection. He just looked down, laughed and started to get dressed. Holden put on a clean, newer pair of boxer briefs, slid on a pair of designer jeans, a t-shirt from a retro rock band and threw a dress shirt over top, which he left open and untucked. Paige watched him intently as he dressed, wishing she could unwrap his pretty package. Holden knew she was watching so he made his moves more deliberately, flexing whenever possible without being too obvious. He pulled out a pair of black Tommy socks and slid them over his feet. He looked up at her; she just giggled and applauded him. He was a bit embarrassed but flattered he could hold her attention; a warm wave hit him as he realized he was falling that much more in love with her. The uncertainty of their relationship and whether or not she should move with him was slowly being replaced with confidence that they were doing the right thing and at that moment all doubt had vanished. He knew he couldn't have done it without her; he wanted to tell her how much he loved her. He wanted to kiss her but he got control of his runaway emotions and instead went to put on some cologne. The phone rang, his buddy Mike was on the other end. "Hey, you guys ready?"

"Ya, what time you getting here?"

"I'm down in the lobby, I'm on my way up, I just thought I'd give you a chance to um, clean up. We'll have a beer and head out to the restaurant."

Holden told him that he didn't have any in the room. "No worries," was the reply, followed by the click of the line going dead. Holden didn't have any time to realize he was hung up on when there was a knock at the door. Rushing to answer the door, Holden was excited to see his friend. Paige began to get nervous and started to doubt her clothing option or if she would fit in with his friends. Holden swung open the door and had to dodge a flying beer cap, he looked behind him to see where it landed then looked at his buddy who was holding a 12 pack in one hand and an opened bottle in the other. "For you my friend," he said. Holden politely grabbed the bottle and took a long drink. He invited Mike in and made introductions. Mike froze when his eyes met Paige's. He pushed the case of beer to Holden who dug in the box and pulled out 2 more bottles. Mike extended his hand to Paige. Paige, beginning to feel more comfortable after watching his comical entrance, reached for Mike's hand and they shook. Mike still staring at Paige said, "Oh my God you are beautiful. Good job Holden. Seriously Paige, how'd you end up with a bum like this?"

"Oh you know, he got me drunk and knocked up, now I'm stuck with him." The expression on Mike's face changed to panic, "You're pregnant? Holden what did you do?" Paige and Holden both almost collapsed with laughter, "No, you dopey bastard, she was kidding, have a beer."

"Oh, I get it," Mike said laughing nervously. "Paige, you remind me a lot of my girlfriend. She is a hopeful on Suicide Girls. As a matter of fact a few hopefuls, models, and members are having a gathering tonight, we'll have to join up with them later."

"I would love too," Paige answered. Holden handed Mike and Paige their beer, then sat and talked. Holden told Mike about the drive, Mike told Holden the ins and out of the office, who to watch out for and who was a good person. Mike finally looked at his watch and said they should go. They decided to walk so that no one had to worry about driving.

They restaurant wasn't that far away, but on the walk Paige and Holden stopped to look at everything. Mike could only laugh at the 'tourists'. The restaurant was filling fast, but they had reservations and the other two members of the dinner party were already seated and judging by the empty beer bottles around them, they had been there for a while. The two men started hooting and hollering when they saw Mike. They stood up and said, "This must be the young man we hired sight unseen. Mike told us what a great guy you are."

"Hello sir, I'm Holden, this is my girlfriend Paige."

"Enough with the sir shit, I'm Charlie and this is Steve."

They all exchanged pleasantries and just as they took their seats, the waitress appeared as if on cue. She took the orders and the night took off from the first toast. Half way through the night Charlie told Holden and Paige that the moving company called the office that night and because of a big job in Vancouver they needed the moving truck and were wondering if they could drop off the furniture sooner than they quoted. Their furniture would be in town in two days, not the week they were expecting. Paige and Holden were ecstatic at the news as Charlie handed them the keys to their new place. Holden and Paige hugged each other and got really excited at the chance to see their home. Holden ordered another round. Several hours passed, they ate until they were stuffed and drank till they could barely walk. Mike jumped up getting the attention of everyone at the table. He fumbled around with his pocket, pulled out his cell phone and started shouting "HELLO, HELLO?" into the phone. Holden reached up grabbed his cell from him and pushed the green phone button. "Hello, you have reached Mike's phone, I'm sorry he is too stupid to own a cell phone, this is Holden how may I help you?" Holden said trying to disguise his own drunkenness. The voice on the other end was shouting back, she sounded like she was just as drunk as the people in Holden's party. "HOLDEN? This Tamara, Mike's girlfriend. Welcome to B.C. I can't wait to meet you, is Mike around?"

"Ya, he's right here, hold on. Dingus, it's for you, its Tamara."

"No shit it's for me, it's my phone," Mike said before he started talking to his girlfriend.

The group went on with their own conversation, ignoring Mike. Occasionally Steve or Charlie would throw a left over fry at him. Not being one to waste food, Mike snatched up the ones he could and ate them; they all had a laugh at "Drunk Mike". Finally Mike pushed the button to disconnect, looked at Holden and Paige and said the SG group was at a dance club called Heaven. It was across town and the lineup was likely to be long but if they told the bouncers they were with the Suicide Girl group they could cut the line. The three looked at Steve and Charlie as if to invite them to the club. The two older gentleman said they would pass but told the trio that they should go as they were soon going to call it a night anyway, their wives would be wondering where they were. They all sat there for about another half hour finishing up their drinks and waiting for the checks. When the waitress who they had befriended over the hours finally brought the tabs, Charlie the senior executive at the table reached for them all. Holden tried to object, but Charlie just said it was a business dinner and he couldn't in good conscience let his newest employee pay for his first dinner in town. Everyone else at the table graciously accepted his offer and they all chipped in for the tip.

Charlie and Steve headed out in the first available cab, the remaining three waited for only a couple of minutes before getting a taxi of their own. Mike sat in the front, letting Paige and Holden cuddle in the backseat. He engaged the cab driver in conversation, asking him the wildest thing he had ever seen and other questions about being a cabbie. The driver was only too happy to tell tales of the road; the long drive passed quickly and soon they were at the front door of "Heaven." There was a huge line up and the threesome hoped that Tamara was right. Mike strutted up to the bouncer and said he was there with the Suicide Girls group. The bouncer eyed up Paige and finally nodded to let them in. They made their way through the packed bar, Mike knew the general area the group was sitting so they headed in that direction. Finally, through the crowd Mike noticed some pink hair bopping up and down, which he recognized it as the wig Tamara had left in earlier. He grabbed Paige's hand, who in turn grabbed Holden's and like a line backer he pushed his way through the crowd until he got right up behind Tamara. She didn't know it was him as he put his arms around her. He put one palm slightly under her short cut shirt, the other well below the belt on her skirt. He pushed up as close to her as possible and started to grind into her. She rested her head on his shoulder, closing her eyes and whispered, "Let's go sailor, but make it fast my boyfriend will be here any minute." She then spun around and hugged him and smothered him with kisses. "It's about time you got here." She said to the three new comers as she led them over to the group and introduced them. Paige and Tamara started talking; they complimented on each other's clothes and as Mike and Holden watched them talk they realized that Tamara was pretty much a blonde version of Paige. The two girls clicked right away, Paige, albeit drunk, was happy to have made a friend her first night in town.

When the waitress came over, they placed their drink order as the song changed to something the girls apparently liked. They let out a shriek, Tamara grabbed Paige's hand and they both ran off to the dance floor. They stayed within eyesight of the two boys as they started to strut their stuff. Both moved very erotically to the music. The drinks came over and Holden bought the first round. The two boys' clinked glasses as they watched their girls on the floor trying to out sexify the other. Finally Paige grabbed Tamara and started dancing close to her, Tamara reciprocated and they began grinding into each other. Now others besides Holden and Mike noticed the dancing display. Eventually every guy in the bar, and most of the girls, were watching. Holden was used to having his girl be the center of attention but, despite Tamara's incredibly good looks, Mike wasn't as comfortable with it. He began getting upset. Holden asked him if he trusted her, he said of course, so Holden told him to sit back, enjoy the show and reap the benefits of it later. The next song came on, the girls tamed down their show so the two guys sat down with the SG group.

When the next song started the lights also began to brighten, Holden looked at his watch. 3 a.m. "Fuck its late," he said to no one in particular. Mike nodded in agreement. By now most of the group, and the bar for that matter, had left or was starting to head for the door. The girls staggered over. The guys overheard Tamara say that she would love to help them move in. She slapped the back of her hand against a half asleep Mike, "Right Mike?"

"Huh? Ya, whatever honey," he replied, not knowing what he was agreeing too.

Tamara dug through her purse and pulled out her cell phone, she fumbled with it for a minute before she eventually dropped it on the floor. She giggled and picked it up. "Okay, what's your number?" Paige gave it to her, but told her it would be changing soon, so Paige got Tamara's number as well. They hugged and kissed each other on the cheek. That got Mike's attention, he jumped up and hugged Holden and pretended to kiss him on the cheek before Holden pushed him away. "Get away from me." Holden said laughing.

"Peace out brother," Mike slurred. He grabbed Tamara by the hand and she pranced behind him showing way too much energy for a girl as drunk as she was. Holden and Paige walked out of the bar. Holden was happy to have everyone see him with her, he was very proud of Paige. The doormen nodded at Holden, it was clear they saw Paige dancing earlier and were nodding the guy 'that a boy' nod. Holden got Paige into a cab, he looked through his pockets until he found the business card of their hotel they were staying at and showed the cabbie. They both reflected on their night, relieved their first night was a success. Paige was happy she met a friend and Holden felt more at ease showing up at work. Charlie and Steve invited them for a tour after their furniture and effects arrived. The happy couple poured themselves into their hotel room and undressed as much as they could before they passed out.

The next day Holden was the first to move, he opened his eyelids and felt a sharp pain in his temples. He laid still looking at the ceiling then mumbled to himself that he needed water. Paige barely moving herself said, "Not so loud, some of us are hung over." Holden tried to laugh but the mere thought caused too much pain. They stayed perfectly still for another hour or so before Paige gathered the courage to get out of bed. She slowly moved to the sink, poured herself a glass of water, drank one glass, took a couple of aspirin, then drank another glass. Before going back to the bed she brought Holden a glass of water and a couple of aspirin.

They tried to talk while they waited for the pain to subside, but neither was very successful. The aspirin didn't take long to kick in and they both felt well enough to go out of the room. They decided the first thing they had to do was go get some fast food. Nothing cured a hangover like some greasy burgers.

After the aspirin kicked in and the burgers filled their bellies, the pair was starting to feel better so they did a walking tour of Vancouver, spending the bulk of their time by the water front. Paige looked in shop after shop, Holden, although pretending he was being put out, secretly enjoyed shopping with Paige. He intentionally picked out clothes that were a size too small when she was in the change room so he could see how great she looked in the extra tight clothing. After they shopped and walked for hours, they decided to go for dinner then head over to their apartment to see what needed to be done before the movers arrived.

They found an ocean side restaurant that had a very comfortable feel to it. They remembered the name and decided they would go back frequently. The pair started the walk to their apartment, saying hi to everyone they passed by as they took in all the sites. Finally arriving at the lobby door, Holden dug in his pockets to find the keys he got the night before. Paige grabbed Holden's hand and squeezed, she was getting very excited, as was Holden, but he was doing his best to contain it. They jumped in the elevator and Paige pushed 10. They elevator gave them a very smooth quick ride to their floor. The bell dinged, the doors opened and Paige burst through the door. Holden laughed and moved much slower. Impatiently, Paige reached into the elevator grabbing Holden. "Come on!" Holden fiddled with his key chain again trying to find the door key. Paige kept urging Holden to hurry; Holden told her he was going as fast as he could. Finally, he found the right key and opened the door. Paige was about to race through when Holden grabbed her by the back of her pants pulling her back, she almost fell down but he caught her. "What are you doing?" she asked. He looked at her, picked her up in his strong arms and carried her through the threshold. She threw her arms over him and once they were in, she gave him a kiss on the lips before he had a chance to put her down. He held her tighter, her small frame was nothing in his muscular arms, he could have held her like that all night. They explored the apartment hand in hand. Opening every door to see where everything was, they planned how they were going to arrange furniture, who was going to get what closet and what art they needed to bring the walls alive. They got so excited arranging their apartment; they didn't really look at the view. Finally, as Holden was looking at the fireplace, planning on what he would be putting on the mantle, something shiny caught his eye. He looked over and had his first glimpse of the breath taking view. He called over Paige. They could see much more of the ocean than they thought they would, the shiny object that had caught Holden's eye was a floatplane taking off. The view they had was of a small bay, and on the other side of the bay were the Rocky Mountains. The locals were used to the mountains so they weren't that big of a deal to them, but to Holden and Paige they were very impressive. Just as they were about to turn and head back to their hotel to get a good night sleep, in preparation of the big day ahead, a bald eagle soared past their window and majestically floated around in an air stream looking for its prey. They watched it for several minutes then Holden scanned the bay hoping to see the famous black fin of an Orca, but they weren't that lucky. He would have been surprised if Orcas ever went into that bay with all the boat and air traffic that occupied the water space, but he was still hopeful. They left the apartment and went back to their hotel.

The next morning came early; the moving company told them they would be there around eight in the morning so Paige and Holden got there just after six to make sure things were ready. Mike and Tamara, in keeping Tamara's drunken promise, called and said they would be there around ten. The movers finally arrived, Holden went downstairs to meet them so he could rig the door to stay open and escort them to the right apartment. Holden got excited when they opened the truck doors and he saw his furniture. As the movers carried up their things, he didn't seem to remember owning so much. The living room began filling up with boxes. Paige was directing the movers to the appropriate locations for each box making sure as many were put in the right rooms as possible. Mike and Tamara appeared out of nowhere; Mike snuck up behind Holden and gave him a small shove and yelled, "BOO!!" Holden jumped a foot, much to the amusement of Tamara and Mike. "Hey man, sorry we didn't knock but the doors were open and we thought you'd be busy."

"No worries, thanks for coming," Holden said.

"Here, we brought you something," Tamara added, and then showed Holden the four Tim Horton's coffee cups. Holden yelled for Paige to come out from emptying boxes in the bathroom. She came running out and gave Tamara a hug and said hello to Mike. Holden passed her a coffee. "Oh thank you, you're a life saver," Paige said to Mike and Tamara. As the bigger furniture was brought up, the four tried to help the movers. They moved boxes out of their way and Holden and Mike helped position the furniture to the spots Paige and Holden decided on the night before. As the sofa and coffee table were set up, Holden and Mike started stacking boxes on both to help make more room for the movers. Next to come up was Holden's queen sized bed. Holden directed the movers to the master bedroom. Holden and Mike began putting the bed frame together as Paige and Tamara went back to the bathroom to finish what Paige already started. When the bed was together, and all the big furniture in its place, there were only a few more boxes left. Holden and Mike began working on hooking up the home theatre. Mike was impressed by Holden's 50 inch HD TV and surround sound. He couldn't wait until it was all hooked up to see its capabilities. Tamara told Paige that now Mike would have to get a TV just as big or bigger, Paige said if they did get a bigger TV, Holden would have to get an even bigger one. They both shared a laugh at the guy's expense and continued working.

The movers came up with only 2 boxes on a cart. "Well this is the last of them," the lead mover said. "Do you want the packers to come in tomorrow to unpack?" The four friends did a quick inspection of what was important to Holden and Paige. Satisfied nothing was damaged in the move; Holden signed the declaration saying everything was accounted for and denied the unpackers. Holden looked at the clock and had to make sure the time was right. It was only three in the afternoon; he thought the movers would take much longer. Since they were all working as the movers brought things up, they already had made a big dent in the boxes but there was still lots to do. Everyone was hungry, so they put the work on hold and walked down to the nearest fast food joint. After lunch the 2 girls said they had an errand to run and would meet the boys back at the apartment.

Holden and Mike made it back into the apartment to start working. Holden went to offer Mike a beer then realized he didn't plan ahead and stock the fridge. Holden apologized and had the bright idea to call Paige to see if she could pick up some beer while they were out on their errands. Holden grabbed his cell phone, hit #1 on the speed dial, and just as he hit "call" he heard the muffled song "Punk Rock Girl" playing. They both searched for the source of the music, Holden found it first on the kitchen counter top under some clothes; it was Paige's cell phone. Holden hung up his phone. "Damn." Mike said that Tamara didn't have her cell phone, so they were shit out of luck. They decided they would wait to let the girls in, then go on a beer run. In the mean time, Mike started playing with the entertainment system. He programmed in local radio stations, tested the DVD player and PS3 to see if they all worked right.

Mike found the CD collection and put in the first Billy Talent album and cranked up the volume as "This is How it Goes" played. The sub woofer had the apartment shaking, Mike was very impressed. Holden turned down the amplifier saying he didn't want a noise complaint his first day. The PS3 games were in the same boxes with the CDs and DVD collection. Mike thumbed through the games, saying that they would have to plan a gaming night. Holden agreed and said they could send the girls out clubbing or something. Finally Mike flipped through the TV channels and settled on a sports highlight program before the two of them went back to unpacking.

The buzzer from the front door went off, it was the two girls. Holden buzzed them in and when they walked through the front door, "Surprise," the girls said as they held up a two four of Bud and two big bottles of wine. Holden searched through the boxes in the kitchen to find the wine glasses and Paige searched through another box looking for a cork screw. Paige was successful, Holden not so much. He found a novelty glass shaped like the CN tower and another oddly shaped glass. Paige and Tamara said they weren't too proud to drink wine from non wine glasses. Holden opened the wine as Paige gave Holden a beer and tossed one to Mike who was sitting on the floor, leaning against the wall. Holden told him to take the couch; Mike said he was fine. After Tamara had her glass of wine she laid down beside Mike with her head in Mike's lap. Mike began to subconsciously run his fingers through her hair. Mike proposed a toast, "To Paige and Holden, to your new apartment and your new lives." They all raised their glasses and when the first drop of alcohol touched their tongues everyone knew that their work was done for the day. Paige and Holden would tinker around later in the evening, but the important things were unpacked and set up. Holden then proposed a toast of his own "To Mike and Tamara, our only friends in BC, thanks for all your help in getting us here and helping us move," again they raised their glasses and took a drink. The next few hours were passed by conversation, watching TV and, of course, more drinks. Mike looked at his watch, "Well, I think we should be going." It was eight at night and the four were drunk and tired. After they left, Holden closed the door behind them and turned to Paige. "Welcome home," he said, as they hugged and kissed. Paige broke the embrace and went into the kitchen to get some more unpacking done. Holden watched her for a minute and finally couldn't take it anymore. Using his arm he cleared off the remaining couple of boxes on the counter. One of the boxes landed with a breaking sound. "Oops, I think I found those wine glasses."

"What are you doing?" Paige asked. Without speaking, he picked her up and put her down on the counter he had just cleared off. Her breasts were at eye level and he couldn't wait to touch them.

"We're living in our new home, vow is over." With that he pulled at her shirt, she helped him get it off as he reached underneath her sports bra and guided it over her head. He took her right breast in his mouth, Paige leaned her head back. She was amazed how great his warm breath and mouth felt on her body after going so long without it. His tongue danced all around her erect nipple, his one hand supported him on the counter top, the other was firmly on her back so she could lean back and relax. He loved the feel of her firm breasts in his mouth. He knew she was self conscious about the size of them, so he tried to reassure her every chance he could get. He legitimately loved their size. He loved how they looked, he loved how they felt, he particularly loved the reaction he got when he touched them. She was the only girl he was able to give an orgasm to by simply caressing her breasts the right way. Giving her another orgasm by licking her tits crossed his mind but after spending the last couple of weeks without tasting her, without being inside of her but being so close to her on the trip, was too much for him to resist. He moved the hand off her back forcing her to lean back on her own hands. His hand ever so gently ran over the perky breast. She could feel no more than a whisper of his hand, it was a huge tease, she wanted him to squeeze it, twist it, to do something substantial; the random touching was driving her wild. He could feel her wanting more, he refused to give it to her but as he was teasing her one tit, his teeth found her other nipple and he gently bit. The unexpected pain kept her guessing and it was that randomness she loved. It kept her mind guessing, never knowing what was going to happen next. He moved the hand running over her tit to the middle of her chest. He gently pushed her back, she took the hint and leaned back until she was eventually was lying down. As she laid back, Holden kept his mouth on her chest, sliding his tongue down her ribs, over her hard stomach until it reached the elastic band of her gray track pants. Holden, not missing a beat, grabbed her track pants and pulled. She helped him by putting her weight on her shoulder blades and lifting her bum off the counter, giving the track pants no resistance to come off. She was already very wet with anticipation. Holden quickly got her pants off and was happy to see the plain white cotton panties. He loved the unusual lingerie, but he also loved the more traditional things. Holden, as he pulled the pants off her ankles, left her 1/4 cut socks on. He kissed her ankle, slid his tongue up her calf, kissed her knee and kept kissing up her thigh with his hands firmly on her waist. He pulled her closer to him; she slid easily on the counter. Finally, his mouth was less than an inch from her wet pussy. The only thing standing in his way was a very thin layer of cotton. His fingers started dancing around her stomach and the waistband of her panties. She reached down to take them off, his hands stopped her, and she took the hint and moved her hands behind her head to support it against the hard counter. Holden satisfied she was going to behave, reached down and took off his own t-shirt. Both were sweaty from a hard days work, but neither seemed to care. With him half undressed, her wearing only panties, he continued. He moved her legs so that they were resting on his broad shoulders. He moved his mouth against her panties; he could feel how moist she was through the cotton. He let out a warm breath; the extra heat going against her hungry cunt made her fidget with anticipation. She was yearning to be filled. His hands ran across her stomach and rib cage. She used her legs to pull Holden in closer and deeper. He used his tongue to move the panties out of the way. They would only move so far allowing him to barely get the odd lick of her clit and penetrate her by a millimeter. That wasn't nearly deep enough for either of them. From the first taste Holden couldn't play the teasing game anymore, he wanted to lick her, he wanted to taste every last drop out of her. He loved her pussy; he could lick her for hours given the chance. He couldn't hold back any longer he groped at her waist band, she moved her legs off his shoulders and in a quick fluid movement he pulled her panties off and threw them over his shoulder. He looked at her for a second before going in for another taste. She had a little stubble growing from not being able to shave for the week, but it was still very soft. Her legs were spread which pulled her lips apart, he could see her glistening in the light, and apparently he was taking too long. "Lick me," Paige moaned. Holden obliged, he put his hands behind her knees and pushed them to her chest, exposing even more of her cunt. His tongue took one long lick of her pussy and then he pulled away, he had a string of her juices hanging off his lips connecting him to her. He used his finger and collected it like one would a dangling piece of cheese from a slice of pizza and, like the cheese, he brought it to his lips and licked it all off. She tasted great. His mouth went back to work, not teasing her clit but penetrating her. It's been to long coming to play around. He had a job to do and he was going to do it. His tongue moved around deep inside her, she placed her hands behind her knees to free Holden's hands. He ran his fingers up and down the back of her legs as he continued to eat her. She pulled her legs back even further allowing him to get deeper inside her. Holden slid his tongue around in every direction inside her, he moved his hands to her ass, raising it off the counter a bit and pulled her cheeks apart. He then pulled his tongue out of her pussy and slid it down to her ass. His tongue made small circles in her ass, she loved the sensation, she also loved that Holden would do that to her, a lot of people wouldn't dream of it but it felt so great. His tongue worked his way in deeper in her tight ass, her hips moved around to let him get a better angle. His nose was buried into her pussy as he continued to lick her asshole. He took one hand off her cheek and moved it to replace his tongue, he put the finger in her pussy to get it nice and wet then slide it very slowly into her ass. He could feel her muscles contract around the foreign object now deep inside her. He moved the finger inside her in a "come here" motion, the movement was very soft, she was so tight he couldn't make a very big curve with his finger but it was enough to get a response from her. His tongue then went back up to her clit and began rolling it around. As his mouth worked over her pussy, his tongue seemed be everywhere at once. The attention Paige was getting after such a long drought was like heaven to her, she laid back and relaxed all muscles and just gave into Holden knowing that she was going to have a massive orgasm if Holden could just hold out a little longer. Holden could feel Paige's body relax, he knew that was a sign she was ready to cum, he took pride in being able to get her off so quickly but he knew it was more attributed to lack of sex. His finger started to ever so slightly move back and forth inside her. His other hand slid 3 fingers into her pussy and he began fucking her with them very hard as his tongue continued to play with her clit, occasionally taking a very gentle bite of it to keep her guessing. She began to moan, her fingers tried gripping into the counter top with no luck, she slammed her hands down hard making a very loud slapping sound. She needed something to hold onto, some resistance so she finally grabbed the first thing she could see, Holden's hair. She grabbed a handful and began pulling hard. He began fucking her harder with both hands, the fingers in her pussy moved around in as many directions as possible, he forced them in deep with one sudden hard jolt. That was what did the trick. The fingers slamming hard into her was unexpected and any resistance she had left in her was shocked away and she began to orgasm. She let out a very loud, "Fuck ya," as she cam. She flooded Holden's fingers, as she was experiencing her orgasm; Holden quickly slid his finger out of her ass, the muscles relaxing in her ass added to her orgasm. Holden took his fingers out of her pussy, her cum chased them out. He pushed his head between her legs and licked up as much of her as he could, his nose accidentally touched her clit which made her jump. She was still holding on to his hair and with the last jump she pushed his head away, she could see his lips and cheeks glistening with her fluids.

She sat up and slid herself to the edge of the counter so she was face to face with Holden and she began running her fingers through his messy hair. She kissed his lips, tasting herself, she then used her tongue to lick every last drop of herself off his face. Holden was so very turned on by her doing that. They kissed a bit longer. Paige looked up at Holden, giving him that mischievous look of hers. She moved and disappeared from the counter top. She was now facing the bulge in his pants. She quickly started unclasping his belt, button and fly. She pulled his pants down and his large penis slapped her in the face. With no hesitation she put her lips on his shaft, kissing it then sliding her lips up to his head again giving it a kiss before taking the full length in her mouth. She bobbed her head back and forth pleasuring Holden. She had just the right amount of pressure on her lips; he felt her lips breaking their seal as they slid by his piercings. He could also feel her breath on his testicles. She then let the cock fall out of her mouth, as she took his length in her small hand and began stroking him. He looked down at and couldn't believe how sexy she looked with his cock in her hand. She kept stroking him as her free hand cupped his balls. She gently blew all over his pubic area; she had a very firm grasp on his cock as she jerked him off. Holden spread his legs getting a more secure stance so he wouldn't lose his balance in the heat of the moment. He let her continue for several minutes before telling her to stop. He told her he was dangerously close to cumming, she said she wanted him to finish in her mouth, but he had other plans. He helped her to her feet, kissed her then turned her around, she bent over onto the counter top resting on her elbows. He looked down; her perfectly heart shape ass and pussy spread open as she spread her legs. Her head dropped below her arms, her long hair draped off her head causing her curly locks to sway as Holden touched her. Holden grabbed the base of his cock and slowly guided his length into her waiting pussy. She could feel all the piercings touching her lips as they passed by. Once he was in nice and deep, he stopped to let her feel him inside, she was already worked up from her last orgasm and he was already close to cumming from the oral he just received. He slowly moved around, pulling his hard cock out of her so the head was just touching her waiting hole. He clenched her hips as he slid his length in again, her pussy contracted around him as he fucked her. She moved one hand between her legs and started rubbing her clit; she let the occasional finger wander so it could graze his bag and asshole. Holden reached up and wrapped his hand in her hair. He gave a hard pull, causing her head to raise back as she continued playing with herself. The force of his hair pulling started her second orgasm. She let out another moan and began convulsing. That was too much for Holden, he exploded inside her. His cock twitched in unison with her as cum came flushing out of him. He let go of her hair and once again her head dropped below her arms. He left his cock in her as he continued to ejaculate. She could feel him coming inside her which kept her orgasm going. Finally, satisfied he was done, he pulled out of her. She turned around and cum oozed down her leg. They hugged and began kissing like it was their first kiss.

They both decided they need a shower, their first shower together in their new place. Holden went in to the bathroom and brushed his teeth; Paige came in, sat on the toilet and began to pee. Holden looked at her; he has never had a girlfriend pee in front him before. She saw the surprise in his eyes. "I hope you don't mind"

"Not at all" He was happy with the comfort she displayed around him. After she was done, she started the shower and disappeared behind the curtain she and Tamara put up earlier. Holden told her he would be right in.

7

Several weeks had passed since Holden and Paige first moved into their B.C. apartment and in that time they both started their new jobs. Holden was really enjoying his job mostly because his coworkers and he really hit it off. The puck hadn't even dropped on the next season and already they were planning the championship party. Holden had more than his fair share of work; he was actually quite busy, but he loved it. He loved being able to contribute in such a substantial way, being able to make decisions to improve the team, instead of just doing the paper work for other peoples' decisions.

Paige was enjoying work as well. The other office assistants made her feel right at home. She had never held down a normal 9 to 5 job before. She wasn't finding the odd jobs challenging, and the early hours were hard to adjust to, but she was doing it all for the future so she tried to make the best of it, and would never complain to Holden. She knew how happy he was, and she also knew he was really worried about her being homesick, and she didn't want to do anything to add to his worry.

Any free time they had, they spent working on the apartment which was starting to look great. They spent their weekends looking through various stores for the perfect things to tie their apartment together and make it theirs. Holden had continued to be worried about Paige; she had been showing signs of stress because of the move, the new job and all the work they had been putting into the apartment. Holden wanted to surprise her with something big as a treat for her for giving up so much to be there with him. He talked to Mike and others at the office and they came up with the perfect plan, a weekend getaway. Holden planned everything out and made all the arrangements. He was able to do everything without Paige getting even the slightest hint of what he had in store.

After meticulous planning, the weekend he worked so hard for, had finally arrived. Holden was sitting in the apartment, his bags packed, waiting for Paige to get home from work so that they could head up the mountain. Holden had been anticipating the weekend for what seemed like an unbearable amount of time. He wanted to tell Paige several times but he managed to keep it a secret, thinking the surprise would make her happier. It was going to be perfect. He had a cabin with a hot tub reserved from Friday night until Sunday morning. He had been listening to the weather reports all week; it didn't look promising for Friday, but if Paige got off work early enough he was hoping they could beat the bad weather. He wasn't as worried about the weather once he was on the mountain because he packed plenty of wine and the hot tub would still be hot regardless of the amount of snow that may fall. The thought of being stuck in the cabin alone with Paige for the night was more than okay, as he didn't plan on leaving the cabin much the first night anyway. It was the drive up he was worried about.

The rain started as he heard Paige's key hit the front door. She was soaking wet and started complaining about the rain and the bad weather, until she saw all the packed bags by the door. She looked quizzically at Holden. Finally Holden was finally able to tell her his secret. She started to cry as she hugged him. She couldn't believe he would do something like that for her. She finally admitted that she was feeling a bit overwhelmed and could use the break. Paige changed and told Holden she was ready to go. She started pulling him towards the door. As badly as he wanted to go, he decided to call the ski lodge's weather report. He dialed the 7 digits and after the first ring, an automated voice answered. "Due to excessive snow, all runs have been cancelled and the mountain trail has been closed." Holden's face dropped and he looked at Paige. Just by seeing his expression she knew it was bad news. Paige sat down and looked like she was about to cry. Holden hung up the phone, sat next to Paige, and put his arm around her. "It is okay, we can try again tomorrow. Tonight we'll cuddle up, sheltered from the rain and make the best of it." Paige choked back her tears, smiled and agreed. Holden said he was going to go grab the bags so they could have toiletries for the night. "Don't touch the small black bag," she yelled at Holden, who was already by the door. Holden looked through the bags he so carefully packed and saw the little black bag beside their luggage. Even though he was curious about its contents he respected

Paige's wishes and left it alone, only taking the small bag of bathroom necessities. He then went back into the living room slapped Paige's knee as he sat down on to the couch, "So, what do you want to do? Wanna go rent a movie?"

"No, it's too wet out; let's watch one we have here."

"Okay, pick whatever you want."

Paige flipped through Holden's movies and picked the perfect one "*Phantom of the Opera*" the 2004 Andrew Lloyd Webber version. She knew it was one of Holden's favourite movies, and Paige thought it would be fun to relive their first date. Holden slapped it into the DVD player, threw a bag of popcorn into the microwave and cracked a bottle of wine from the fridge. Smiling, Paige said it was getting cold in the apartment as she grabbed a blanket, ALL of the blanket, then she snuggled in and got cozy. Holden took the hint and handed her a glass of wine and dutifully went to the fireplace to start making a fire. He looked back at Paige who was cuddled up beneath her blanket. She had her trademark devilish grin on her face, that look she made when Holden was catering to her every whim. The fire flamed up fast, the microwave dinged and the wine was cold. 'Okay, it's not a cabin overlooking a ski mountain but it is a quiet night with Paige so it was already perfect,' Holden thought to himself, as he poured the popcorn into a bowl, grabbed his glass of wine and took his place next to his girlfriend on the couch, blanket less. Holden reached for the remote, hit play, and switched the amplifier over to 'DVD' as the movie started. Paige commented on how much harder it was raining as she cuddled up next to him. Not even halfway through the movie, the lightning started and it was fierce. Since lightning was rare in Vancouver, Holden opened up the curtains to the patio so that they could watch the show. When Holden sat back down, Paige grabbed Holden's arm and held him closer, showing her discomfort with the lightning. He told her it was okay and to enjoy the beauty of it. As he spoke his last word, lighting cracked and lit up the sky showing the mountain range; it was fantastic. At that point the movie became merely background noise. The storm moved closer to their place and the rain was pouring down hard. The lightning was getting more frequent and with one very close strike, the power flickered and the room went black. The hope for the power outage to be short term faded after a couple of minutes. Once again Holden could see the disappointment in Paige's eyes. First a delay on the ski weekend and now sitting in a room with no power, which meant no more movies, not even a hot shower before bed. She gave Holden that 'what are we going to do now' look. He had so wanted this weekend to be perfect, and refused to give up. All of a sudden Holden got a brilliant idea. He begun lighting candles, handed one to Paige and told her to go into the bedroom, change into something super comfortable and not to come out until he called for her. She asked him why and with a smile he said, "Just do it." She hesitantly listened to him.

Holden quickly ran to the hallway closet and the spare bedroom, grabbing all the blankets he could find and took them to the living room. He started rearranging the furniture. Paige heard the commotion and asked if everything was ok. "FINE HONEY," he yelled back.

Several minutes later he went into the bedroom and opened the door. Unfortunately Paige was already changed and Holden missed the opportunity to catch her in the act. That disappointment turned quickly to arousal when he saw what she was actually wearing. She found an old pair of his grey sweatpants he had forgotten he owned, one of his old roller hockey jerseys and her hair was in pigtails. Looking at her, lit up by candlelight, she had never looked sexier. She could tell by his opened mouth stare that he was happy. She walked over to Holden causing the candle to flicker on top of the antique dresser, hugged him and whispered in his ear "I hope you don't mind me grabbing one of your precious jerseys," she said sarcastically. The jersey was white with small perforations in it and even in the candlelight he could see through them well enough to tell she wasn't wearing a bra. As tempting as it was to throw her on the bed and ravish her right then and there, he fought the urge and instead grabbed her hand, the candle and led her into the living room. She saw the furniture moved around, blankets all over the place and at first it wasn't clear what was going on. Holden took her around the blankets to where the fire lit up the area and it became clear to her. "Oh my God, it's a little fort!" Paige said with excitement in her voice. Holden smiled and placed the flickering candle back onto the fireplace mantel and followed her into the fort. He had placed the cushions from the couch and love seat on the floor with a sleeping bag spread out over top of them. The pair sat down and looked at each other. With no words spoken they leaned in and started kissing; the fire and lightning creating a romantic back drop. They lowered each other down, lying so their heads were by the door. They stopped fondling each other and started looking at the lightning show that had created the situation, with every flash the mountains were silhouetted. Holden placed his arm gently over her back, wanting to be as close to her as possible. They weren't too sure how long they sat in silence watching the weather, eventually they start talking, nothing to serious, just life in general. Holden then said he had another idea. He crawled out of the comfy fort and returned with his favourite book. He laid back down as close to Paige as he could and opened the book up to a random chapter and started reading to her. After several chapters and an undetermined amount of time Holden closed up the book, Paige bit her lip and it was her turn to disappear out of the fort. She came back in holding books of her own, but hers weren't novels. They were yearbooks. Holden had never seen them before. Paige said she kept them in a small suitcase along with other mementos from her childhood. Holden asked her if he could see what else was in the suitcase, to which she replied maybe someday. Holden began flipping through her yearbooks. First trying to find her posed picture, then looking for any candids of her and finally reading all the quotes her classmates wrote her. She had to point out her picture, as he wasn't able to pick her out of the first two books he looked through. She had definitely changed over the years; the quotes in her book were as equally funny as her pictures. Holden read the ones that were legible. Paige shared stories of high school, telling him who some of the people were and the meanings of the inside jokes. Paige got really excited with her trip down memory lane. Holden wasn't sure if that was going fuel her feelings of being homesick or if it was just the thing she needed, but he enjoyed hearing her stories and definitely loved seeing her pictures, so he let her continue. The last book was pink; he picked it up and flipped through the first few pages. He stopped on page 20; his eyes were drawn to the bottom third of the page. The last girl in the row was stunning; he couldn't stop looking at her. He finally let his eyes drift over to the left hand column to read the name. It was Paige. She looked different, her hair was long and her natural colour, she had big bangs but he could definitely see the resemblance between the girl in the picture and the girl that was sitting by his side. She pointed out other people throughout the book, showed him candid pictures of her and her friends. She was by all appearances a tom boy who seemed to be hiding her femininity by wearing clothes that were too big for her. The generic jeans and t shirts were better suited to an awkward teenage boy, not the beautiful woman that she had become. She was, however, still wearing her familiar Chuck Taylor's. Paige shuddered with every new picture, laughing at the memories and her self-described horrible style. He began to wonder if the weather had allowed them to go up to the mountain, if they would have had the same bonding experience.

Paige began to yawn, Holden followed suit. He closed up the books, their eyes met and Holden said it was time for them to go to sleep; they had a long day ahead of them. Paige agreed, they shared another kiss, embraced each other and fell asleep in their living room fort.

The sun beaming through the balcony doors woke up Holden first. He looked over to see if Paige was awake yet, she wasn't, she was sleeping so peacefully he almost hated to wake her. As gently as he could, he put his arm on her shoulder, shook her hard and yelled "HEY WAKE UP!!" She jumped to the roof of the blanket fort and let out a scream. She looked around, realized what was going on and slapped Holden playfully. "Ass." He laughed and said that they had a busy day and that they had to get going. A quick brush of the teeth, a joint shower and they were headed out to the car. She made sure she picked up her black bag, which made him even more curious as to its contents. The sun was shining making it warm out, not a sign of the terrible storm the night before. Even the weather report from the ski hill reported ideal conditions. She threw the bag in the trunk, Holden started up the engine and they were on their way.

Holden noticed the drive started off in beautiful weather. Lush green grass, sunny, warm and not 20 minutes into the drive up the hill, the scenery was starting to show signs of colder climate. Minutes later, snow banks were starting to appear on the shoulders of the road. Paige reached for the climate control in the car and turned up the heat.

In no time the two arrived at the lodge. The sun was still shining, but it was definitely colder and because of the storm the night before everything had a thick clean white coat of snow. They checked in and decided not to go out to their cabin right away, but instead start their snowboarding lessons. Since it was a weekend full of new adventures, they elected to try their hand at snowboarding as they were both decent skiers. With their helmets and suit of armour on they went off to find their class.

Because of the delay getting to the hill that morning, they extended their snowboarding lesson until mid afternoon. Exhausted, sore and bruised, they decided to hit the lodge for a bite to eat. The dining room was beautiful with oak trimming, a roaring fireplace and a lot of happy people that left their cares at the base of the hill. The meal was fantastic and after charging it to their room, they headed off to finally see their cabin. The drive to their lodgings was encouraging; the road led to the top of the hill, the view was increasingly spectacular with every turn and the cabins themselves looked like small homes. After a couple of wrong turns they finally found their number, pulled into the lane and grab the bags. Holden took the key out of his pocket, slide it into the lock and looked into Paige's eyes. She saw the excitement in his eyes and very spontaneously dropped her bags, put both her hands on the sides of his head and kissed him. The intensity caused him to drop the bags but he still managed to get the key turned as they fell into the cabin, causing her to land on top of a laughing Holden. They continued laughing and then he realized he was still holding the key or, at least, part of the key in his hand. Paige looked at his hand, then back at him, trying to gauge his reaction. He looked at the key and then at her and started to laugh. Paige hugged him and kissed him on the cheek. "Oops." When they stopped laughing, they both looked up towards the room. 'Wow' was the only thing they could manage to say. Holden tossed Paige lovingly off him so he could roll over and see the room better. She landed with a thud and gave him a kick. Holden smirked back at her. Holden was the first to get to his feet and started walking into the room; Paige followed leaving the bags just outside the door. The cabin was huge with one very large bed, a 46-inch TV with a Blu Ray player and a fireplace. They went to the patio, opened the large glass doors and saw the most amazing view of the mountain and the ski hill. The yard had fences on the two sides, blocking out the neighbours but was open towards the hill. There was only a couple of hundred feet of forest going down a very sharp drop between them and the upper most run. They could see down the entire hill at all the skiers. The name of the resort was just up the hill, not far from them, in huge letters comparable to the size of the Hollywood sign. They walked through the freshly fallen snow to the hot tub. Holden removed the cover and started it up so that it would be nice and hot for later. They walked back inside; Paige turned around and said she was going to have a quick shower to rinse off all the sweat from their day of snowboarding. Holden said okay then they gave each other a quick peck on the lips. Holden went to sweep off the deck so they wouldn't have to walk through a lot of snow later. It only took him ten minutes or so to clean off it off, get their things from outside the door, unpack, and start chilling the wine. Holden heard the water shut off and Paige leave the shower. She came out wearing a housecoat that looked incredibly comfortable and drying her hair with a provided towel. "My turn," Holden said as he started to undress before hitting the bathroom. He closed the door behind him and looked around the bathroom. The tub was a huge Jacuzzi style and that brought a smile to his face, thinking of the endless possibilities that night held. The bathroom itself was big, the mirror took up the wall in front of the sink, which had gold plated faucets, and the counter top was marble-esque. He almost felt guilty dirtying up the place.

But he did anyways. The shower was hot, the water pressure was strong, he didn't want to get out but he knew he had a hot girl waiting on the other side of the door for him. He turned the taps off, opened the shower curtain and grabbed a towel. He dried himself off, wrapped the towel around his waist and walked into the living area. He stopped dead when he saw a tall, very well built blonde girl standing in the middle of the room. Her pure white outfit clung to her hard body. She had a couple of buttons undone to show off her ample cleavage and her white skirt barely hid the top of her thigh highs. Holden wondered what was going on as he looked around and saw a man almost a foot taller than himself wearing a very tight, thin white t shirt that showed off every muscle in his perfectly formed body as well as amplified his golden tan. His biceps flexing as he dug his powerful hands into a nearly naked Paige. Paige was lying on a portable massage table wearing only a tiny towel over her ass. From the angle Holden had, he could see underneath it but he knew the tall stranger couldn't, for the moment anyway. The girl said, "You must be Holden, come lay down." Holden, trying to hide the tent he was pitching under his towel, awkwardly walked over to the massage table and laid down. Paige looked over at Holden, "Surprise, I thought it would be a nice treat for you after snowboarding." Paige said with a smile. The girl flicked her long blonde hair off her shoulders as she took her spot beside Holden. Paige and Holden were positioned so they could see each other. Holden felt weird watching his naked girlfriend get touched in such a pleasurable way by a total stranger, especially one as hot as the guy working her over. He mostly felt weird because he was enjoying the show so much. It was hard for him to focus on Paige once his blonde angel began massaging him. Her tiny hands were much stronger than he imagined and they danced over his sore body. Holden began to fade away when he was brought to reality by a moan Paige let out. Holden began watching the guy run his hands all over Paige. Paige too was enjoying the Swedish masseuse rubbing Holden, she got caught a couple of times looking at the masseuse's cleavage. The woman didn't seem to mind; she even seemed to encourage it. Taking Paige's cue, the blonde girl took every opportunity to sneak a peek at Paige and Holden as well. Holden was not in a very good position to check out his masseuse, he could only settle for watching Paige get pleasured from her tall dark stranger. As the two professionals kneaded, rubbed and stretched the couple, Holden could only think of the nasty things he was planning for Paige later on that evening. Paige was wondering if a happy ending was included in the massage, and if it wasn't, she was wondering how to approach the subject of them staying after for a drink and possibly some more fun. She just wasn't sure how Holden would react to a three or four-some. The thought of Holden fucking his masseuse on her massage table while Paige watched intrigued her so much, she found herself getting wet. She couldn't help but wonder what the muscular guy rubbing her was packing. Her imagination began to work over time; her masseuse began running his hands up her legs, close to her ass. She imagined Holden's cock between the other woman's perfectly round tits while her masseuse feed her his gigantic cock. Holden's girl told him to turn over so she could rub his chest and legs. Hesitantly, he rolled over; making sure the towel was covering him. Much to his embarrassment, the weight of the towel wasn't enough to counter the force of his erection. The masseuse looked down at the large bulge in the towel. "Impressive," she said as she looked up at Paige. Paige was already on her back, her small but firm tits exposed to everyone in the room. Paige met her glance, acknowledging the female masseuse as she was checking out her tits. Holden caught the glance knowing what was going on. He continued to watch the man touch his girlfriend; rubbing her shoulders, her stomach and then he started giving her lymph nodes a massage. His strong hands dug deep into Paige's tits; she definitely reacted positively, letting out frequent moans of pleasure. The man moved down her stomach to Paige's legs. Holden's masseuse was working on Holden's limbs, making him feel very relaxed. He was resisting the urge to fall asleep so that he could watch the show on the next table. Finally, the guy got to Paige's legs; he worked down her thighs, each calf and he began rubbing her feet. Holden knew he could see under Paige's towel, but neither Paige nor Holden cared. Holden looked up at the masseuse, their eyes met. Unexpectedly, the guy raised his eyebrows twice in an 'I'm the man' kind of way. Then with his eyes, he directed Holden's eyes downwards. Holden followed his gaze down to the masseuse's waist. He could see the massive bulge in his pants and, to Holden's shock and horror, the guy reached down and pulled out his massive cock. It was fully erect and looked very angry. His cock had to have been about a foot long and very thick. Holden looked at it and was very impressed. He was so captivated with it, he himself wanted to go touch it. Before either of the girls noticed, or Holden could object, the guy grabbed Paige's legs and pulled her tiny frame until her small ass was on the edge of the table. The man forced the monster into Paige. She winced as it tore into her, but she didn't do anything to stop him. Holden felt helpless, he just sat there watching his girlfriend wrap her ankles around the masseuse's muscular thighs. She raised her hands over her head, grasping the sides of the table. The female masseuse looked over and began getting herself worked up as she watched the python penetrate Paige. Holden laid still, paralyzed with fear, anger, but mostly curiosity. He couldn't stop this man from violating his girlfriend. Paige winced in pain and moaned like a whore as the man thrust into her over and over again. Holden felt his towel fly off. He looked down as the blonde masseuse jumped up on the table and crawled up Holden's body. She pulled her skirt up over her waist exposing her white sheer thong. She then pulled it aside as her waist lined up with Holden's. Holden could see the small 'landing strip' shaved in her pubic area. The woman reached down to Holden's hard rod, wrapped her fingers around his length and guided it into her wet, willing pussy. As soon as it was as deep into her as possible, she looked down at Holden, put her fingers in between the buttons of her white blouse and, with a lot of passion and force, she pulled. Buttons flew everywhere. She began to grind her hips hard onto Holden; she was tight and wet. Holden resisted the urge to cum early, but he found it difficult because that was the first pussy he had been in other than Paige's for almost a year. The subtle differences were enough to set him off, but he fought it with every ounce of strength he had. Paige didn't see or at least care that Holden was being fucked; she was concentrating too hard on her own pleasure. The vein in the man's forehead began to throb; he let out a moan. Holden could tell the signs that the man was about to orgasm. Holden was still mad at himself for letting this happen, but was helpless to stop it. Finally, the man freed his cock from Paige's tight hole and scrambled to her side squeezing the tip closed. He slapped the baby elephant's trunk down onto Paige's chest and began to cum. His load was thick and ample. Paige released the table from her clenches and began rubbing her tits, smearing his cum all over. Holden found the sight of Paige's tits glistening with another man's cum too much to take; he was about to cum himself. Just before he released his load inside the gorgeous blonde masseuse he heard Paige's voice. "HOLDEN!" He looked around. "HOLDEN!" Holden came too and looked around again. He saw Paige sitting on the side of the table in her housecoat, the two masseuses with their jackets on, standing at the end of the table. "You were snoring," Paige laughed. She also made Holden aware that everyone could see his hard on. Self-consciously Holden covered up and leapt from the table so the two masseuses could pack up and be on their way. Holden was embarrassed, yet amazed, that the dream felt so real and he was even more ashamed that he almost had a wet dream at the thought of his girlfriend being violated by another man.

Paige and Holden thanked the pair for their work and tipped them generously. As the door closed, Holden turned to Paige and told her of his dream. Paige agreed it sounded hot and admitted she often fantasized of watching Holden fuck another woman. Paige moved to the bed and laid down. Holden, still feeling playful from the sexually charged massage, pretended he didn't notice her eyes burning into him. After he got dressed, Paige looked at him with a laugh in her voice and said, "What was the point of that, you're not going to be in them long anyways." The housecoat Paige had put on after the massage fell open. Holden crawled over to her, put a hand onto her hip, leaned in and kissed her. "You wish." Paige jumped off the bed laughing at Holden. He was left lying on the bed looking at her with frustration and confusion. She continued to laugh at him and grabbed one of her bags, dug out some clothes and continued to tease him further by slowly dressing in front of him. "TEASE!" Holden yelled. She threw the panties she was just about to put on at him. "A little something to tide you over until later," she said.

"What?!?" Holden said. Paige's attempt at teasing worked perfectly. It was now around suppertime, but since they had a late lunch neither of them were hungry. Holden poured Paige and himself a glass of wine and they sat on the leather couch that was directed towards the fireplace, but also had a perfect view of the mountain. The fireplace was gas and Holden had already turned it on while Paige was showering and they left the TV on for background noise. Holden placed his arm around Paige's shoulder; she snuggled up tight into him. With their glasses of wine empty, the sun was starting to set. "So, your masseuse was hot," Holden said.

"Yup, I'd do him," Paige shot back "I would have done the girl that was massaging you too."

"Yup, me too," Holden said casually.

"Too bad neither are coming back," Paige said with an inflection of disappointment in her voice.

"Yup, hot tub?" Holden asked.

"Yes," Paige replied.

With that they popped up, Holden grabbed a couple of bottles of wine and headed for the hot tub. Paige said she was going to take a quick pee and that she would be joining him in a second. "Better now than in the tub," Holden quipped.

The tub heated up nicely; Holden slid the bottles of wine into the snow built up around the edges of the tub, filled their glasses and slid into the water. It was hot at first, especially compared to the frosty mountain air. Holden sat enjoying the view, anxious for Paige to join him. He heard music playing and looked around to see where it was coming from, and then heard voices over the music. The cabin next door was having a party and it sounded like a bunch of teenagers. Holden was upset at first, thinking that the unwanted distraction may take away from their 'perfect' weekend, but then decided nothing could ruin the amazing time they were already having. Eavesdropping on their conversation gave Holden a couple of laughs. "Oh those crazy teens," he thought. Drawn back to his own cabin, he heard the patio door open and whatever he was thinking vanished as his eyes and thoughts were trained on Paige. She walked towards him, wearing the robe that she had on earlier but she left it open. She got to the stairs into the hot tub and noticed Holden's robe on the patio. She smiled and let hers drop. Just as it hit the ground they could hear some boys at the cabin next door make a commotion and bang against the fence. A series of shhhs then filled the air. Paige started to blush and then laughed. Holden tried not to hurt something by holding back his laughter. Paige didn't hurry into the tub; between the low light, angle of the fence and the steam they weren't going to see much, so Paige decided to give them a little bit of a show. She bent over at her waist to pick up her wine and accidentally spilled some onto her bare breast. She made a production of wiping the wine off of herself. She bent over the tub and scooped handfuls of water to her chest and used her fingers to gentle clean her tender skin. Finally, she lowered herself into the water and leaned against the back of the tub. She grabbed her wine, took a sip and then completely relaxed. It had been an adventure getting there, but now they were right where they wanted to be. Not saying a word they sat there, sipping their wine, taking in the sights, aware that there was no doubt some horny teen boys still watching their every move. The sun had set but it wasn't dark out and just as Holden noticed the lack of natural light, 3 big spotlights lit up the big resort sign. The lights were soft enough as to not ruin the view nor distract them. Paige slid around the Jacuzzi to be next to Holden, as she sat in the tub her beautiful tits were magnified just below the water line. She put her hand on his lap and gently caressed his leg. Holden put his arm around her neck and leaned in to start kissing her neck and ear. Since there were no noises from the peanut gallery, they assumed their spectators had moved on to something else. Paige's hand slid further up Holden's leg to his cock "What do we have here?" Paige said with an innocent smile. Holden grabbed a handful of Paige's hair and moved her head so she was looking at him. He kissed her; her hand grabbed onto his cock and softly stroked it under the hot, bubbling water. Holden kissed her lips before moving to her cheek and ear down to her neck. Holden was still pulling her hair; Paige loved the forceful feeling of having her hair pulled. The pressure was enough to distract her mind from other sensations, allowing them to heighten and eventually lead to a more powerful orgasm. Also, it was a small act, but it made her feel like she was filling the submissive role, a role she enjoyed playing more often than not. Holden's other hand reached over to her wet tits and started slowly rubbing his strong hand over them. He pushed and squeezed her, as his other hand was still playing with her hair. Paige's hand got tighter on his cock as she got more and more aroused. Without warning, she stopped. Holden looked at her, she didn't say a word; she just straddled his lap and used her hand to guide his throbbing cock into her pussy. She rode him without consideration for Holden's satisfaction; she went to town on him like he wasn't even there. Holden then realized that it wasn't just him that was getting lost in the romance of the weekend, and that the weekend was just the thing to relieve the stress of the move and their new jobs. Paige grabbed both Holden's hands and forced them to her tits. "Fuck me," she kept saying over and over again. He looked deep into her eyes. He loved watching her fuck him; her face, the way her tits moved, it was all very intense. She looked possessed, lost in the mood, unaware of her surroundings and taking in all the sensations as best she could. The heat from the hot tub was wearing Holden out. He didn't want to stop, and Paige seemed to be enjoying herself way too much. Apparently though, the heat was affecting Paige as well; she collapsed beside Holden. Exhausted she mumbled, "This isn't over by a long shot." She grabbed for her glass of wine, Holden grabbed his, and they slammed back the remaining drops, poured another glass and quickly drank that too. They were breathing so hard they didn't even notice the clear moonlit night had turned to snow. It wasn't the blizzard like the night before, but the flakes were still large and puffy. They leaned their heads up at the same time, trying to catch them with their tongues, but the heat from the tub melted them before they got to the couple. The visibility was dwindling; they could barely read the sign that was once so prominent. They caught their breath, finished yet another glass of wine, and Paige suggested they head back inside. Holden agreed; on the way in Paige said she had to pee again. Holden turned off the tub. The party next door was dying down, so Holden felt comfortable walking around naked. Holden got into the cabin and closed the door behind him. The room was still warm from the fireplace, so he lied naked on the bed.

He looked around and noticed the mysterious black bag Paige had been so concerned about was gone.

Holden heard the bathroom door open and even without seeing her, the anticipation started his blood flowing. Paige walked around the corner from the bathroom and left Holden speechless. There was the girl he loved standing in front of him wearing a pink bustier, her tits exposed, pink thigh highs attached to the bustier by its built in garters and no panties. Her hair was in her trademark pigtails. She saw the reaction and any hesitancy she had about whether or not Holden would like the outfit was all gone. "You weren't the only one who had something special planned for the weekend. I guess great minds think alike," she said. No other words were spoken as she walked over to the bed, crawled up to Holden and said, "Now then, where were we"?

A series of babbles was all he was capable of.

"Right about here I think." She straddled him again and guided his cock into her pussy. "Yup, that feels right," Holden said. She started riding him again. This time she grabbed his arms and pinned them above his head. He was helpless and could only watch as she fucked him. Her breasts moved around ever so slightly, being held firmly in place by the bustier. Holden didn't know how much longer he could take of Paige's attention, but he was holding on as best he could, at least until Paige was able to make herself cum first. Paige leaned down; her hips were moving much slower, feeling every inch of Holden's pierced cock inside her. Holden was thinking Paige could tell he was about to cum and wasn't ready to let that happen. She pulled herself off him; his cock fell out of her and slapped against his stomach. Holden stared at her, amazed how fantastic she looked in her new outfit. She crawled up his body; he felt her wet pussy on him as she made her way up him. She knelt over his face and let him taste her soaking wet cunt. Holden could feel the thigh highs against the sides of his face as he licked her, taking long strokes up her pussy to her clit. He could feel her pussy splashing on him; it got him harder knowing she was so wet. He wanted to make her cum so badly. He licked her faster, harder and deeper. Paige grabbed her own tits as she rode Holden's face. Her moans were getting louder; her hips were moving more sporadically like she wasn't totally in control anymore. Fair is fair Holden thought, and before he gave her satisfaction, he threw her off of him. She had a bewildered look as he moved her onto her hands and knees. He positioned himself behind her and grabbed her hips firmly before sliding his hard cock into her pussy. Holden reached up and grabbed her pigtails as he began to slowly fuck her. They both found their rhythm and moved their bodies in unison. Holden pulled her hair harder, and with one hand, ran his fingernails down her spine. Her back arched and her pussy tightened. Holden thrust very hard and deep into her; he felt her legs tremble as his own orgasm was mounting. Paige surprised him again by wiggling away and jumped up out of bed. "Don't you dare move," she said. Again, he was left wondering what the fuck had just happened. She ran over to the table, grabbed his glass of wine and returned. 'A hell of a fine time for a drink,' Holden thought. Paige joined Holden back on the bed, placing her pussy beside his head. "Finish me," she ordered.

"Okay," Holden replied, as he slid his fingers inside her and with the other hand he started teasing her clit. Holden loved her sexy pink bustier outfit, as great as sex normally was with her; he thought the outfit amplified the perfection of the weekend. Paige was getting further worked up as his fingers danced around inside her. She took his cock in her mouth and started working him over, one hand holding the wine glass the other playing with his balls and ass. As she felt her orgasm growing again, she made him remove his mouth, grabbed his cock and jerked it off incredibly fast and so hard. Holden rubbed her clit just as fast and as hard as she was rubbing him. Her orgasm ran like wave through her. The sight and sensation of her cumming finished off Holden. Paige could feel that his orgasm was close and she put the wine glass over the tip of his cock, still jerking him off hard. The first squirts of cum exploded into the glass. That didn't stop her; she kept beating him harder and faster as long as he continued cumming. Breathless he laid back, looking at her as she adopted a kneeling position next to Holden. She held the glass half filled with wine and almost a third of Holden's cum to her lips and poured it all down her throat. When it was empty, she threw the empty glass over her shoulder, letting it crash to the ground. "I saw that in a porno once," she giggled just before she collapsed next to Holden. "I love you," Holden whispered to Paige, Paige said it back and then the two lovers collapsed, entangled in each others arms for the night.

8

Holden slid his key in the door and walked inside the apartment. He was happy to be home, as much as he loved his new job one of the down falls was the constant traveling. Paige had never said anything but Holden didn't like being away from her so much. He wasn't worried about her being alone because Paige and Tamara had become very close and spent a lot of time together. He did however know Paige was nervous being in the apartment alone at nights. He left his suitcase in the hallway and started to walk towards the living room to find his love. He made it a step or two when Paige popped around the corner; she had her head down selecting a song from her MP3 player. She had her headset on and didn't hear him come in. He didn't make his presence immediately known, instead he watched her for awhile. She was wearing white running shoes and black yoga pants that fit tightly to her perfect form. The lines of her sports bra were clearly visible under her equally tight white shirt that compressed her tits to look like two perfectly round peaches. Her hair was tied back into a pony tail which she had running through the back of her black hat. She walked closer to Holden and just as she was about to run into him she looked up. She let out a scream and jumped which caused her to fall to the floor. Holden tried not to laugh despite her comical reaction. He knelt beside her; he put his hand under her head and asked if she was okay. She slapped his arm, feeling embarrassed. She then reached around and gave him a hug. "I missed you," she said. He hugged her back squeezing her real tight. "I missed you too honey," then he leaned in and kissed her. Her heart was still racing from the fright. Holden laid down beside her as she snuggled up close to him. He had only been gone a week but to Paige it felt like a life time. They continued to embrace each other and kiss deeply.

In between kisses they talked about what happened during the past week even though they talked on the phone every night.

Holden was being sent away more and more and the frequency of the trips wasn't making them easier to deal with. They got to talk on the phone every night but the lack of intimacy was hard on them. Holden had the internet to tie him over and Paige had her tickle trunk of toys to relieve her stress but neither of those was as good as the real thing. Holden moved his hands all around Paige's back, down to her ass, he gave her a good squeeze and Paige's fingers ran through Holden's hair as their lips locked. Holden rolled over onto Paige; she wrapped her legs around his. She could feel the familiar feeling of Holden's pierced cock against her. Even though it was through her yoga pants and his jeans she could feel it and she yearned for it to be inside her. Holden started moving his hips around, trying to fuck her through their clothes. Paige did the same; their hands were moving all over each other's body. Holden ran his hands over her firm tits then down her ribs, stomach and into her pants. He awkwardly slid his hands deep into her waistband and tried to get his fingers inside her but at their body positions made it impossible. She reached into Holden's pants and grabbed his ass. Unhappy that he wasn't able to penetrate Paige in their current position, Holden leaned to one side and rolled Paige over so she was on her stomach. He reached down and unzipped his pants, one hand opened the zipper the other reached into his boxers and pulled out his thick meat. Once his erect cock was free he pulled Paige's stretchy pants over her ass, she was wearing a very small G string that he pulled that to one side exposing her pussy. He straddled her waist, leaned forward and slid his cock inside her eager pussy. She let out a soft moan as she finally got to feel his piercings again. He plunged deep inside her and began fucking her on the hallway floor. The act was very spontaneous, neither had a chance to get out of their clothes. Holden could feel the waist band of her pants sliding up her ass and rubbing against his cock. The foreign sensation heightened Holden's sensitivity and the random passionate act had Holden very close to cumming in record time. Paige was feeling the same; the adrenaline rush she experienced earlier from the scare Holden gave her and the desire to be touched had her had blood rushing directly to her pussy. She too was turned on by the spontaneity of their love making. Holden began to cum hard, filling her pussy, the semen spraying inside her which made Paige orgasm as well. Within minutes of their first embrace the pair were laying on the carpeted flooring in need of a cigarette. Paige was the first to move; she adjusted her pants and underwear and stood up.

Holden layed on his back looking up at her. "I'm going for a run; I'll be back in half an hour." Putting in her earphones, she turned on her MP3 player went into the bathroom to clean up before running out the door. Holden tucked his now flaccid cock away, grabbed his suitcase and began unpacking, happy to be home.

He connected his laptop to speakers in the bathroom and cranked his rock play list, knowing Paige was out for her run and wouldn't be disturbed. The extra adrenaline coursing through his veins motivated him to crank the speakers louder than normal. As the songs played, he sang at the top of his lungs and thought to himself if Canadian Idol was held in his shower he would win easily. Finally, feeling his fingers and toes wrinkle he decided it was time to get out of the shower and make himself pretty for Paige before she got home.

He turned off the water, opened the curtain and started to dry himself. Over the music he heard a faint "Holden." He turned down his speakers and sure enough Paige was yelling for him. Leaving the bathroom still partially wet and wearing only a towel, he followed her voice. It led him to their spare bedroom; he opened the door to see Paige standing by the head of the bed wearing fishnet thigh highs and the same knee high boots she wore to the park on their third date. On her upper body she wore an open bust lace teddy and crotch less panties, her arms were accessorized with fishnet loop gloves and her tiny fingers held a riding crop. Holden stopped dead in the doorway. "Nice singing," Paige said with a smile. Holden was embarrassed but quickly got over it; Paige used her riding crop to point to the bed. "Lay down." She commanded. She reached towards him and tapped the towel with her crop. "Good boy," she said acknowledging his erection. She then steered him to the bed with her eyes. He walked towards the bed and noticed four ropes, one on each corner and just by her feet was her tickle trunk of toys and various lotions. The tickle trunk always intrigued him as he was forbidden to go anywhere near it without her around. He took his spot on the bed; she grabbed his towel and pulled hard like she was doing a magic trick. In an instant he was laying on the bed completely naked at Syn's mercy. She held the feathery tip of the crop over his body so it was very gently touching him. She dragged it all the way up and down his body, teasing his balls and cock before continuing. Once it was up by his ears she raised it high in the air and slapped it down hard against his cock, it didn't hurt as much as he anticipated which he figured was the point. It very slightly grazed his sack and that sent a wave of discomfort up his body but he assumed there was a lot more of that in store for him. She then gripped his shaft in her hand and squeezed. Kneeling beside Holden, she leaned over his body, her tits pressed into against him as she reached for one of the ropes meant for his left arm. She tried tying it but was unsuccessful, Holden couldn't help but laugh. She decided to try the rope closest to her and as she was struggling with that rope, Holden said he would show her how to tie the proper knot. With that he used his free arm, grabbed the rope made a quick loop and before Paige realized it her wrist was now bound, Holden squirmed out from under her and jumped off the bed. He used his body mass to push her over so she was now lying on the bed. Continuing to use his body to hold her down, she could feel his bare cock pressing into her waist as he quickly tied her other arm. She was now bound to the bed, not at all what she was expecting. He then moved to her feet where he tightly secured the ropes over her boots. He stood at the base of the bed looking at her. As much as she was looking forward to making Holden her slave, the sudden change of rolls, the helplessness and vulnerability she was feeling made her enjoy the reversal. "Well, Well, Well, what do we have here?" Holden asked as he picked up her riding crop, he did the same trick she did. Starting at her knees he ran it over her thigh, he forced it into the open slit in her panties, up her stomach, over each nipple, up her chest to her neck. He then put the tip against her lips and leaned in to kiss the other side. Standing up again, he raised the crop in the air like she did and abruptly brought the crop down hard against her pussy. The bristles made a loud snapping sound against her leather panties. He then dropped the crop on the bed beside her, stood up and left the room. Paige started yelling as he left. He was gone for several minutes. He reentered carrying his digital camera and tripod. She melted at the sight of the camera, she has never been taped before but they have discussed how erotic it would be to "perform" for the camera and she certainly trusted Holden enough to allow him to tape her.

Holden extended the legs on the tripod, looked through the view finder and angled the camera to get the best possible view of his slut tied to the bed. She became very wet when she saw the red light come on, that very little addition to their love making made everything different. Holden felt it too; like they were strangers in a porno. He walked around the bed until he was beside her tickle trunk and he looked down. "What's all this then?" he asked as he picked up the bag and emptied it out beside her. Inside was several vibrators/dildos all different shapes and sizes, other bondage cuffs and collars, hand cuffs, anal beads, egg vibrators, clit stimulators, even long thin metal rods that Holden could only assume were Urethral Sounds.

They were something Holden has never experienced before but was very intrigued. The one that stood out was a huge dildo, it was two feet long and very round. Paige laughed when Holden picked it up. "What? That one was more of a gag gift for my birthday; I have been to scared to use it."

"No shit." Holden said with a laugh then dropped it to the side. Holden methodically picked up each toy, examined it and turned them on so Paige could hear the vibrating. All this was building anticipation to the restrained Paige. She started to talk. Holden turned to her "Shut up whore or you'll get this!" He said as he held up a ball gag and blindfold. Holden had never talked to her like that before but it fit the situation and she really liked the idea of being his whore.

The bag of toys contained another smaller plastic bag; Holden dumped out its contents to find several clothes pins. "Hmmm," was all he said as he grabbed one of the pins. He pinned it to the fleshy part of his hand between his thumb and forefinger. He let out another "hmm," as his eyes widened. Paige knew what he was thinking, she tried to squirm around, but the ropes did their job keeping her in place. She wanted to object but her lips remained sealed. He took the pin off his hand, squeezed the end between his fingers so it opened and closed as he brought it to her body. He pushed the hard wood into her flesh, she could feel the rough texture against her soft skin, causing goose bumps anticipating the pain that he was about to inflicted upon her. Holden dragged the clothes pin to her ear and attached it. She felt a slight pinch but it didn't hurt as much as she though, he clipped another to her other ear. She assumed that because of the amount of piercings she had in her ears they were desensitized to pain. He reached into the plastic bag and pulled out two more pins. She saw his eyes staring at her nipples; she knew what he was thinking so she braced herself for it. Helplessly she could only watch as the jaws of the wooden clothes pin clamped down onto her nipple. Again, the pain wasn't as much as she thought it would be, as a matter of fact it was just a slight pressure, no real pain at all. With the second pin clapped down on her erect nipples, Holden began digging through the tickle trunk, pulling out a small clit stimulator. He turned it on and sat beside her with his head on her stomach. Aware of the camera, he positioned himself so the camera would catch everything he was doing. He smiled at the lens as he extended his tongue and began teasing her clit, the hum of the vibrator filled the air. Holden left it on the bed and as he rolled around the toy rolled against Paige's ass cheek, the surprise sensation made her jump. Holden knew what happened but elected to keep the vibrator where it was. His fingers buried themselves deep into her calves as he did his best to lick her. Paige wanted to reach down and play with Holden's hair or reach around and grab his cock but all she could do is lay there helpless, allowing him to use her body like his personal playground. Holden finally reached for the toy, he pressed it hard against her clit. She began moving her hips around to fuck the toy, Holden turned around sending the riding crop across her face. "NO!" He ordered. The theatrics of being dominated was driving her wild. Holden moved the tickle trunk and all the contents under her leg so it wouldn't block the view of the camera also so she couldn't see what he was grabbing next. Holden left the clit stimulator in place, changing the speed and pressure trying to be as unpredictable as possible. After several minutes of pure clit teasing, Holden reached into the smaller plastic bag and grabbed another clothes pin which he clamped to her swollen clit. Expecting a reaction Holden was surprised when Paige didn't seem to notice. Happy he didn't hurt her, he reached into her bag of tricks and pulled out a long rubber vibrator with a smaller attachment on the bottom. Not sure if the smaller piece was for her clit or her ass, he did know what he was going to use it for. Using the lube from her tickle trunk, he poured some into his hand and began stroking the toy. Paige was already wet but he wanted to make sure the long vibrator would fit smoothing inside her. When he was satisfied the toy was sufficiently lubed he put his hand on Paige ensuring she too was well lubricated. She jumped when his finger slipped inside her ass. She really didn't like not knowing what was happing to her but she couldn't stop him, nor would she if she could have. He pressed the tip of the toy against her hole; with sufficient force he was able to slide the length inside her. He loved watching her pussy spread to take the foreign object, the way her labia wrapped around the toy was as if she was hugging it. Paige felt the penetration; it was going in deep filling, her to the max. The surprise happened when the secondary attachment poked at her ass then it too easily penetrated her. Holden adjusted the vibration setting to a random pulsing; a pulsing that worked its way through her body to her core. Holden stuffed the toy in as deep as he could, confident her tight pussy wasn't going to force it out, he took his hands off it. He went back to the bag of clothes pins and placed one on her labia, again she didn't acknowledge the pin so he continued to line them around her pussy. He managed to get five on each side. Looking at his work, he laughed when he realized her pussy look like an evil jaw with its straggly teeth devouring the vibrator. While he was moving around he accidentally pushed hard on the top of the toy, forcing it deeper into her pussy. She jumped but the momentary pain seemed to have increased her pleasure. Holden elected to get rougher with her as she seemed to be responding to it. Not wanting to hurt the girl he loved he escalated his aggressiveness slowly, seeing how she would take it. Never being able to talk derogatorily to someone he cared about, he was stepping outside his comfort zone by calling her names and slapping her around ever so gingerly.

Certain her pussy was taken care of for now, his focus turned to Paige. He moved around looked up at her, their eyes met. Paige could barely focus on Holden until he shouted, "You like that, you fucking bitch?"

"Yes sir," was all she responded.

"I like that. Sir. From now on you call me sir. You got that whore?"

"Yes sir." Paige quietly responded.

Both of them were enjoying the trust and boundary exploration.

Holden crawled up putting his hands on her cheeks squeezing them together. "You fucking got that?" He said with an angry inflection

"Yes sir." She responded.

Momentarily Holden broke character, leaned in and gave her quick peck on the lips. That simple act of tenderness made Paige smile.

The vibrator continued to work away inside Paige and she still hadn't mentioned the clothes pins. Holden was thinking of what he could do next to Paige. He leaned beside her and removed the pin dangling from her lobe causing Paige to jump. "Ow." Holden again breaking character asked if she was okay. She said that the clothes pin numbed the area; it didn't hurt when it was attached but the tingling sensation of the blood flowing back to her ear stung a bit. Holden thought about the pins lining her pussy and thought there was nothing he could do about it now. Shrugging it off, he whispered in Paige's ear. "You want my cock?"

"Yes sir."

"You want to fuck me like the whore you are?"

"Yes sir."

"You want to feel my cum on your face? On your tits? Inside you?"

"Yes sir."

"Well which is it bitch?"

"On my tits sir."

"Your face it is. Unless, of course you have a problem with that."

"No sir, anywhere you wish sir."

"Damn right."

Holden knelt beside Paige, he reached down and began fucking her with the vibrator that was still alive inside her. Every time he pulled the toy in or out of her, it would hit the clothes pins, giving her a hint of the pain to come. Paige couldn't understand the burning she was feeling in her pussy, it wasn't constant, just enough for her to notice. She soon connected it to the sensation that she experienced in her ear, except amplified, making her realize what Holden had done. Holden, oblivious to Paige's reaction to the clothes pins continued to work the toy forcefully in and out of her. He was fascinated watching the way her pussy changed shape to accommodate the oversized toy. He did however use care making sure the piece in her ass wasn't going to hurt her. Paige began to moan, Holden looked at her. "I didn't tell you that you could make a noise did I?"

"No sir"

"Then shut up."

"Yes sir. Sorry sir."

Holden let go of the toy, reached up and put his strong hand across Paige's throat and squeezed it to cut off her air. She tilted her head back, her mouth opened, eyes widened, she wanted to grab his hand and move it but her own hands were bound too tightly. She wanted to tell him to stop but his grip was too tight. Holden leaned in and put his mouth over her open mouth and licked her lips as he continued to deprive her of oxygen. Cautious not to hurt her, he released his grasp. He had limited experience with asphyxiation so he erred on the side of extreme caution and only chocked her for about five seconds. A five seconds that felt like an eternity to Paige whose experience with asphyxiation was even less extensive than Holden's.

As Holden's clench weakened, Paige grasped for air, the oxygen filled her blood and rushed through her body which heightened all her sensations. She was now very aware of the clamps on her pussy and the toy that was in her ass. "OH FUCK ME!" She yelled as she fought to get her breath back. Not sure how she would respond to being chocked Holden asked her if she liked that. "Oh fuck yes," she replied. Holden gave her an open palm slap across the face making a loud noise but again not hurting her. "Oh fuck yes what bitch?"

"Yes sir."

"That's better."

Holden looked through her bag of tricks to see what else he could do to her; he found another small clit stimulator that attached to a finger tip. He slipped it on his right hand and with his left he removed the clothes pin that was attached to her clit. Paige jumped and moved her hips around as the blood rushed to the area, it felt like a thousand needles were running through her clit. Holden gave her a couple of seconds to get over the pain, and then he turned on the finger held device and pressed it hard against her already very swollen clitoris. He moved it around like he would if he was simply fingering her. The bigger toy was left inside her to do its thing. He felt the familiar feeling of her orgasm growing. The vibrators were a tease at best and despite her building orgasm she knew they wouldn't be enough. Holden felt her writhing around trying to free her limbs. Ignoring her, he just fingered her faster. He reached up and began to chock her again; Paige went silent as she fought for air. Holden knew she was close, with his spare hand he grabbed the vibrator, moved it around a bit so she felt it hit every wall inside her pussy and ass and then he tore it out of her knocking two clothes pins off in the process. At the same time he let go of her throat, so many different feelings rushing through her body cumulated into her second orgasm of the day. Holden, being proud of himself lied down very close to Paige, his face near hers, he hugged her and although she tried to reciprocate she wasn't able to. He kissed her and she kissed him back just as hard. "I love you," they said at the same time. Holden then positioned himself between her legs again and began to remove the clothes pins, one after another. Each one made Paige jump. She was in awe at the amount of clips that were attached to her. She felt a weird rush come over her as Holden continued to remove the pins; getting the last one off her pussy he then removed the two remaining pins off her nipples. Paige let out a deep moan as she began to tremble as a smaller orgasm rushed through her body. It surprised them both, Paige began to giggle like a little school girl. Holden was really proud of himself now; he was also surprised by her reaction to the derogatory talk and pain. Something he would keep in his back pocket for another day. Holden then began to untie Paige, slowly starting with her feet. She wanted to be untied and he was taking a painfully long time. He was looking back at her so she was well aware of his action. Finally he had the last hand free and unexpectedly Paige pulled Holden's hair forcing him to the bed, she jumped on him with her legs straddling him. She leaned in and started passionately kissing him, his lips, his cheeks, his face and finally biting his ear. "How long did you think I was going to let you get away without fucking me?"

"As long as I had you tied up?" Holden said with a laugh.

"Well, I'm untied now, wait a minute..." She said looking at the ropes.

She dragged Holden into the position she was just lying in, grabbed the ropes and learning from Holden's tying ability quickly had all four of his limbs secured.

"Now, what am I going to do with you?" She asked as she stood up, "I think someone needs a lesson in manors, tying me up like that." She grabbed her riding crop. "This is more like it," she whipped him across the face and again, it was all sound and theatrics; the very slight sting did arouse him though. She straddled him again; his cock felt the leather of her crotch less panties and just a slight hint of heat radiating from her pussy. She grabbed his cock and started to guide it towards the slit in her panties. At the last second she pushed his cock away. "You wish." Reaching between her legs, she let her fingers slide up her wet cunt; she then raised them to Holden's lips. "See what you're missing?" Holden gladly licked her fingers. She tasted great, he really wanted to bury his face in her and taste her first hand but he was at her mercy.

"What to do with you?" She contemplated. Holden intently watched her as she moved around, she looked back at him. "What you looking at?" She asked him, Holden remained silent. "I have just the thing for nosey boys like you." she said as she grabbed the blind fold, securing it to his face she warned him that if he wasn't careful the ball gag was next. Holden kept quiet. Paige knelt beside Holden thinking about what she could do to her sex slave. She was happy Holden set the bar with the dirty talk and aggressiveness; it was now her turn to push the envelope. She had often fantasized about a day like this, where anything went and she was in complete control but now that it was happening she wasn't sure what to do.

Holden felt the bed shake as she moved, finally the bed bounced up when Paige jumped off, he heard the door open and close and he knew she left. After a couple of minutes he heard the door reopen and Paige's footsteps getting closer to the bed. He then heard a metal ball banging around in a tin can. He began to wonder if she was about to spray paint him, he knew he wouldn't have to wait long to find out. Paige pushed the plastic top of the can causing the familiar swoosh that only a can of whip cream makes. She sprayed a heart on his chest, a line up his hard cock and a small dab in his shaved pubic area, like the cherry on top. Holden heard the sound, felt the sugary toping against his skin and the cream on his cock slowly sliding down. It was definitely a new sensation, one he knew he was about to really enjoy. He heard the can drop to the floor and felt Paige's weight shift around as she searched for her most comfortable position.

Paige looked down at Holden wondering where to start, she saw the whip cream sliding off his cock and she decided that was just a good a place as any. She laid down the best she could between his legs, she was trying to keep herself on the foot of the bed as well as making sure the camera could watch her suck him like a porn star. She put her tongue on the base of his cock and ran it up the full length licking up as much of the whip cream as possible. When she got to the tip of his cock she swallowed the mouth full of cream then put her lips around his head and took his length in her mouth. She then let her tongue dance away on his shaft trying to get all the sticky cream off him. Holden, who was getting cold positively reacted to Paige's hot mouth on his cock.

Paige, satisfied his cock was as clean as she was going to get it let his cock slide out of her mouth. She kept it under control so it wouldn't slap against his stomach and ruin the dab of whip cream on his pubic area. Her hand stroked his cock a couple of times, she couldn't help herself, she loved it so much she didn't want to let it go. She wanted to touch it, lick it and fuck it. She knew that she could at anytime but there was a long way to go before she would let herself. She then knelt beside Holden and began to lick the heart off his chest; she loved the way Holden responded to her touch. Even though she wasn't touching anything one would consider sexual it was an intensely erotic moment. It took her several minutes to get the heart all off him.

She thought she'd share some of the whipped topping with Holden. She grabbed the can off the floor and then laid down, ensuring the camera had a good view of her spreading her legs. She than sprayed a small line onto her pussy. She carefully positioned herself over Holden's head until she could feel his breath on her and then gave him the order to lick. Holden tilted his head back, stuck out his tongue and lapped up every bit of the whip cream. He really wanted to grab her ass and force her hips further down onto his face so he could get deep inside her but he was unable. The frustration was part of the build up and something he had to put up with. Paige wanted to sit back and let him lick her but she knew she had to seek her revenge. She grabbed his cock by the base and squeezed firmly as she moved it out of her way. Leaning down, she opened her mouth and put her lips around the gob of cream taking most of it in her mouth like she just ate the top off a soft serve ice cream cone. She then began licking the whole area clean, not letting go of his cock; she forced it around as rough as she could, trying to abuse and punish it. Holden could feel the force on his cock, he was happy she stopped treating it like a delicate china doll but he was too involved with licking Paige's cunt to fully focus on what she was doing to him.

After Holden was licked clean, she sat up, starred at the camera and gave her clit a quick tickle before inspecting how well Holden did cleaning her off. Confident he had done a good enough job; she raised her left leg and swung it over his head. Holden wasn't nearly done tasting his lover but again it was well beyond his control. She figured it was time for her to dive into the tickle trunk. Following Holden's lead she put the big bag of toys on the bed beside his legs well out of view of the camera. She wasn't sure what she wanted to use on him. Her focus was going to be his ass, she grabbed some lube, pressed the tube against his ass and squeezed. Holden jumped as he felt her finger penetrate him, her finger nail scratched him a bit but remembering the ball gag threat he remained silent. Paige then went back into the bag and saw the obvious choice. It was a long chord of anal beads; she pressed the first and smallest ball against his hole and forced it into him. She was fascinated as she watched them disappear inside him. With a lot more beads to go so she continued to push bead after bead in. Each bead was bigger than the last making the last ones harder to force into him. Holden reacted as he felt Paige filling him up. He was wondering how much more he could take. She too was wondering if he could take them all. Assuming he could, she pushed as hard as she could forcing the last bead inside him until all that remained was a string with a finger loop on the end. "Do you like that?"

"Oh Ya." Holden said.

"What did I say about you talking?" Paige said sternly.

She grabbed the ball gag, forced it into Holden's mouth and tied it behind his head.

"That's what you get slut," she said to him.

Holden loved the way she was talking to him, so out of character for what he knew of her. It was like he was with a different girl and since he couldn't see her, she could very well have been. Paige looked at the bag and wondered what else she could do. She saw the bag of clothes pins and figured he should experience them as well. She placed them on both his nipples then she clipped one on each one of his penis piercings. They didn't cause him pain but the slight pinch made him well aware of what she was doing.

Holden could feel Paige moving around again. She grabbed the camera off the tripod and started at his bound ankles. She moved the camera up his body, just a couple of inches off his skin. She made sure his cock, clothes pins, the blind fold and ball gag were all captured by the camera. "This is what happens when you don't listen to me," she said to the camera. She then laid her head by his penis. Putting the camera on the bed, she used the covers to angle the camera up to her face. She talked to the camera in a whisper so Holden would only be able to hear what she said during the play back.

After she was done her speaking role, she kissed his head and then put the camera back on the tripod ensuring it was repositioned to see everything she was doing. Happy it was set up perfectly she laid back down so her head by his waist with her leg resting against his arm. He could feel the rough texture of her boot against his arm; he knew her pussy and ass were close but yet so far away. Paige grabbed the same finger mounted clit stimulator that Holden used on her. She turned it on high and slid it onto her middle finger before she wrapped her fingers around his cock. Each finger fit perfectly around the well spaced clothes pins. She started jerking him off, her grip was firm and the jaws of the clothes pins pulled at his skin. Holden loved the vibrator on his cock. Every time he moved; the anal beads rubbed his prostate. Paige then stopped, Holden was disappointed, he really wanted to cum. Paige sensed he was close; she leaned in and kissed the tip of his cock licking all the precum dripping from him. Reaching back into the bag she grabbed a urethral sound, the skinniest and longest one she had. She turned off the vibrator and took it off her finger. Very slowly, she slid the sound inside him. It felt much better than he expected. As Paige ever so gently slid the metal object into his cock she said, "We don't want you making a mess now do we?" The sound was forced as deep into him as she could get it. Since she had no experience with sounds either she turned to Holden with great concern in her voice and asked "Is that ok, if it is nod yes," Holden nodded. "Does it hurt at all?" Holden shifted his head side to side to indicate a no. "Good." She then turned her focus back to his cock. She put the finger vibrator back on her left hand this time and instead of pressing it against his shaft; she pressed it hard against his scrotum between his testicles. The vibration radiated through his scrotum, through the beads that were still forced into his ass and directly to his prostate. To increase the intensity Paige grabbed his cock and started jerking him off with so much force it felt like she was going to rip it off. Paige used the tip of her tongue to push the sound back into him as it continually tried sliding out.

Although Holden was incapable of talking, his body began thrashing around, Paige knew he was close. As he felt his cock tighten up she knew he was seconds from orgasm. She put her lips over the head of his cock and used her tongue to keep the sound in place while looking down at the finger loop still protruding from his ass. Should she, she contemplated. Not having much time, she decided to go for it. She put her index finger in the loop and pulled hard like she was starting a lawn mower. The over stimulation of his prostate was enough to start Holden's orgasm. Paige kept her mouth over his cock; she could feel it twitching as his building orgasm was realized. She was amazed and disappointed that she didn't even taste a drop. Once his orgasm subsided, her lips unwrapped around his cock, she turned the vibrator off and placed it beside her. Not sure what to expect, she began sliding the sound out of his still erect cock. She wondered if the built up pressure would explode out of him like a volcano as the sound unblocked its passage. She quickly found the answer to her question. Nothing happened; the only evidence of his orgasm was a small trace of cum at the end of the tool. She brought it to her mouth and licked it in its entirety like a thin Popsicle. She then gripped his cock again giving it a couple of tugs wondering where the cum went. Giving up the search she turned around and removed the ball gag and blind fold from Holden. She left his arms and legs restrained. "Where's your cum?" She asked Holden.

"I don't know, I thought you had it." He laughed, they both looked down at his cock like it was going to give them the answer.

"Well, there is only one way to find out," Paige swung her leg over Holden's head, he could see her perfect ass, he wanted to bite it or spank but he couldn't. She stopped so her pussy was pressed against his chest just out of tongue reach. She unclipped the clothes pins from his nipples and from his cock. Holden than realized what Paige was talking about, the blood returning tickled, burnt and in all was very unpleasant but he didn't dislike it.

Paige was happy to see Holden was still hard because she was on a mission to find out where his cum went. She crawled down his body until she was able to lower herself onto him in a reverse cowgirl position. She grabbed the finger vibrator and turned it back on. As she began to fuck Holden she made sure the camera could see his entire length penetrating her. She pressed the vibrator against her clit and moved it between herself and Holden's cock and balls. Holden responded well to the toy but was just happy he could see Paige; he loved watching her fuck him, especially in that position. He watched her perfectly round ass, he could see his cock disappear and reappear, driving Holden wild. Paige too was sexually overcharged, the camera watching her fuck, felt like a voyeur watching them from the shadows. She was about ready to orgasm yet again. Holden too was ready to explode; he was overfilled with cum and needed to release it upon the world. Paige laid back; her hair tickled his chest as she fought to keep the vibrator on her clit as long as possible. She began to orgasm. She collapsed onto Holden. Her pussy contracting and the new body position forced his cock to slip out of her. Since the gears of orgasm were already set into motion, Holden cam with all the pressure of a fountain. Paige had a long thick stream of cum up her entire body, which was contrasted against her black teddy. Paige was still collapsed onto Holden; her head was now beside his. "Oh, there's that cum we were looking for."

"And then some," he added.

Paige remained motionless for several minutes. "Wow," was all she could mutter.

Holden laid quiet.

"Oh crap," Paige said and spun around. As she laid flat onto him, the cum that was once solely on her teddy smeared against his chest. She looked directly into his eyes and smiled as she so often did. "Nice," was all he said. She untied his arms; his legs then stood up to and turned off the camcorder. She began to undress, first taking off her bulky boots and then Holden watched intently as she slowly slid the fishnet stockings off her long well defined legs. Bending at the waist to tease Holden, she showed him her ass as she helped the stockings off her feet. She looked deep into Holden's eyes as her fish netted arms reached up to the satin bows of her teddy, slowly untying each bow until it was open. Pushing the cum soaked teddy and crotch less panties to the floor, she declared that she needed a shower. Holden thought it was a great idea and said that he was going to clean up the room and would join her in the shower. She happily agreed.

While Paige was in the shower Holden put all the toys back into Paige's not so forbidden tickle trunk, took the camera off the tripod and put the tripod back in the closet. He then took the camera to their big screen TV and connected the RCA cables to the video in ports. Once it was ready for it to be watched, he paused the playback and joined Paige in the shower.

Being exhausted from their afternoon sexcapades the shower was uneventful. Paige helped wash Holden to make sure all the whip cream residue was gone. Holden rubbed his soapy hands all over Paige's breasts and ass but mostly they just got down to the business of cleaning themselves.

With the shower off, the pair toweled dried and dressed in their comfiest clothes then they made their way to the living room. Paige laughed as she saw herself naked on the bed and Holden's back facing the camera. "Wait, I'll make popcorn," She threw a bag into the microwave, grabbed a couple of beers from the fridge, dumped the popcorn into a bowl and joined Holden on the couch. He grabbed his beer, they touched the long necks together to cheers their porn debut and then he hit play. For the next two hours they watched themselves on the big screen in surround sound. They laughed at how funny they looked. At the time they thought they were just as good as professional porn stars but the replay showed quiet a different story. Paige watched in amazement as Holden clipped all the clothes pins on her, it didn't hurt at the time but watching it made Paige shudder in retroactive pain. Holden gave Paige a look as he saw the heart on his chest, Paige smiled back at him and snuggled up closer to him. Holden put his arm around her and reflected on how happy he was and how much he loved Paige. The video started moving around; Holden looked away in embarrassment as he watched the camera run up his body. He was suitably impressed at how big his 'manhood' looked when Paige had the camera between his legs. They watched her suck him then he finally heard what Paige whispered to the camera. "I love his cock," she said shifting her eyes over his length. "Don't tell him this but I can't get enough of it, I could suck it all day every day if he would let me." Paige put her hands over her face trying to hide her embarrassment. "Is that right?" Holden asked, teasing Paige.

"Shut up and watch the TV," she responded.

Finally the screen went black; they both took a drink of their beer and laughed.

"We'll keep that for a cold rainy day," Holden said.

"Okay, but don't be having your little friends here watching it without me."

"Never."

"Ya right," she laughed.

They watched a bit more TV before Paige said she had to go to bed, she had to get up early to start her first day back to university. She also was keeping her job with the roller hockey team. She managed to change departments but that meant she would be working evenings. Holden felt bad for her but it was her choice to continue working.

The alarm went off, telling them both it was time to get up and start their day. Holden drove his university girl to school, disappointed she wasn't wearing the traditional school girl uniform. She said she would for him another time.

Holden made it home from work, he looked at the clock knowing Paige would be just getting out of school and heading to work. He felt bad for her as he sunk into the couch, turned on his video games and cracked a beer. He knew he had a couple of hours before she got home.

Holden finally heard her keys hit the door; as she got home from her long day of school and work. Holden had been off for hours and anxiously waited for her to get home. Paige looked tired; Holden greeted her at the door and gave her a hug and a kiss. He also told her he had a surprise for her. Paige objected saying she had a long hard day and just wanted to veg on the couch and watch TV. Holden stopped her from going into the living room and instead guided her to the bathroom where he had a hot bubble bath waiting for her. He kissed her and gave her time to get undressed. He returned a couple of minutes later with a glass of wine. Paige was already fully submerged in the tub almost invisible by the bubbles that were now overflowing the tub and spilling onto the bathroom floor. Holden reached in the tub, water came up to his shoulder soaking his sleeve as he leaned in and kissed her deeply on the lips and handed her the glass of wine. Paige smiled and gratefully accepted the drink. She leaned her head back into the water; she had the most beautiful smile on her face that made Holden melt. She sipped her wine and began to drift off into her own world. Holden told her to relax, take her time and that dinner would be ready in an hour. Paige closed her eyes as he left the bathroom which is why she didn't notice the amazingly comfortable new bathrobe hanging behind the bathroom door. She also didn't notice the fact that Holden took all her clothes, with the exception of her panties, with him when he left.

Roughly 45 minutes to an hour passed when Paige came out of the bathroom wearing the long thick white bathrobe, her hair was slicked back and still wet. With a smile she asked Holden what happened to her clothes. Holden casually said he put them in the wash and told her to take a seat at the table because dinner was ready. "Oh the table, like grownups," Paige laughed. Their normal dinners consisted of sitting at a fold up living room table while they watched TV. Paige took a seat at the large dinner table which was almost never used except for mail, keys and other odd bits of household items. Holden bought a beautiful flower arrangement on his way home from work which he used as the center piece. He also had two very large candles lit on the table. Paige sat down with one foot on the chair. She innocently gave Holden a quick glance of her panties. Paige told Holden about her classes, her professors, classmates and her new job. Holden told her about his day and about the video games he played after work.

    After dinner they moved to the couch. Holden sat on one end and Paige laid down and put her feet up on Holden as they started to watch a movie Holden rented. He began to rub her feet; he found that he was looking at Paige more than he was watching the movie. Her robe was open slightly and he could see the outline of her perfect breast. Once again Holden had to control the passion he was feeling for her at that moment. His self control was getting harder and harder to maintain. Paige complained about tension in her shoulders. Taking the hint Holden sat on the back of the couch; she settled between his legs and lowered the robe to her waist. Holden began to give her a long deep massage. Paige, getting aroused as well twisted her neck around to kiss Holden but he grabbed her chin and pushed it forward telling her "Not yet." After a very long deep shoulder massage Holden asked Paige if she wanted a full body massage. Without answering him she jumped up, grabbed Holden by the hand and they ran to the bedroom. She dove on the bed and in one quick motion she ripped off her panties and playfully threw them at Holden as he ran through the open door. Holden reached into the nightstand drawer where they kept some of their toys. "Oh, what you gonna do?" Paige asked hopefully. Holden pulled out the baby oil and said he was only going to give her a massage. She huffed and rolled over on her stomach. Holden straddled her bum and poured the oil all over her back. She tensed as the cold oil hit her warm skin. Holden's hands slid magically all over her body, touching her in all the right places while adjusting pressure and intensity, then he slid two fingers down her spine. His thumbs dug deeply into the small of her back, his body was positioned just below her gorgeous ass. He leaned over, she could feel his chest on her ass, she tried to spread her legs but his legs stopped her. Holden took off his t shirt and leaned even further down and began rubbing her back, shoulders and arms right down to her wrist. She could feel his naked chest on her back. He kissed Paige's ear and she told him she wanted him inside her. Holden told her "not yet," and he went back to massaging her. He worked his way down her body. His oily hands slid down her ass cheeks and started rubbing each leg. Paige spread her legs slightly and he could see her glistening pussy. He fought the urge to lean in and taste her. He thoroughly rubbed each leg, her thigh, calves and feet. Finally Paige rolled over and commanded him to kiss her. Holden slowly slid his body up hers; his hand grazed her pussy and tits. Holden then placed one hand behind her neck, firmly but gently gripped it, leaned in and kissed her passionately. With the previous day's events still very fresh in their minds, they both were already close to orgasm. Paige forced Holden on his back, fumbled at his belt buckle and pulled his pants off leaving his boxers on. Paige rubbed her hand over his boxers than she did something Holden loved. She slowly folded his boxers down exposing his dick. He felt vulnerable, but not in the same way as the day before. Paige took one hard lick up his shaft. Before Paige had a chance to take Holden deep into her mouth, Holden grabbed her hair and pulled her back up to him. "No," he said, today is all about you. He began to kiss her, then slowly twisted around until he settled down on top of her. He paused; she could feel the head of his cock just touching her pussy. She wanted him inside her so badly, Holden wanted to be inside her as well but the pause was to build anticipation, making her want it even more. Seeing the anticipation building in her eyes Holden began to very slowly slide his cock inside her. She could feel every millimeter of his cock enter her. It seemed to take forever but Holden was very careful not to go any faster. Finally he had his whole length penetrating her, he paused for a second and he could feel her pussy contract as he kissed her neck and gently squeezed her breast. Then he slowly pulled his cock out again. She felt each piercing touching the walls of her pussy and lips as they slid out of her. A feeling she had felt several times before but never this slow and with such clarity. She wanted him to fuck her fast and hard but Holden refused. He repeated that move several times; it took him roughly five minutes just to get three full thrusts into her. He made sure he forced his cock in as deeply as possible and then as they were both getting worked up, he started to fuck her faster, only slightly faster though. Her nails dug deep into his back as she dragged them down his flesh trying to force him to fuck her faster. He could tell the sensation of his cock slowly penetrating her was driving her wild, just as wild as it was making him. With a quick hard bite of her neck Holden thrusted his cock deep into. Her nails dug deeper into his back drawing blood as she felt his cum shoot inside her. The unexpected thrust and his cum filling her up was enough for Paige, her orgasm shuttered through her body. Holden collapsed onto Paige, his sweaty body pressed firmly against hers. They kissed passionately, Holden began running his fingers through her hair as he looked into her eyes. He was falling deeper in love with her with every passing day.

She could feel his once mighty cock get smaller as the blood rushed out and back into other vital organs. Holden's hand ran up her thigh, over her soaked pussy and grazed her clit with just enough force to make her jump almost to the roof. He continued to pull his hand over her belly, her breast, over her lips to his mouth. Paige leaned up and kissed the finger that was in his mouth, she used her tongue to taste what he tasted. They then rolled over towards each other and held each other in a long tight embrace. Holden reached down pulled the comforter over them as they fell asleep. They woke up to the alarm the next morning, holding each other just as tightly.

9

The wind blew through the car as Holden maneuvered it down the road. It was a perfect Sunday for a lazy drive up the coast. Holden threw the map in the back seat, Paige plugged in her MP3 player and they decided to drive up the highway for a few hours to explore as many side roads as they could. The BMW twisted and turned down the highway as Holden and Paige took in the sights. Paige reached deep into her purse and pulled out a couple of soft drinks and a bag of chips. They snacked and talked, mostly about passing motorists and the brilliant scenery. "It's like we're living in a postcard," Paige remarked. Holden agreed with her. The mountains were still snow covered but the rain and chilly BC winter had finally past, spring was in the air and the couple wanted to take advantage of the beautiful weekend weather. Holden was going away on yet another business trip that coming Monday morning so they wanted to spend as much time together as possible. Paige was sad but she was slowly getting used to having him gone so often.

    The kilometers clicked by on the odometer and the hours clicked by on the clock. Holden and Paige found themselves far up the coast, the city was well in their rearview mirror and only the odd gas station indicated any signs of life in that remote part of the province. They decided it was a good time to veer off the highway and go exploring on some back roads. Holden turned on the blinker and turned off the main highway heading west on a secondary road. Not sure where they were or where they were going, all they knew was the ocean was west. As Holden drove the car around corner after corner he started to pick up speed. As the roar of the engine's RPMs vibrated through the car, Paige's heart began to race as she swayed side to side with each corner. The trees became a blur as they whizzed past. Holden began to go faster and faster, the tires on the car squealed as they struggled to grip the pavement. Holden was being motivated by Paige's excitement for speed. He down shifted and turned the car to the right around a sharp corner, up shifted on the roll out and accelerated. The car caught air over a small hill giving them that floating sensation in their stomach. The road opened up to a long straight stretch, the forest also broke and turned into fields on either side. Holden took advantage of the open road and quickly up shifted pushing the classic cars engine to the limit. Paige grabbed the 'holy shit handle' on the door as she braced herself against the opposing force of the car. Before Holden entered the corner at the end of the straight stretch he caught a glimpse of head lights floating over the same bump he just passed over. Worried it might have been a cop Holden throttled back a bit. Paige was unaware of the company and didn't really notice the car slowing. She was drinking in as much of the passing scenery as possible; she was also reading signs of upcoming tourist spots, shops and towns ahead.

As Holden continued to drive he kept his eye on the rearview mirror to see if he could catch another glimpse of the trailing car. If he didn't see it after a few more turns he would feel confident the car wasn't gaining on him and he could again speed up. Just as he exited the next turn he had a mirror full of headlights, giving him a better look at the car that was now on his bumper. It was a new convertible mustang, the driver was a young man and like Holden he had a beautiful young girl in the passenger seat. He saw the driver's frustration when he pulled up on the slower Holden. Holden, relieved it wasn't the police, put his foot to the floor and the mustang kept up to him through every turn. Confident his BMW could easily out maneuver the much newer domestic car, Holden toyed with his young challenger, letting his car roll out of the corners before accelerating allowing the less agile mustang to keep on his tail. Paige started to clue into what was happening, she began to cheer Holden on. She was acting as his spotter and cheer leader. Holden's heart started racing only after seeing Paige's intense reaction to the car race. The girl in the passenger's seat of the other car was as equally as excited. The drivers did their best to remain focused. Holden easily kept the mustang at bay in the tight corners but as the road opened up for another lengthy straight stretch the mustang got a jump on Holden and pulled up beside him. The roar of the powerful American engine drowned out the quieter but just as powerful BWM engine. Even Holden had to admit the sound of the raw power of the car next to his got his blood flowing. Paige leaned forward looking over at the car next to theirs, the female passenger looked back at Holden and Paige, the two drivers glanced over at each other but remained focused on keeping their cars on the road. Paige licked her lips seductively at the young girl, the girl countered Paige's taunting by kneeling in her seat and flashing Paige. Holden almost lost control of his car when he caught a glimpse of the bare breasts next to him. His momentary lapse almost allowed the mustang to overtake him but he managed to stay door to door with the mustang as they entered a gentle left turn. Because the turn was to the left it gave Holden's opponent the inside lane but the BMW's much greater cornering ability still gave Holden the edge through the turn. As the mustang's driver let off on the gas to hold the car on the inside, Holden kept his foot pressed to the floor and roared past the 'stang. Paige completely wrapped up in the moment gave the female in the other car the finger as they passed. The young girl reciprocated the motion. Holden was unaware of the spirited exchange between the two adrenaline rushed girls. As the cars exited the corner Holden caught a glimpse of a van coming towards them, the other driver had quick reflexes and powered the mustang inches behind Holden's bumper allowing the van to safely pass, with its horn blaring. Holden felt his legs tingle with the close call, Paige began yelling with excitement. They could only imagine the other two were just as jacked up if not more so but if they were, the ice flowing through the other drivers veins didn't allow it to show. He wasn't happy on Holden's bumper and pulled out to pass again just before they entered a tighter right hand turn. Both drivers under estimated the turn, the Mustang driver knew he had no chance on the outside of the European sports car so he pulled in behind Holden again. Through the center of the turn Holden felt the back end of the car start to slide out after losing traction on some sand. Worried that the Mustang, which was only inches off his bumper, wouldn't be able to react quickly enough to avoid a collision, Holden kept his foot on the gas and he drifted through the turn. All four tires squealed and smoke poured out of the rear wheel wells. As the car straightened out, Holden check his mirrors and saw he not only gained on the Mustang but it was drifting through the corner as well. Holden had to resist watching the car in the rear view mirror. All he heard was Paige next to him fixated on the passenger side mirror. "That was fucking cool!" Her fingers were still clenching the holy shit handle. Her leg was bouncing up and down as her nerves began to get the best of her. She was quiet confident in Holden's driving abilities but she was scared of the unpredictable road conditions, other vehicles and the occupants of the other vehicle. She wasn't going to tell Holden to slow down, her adrenaline had taken over her and she wanted more. She liked to be scared; it awakened senses in her that were rarely touched.

Holden shuck off the most recent close call and kept his foot on the gas. He had a big lead on the mustang but the hard charger behind the wheel of the mustang was pushing his car to its limits in an attempt to catch the BMW and impress his girlfriend. Holden ducked into yet another corner and had to hit the brakes hard to slow up for a much slower car in his lane. When it was as safe as possible on the windy road he down shifted and easily passed the obstruction. The mustang's timing was perfect as it came around the corner. The driver noticed the slower car, saw Holden passing it and kept on the gas, easily following Holden around the car. He was again only inches away from Holden's bumper. Paige's eyes were glued to the side mirror watching the other racer. The engines continued to roar, tires were squealing, the smell of burning rubber filled the BMW. Paige unwittingly pulled up her shirt slightly and began running her fingers over her stomach as she held on dearly to the handle. Holden noticed but tried not to get fixated on Paige getting worked up. As they drove through corner after corner Holden began to open up on the mustang until it was almost out of sight. After yet another very tight turn Holden shifted down to kill momentum and to get the most power out of the engine at the end of the turn. When the car started to straighten out, he once again slammed on the gas and worked his way through the gears. The car caught some air before the end of the corner, the BMW lost traction momentarily but regained it quickly as the tires once again made contact with the pavement. The momentary loss of control spooked both him and Paige but knowing there was another car coming up fast behind him Holden had no choice but to keep his foot on the gas to clear a path for the competitor. Holden decided that the fun was up and things were getting too dangerous, he wasn't as worried about himself but he would never forgive himself if anything was to happen to Paige. As he was about ready to pull over and concede the race when he saw the mustang come speeding around the corner and over the same bump, catching air in the same spot he did. But instead of a non eventful landing, the heavier mustang's rear end had too much momentum and began to pass the front end. Holden and Paige could only watch in horror as the car disappeared into cloud of smoke. Holden stopped in case they needed help but when the smoke dissipated both Holden and Paige could see the headlights of the mustang stopped in the middle of the road, the car was angled about 45 degrees off center. Holden stayed put as the driver of the mustang selected a gear and slowly began rolling towards the BMW. Holden and Paige were curious to meet the other couple but were nervous as well, unsure how they would react. The recent road rage horrors in the news had them a little nervous. The convertible pulled up alongside Holden, the driver yelled over "That was intense, awesome."

"Hell Ya!" Holden shouted back "You guys alright? That was a hell of a spin."

"Ya, we're good, I think we're going to take it easy from here on in though, great driving."

"You too," Holden replied. The young driver swallowing his pride waved his arm allowing Holden to take the lead. Just as Holden released the clutch, he and Paige looked over again at the Mustang. The young girl was kneeling on the seat with her shirt up over her head. This time Holden was in a much better position to see the show. He and Paige laughed as they drove off, Paige waved back, this time much more politely than the last. "Wow that was intense." Paige said repeating the other drives words.

"Yup, how are you doing? Are you okay?" Holden asked.

"Oh Ya, I'm good," Paige said gently fanning herself with her hand. As Holden drove off the mustang quickly disappeared from the rearview mirror and he and Paige were once again alone on the road.

The drive turned into a lazy Sunday cruise through the country side, the air started to get cooler, the smell of the ocean filled the car and they knew they were close. They took a couple of more corners and found themselves at a T intersection. They could see the ocean peaking through a patch of trees; they just didn't know the best way to get to it. Taking a chance, Holden turned the car left, they drove less than a kilometer before they found a trail just big enough for a car. Deciding to drive down the path, Holden cringed as he heard the sound of branches dragging along the side of his pride and joy. He continued driving forward despite the teeth clenching sound. Finally after only a few minutes the trees opened up and they found themselves in an open clearing with a picnic table in the middle of a grassy area. They couldn't have imagined a more perfect spot. With the car parked, they popped out and unpacked their provisions. Even though there was a perfectly good picnic table, Paige spread out a red and white checkered table cloth on the ground at the spot where the grass met the beach sand. Holden questioned her and Paige simply said when she started the day she pictured sitting on the grass next to the ocean and nothing was going to change that. Holden knew better than to question Paige when she had her mind made up, he just smiled and began unloading the cooler. The night before, they bought a precooked chicken from the grocery store as well as a couple of varieties of salads. Paige pulled out the paper plates and plastic utensils as Holden grabbed the bottle of white wine and the cork screw that he tossed into the cooler. The cork popped out and they both giggled at the sudden noise, it was very apparent they were both still riding the adrenaline rush from the race.

Neither spoke much as they ate, they spent time gazing off into the ocean, staring at each other and at the clouds. The sounds of the waves crashing onto the beach mere feet from them and the birds fighting for whatever scraps of fish washed up on the shore was hypnotic. Paige was the first to break the trance. "You never did tell me the dream you had about your masseuse that had you so worked up."

Laughing, "It wasn't just about her, you were very much involved." Holden said. He began to tell her his very vivid dream, Paige listened intently to Holden's every word as he described the fantasy in pain staking detail. Paige recalled the night, the room, the sounds and smells as Holden talked on. Paige stood up, grabbed Holden by the shirt and dragged him to the picnic table, all the while listening to Holden. She pushed him down on the table, Holden adjusted himself so he was lying down in the middle. Paige opened the button on Holden's shorts, unzipped the fly, reached into his boxers and pulled out his flaccid cock. She used her mouth to get Holden hard; finally he got to the point of the story where the female masseuse began riding him. Paige began acting out the story; she hiked up her thin sundress, placed her knees on the hard wood of the picnic table, on either side of Holden's legs. Holden kept explaining his dream as Paige reached for Holden's exposed cock, she looked down as she pushed his penis against her panties, Holden paused his story. Paige looked back up at him smiled as she said, "was it something like this?" She pulled her panties to one side, wrapped her hand around his thick meat and raised her body an inch over Holden's full length. Using her hand she guided his cock into her well lubricated pussy. Both sighed a very pleasurable sigh as they became one again. Holden resumed his story; Paige continued acting it out as best she could. Instead of ripping her dress, the only clothing she had with her, she let the straps fall of her silky shoulders. She pushed the dress down over her chest, reached back, unclasped her bra and tossed it carelessly to the side. Her breasts were highlighted in the hot spring sun. As Paige took Holden's cock deep inside her, she began gazing into the surf; lost between the scenery and Holden's words she let the sun warm her body. Her mind was torn between so many different images, the adrenaline of the race, the spectacular scenery, Holden's dream; having the man she loves inside her and being fucked outside with the possibility of having someone catch them at any minute. She felt a very intense pleasure, she wasn't even close to orgasm but her pussy was very sensitive, she felt a tingling sensation that was foreign to her, her legs were getting weaker by the minute. Holden, now finished with his story, watched Paige. Paige's hips rhythmically grinded onto Holden. She was still focused on the nearby ocean and out of nowhere she came to. She reached down and pulled her sundress up over her head and carelessly tossed it on the ground by her bra. She continued to work over Holden, like dinner they didn't exchange any words, the normally vocal Paige remained silent. Holden too kept his normal enthusiasm low key because he was worried that he would ruin Paige's moment. He fought to stay hard, he had never seen Paige so distant yet so focused, he didn't want to cum, not just yet.

Waves from a passing cruise ship thundered into the beach, Paige synched her thrusts with the beats of the waves and as they got faster so did Paige. She stopped and spread her legs to get lower onto his cock. She leaned her head back causing her long hair to tickle her back. She didn't move. Holden was just about to talk when he felt a deep long shiver coursing through her entire body, she shook her head and refocused back onto Holden. "Wow," was all she said. She rolled over onto the picnic table top and snuggled up next to Holden. She began to lightly caress his still hard cock, "Oh, you didn't finish yet?"

"Nope" he said with a smile "Did you?"

"I don't know what I did, it wasn't an orgasm but it was very intense."

Holden then rolled off the picnic table, stood at the end of the table, put his hands on Paige's thighs and twisted her around so she was lying on her stomach. Paige instinctively knew what Holden wanted so she got up on her hands and knees. Holden grabbed the waist band of her panties, pulled them over her perfectly round ass and past her knees. He then placed his strong but soft hands firmly on her ass checks and spread them apart. He lowered his head to her ass and began gently kissing her bum, her asshole and freshly fucked pussy. His lips touched her sensitive skin, then spreading her cheeks apart even wider he extended his tongue and took a long hard lick of her pussy. He then slid his tongue up past her pussy to her asshole. His tongue danced around her hole getting deeper and deeper, as he licked her ass, she leaned forward and rested on her shoulder. Her free hand appeared between her legs and she violently began rubbing her clit.

He knew she was ready to orgasm as she was riding him and he wanted to finish the job for her, he wasn't as worried about himself, he knew he could take care of that later.

Her hand worked faster and harder, Holden tried to match the pace but his tongue was getting tired and sore from working away in her tight button. Just as he thought she was going to orgasm, he moved his mouth down to her wet pussy and began licking everything that was splashing out of her. Like earlier she just stopped and rolled over kicking her leg over Holden's head. "Wow," she said again.

"What happened?" Holden asked.

"I don't know, I feel like I'm having an orgasm but I don't, ya know?"

"No, no I don't" Holden laughed. "You're fucked up." Paige laughed then her eyes widened. "LETS GO FOR A SWIM!" She said excitedly.

"Not only no, but HELL NO, it'll be freezing."

"Oh you big baby," Paige said as she jumped up and ran down the beach. Holden couldn't do anything but shake his head. He watched as Paige ran and jumped into the ocean. Her head disappeared under the water and reappeared with a shriek. Holden laughed as he saw Paige run out of the water twice as fast as she ran into it. He found it incredibly sexy watching her naked body wiggle around as she was in full sprint to the car. He casually walked to the car and opened the door for her as she dove in. He reached over her and started the ignition and cranked the climate control to fully hot, he also clicked on her seat warmer. After closing the car door to let his crazy girlfriend warm up, he went back to where they had their picnic set up and cleaned up the area throwing everything in the trunk. He made sure to grab all their clothes and threw them into the back seat. Paige was shivering on the front seat cuddled up in the fetal position. Holden covered her with the blanket they just had their picnic on. It wasn't very thick but it was all they had. He couldn't help but giggle at his wet naked girlfriend. She looked at him with her big sad eyes. "Told you it was cold," he reminded her. She looked back at him with fuck off in her eyes but she didn't say anything. Holden began the drive home.

Taking their time on the drive home, the telephone poles no longer looked like a closely spaced picket fence. Something on the shoulder of the road caught Holden's attention. When he looked over his shoulder he saw Paige's dress and panties on the back seat, just the sight of her clothes made him hard. He then looked at her asleep under the blanked, forgetting all about whatever it was that caught his attention in the first place. He saw she was no longer shivering so he began to turn down the heat and the fan, it was feeling way to much like a sauna for his liking.

Paige woke up halfway home, she too was feeling the effects of the heat, mostly because Holden had forgotten to turn off her seat warmer. She looked around and found her clothes, first she pulled on her tight white panties then she pulled her sundress over her head, leaving her bra on the back seat. Holden fought to keep his concentration on the road. It had been almost a year since they have been together but Holden still couldn't get enough of Paige, in his eyes she was getting more and more beautiful each time he saw her.

Their day finally came to an end; they pulled into their condo parking lot and headed upstairs. The sunset roughly an hour earlier and Holden had some packing to do. With the start of the roller hockey season only a week away he had to go away for yet another meeting so all the teams could iron out last minute problems. Paige and Holden didn't talk about the upcoming trip very much, Paige knew with the season starting she would be seeing less and less of Holden. That prospect made her sad but she did know what she was getting into before she moved to BC with him.

After they unpacked the car, Paige shed her clothes and crawled into bed and watched as Holden packed his bags, something he did very quickly now. When he was all done he undressed and joined Paige in bed. The fresh air and days activity had them both exhausted, Holden set the alarm, rolled over and fell asleep in his lovers arms.

The alarm sounded, Holden jumped and made sure the time was right, it felt like they had just gotten to sleep. Paige let out a cute little hmmmpff then told Holden to turn the alarm off and go back to sleep. Holden told her he couldn't; the cab would be there for him in 45 minutes and he still needed to shower. Paige reluctantly let Holden go and as he walked out of the room she rolled over and closed her eyes. Holden paused a moment and watched her. He then turned and jumped into the shower. He no sooner had his hair lathered with shampoo when the shower curtain quickly opened, Holden jumped and Paige let out a laugh. She stepped into the tub and put her arms around him. Holden tried to fight her off for half a second or so until he gave into her advances. "You think you were going to go away for an entire week and not say goodbye?"

"What was I thinking?" Holden replied. He grabbed Paige's ass, picked her up and pushed her against the cold shower wall. He tilted the shower head so it was spraying on both of them. Paige wrapped her legs around Holden's thigh as he began to fuck her. Paige wrapped her arms around Holden's broad shoulders giving into his powerful thrusts. The hot water splashed over their shoulders and dripped down their bodies. Paige clenched Holden tighter, her legs flexed and he could feel she was getting ready to orgasm, which in his opinion was a good thing because he too was about to cum and he didn't want to leave her high and dry before he left. Holden, after hearing a particularly deep moan from Paige, released his cum inside her. Paige felt his hot semen filling her up, she felt the same deep intense wave rush through her body but like at the beach it wasn't an orgasm. Holden hated to rush off but the delay in the shower had him now running behind. He washed himself off quickly, grabbed his towel and then got dressed. He no sooner had his shirt buttoned up when his phone rang, it was the cabbie telling him that he had arrived. Holden grabbed his suitcase, gave Paige a kiss on the cheek and ran out the door. Paige was left all alone in her condo again. She had a busy week of school ahead of her and she was happy for the distraction.

Paige got home from school; she fumbled through her bag for her keys. Just as she was about to place the key into the lock she noticed the door was left slightly open. She slowly pushed the door open, something didn't seem right to her, she looked around and quickly dismissed her uncomfortable feelings as her being crazy. She was just missing Holden and didn't like the idea of being in the apartment alone. As Paige moved around the apartment her discomfort grew, something just wasn't right. She wanted to call Holden but she knew it was nothing more than silly paranoia. She reached for the hallway closet door, as her hand touched the knob she took a deep breath and opened the door. With a quick fling of the door, she saw nothing. She let out a loud laugh and put the weird feelings behind her once and for all, as she hung up her jacket she noticed one of Holden's favourite coats. 'Weird, I thought he took that with him,' she thought to herself. Paige then moved freely about the apartment with her new found sense of security. She didn't have to work that night so she decided to go for a jog. Moving into the bedroom she pulled out her jogging clothes and began to undress. As she had her shirt over her head when she heard a sound coming from the bedroom closet, she turned quickly with her breasts exposed. She looked long and hard at the closet door which was left slightly open. After letting out a giggle and a sigh of relief as she continued to change. She was embarrassed about her ever growing paranoia; she was going to tell Holden about her silliness that night on the phone. She unfastened her belt, the button to her jeans and unzipped the zipper. She reached her thumbs into the waist band of her jeans and underwear and pulled them down. She no sooner had her pants around her ankles when she heard a much louder bang coming from the closet. Before she had a chance to turn to investigate she felt a large force slam into her back, knocking her frail naked body to the ground. She was winded and fought to catch her breath. Before she could regain her composure she felt a hand cover her mouth and breathe on her neck. Paige began to struggle causing the assailants grip to tighten. Paige grasped for a breath when she felt sharp cold steel pressing against her throat. She began to cry but stopped, not giving the attacker the satisfaction of seeing her weak. Paige tightened her body to be strong in defiance. "Tough little whore aren't you?" The deep voice said. "On your knees bitch." Paige didn't move, trying to stand her ground. She felt his hand reach into her hair. Forcefully grabbing a handful, he pulled her to her knees. Paige still refused to show any pain. She tried to twist to look at her attacker but was met with a hard pull of her hair. "DO NOT fucking look at me!" The attacker said as he began pressing the knife harder against her skin. Keeping his grip on her hair he leaned in. "We can do this the easy way or the hard way, which is it going to be whore?"

Paige angled herself and spit in his direction. She then felt a sharp sting across her face. "The hard way it is," the attacker said. He then shoved her head towards the floor. Paige nearly lost her balance but managed to stay on her knees. She felt a bag slide over her head and it being tied around her throat, tight enough to remain in place but loose enough to allow her to breath, all be it laboured. Paige then realized the seriousness of her predicament, she became anxious and claustrophobic. Paige lost her bearings as the attacker grabbed her by the hair and pulled her to her feet. She reached up to grab the man's hand so he didn't pull all her hair out. He then flung her onto the bed like she was a rag doll, Paige propped herself up onto her knees and she heard a snap, then felt a burning sensation in her jaw. The force of the hit was enough to knock her backwards onto the bed. Still dazed she felt the man moving around her, he grabbed one of her arms and she became panicked as she felt the cold steel of a handcuff attaching itself to her wrist. He pulled her arm over her head and she heard the hinges of the handcuff again, then the man let go. She tried to move her arm and she couldn't, he apparently fastened the other end to the bed post. He then grabbed her free arm and affixed it to the opposite bedpost. Unable to move Paige did her best to not give in and cry. She began thinking about

Holden and how she hoped he would barge into the room and save her; then her thoughts turned to Holden and their happy times together, she did everything she could to take herself out of the current situation. She felt the man tie rope around both her ankles and secure the ends of the rope to the bed posts. Paige was tightly bound to the bed, completely naked, legs spread and she now knew she was helpless to stop the man from violating her. As she was contemplating all the horrible things that he was about to do to her, he once again leaned in, "Pamplemousse," he said before she heard him stand up and walk out the door. Several minutes passed since she heard anything else, those minutes felt like an eternity. She focused on the word he just whispered to her.

Foot steps approached the door, Paige began to pray he left and this new person was a rescuer. Hope began to fade as she felt the weight of someone climbing on the bed. She again almost began to cry as she realized that it wasn't help nor was help likely to come. Paige felt a hand press against her stomach, up to her tits and back down to cup her pussy. "How is it? Nice and wet for me bitch?" Paige winced but was unable to move. "Now, now, that's a good girl," the assailant said with a laugh.

Paige unable to see, she could only feel him moving around again. Paige held her breath as she felt something slap across her throat, it was very heavy but she could recognize the texture as leather. The man walked around the bed and back to the opposite side. He pulled the leather strap tight almost to the point of fully cutting off her air and circulation. Paige knew she was in a lot of trouble. She let out a squeak "I can't breath."

"Not my problem whore."

Paige was completely helpless, unable to move, talk or even breathe for that matter. Her heart began to race even faster as she felt sharp metal of the knife on her cheek. He moved the metal blade to the top of her head, slid it down her forehead, across her eye lid, down her cheek and to her chest. The blade began to work its way across her tits. "Kinda small but they'll do," the man said harshly. "Let's see what the rest of you is like." He began to move his hand down her stomach to her crotch, the knife that was also in his hand poked her thigh. She jumped but the restraints did their job keeping her firmly in her place. He dropped the knife but she could feel the cold metal handle against her thigh as a reminder. He moved his hand between her legs and began touching her, letting the odd finger penetrate her. Her pussy was extra sensitive with the blood racing through her body, there was no way she was going to let him think he was pleasuring her though. As his fingers moved around her pussy she got wetter and wetter.

Her attacker felt it. "I knew you were a whore ripe for a fucking," he said as he brought his hand to his mouth. "Tasty little fuck aren't you. Well it's my turn to get off now, how do you like that?"

"Fuck you!" Was all Paige could muster.

The man became very angry; he grabbed the knife and poked it into the bottom of her chin. "Why do you have to be like that? Just lay back and enjoy." Paige remained silent; the point of the knife was already very close to puncturing her. The man regained his composure, crawled off the bed, and Paige could hear him taking off his clothes. She winced as she felt him crawling back onto the bed, this time from the foot of the bed, between her legs. She felt him move around and then felt his breath on her pussy. Instinctively she tried to close her legs but she was unable, she was bound just too tightly so she began twisting around, anything to stop this madman from violating her. As she flailed uselessly around she felt a very painful slap on her chest. "STOP FUCKING AROUND!" The man yelled. Paige stopped moving and started to wonder what just hit her. It was too sharp to be a hand and she didn't think it felt like a knife stabbing her, could it have been a whip? She stopped thinking about what happened and began thinking about what was happening when she felt his tongue press against her pussy. "Nice, I knew you wanted me, you really are a dirty fucking whore aren't you?" Paige, not being able to take anymore, began to cry. The assailant slide his naked body up hers, she felt his cock press against her pussy. "Let's have a little fun shall we?" He said. Paige tightened up as she felt the familiar cold steel sliding across her face, down her chest to her tit. He grabbed one and pulled it hard making Paige wince in pain. She felt the blade slide underneath "You call these tits?? I'd be doing you a favour cutting them off." Paige then felt the knife press even harder against her bare breast. Paige barely let out a whimper of "no," she couldn't say anything more. "Alright, you can keep them for now," he said.

The sharp tip of the knife circled around her belly button then down to her clit. "How wet for me are you whore?" The man penetrated her again, this time with several fingers. "YOU CALL THAT WET? EVERYTHING I'M DOING FOR YOU AND THAT'S ALL YOU GOT?" Hastily the fingers that were just inside her pussy slide under the hood and touched her lips. "HOW DO YOU TASTE SLUT?" His voice was becoming louder and angrier. Paige was becoming increasingly scared with every second. Paige felt something slide into her, it was cold and metal feeling. Is it steel? She thought to herself. As she tried to figure it out or if she felt any pain at all, she did feel that she was becoming increasingly wet, way wetter than she should be. After several minutes the torture stopped. "There you go, nice and wet for my cock." The attacker rammed his cock deep into her pussy, very hard, not concerned for her comfort at all. It hurt her at first but as the cock worked in and out of her she could feel an orgasm building and she hated herself for it. The large cock continued to violate her again and again; Paige's orgasm was building. She fought the sensation but the leather strap began to chock her to the point of being breathless. He grabbed her hair and pulled hard. That was one sensation to many for the already over stimulated Paige, she began to have an orgasm. She realized that the day before at the beach, the morning in the shower, the orgasms that didn't happen were in a reservoir and they were all coming together at that moment in one mammoth orgasm. Paige hated that this man was not only getting her off but he was getting the result of her and Holden's passion and love making. It almost made her physically ill. She heard the man's voice "I told you, you were a whore." He became faster and more erratic as he fucked the unwilling Paige. "I'm going to cum," he said as she felt the cock quickly exit her. She could then feel a warm puddle form on her stomach. 'At least he didn't cum inside me,' she thought. She felt fingers run through the warm cum, the hand once again slid under the mask. "How do I taste bitch?" The fingers forced their way into her mouth. Paige took the fingers and licked all the cum clean off. Despite the leather strap across her throat she began to laugh. "What's so fucking funny bitch?"

"I love you." Paige said "why didn't you leave?"

"I'm glad you remembered pamplemousse," Holden said as he removed her hood. "I was worried you forgot, you were getting so worked up, I almost pulled the hood off several times but didn't want to ruin the fantasy."

"Even without the safety word, I knew it was you from the beginning. I'd recognize your touch and scent anywhere."

"Really? You were a good actress then, you had me freaked out a couple of times, I wanted to say pamplemousse the second I popped out of the closet but I wanted to create a little bit of doubt to get your heart racing." Holden said.

"I admit, I was scared a bit at first, but ya, I didn't want to ruin the fantasy either," She said. "Thanks for doing that for me, but we don't have to do that again."

"Fair enough, I hope knowing it was me didn't ruin it for you."

"NOOO, knowing it was you was the only way I could have possibly enjoyed it." Even though she knew it was him she was still relieved to see him. After their earlier experimentation with domination, they talked in depth about fantasies. Paige reluctantly admitted that she had a rape fantasy; she said she wanted to be taken by force and made to submit to her lover. Under very controlled circumstances with someone she loved and trusted. They decided on the safety word of pamplemousse because it wasn't something they wouldn't normally say in the throes of passion. Even with a ball gag, the amount of syllables meant the word could easily be identified when they were being pushed past their comfort zones. Holden quickly unfastened all her restraints, then he smiled sheepishly and pulled out a new steel vibrator she had never seen before. "I bought it for you before I left, I was going to call you tonight and tell you where I hid it."

"Is that the steel I felt? How'd you get me so wet?" Paige asked. Holden reached to the side of the bed and pulled out a bottle of baby oil. "About half a bottle of this," he said with a laugh.

Exhausted Paige collapsed against Holden. "You're an ass, but I'm glad you're home. Thanks again." She draped her arms around his neck. Holden leaned in and kissed his love, he returned her embrace and they fell asleep tightly in each other's arms for a much deserved midafternoon nap.

10

Paige was standing at the bus stop for what seemed like forever before she finally saw the #3 round the corner. She gathered her things and walked to the curb to await her chariot. The airbrakes hissed, the door opened and Paige climbed aboard. She was the only one waiting at the stop so as soon as she was clear of the doors; the bus was on the move. Paige found her seat and turned up her MP3 player to drown out the city sounds. At the next stop a young woman boarded. Paige looked at her, she thought she looked incredibly beautiful, she couldn't pin point what it was about her but Paige couldn't look away. The young woman put down her bag and took a seat across from Paige. The woman looked over and smiled. Paige smiled back, just then she noticed the girls firm round belly, she was pregnant. "It's kicking, do you want to feel it?" The girl asked noticing that Paige was staring at her belly. Paige hesitantly reached over and put her hand on the beautiful girl's belly. Paige giggled as she felt the tiny life under the girl's skin. The two talked for several blocks but the conversation was interrupted by Paige's ringing cell phone, she excused herself and answered the phone. "Hello……Just riding on the bus…shut up…..shut up…..OH MY GOD, that is fucking awesome….Ya, definitely……talk to you later." Paige hung up the phone and looked over at the pregnant girl, smiled and began dialing her phone. "Holden?"

"Ya, what's up?" He answered.

"Tamara just called, guess what."

"What?"

"She told me Mike proposed last night and they are getting married in two weeks."

"Oh Ya, that, didn't I tell you he was going to do that?" Holden asked with mock sincerity.

"No! You did not. How long did you know?"

"About a month or so, you sure I didn't mention it before?" Holden asked again playing with Paige.

"I'm pretty sure you didn't tell me, that's awesome. Her Stagette is Saturday
night."

"Ya, Mike's bachelor party is Saturday as well. We'll have to make sure we don't go to the same places." Holden said.

"We'll have to go get them something after work." Paige stated.

"Sounds good, I have to run honey, love you."

"Love you too," Paige said then hung up her phone. While she was talking she didn't realize the pregnant girl got up and moved to the door. As the bus stopped she turned and waved goodbye to Paige then she disappeared down the stairs. Paige spent the rest of the bus ride thinking about how happy the pregnant girl looked, how happy Tamara sounded when she was telling Paige about her engagement and upcoming wedding. She saw her stop; rang the bell then grabbed her bag and got off the bus in front of her school. Her day at school was pretty much a waste as she daydreamed about being pregnant and being at the altar walking towards Holden.

She called Holden at lunch; they agreed to meet up at the end of the day so they could go shopping. Holden asked Mike where they were registered, Mike said the beer store but when Holden pried further he found out that they were having a very low key intimate wedding. They weren't expecting a lot of people nor did they want their friends buying them a lot of gifts. Since neither of them was religious Mike explained it was more of a party to celebrate their love so they wanted to keep it very informal. Holden laughed and asked how he managed to get away with it. Mike said it was mostly Tamara's idea and that the subliminal tapes he played her at night seemed to work. Even though Holden knew Paige wasn't going to be happy with his answer of "they aren't registered anywhere and they don't want a fuss made," he dropped his line of questioning to Mike.

Holden and Paige spent several hours after work going from porn store to porn store looking for just the right gifts for the upcoming bachelor/bachelorette parties. They spent most of the time adding to their own wish lists and laughing at some of the inventory. Finally, they were confident they found just the right things and they moved on to the mall to find something for the wedding. Paige began trying on clothes, Holden spent most of the time bringing Paige clothes that were one size to small so he could see her in the overly tight garments. They both enjoyed themselves. Finally after carefully selecting something returnable for Mike and Tamara they went home.

Saturday rolled around and they were woken up by a ringing doorbell. Holden had an idea who was at the door while Paige had no clue. Holden did his best to keep the surprise visitors just that, a surprise. Holden climbed out of bed, threw on some pants and an old T shirt and ran to the door. He opened it up to see his old friends Pete, Andrew and Jeff standing in the entrance. Andrew handed Holden a beer and smiled. Holden looked at the beer. "Dude, its 9 a.m."

Andrew shot back "It's noon in Toronto, don't you ever forget where you came from."

"Fair enough, come in," Holden said as he took the beer and showed his guests into the living room. They all made sure to peak their head in the bedroom to say hi to Paige who was still in bed. Taking the hint, she got out of bed and dressed then joined the boys in the living room. They all exchanged war stories. Pete had some amazing stories from his adventures on the police force, Andrew told stories of his conquests at the resort and Jeff simply said the law firm was busy representing clients with suits against Pete. Holden and Paige told them how great life in B.C. was. Holden told them embarrassing stories about Mike and they were looking forward to meeting his bride to be. They all asked Paige if she had met any single friends yet, she just told them no one she would subject them to. Pete said that was probably a wise choice. Several more beers went down range as Holden and Paige took turns showering. When they were both ready the guys decided they wanted to go for lunch. Holden kept looking at his watch and stalling. Finally just as he was about to lose the battle to stay put, the doorbell rang once again. "Paige honey could you get that?" Holden asked.

"Yes sir, anything you wish." Paige said playfully.

Holden just smiled, the guys asked who it was. "Just wait and see." Then they heard a shriek come from the front door. Holden could only laugh. They heard two sets of footsteps running down the hall. It was Paige's old roommate Melanie or "Sunshine." Jeff froze as he looked at his past crush. He then shot Holden a dirty look for not warning him. They all talked, Holden took Mel's bags and put them in the spare room then went to offer her a beer. Pete spoke up and said he would buy her one at the restaurant but they had to go because he was starving.

Over lunch they all continued talking and sharing humourous stories. Jeff was disappointed to hear that Mel was only in town for the weekend for the bachelorette party. Tamara invited Mel to come to the party because she knew Paige didn't really know any of the other girls that were going to be attending the stagette. She wanted Paige to have a close friend there too. The guys were staying the entire week so they could attend the wedding as well. Andrew was pushing Jeff to make his move on Mel while he had the chance and he reminded him that they still lived in the same city. Jeff took a drink to contemplate his options. Paige looked at her watch and said they had to go and start getting ready. They paid their bills and headed back to the apartment.

The boys sat in the living room watching TV while the girls took over the bedroom and bathroom. They took the better part of the afternoon getting ready but the time turned out to be worthwhile. According to the guys, they looked stunning when they were done. The boys however took separate showers and inside of 30 minutes all 4 guys were showered and dressed. They all looked the same, just smelt a little better. The taxi's arrived. Paige and Holden locked up, they said that both parties had hotel rooms so neither would be back at the apartment that night.

Paige and Mel headed for an extravagant hotel downtown Vancouver. The girls all chipped in and got Tamara a suite for her party. When they arrived at the room, all the other girls were there with the exception of Tamara. Paige put her party gifts in the corner with the rest. One of the girls phones started to ring, on the other end of the phone was the girl assigned with the task of not only distracting Tamara for the day but to figure out a way to get her to the hotel. The girl who received the call said Tamara was on her way up. All the girls started to get excited as they pulled out Tamara's outfit for the night. There was a knock at the door, Mel answered it. They chose Mel because she was the only girl in the room Tamara didn't know and they thought it would be a good way to confuse her further. Even the girl escorting Tamara was a bit confused when the door opened, she looked at the room number written down on her page, back up to the door and finally verbally confirmed that she did indeed have the right room.

Mel opened the door wider to let them in, the girls yelled surprise and Tamara walked in hugged all her guests and thanked them for the effort. Before she could finish, one of the girls handed her a glass of wine.

Tamara quickly drank that glass and asked for another. As the girl topped up Tamara's glass, another girl grabbed Tamara by the arm and escorted her to a chair they put in the front of the room. They arranged a couch and other chairs around the seat of honour. Tamara quickly sunk into her chair as she felt the warmth of the first glass of wine rush through her. One of the girls ran to the freezer and brought out a tray of penis shaped ice cubes and splashed a couple in Tamara's glass then passed the tray around to the other girls. Once all the girls had a drink they brought out their gifts and laid them around Tamara. Before she could start opening them Paige brought over a cheap wedding veil and put it on Tamara's head instructing her that she couldn't take it off for the rest of the night. Tamara reached into the first bag and pulled out an oversized dildo. She held it up for everyone to see and moved it around so the head flopped around all crazy like. They all laughed. Tamara put it on a table beside her, the next gift was a Chippendales calendar. It was passed from girl to girl for them to oogle the buff men on each page. The girls found their birthday months and said why their month was hotter than the next girls. The next was a card with a man on the cover equally as buff as the men in the calendar and inside was a coupon for DVD rentals at an adult store. The rest of the gifts were the same, novelty gifts from various adult stores. Tamara said she needed another drink; two girls got up and went to the fridge. They pulled out a glass that was shaped like a foot long penis with a white curly straw coming out the urethra. Tamara fought them saying she wouldn't drink out of it. The girls told her that her only other option was to not drink at all. Tamara put her lips on the straw, took a big gulp of the alcohol inside and said "mmm mmm good," to the amusement of the girls.

    They continued to laugh, someone turned up the music and there was a knock at the door. Paige opened it to be met by a police officer. He said there were some complaints and they would have to keep the noise down. Paige apologized; the cop ignored Paige and peaked around the door. "What's going on in here?" He asked.

    Paige told him it was just a stagette and they would keep the noise down. The cop asked if there were any drugs in the room and radioed something into his walkie talkie and very quickly he was joined by two more cops. All 3 were tall, ripped men in tight uniforms. One of the men was a light skinned black man Paige thought was particularly hot because of his steel grey eyes. The cop that first knocked on the door asked if they could come in to look around. Paige said she would rather they didn't. The cop forced his way through the door almost knocking Paige down. "I'm sorry ma'am, I insist. We had a call and we have to do our duty." The three men stormed in and surrounded the girls. Everyone was silent, only the music broke the tension. One of the girls went to turn off the tunes when the black man told 0efully back into her chair the music turned from rock to a dance beat. The cop who had Tamara cuffed turned to his partners. "Frisk 'em boys." In unison the cops ripped open their shirts to the cheers of the girls. Only two girls knew about their special guests and they were very impressed with the guy's performance. They were hoping to get even more impressed very soon. The 'star' of the show kept his focus on Tamara while the other two men entertained the rest of the girls. Each girl had an opportunity to run their fingers down the men's six packs. Mel grabbed one guy's waistband and tried to sneak a peek but he backed away from her wagging his finger in a no motion. The other girls laughed at her failed attempt. Mel playfully pouted and sat back, taking a sip of her drink and waited for the rest of the show. As the first song ended, the men gathered in a line facing Tamara. Another song started and in unison their police belts fell to the floor and then they ripped their Velcro pants off and tossed them. They were each wearing the same styled thong, only in different colours. The girls on the couch and chairs only had a view of their perfectly shaped tight asses, Tamara's eyes widened as she looked back and forth between the three well endowed men. Giving her ample time to spectate, they spun around causing their mighty cocks to fly straight out and slap against their thigh. All the girls were suitably impressed. Mel, after taking a sip of her drink, which was getting stronger and stronger each time she got a refill simply said "Now THAT'S what I'm talkin' about."

The other girls gave a small applause. The star of the show turned around again and began giving Tamara a lap dance. The other two walked up and down the line of ladies letting them all see what they had to offer. Each girl reached out, some to touch their abs again, one or two slapped their tight butts but Mel, sitting pretty much in the middle waited until the guys were standing beside each other. She reached out to each man, placing her hand under their cocks and bounced them in her hand as if she was comparing them for weight, size and balance. "Hmm," was the only sound Mel made. Paige laughed; she was always amused by her antics. The other girls were also finding Mel quiet humorous. The guys took an immediate liking to her too, almost like they could sense one of their own. They two guys kept up their feeble attempt to dance, which mostly consisted of them shaking their ass and walking back and forth in front of the line of girls they guys started calling the wolf pack. The other guy was still focused on

Tamara; he put his feet on both sides of the chair and raised himself up so her face was lined up with his waist. He met her eyes and then directed them to his crotch. He told her to take off his thong. She said she would like to but she couldn't as she looked down at her shackled hands. The guy just looked back at her and made a biting motion. Tamara taking the hint leaned forward and took the waist band in her mouth. The guy did the rest. He continued to stand up and lean over her head until the thong slipped off his ass, he then backed away from Tamara letting his thong fall to the floor. The other dancers took their cue. They turned their backs on the wolf pack and pulled their thongs off, letting the girls see their asses. They applauded. They were impressed when the guys turned around; each one had a hammer of almost a foot long. The guys again walked back and forth in front of the girls allowing each one to poke prod and lick whatever they wanted. Each girl couldn't resist at least feeling the mammoth cocks in the hand. Tamara tried not to do anything to inappropriate electing to just stare; she was unable to touch anyway. The guy servicing Tamara moved behind her, he started whispering in her ear, he lowered his cock until it was touching her hand. Tamara opened her palm allowing the cock to slide up and down her hand until she gripped it firmly. "Very nice." She said.

"Thanks." He said as he quickly spun around to the front of the chair and danced a couple of paces in front of her. After all the other girls had their opportunity to visually molest the dancers, the guys gathered in front of Mel again. "Don't be shy." Paige said grabbing one of the mighty cocks and pressed the head against Mel's cheek. The other guy took Paige's cue and grabbed his own cock and brought it to Mel's face. She kissed the tip of each one before suddenly taking the black guys cock in her mouth. The girls intently looked on as they watched Mel not only perform oral sex on the man but they were very impressed she could make the foot long disappear. The man looked down, impressed he turned to the other girls "Oh, I see you have had your tonsils removed." He joked. The other guy still had his cock to Mel's face, Paige had her hand on the back of Mel's head forcing it even deeper onto the cock. Mel finally pulled away letting the cock fall to his knee. She turned to the other cock and offered it to Paige. Paige politely declined saying they were very nice but Holden's was enough for her. "Whatever, more for me," and then she laughed. Looking around at the other girls Mel asked "Anyone else care for a taste?" Mel could see that a couple of girls wanted to but were too shy to act on it or too embarrassed to follow Mel's expert deep throating. Mel, not wanting to make the poor guy feel neglected she put her hand at the base of the dancers cock and took him deep in her mouth. Paige cheered her on as she watched inch by inch slip down Mel's throat. Even Tamara struggled to watch Mel's performance. The guy giving Tamara his attention turned to her and whispered "Wow, girls got skills."

"No shit," Tamara replied.

"You know you could…" The guy began to say

"Nice try, not a chance." Tamara said laughing.

"Can't blame a guy for trying."

"Nope, I couldn't top that anyway."

The dancer turned around and continued dancing. He was rubbing his cock all over her chest and lap, dragging it up her bare knees and just under her skirt. Tamara took the antics in stride. She was even having a lot of fun and was mildly curious what a huge cock like that would feel like. Mel let the cock slide out of her mouth and reached up to her lips whipping the spit off with the back of her hand. "Okay, that was fun, now what we going to do?" The girls looked at the clock, as did the dancers. The dancers informed the girls their hour was up and if they wanted them to stay it would cost extra. The girls agreed the hour was enough, thanked them for their time as each girl slipped some cash into the guy's pants and told them where they'd be later in the night if they cared to join them. With that, the guys left and closed the door behind them. Tamara now free from her cuffs slapped the two girls responsible for the strippers on the shoulder. "Bitches." She said with a laugh. The girls gathered up their things and Tamara was forced to put on a white T shirt that each girl wrote something dirty on. Paige drew two large nipples. They gave Tamara a black marker and instructed her to get 100 names on the shirt before the end of the night. Confident they had everything, the girls headed out for their night of drunken mayhem. The bridesmaid called ahead to 10 different places saying they would be coming so they could get priority in line ups. Bars, which were always eager to have drunken women in their establishment gladly, obliged their requests. The first place had a huge line but the girls walked right past to the doorman who waved them all in and congratulated the bride to be as she passed by. The DJ saw the group enter and an announcement over the microphone. "Ladies and gentleman, I would like to congratulate Tamara on her upcoming wedding. If I could give you some advice, RUN. I kid, I kid, if any of you nice people would like to wish the bride to be well I'm sure she is taking gifts in the form of free drinks." Tamara was embarrassed at the extra attention the DJ just gave her but his words worked. A wave of guys rushed to the bar and brought the party drinks, each guy hoping to cash in on the girls decreased inhibitions. Each girl found a guy and they danced a couple of songs, Mel pushed her guy away as he was beginning to get too frisky and she grabbed Paige, stealing her from her dancing partner. "Mind if I cut in?" She said to no one in particular as she didn't care to hear a response. Mel got the rooms attention as she grabbed Paige's ass and pulled Paige into her thigh. They started grinding each other. Mel was breathing heavily onto Paige's neck. Tamara feeling left out joined the two girls. She pulled up her skirt allowing her legs more flexibility and entangled her legs in with Paige and Mel as they all began dancing. Every guy in the place watched on, jaws opened. As everyone lost track of time, the maid of honour announced to the party that it was time to move onto the next bar. Half the guys in the place wanted to know their schedule so they could meet up later but none of the girls would tell them.

The girls went to bar after bar, getting drunker. Tamara continued to collect names at each stop, while drinking from her penis cup. Although the original plan was to all head back to the hotel for more drinks and partying, the later the night went on, the drunker everyone got. The last bar was close to Paige's apartment, she and Mel decided to just walk back there at the end of the night. The place would be empty so they had all kinds of room to sleep.

Mike's gang all met for pre-drinks at a hotel. The room wasn't nearly as luxurious as the girls. The groomsman started talking a lot of flak from the guys for getting such a seedy room. "Don't worry guys, you won't be complaining for long," and as if on cue there was a knock on the door. "Ladies and gentlemen the entertainment has arrived." The best man rushed to the door and opened it for their guest. He was startled to see a woman that had to have been in her 50's escorted by a very large man with no neck. The man spoke up first. "This the Mike bachelor party?"

"Yes."

"200 dollars for the hour." The man with no neck said. Once the best man paid the bodyguard, the girl took her spot at center stage. The guys all glanced at each other assuming this was a joke before the real entertainment arrived. The dancer called up Mike as she pulled out a cheap wooden chair for him to sit on and once he was seated she straddled him. The guys all felt uncomfortable for Mike. As the music played the woman shed her clothes. She first exposed her aged breasts which sagged down to her belly button. "Do you want to touch them?" She asked Mike.

"Oh no, I'm good thanks. My fiancée would kill me."

"Oh, she isn't her and I won't tell." She said flashing Mike a smile with several teeth missing. Mike did his best to not cringe. He had never felt more uncomfortable. Next she pulled off her jeans and then her control topped panties. She laid on the floor putting her fingers on either side of her pussy and she spread it apart. Mike could only relate the experience to watching someone spread open a grilled cheese sandwich. The guys fought to hold back their laughter. The dancer then stood up and tried doing her dance routine. They all watching on as her loose skin flew uncontrollably in every direction. The straw that broke the camel's back was when she tried to do the splits. She made it about a quarter of the way to the floor and just fell over. They were amazed that not only did she try one and fail, but she tried over and over again to get the splits down. Finally, she stopped and nodded to her security before she disappeared into the side room. "Okay guys, for $50 you all get a private dance with the lady." The guys awkwardly looked at each other. Pete, acting as the spokesmen for the group, "I think we're good, but thank you for the offer." The guys started to let out their laughs. The security then tried to intimidate the guys into forking over more money. Pete finally had enough and reached into his back pocket pulled out his badge and told him that they were good. The girl hurriedly gathered her things and barely got dress before the two scrambled out of the room. The guys then turned to the best man. "What the hell were you thinking? NEVER go to discount escorts for a stag party you dopey bastard." They said, and began teasing him relentlessly, giving him idol threats that the night had better get much better or he was in trouble.

They cut their losses from the stripper and headed to a gentleman's club. They told every girl that would listen that it was Mike's bachelor party and each one sat and chatted with him. The odd girl even gave him a free dance. Finally the headliner came onstage, she called Mike out of the audience and sat him down on a chair, tied his arms behind his back and his feet to the legs of the chair. She then gave him the lap dance he was looking forward to in the hotel. Her perfect body and large implants rubbed over his body which made him hard. She noticed his erection and rubbed her tits on his cock over his jeans. She then turned around and sat on his lap, grinding her prefect ass into his crotch. The song ended marking the end of the show but before she left she called every girl on stage. They came up and one by one rubbed their tits on his head. It was very apparent Mike was in his glory on stage. He was sad as the last girl moved on; the headliner turned to Holden "Come get your guy off the stage." Holden laughed and contemplated leaving him up there. Mike looked at him with rescue me in his eyes. Holden finally gave in and went up on stage enduring the cat calls of all the other guys in the audience. He untied Mike and turned to the crowd and took a bow to even more applause. They watched a couple of more sets and bought Mike a couple of more lap dances. He told every girl that he talked to about the horrid stripper from the hotel. Most volunteered to come by after for a private show. Getting all worked up they decided it was a good time to head to the bar. The old married guys from the party scattered as the party moved to actual dance bars. The bridesmaid and the best man made sure they booked reservations at separate bars so they wouldn't have to worry about running into each other. The bars the best man got were all seedy dives full of cougars. The night was slowly making a turn for the worse. They had a couple of drinks in each place, the last place on the list was a decent dance bar but it was close to the end of the night and it was starting to clear out. Pete, Andrew and Jeff were frustrated they didn't have a chance to pick up. The guys reminded Jeff he still had Mel, who they were meeting up with for breakfast. As the lights of the bar turned on, the guys decided to go home instead of back to the hotel. Assuming Holden's place was empty, between the spare room, the couch and the inflatable bed, there was more than enough room for all the guys.

Holden opened the door to the apartment and the guys followed him in. Holden grabbed them all a beer as Pete claimed the spare room. He opened the door and was startled to see a naked Mel sleeping on the bed. She looked at him; she didn't bother to cover up. "Taken." Was all she said before rolling over and falling back asleep.

"Can't we share? I don't bite." Pete said playfully. Mel just got up, walked past Pete and into Paige's room and slammed the door behind her. The guys could hear the girls talking in the next room. Pete came back into the living room and told him what happened. Holden was surprised the girls were home so he went into the bedroom. He saw Mel cuddled up next to Paige who was also sleeping sans clothes. He temporarily had some very bad thoughts run through his head. "Hey honey what's up?" Paige asked.

"Just got home, what you doing here? How was your night?" Holden asked.

"Good, we'll talk in the morning, can you make room for the guys?"

"Ya, Pete can have the spare room, I'll take the couch and Andrew and Jeff can share the inflatable bed, you two can stay put in here."

"Cool, night."

T-shirt and tiny cotton shorts. She sat on the couch and cuddled up next to Holden. She told them about the girl's night, leaving out crucial details. Mel slept for another few hours before Paige told Jeff to go wake her up then she winked at him. Not needing much urging, Jeff went into the bedroom where they stayed for over half an hour but no one could hear any "commotion" coming from the next room. Finally they walked into the living room, Mel looked very rough, her long blond hair was messed up, her shirt hung off her small frame like it was 3 sizes too big and under the shirt she was only wearing her boy cut shorts.

After everyone finally got showered and dressed, they all went for lunch and a walk around Vancouver. Mel had a late night flight back home so she wanted to see as much of the city as she could.

After the tour of the city it was time to take Mel to the airport, Jeff and the boys volunteered to accompany Holden, Paige and Mel. Holden could see right through Jeff's offer but he wasn't about to cock block him so he let him come. Jeff escorted Mel to the security gate but before she disappeared into the line, she reached into her pocket and handed Jeff a piece of paper. He slipped the note into his pocket and gave her a hug before she turned to leave. After they left the airport, Holden and Paige dropped the three guys off at the hotel that they booked for the week. It was the same hotel Paige and Holden stayed at their first few nights in the city. Holden took the week off to act as tour guide, Paige was happy that she had a busy week of classes ahead, she didn't want to spend the week in and out of hooters and various strip clubs.

The week sailed by, the four friends spent every day out and about seeing the sites and touring different bars. The day of the wedding finally arrived and the three Ontarioians planned to head home the next day. As sad as Holden would be to see them go, his liver couldn't wait.

Holden started to get dressed in his suit and Paige was taking her time in the bathroom. She yelled to Holden that she would be a few minutes and told him to go into the living room and have a beer. Not needing further incentive Holden strolled into the kitchen to grab a beer then he turned on the TV. Nothing special was on but it did the trick to kill time. After about 20 minutes Holden could hear Paige walk down the hallway, he looked at his angel dressed up. She was wearing fishnet nylons under a very sexy short black dress that showed just a hint of cleavage. Holden looked at her and he knew he wanted her very badly. Paige smiled reading Holden's thoughts, she looked into his eyes and said "not yet tiger." Before they left, Holden put on his dress shoes, which were his black leather chuck tailors. Paige laughed at the contrast between the expensive suit Holden was wearing and his chucks. As Holden was putting on his shoes, Paige moved close to him and bent at the waist to put on her Mary Janes. As she bent over her skirt rode up her thigh, completely unintentionally she claimed. Holden could see that the fishnets she was wearing were thigh highs attached to a garter which she knew was his kryptonite. She smiled a coy little smile as she caught him in her peripheral vision. Holden was frozen staring at her exposed leg and garter belt. Paige finally stood up with a devilish grin and asked "something wrong?" Holden snapped out of his trance, grabbed Paige threw her up against the wall. He lifted her skirt up to expose her panties. Paige reached down and began rubbing his throbbing cock through his dress pants as they began to kiss passionately. Paige then turned and threw Holden against the wall still rubbing his cock. Then she pushed him away and said "not now slugger, we're going to be late." She then walked out the door giggling as she left him with a what the fuck look on his face. Holden gathering himself together and quickly joined Paige outside.

The wedding was very small and intimate. Andrew, Jeff and Pete sat next to Holden and Paige. Holden caught all of his friends checking out Paige, it made him proud, he knew she looked hotter than hot. They also made fun of Mike standing up in front of the justice of the peace. The organ began to play "here comes the bride," and Pete yelled out "run!" To Mike, he laughed and Andrew hit him across the chest "shut up." The group all laughed at Pete. As Tamara walked by she glanced over at Pete. "Ass, if anyone's running it's me," she said. The group broke out in laughter; Mike who missed the exchange looked at Holden. "What?" He mouthed. Holden just shrugged his shoulders like he had no idea what was going on. Tamara finally reached Mike and the J.P. started the intimate ceremony. Paige gripped Holden's hand tightly as she put her head on his shoulder. Holden even caught Paige shedding a tear. Finally, the J.P. finished, the newly married couple kissed to the cheers of the crowd. Everyone in attendance left the building and headed to the dance hall where they were expecting a much bigger gathering.

At the reception, Paige and Holden found a seat and talked to the few mutual friends they shared with Mike and Tamara. Andrew, Pete and Jeff took seats near the bar where a couple of attractive young waitresses were working. Holden slid his hand into Paige's which was daintily folded on her lap. He began to casual rub her garter to remind Paige that he did indeed remember what she was wearing and that she still owed him for her quick exit earlier. She stood up, kissed Holden on the cheek and excused herself from the table and headed to the ladies room. She came back when one of their favourite songs started to play. She reached out to grab Holden's hand and said let's dance. Holden took her hand and he quickly realized it wasn't empty. He looked down as she shoved her hand in his pocket. Curious, he reached in to see what she just slipped him. Whatever it was, it was damp. It didn't take him long to realize she slipped him her panties. Laughing, she grabbed his hand and led him to the dance floor. The lights were almost off except for a single mirrored ball. Holden held Paige close, close enough even air couldn't get between them. Holden ran his hand up her back and squeezed her even closer. She responded by burying her head into his shoulder. His free hand was gently caressing her neck and hair. As if by magic the packed dance floor seemed to have emptied, Paige and Holden felt as if they were alone in the room. As the song ended, he hugged her as tight as he could without hurting her; neither of them wanted the song to end. Holden looked deep into Paige's eyes. "I love you," he said. The words have never meant more to him. Paige smiled a very sweet smile and pushed her hips into his hardening cock to tease him once again before they returned to their seats. More songs played, Holden danced with Tamara congratulating the bride, Paige danced with Mike. Pete, Andrew and Jeff all had their dance with Tamara and Paige. Pete even danced with each of the waitresses. The night started to wind down and Paige and Holden said their goodbyes to the newlyweds and asked the 3 boys what their plans were for the night. They said they were invited to an after party that the wait staff were attending.

Holden wished them luck as he and Paige headed out. Holden couldn't get home fast enough. They held hands in the cab in the entire way home. Both of them drifted off into their own little worlds, Holden was thinking about what he was about to do to Paige. Paige thought about the wedding, she imagined her own wedding then thought about the pregnant girl she met on the bus. She also thought about what Mel said to her, about her past. A thousand thoughts a minute were racing through her mind, she also thought about Holden and how badly she wanted him just then. The cab stopped, Holden threw a handful of money at the driver and Paige pushed Holden out of the car. As she did her skirt rode up giving the cab driver an unsuspecting peak at her perfect ass and her garter. They finally got inside and she was now in his arms. They were kissing as they were walking. His tie came off, she ripped open his shirt and buttons flew everywhere. Paige starred at Holden's muscular chest as she ran her fingers down his abs. She bit her lip as she backed away. "Can I get you a drink?" She asked.

"Uh, I thought we were in the middle of something?"

"In time." She then went to the kitchen and poured them both a glass of wine. "Here drink up," Paige instructed Holden. "I'm going to change into something more comfortable." With her wine glass in hand, she ran into the bedroom. Holden sat on the couch and turned on the TV, flipping through his DVDs to see which would be the perfect one to watch when Paige finally returned.

Several minutes later Holden heard Paige yell with a sense of urgency, "Holden, come here a minute." Holden ran into the bedroom. He saw that Paige lit several candles all around the room and she had some classical piano playing on their CD player. She was lying on the bed seductively wearing only her fishnet nylons and garter belt. On her chest with edible sex paint she wrote I love you, substituting the shape of a heart for the word love and a U for you. The U was in her pubic area. Holden paused for a moment, taking in the sights and smells. Paige looked gorgeous lying on the bed lit up by the flickering candles. Paige tapped the bed beside her. "Come here big boy," she said in a whisper. Holden scrambled out of his suit as fast as humanly possible and joined Paige on the bed. He reached under her chin and put his hand on her ear. They leaned into each other and began to kiss. Paige rolled over carefully trying not to smudge her art work. Their kiss was long, deep and passionate. After the kiss they began to talk. They told each other how much they loved each other; they talked about the wedding and fantasized about theirs if they ever got married. Paige brought up the pregnant girl on the bus and how beautiful she looked. They also talked about their future hopes and dreams. When there was a pause in the conversation Holden kissed Paige's luscious lips then moved down her cheek and kissed her ear. After kissing it and softly blowing in it for some time he let out a very faint whisper "I love you." He then put his finger on the edge of the heart and brought the sticky strawberry candy to his tongue. "Yummy," he said. Paige smiled at how playful Holden was being. "Well, there is more where that came from," She said looking down at her body. Holden looked at Paige and rolled his eyes. "Oh okay, if I must," he said with a big smile. He then repositioned himself between her legs, up far enough so that his chest was pressing against her pussy with his face directly above the U. With small gentle flicks of his tongue he licked it off her freshly shaven mound. Each gentle touch drove Paige crazy, she wanted him inside her badly but it was her game and she was going to see it out until the end. Holden was in wonderland, his two favorite things, candy and a naked Paige; both of them were just a tongue stroke away.

With the U gone Holden slid up Paige's body even further so his stomach was now firmly between her legs. He could feel the fishnets rubbing his sides and it was driving him crazy but he persisted on. He started at the bottom of the heart and with one long lick he traced it to the top. He left a long sticky trail behind, one he was only too happy to clean up. As he began to, his fingers dug firmly into Paige's hips. Paige put her hands over her head to grip the headboard ensuring Holden had complete access to her body. Holden's tongue flickered and danced its way up her hard abs, tickling Paige along the way. Satisfied that that half of the heart was cleaned up as much as possible he repositioned himself once again, this time he was lying perpendicular to her body. His hand reached under her thigh so the side of his palm could occasionally graze her pussy. His chest was resting in the sticky mess that used to be the first half of the heart. This time Holden used small kisses to pull the candy gel off her chest. His full lips softly caressed her stomach. She wanted to reach out to grab his cock and massage it until she could feel his own candy treat in her hand but she resisted, knowing it would be hers very shortly. He slowly moved up her stomach, the small kisses did their job and all the gel from the heart was gone. When he was finished he leaned back to look into Paige's eyes and licked his lips. "Delicious," he said and then he once again repositioned himself so that he was lying parallel to Paige. She was flat on her back; he was on his side tucked in tight to Paige. She could feel his cock pressed against her hips. He reached his hand across her stomach to the side of her left breast. He used his chest and hand to push her tits together. They both looked down at her cleavage. "Very nice," Holden said.

"Ya, if only you could follow me around all day holding them like that, I might do better at school." She laughed.

"I wish," was Holden's reply.

"You wish I was doing better in school?" Paige shot back

"No I wish I could…HEYYYY." Holden said as he saw the smirk on Paige's face. He then turned his attention to the I. When he let go of her tits he saw that the I squished between them leaving residue on each breast. Holden used his tongue to quickly clean them off, making sure he gave each nipple a kiss. He then lied back and used his right index finger to collect all the remaining candy from the I. As the red gooey substance began to drip from his finger he slowly brought it Paige's lips.

She dutifully opened her mouth to accept the candy treat and let out a very long seductive "mmmmm," as she began sucking Holden's finger. Once she was willing to give his finger back to him he crawled on top of his princess. She could feel the head of his cock pressing against her and it was very close to penetrating her. She wanted him to give it to her hard, but she didn't want to spoil the anticipation for either of them. Holden was now resting on his elbows so he didn't crush her. He put his hands by her ears and brushed the hair off them as he gently kissed them. He purposely pushed his chest into Paige's, because he loved the feel of her small breasts against his skin. Still leaning into Paige's ear he let out a small cat purr. She laughed because the vibration tickled her ear and the sound was unexpected. "Oh you're an animal." Paige said between her laughs. Holden enjoyed being called an animal so he let out a small roar in her ear. He sounded less like the king of the jungle and more like baby Simba discovering his first roar. Paige began laughing even louder; she then used the distraction to roll over so she was now lying on top of Holden. It was her turn to lean in and kiss Holden. She gave him a series of small pecks on the lips. She then straddled his stomach as she leaned over to the bedside table and picked up the paint. "Your turn." Paige dipped her finger into the paint and brought a dap to her extended tongue and with a curl of the tongue she lapped up the oozing mess. She then began to paint Holden. She dabbed a small amount on both his nipples and drew an arrow down to his cock. With a big finger full, she ran her digit down his cock between the beads of his piercings. Starting with his nipples she gently used her teeth to bite them and pull the candy paint off. For the other nipple she wrapped her mouth around it and began sucking until the candy was all gone. Then, copying Holden she used small kisses at the top of the arrow until she got half way. She then slid down his body and used her tongue to lick up the arrow. With only the two points left she put her tongue flat against his hard body and dragged it across his stomach until it was all gone. Proud of her job, she was very happy knowing that she could now concentrate on the only remaining paint left which was on his penis. She was now between his legs and her face was only an inch from his cock. Her hand reached around his leg and grabbed the base of his cock. She did the same trick as she did with the ends of the arrows. She flattened her tongue on his cock and licked up. Although she got a good mouth full of the paint, there was some remaining. She opened her mouth and lowered it down around his shaft. Once she had the entire length in her mouth, she used her tongue to clean the rest of him off. Her tongue was like magic to him. He didn't know how much he could take but he soon found out. She popped up so that she was kneeling between his legs. She used her finger to collect the spit and paint that formed on the corners of her lips. "All done, nice and clean." She said with a smile. "I'm going to shower to get this stickiness off me." She crawled off the bed and walked towards the bathroom. Looking down at his cock, he asked "What the hell?"

Holden could hear the shower start and after just a couple of seconds he heard Paige yell for him once again. "Care to join me?" Without hesitation he ran into the bathroom. She was standing in the tub with the water running down her body, the curtain was wide open and she was still wearing the garter and thigh highs. She grabbed the soap and slowly lathered herself up; her eyes never once left Holden's. Holden watched on intently, not saying a word. Instead he stood there with his mouth gapping. Once Paige had all the soap lathered on her body, she began rubbing it in concentrating on her tits and pussy. Confident she was clean she turned around; water was spraying everywhere, causing a big puddle on the bathroom floor. It was a small price to pay Holden thought. Paige lathered up her ass, then bending at the waist she worked her hand up between her legs. Her fingers worked in and around her pussy causing the view to become very obscured by the bubbles. With teasing phase two complete, she turned around and slowly unclasped the thigh highs, pulling each stocking slowly down her leg and tossing the wet garments at Holden. Each hit him with a slapping sound. Holden just let the first one fall to the floor and the second one hung over his shoulder. She finally removed her garter and tossed it with much more care towards Holden. She was worried the straps and buckles would make him lose an eye or knock out a tooth. The garter fell well short of Holden. Paige, now completely undressed quickly closed the shower curtain; she extended her hand and gave Holden the come here signal with her finger. Holden paused, trying to create doubt into Paige's mind as to whether or not he was going to join her. Of course, he did. Paige wrapped her arms around his neck and kissed him. "I love you so much," she said. Holden, gripping her hips squeezed her tightly against him "I know baby, I love you too." Paige jumped up, wrapped her legs around Holden, Holden slammed her against the shower wall and slowly slide his now very worked up cock inside her. As he began thrusting into her, she reached up, grabbed the shower head off the holder and positioned it under her leg and focused the stream of water up into them. The spray of the warm water against Holden's balls and ass put him over the top. He cam hard inside her. Paige felt him filling her up as she moved the shower head between their stomachs so the stream was focused onto her clit. Holden, realizing Paige wasn't done yet, did his best to keep his cock hard and continued to fuck her. He began biting her neck. Paige was pressing the showerhead hard against her clit which set off her orgasm. She dropped the showerhead; it swung back and forth inside the shower spraying water everywhere. Paige reached around grabbing Holden's muscular ass and pulled it tight towards her, hoping to get his now flaccid cock further inside her, to no avail. Holden lowered Paige until her bare toes touched the porcelain. Their grip on each other loosened as they leaned it kissing each other deeply. All the while Holden's cum was coursing their way deeper inside Paige.

11

As their one year anniversary approached, Holden began teasing Paige with hints of his special plans for the evening. Paige's mind began to wander. Although it has only been one year, they went through a lot as a couple. With the excitement of Tamara and Mike's last minute wedding, Paige's thoughts began to drift to her own wedding and she convinced herself Holden was going to propose on their anniversary. She even told her mom and Tamara what she was thinking. Everyone was excited for her.

She dressed up in a nice black form fitting dress and her Mary Jane shoes. Holden put on a nice shirt and tie with a fun sport coat he purchased earlier in the week. They arrived at the restaurant. Neither had been to that particular restaurant before but it had the reputation of being the nicest in town. Holden had to use some recently made connections to even get a reservation. If first impressions meant anything the establishment was well worth its reputation. Behind the large solid oak doors was the lobby complete with a wall sized fountain, a handsome man in a tuxedo standing behind a small podium and classical music playing softly in the back ground. As the couple walked in the Maitre D greeted them and asked their names. After verifying the reservations he turned and showed them to their table. Holden and Paige became very giddy as they got caught up in the ambiance of the classy establishment. They tried to hide their excitement and pretended they were well accustomed to such places. Holden held out his elbow so Paige could slide her arm through his as they followed the Maitre D.

He finally stopped at a very beautiful and private corner table overlooking the ocean. He pulled out Paige's chair and gentle pushed it in as she took her seat. He then turned to the already seated Holden and after unfolding the napkin he laid it out in Holden's lap, much to Holden's surprise. Paige laughed at Holden's expression. Once they were settled Paige began looking all over the table for anything that might be out of the ordinary. Seeing nothing that may contain a diamond, Paige convinced herself that the "surprise" would come with dessert. Over the next couple of hours the two enjoyed their dinner and several glasses of wine. As they talked, the only time their gaze broke lock was when they looked out the window to enjoy the tremendous view. It was a beautiful night with a gentle breeze that caused the waves to crash against the beach. The hypnotic sounds of the ocean held their attention for some time. Once the last of the wine was drunk, the waiter brought them some coffee along with a dessert menu. Holden took his time ordering and the anticipation was now killing Paige. What was the big surprise Holden had in store for her she wondered? Finally, Holden ordered something for the two of them to share. Paige's legs became weak with nerves, she was getting very excited. The dessert was delivered and they began to eat, once it was gone there was still nothing. The waiter came around and asked if there was anything else. Not wanting to leave right away Holden ordered two glasses of champagne and he made sure to point out to the waiter that they were celebrating their anniversary. Paige began to get her hopes up once again. When the drinks arrived the waiter informed them that the champagne was on the house with their compliments. Holden and Paige tapped glasses to cheers their year together. Holden was amused when he caught Paige looking hard into her glass, her look of disappointment wasn't lost on him. They sipped their drinks and as the last drop was downed, Holden gave the waiter his credit card, signed the slip and the pair was off. Paige, despite the fantastic meal and the great ambiance, felt the dinner was a bit anti climatic. On the way to their car, Paige suggested a movie. Holden told her he was too tired and that they should just head back to the apartment, reluctantly Paige agreed. Then it struck Paige, maybe the surprise was really waiting for her at the apartment.

 Paige didn't even wait for the car to be turned off. She bounced out of the car and headed for the door. Holden purposely took his time walking to the door with his keys in hand. Looking up at Paige he asked her what her problem was and then asked her if she had to pee. Paige just told him to shut up and open the door. Not being one to argue, Holden obliged. Paige ran into the apartment to look around. She didn't see anything out of the ordinary nor did she notice that Holden disappeared into the bedroom for a minute then rejoined her. Holden stood behind Paige, wrapped his arms around her waist and kissed her neck. She leaned back against him and thanked him for a wonderful dinner and a wonderful year. Holden squeezed her tightly and returned the sentiment. Holden then asked Paige if she was ready for her surprise. Paige tried to turn around to face him but his grip on her tightened to hold her securely in place. Paige wasn't sure what the surprise could be but she was sure there was nothing in the living room for her. Holden reached into his pocket and pulled out a mask which he slipped over her head. Paige was really becoming unsure of what he had in store. Holden asked Paige if she trusted him, she of course said she did. Leading her by the hand, he escorted her into the bedroom. She felt the bed at her knee and she started to lower herself but Holden stopped her. Holden slowly unzipped her dress then slid it if off her shoulders, down her body and to the floor. Paige didn't want to show any lines under her tight dress so she elected not to wear a bra or panties to dinner. She was now standing at the foot of the bed blindfolded and completely naked. Holden wrapped his arm around her waist as he kissed her shoulder and asked if she was okay. Paige smiled and gave him a nod as Holden slid his hand down her tight stomach which sent shivers through her as he gently touched her. Holden carefully guided her to the bed then he paused to look at his beautiful girlfriend. Paige wasn't sure where Holden was and her mind started to wander as she began to think of him staring at her. She started to anticipate what he was going to do to her, what part of her body his eyes were looking at and what he was currently doing. She could hear him fumbling with something across the room. She wasn't sure what it was until she felt the fibers of the rope slide over her hand and wrist until her arm was restrained above her head. She could hear him walking around the bed to work on her other arm. After her arms were secured she could feel him pull on her legs, one at a time tying them up so they were spread open. Once the last knot was tied and Holden was satisfied she couldn't move, he stood up to appreciate his work. She couldn't hear him nor could she feel him and she definitely couldn't see him but she could feel his eyes burning into her naked vulnerable body. She could hear sounds of what she guessed to be Holden taking off his clothes but that was mere speculation. Paige was now eager to have Holden touch her in a way only he could. Holden moved around the bed so she could only feel small grazes of his touch. His fingers ever so softly ran up her thigh and caressed her stomach to her now heaving breasts, at the same time she could feel his breath on her neck moving down her body past her nipple until she felt the touch of his tongue on her pussy. She didn't know when or where the next touch would be but she wanted it soon. She was already very wet and in need of release. Paige tensed as Holden's tongue met her clit. Holden took one, maybe two very hard licks the entire length of her pussy. Paige begged Holden to fuck her, "In time." Holden responded. She then felt his body slide up hers. Paige felt Holden's nipple ring slide past her own nipple at the same time she felt his cock pressing against her pussy but was helpless to guide it into her. She didn't say anything but she moved around as best she could to get him inside her but he wasn't cooperating. Holden whispered that he was in control. Paige took the hint and stopped moving as she felt his hand move towards his cock to aid it in penetrating her. First his head slipped inside her then she felt the familiar feeling of the piercings. Just as Holden started to get a good rhythm going, the doorbell rang. At first Paige was upset by the unwelcome intrusion until Holden stopped fucking her, whispered in her ear. "Right on time." He got up; she could hear him put on some clothes and the last thing she could hear was Holden say "Don't go anywhere." She then heard his footsteps run down the hall. Paige was now nervous but still very horny. She could hear Holden outside the bedroom talking to an unfamiliar voice. The bedroom door opened and panic set in as she realized there was now a 3rd person in the room. She moved the best she could to cover herself up but to no avail. Holden could see the discomfort in her face so he sat down next to her, whispered in her ear "do you trust me?" Paige seemed hesitant to answer so he simply said "This is for you, enjoy but if you aren't comfortable, tell me and we can stop it right now." They have talked about 3somes before, more of a fantasy something neither expected to really take place. She was upset that Holden didn't consult her first but she did have the fantasy regularly and she also really needed to be satisfied. Since she trusted Holden completely she nodded, giving him the okay to proceed. Her mind then started spinning, she started working herself up at the endless possibilities of what the evening had in store. Who was the 3rd person she wondered, she was pretty confident it was a guy but did she know him? The questions running around her head disappeared when she felt the first set of hands touch her body. She wasn't sure if they were Holden's or the mysterious other person but they were definitely male hands. They began to work from her knee to her thigh and to her pussy. Music started, it was a bit loud, Paige could barely hear what was going on in the room but she could definitely feel it. She felt the weight of a person on the bed beside her head which startled her. When a cock touched her lips she could feel the piercings so she knew it was Holden in her mouth, meaning the hands on her pussy had to belong to the stranger. Paige opened her mouth and accepted Holden's very hard cock into it. She began to suck him while he leaned over and began playing with her tits as the stranger explored inside her. Over the music, she could barely make out Holden saying "beautiful pussy isn't it?" She couldn't hear the stranger's response but by the more energetic fingering she knew he agreed. Holden pulled his cock out of her mouth and twisted around as the mystery man pulled his hand out of her pussy. Holden kissed her lips. "I love you, ok." Paige, still very hesitant let her imagination and curiosity get the best of her. "I love you too." Was all she said. Holden crawled off the bed; Paige heard some commotion in the background. The thought of two men staring at her helpless naked body, both waiting to fuck her was eating her up, she wanted to be ravished. Then she could feel knees on the other side of her head and then a cock press up against her lips. She wasn't sure what to do until she heard Holden reassure her that it was going to be great. She spread her lips hoping to once again feel the metal of Holden's cock but as it got deeper and deeper inside her mouth there was no piecing. She felt guilty at first because it was the first cock, besides Holden's, she tasted since they started dating. All doubt was removed when she felt Holden's cock sink inside her, very quickly and very forcefully. She was surprised because she didn't feel Holden move between her legs. With Holden fucking her with extra intensity, she knew he was enjoying watching her suck someone else's dick, which in turn made her put more of an effort into pleasuring the cock in her mouth. She wondered what she could do with both her hands tied above her head. Holden fucked her harder and harder which brought Paige closer to orgasm. She felt Holden pull out of her and cum across her stomach, she still continued to suck the strangers cock. She knew with Holden finished he was watching her suck the cock and she wanted to put on a good show for him, knowing it was her show that made him cum quicker than normal. Even though she was flattered she was also annoyed, she still needed to get off. Holden knew he didn't make her cum and he wasn't about to let her down. She could hear Holden tell the other man it was his turn to fuck her. Paige was reluctant to let the stranger penetrate her but she had no time to object before he was between her legs and fucking her hard. Paige enjoyed the feeling of the other man's cock inside her, being tied up, the helpless feeling and fucking 2 guys at once made her feel so dirty. She liked exploring her dirty side and she loved that Holden encouraged her to do so but she still felt guilty regardless. She felt 2 hands grab her tits, she wasn't sure who's they were until she heard Holden speak. "Do you like his cock? Does it feel good? Tell him how good his cock is." Paige let out a guilty moan as she was about to cum, she didn't want to, she didn't want to cum for the stranger, she wanted to save it for Holden but she had no choice. She couldn't hold back, she felt Holden's teeth gently clench her nipple as he bit into her. The unsuspecting pain allowed her mind to clear and she began to orgasm. She began to vibrate and she cam hard, very hard, the man inside her didn't lose a beat. He continued to pound her making her orgasm that much more intense. Once she was done, she heard a moan and then she could feel the strange cock inside her release, filling her pussy with his cum. Once the adrenaline began to subside she began to feel even guiltier. All kinds of bad thoughts ran through her mind, what if this guy had something or what if he made her pregnant, she was mad at him for thinking he could cum inside her. Holden leaned in and hugged her, he told her he loved her and thanked her for keeping such an open mind. Holden slowly started to untie her, legs first then the arms. Once she had a free arm she tried to rip off her blind fold but Holden stopped her. "Wait, you ready to meet the guy that was nice enough to join us on our special occasion?" Feeling embarrassed but curious she really wanted to meet the mystery man that just pleasured her so wonderfully. Holden removed her blindfold, shyly she looked around the room but she didn't see anyone. She wondered where he went; she knew he didn't have time to leave. She looked at Holden in bewilderment "Where is he?" Holden just smiled and pulled out a dildo she had never seen before. It was a replica of Holden's cock, complete with piercings. She was still confused, Holden tried to make her understand. He played a recording of some voices he made earlier in the week. She asked who was at door. Holden told her there was a pizza waiting in the kitchen if she was hungry. Holden then directed her eyes to the nightstand where she could see his 3 piercings. He then filled in the rest, how the blindfold and music were designed to disorientate her, he then told her how he planted a couple of small details and let her mind fill in the rest. Paige loved the effort Holden put into her surprise, she also had to laugh at the thought of Holden making the replica toy. The two went into the living room, snuggled up naked in front of the TV and watched an old Marx brother's movie.

They woke up the next morning, spooning on the couch. Neither of them were feeling too great from the wine and champagne from their dinner so they both just stayed on the couch until lunch time. Paige was the first to move, she rolled off the couch and barely avoided falling onto the floor. Holden wanted to laugh but the urge to not move was greater.

Paige stood; Holden stared at her naked body. She didn't say anything; she just walked to the bathroom and jumped in the shower.

Over the next few days Holden noticed a change in Paige, she was becoming more distant. Holden tried to talk to her about it but she just brushed him off saying it was nothing. Holden asked her if she wanted to go home for a visit or if she wanted her parents or sister to come visit them. She said having her sister there would be fun. Holden knew she was getting stressed with school and she had to have been getting home sick so having her sister there might be the thing to cheer her up. He called Paige's parents and set everything up. With school getting out for the summer, the timing was perfect. Holden even discussed the possibility of Chelsea coming and working at the rink selling tickets or something for the summer. Paige, even though she loved her sister thought that much time together would be too much. Holden didn't argue. He was on the phone with Paige's mom who thought the visit was a great idea. Holden knew she just liked the idea of having a spy to check up on everything. She also told Holden that Chelsea's birthday was coming up in a week so the timing couldn't be more perfect.

Holden bought the ticket and before they knew it they were at the airport waiting for her flight. The two sisters greeted each other with a hug. Holden simply said "hey." Since Chelsea had never been out west before Holden took the two girls for a drive around town. They showed her the main tourist sites and the arena they both worked at. They also drove Chelsea to Paige's university before they finally made it back to the apartment. Holden carried Chelsea's bags into their home. They were heavy and he was wondering exactly how long she planned to stay. Paige informed Holden that a woman needed to pack for all possibilities and accessories for those possibilities.

Holden had to work the whole week but since he took a week off for Mike's wedding and Paige just finished a grueling semester of school she took the week off to entertain her sister. Tamara had to work most of the week but managed to scam that Friday off. Paige made reservations for Thursday night, they were going to go out too cut loose with just the girls.

Paige showed Chelsea around the apartment while Holden fired up the BBQ. When Holden looked back into the apartment from his smoke filled balcony, he saw that the drinking had already begun, Chelsea was holding a beer and Paige was sitting next to her, drinking what looked like a rum and coke. Holden stayed out on the balcony watching the meat and enjoying the view. After a few minutes of girl talk, they joined Holden out on the balcony. Paige handed him a beer for which Holden was grateful. Chelsea admired the view. It was a beautiful night, not a cloud in the sky and the sun was setting behind the furthest most mountain range. Holden ran back into the apartment and brought out an extra chair. The three sat down as their supper cooked. Chelsea told them about her new boyfriend. One her mother doesn't know about. Holden and Paige laughed at the fact she was worried to tell her mom then Chelsea dropped the bomb that she wouldn't be sure her mom would like her dating one of her teachers. Holden casually said that was one way to get good grades then took a sip of his beer. Paige hit him across the chest. "CHELSEA, what are you thinking? Is he married? How old is he?"

"NO, he isn't married and he is only 28 and hot."

"You're only 18…." "19 in 2 days." Chelsea interrupted.

"So, it's still 10 years older than you."

"Ya, but he's hot and is great in bed."

"I don't want to hear that."

"Here, look at his picture."

"Oh he is hot," Paige said and handed the picture to Holden.

Holden reluctantly grabbed the picture; he managed to stay out of the argument until then. He looked and said "well damn, he is hot, I'd do him," and passed the picture back to Paige and took another much bigger gulp of his beer as he tried not to laugh. Paige looked at him "you're not helping."

"Not trying too. Seriously, what's the big deal, she's graduated so technically he isn't her teacher anymore, he has a job and things could be worse, he could be a drummer." Holden said mockingly.

"Ya, true, well whatever, as long as you're happy," Paige said.

"Well thank you," Chelsea said looking appreciatively at Holden.

Dinner was cooked to perfection, according to Holden. After dinner Holden didn't want to waste a beautiful night so they drove Chelsea to the water front where they walked around the board walk. It seemed like everyone in Vancouver was thinking the same thing, the boardwalk was full of activity. There was a young man leaning up against a tree playing the saxophone, they all had to stop and watch. He played amazingly. Holden gladly tipped the musician $10. The man, not missing a note, nodded to Holden and the girls before they turned and moved on. There were also some carnival style games lined up on the board walk complete with the hustlers trying to bait Holden into spending his money to win cheap prizes for his women. Holden resisted despite being teased by Paige and Chelsea for being cheap and scared. Holden instead led them to an ice cream truck. They all got vanilla soft serve and after Holden paid he turned and ran into the Witch Doctors goalie. He was taking a late night skate along the board walk. Holden introduced the star goalie to Chelsea, Paige and he had already met on several occasions. The goalie was only 20 and despite being a remarkable goalie he was social awkward. Normally the clown in the dressing room he clamed right up when he saw Chelsea. Holden and Paige continued to talk to him; Chelsea quietly ate her ice cream. Holden tried to get Kurt into a conversation with Chelsea but he didn't take the bait. Finally he bashfully looked up at Chelsea, their eyes met. Kurt put his finger to his lip and told her she had some ice cream. Chelsea, being Paige's sister looked hard back into his eyes and slowly and deliberately licked the vanilla from her lips. Paige laughed at her sisters antics. Kurt just blushed and stopped talking. Finally Holden let him off the hook and told him that they should move on and invited him to join them but he knew he wouldn't. Kurt told them he was just about done his skate and was heading home. Holden couldn't wait to get back to work to let the team in on the story. They walked around the boardwalk and neighbouring park for an hour before they decided to head back to the apartment.

Once they got there, the two girls went out to the balcony; Holden joined them with three beers. Paige turned him down. Holden and Chelsea looked at her and gave her a hard time, Holden put the extra beer beside him and told Chelsea it was up for grabs for the first one done. Taking him up on the challenge they raised their bottles and had a chugging contest. Paige was the unbiased judge. Holden won hands down but still tossed the beer to the runner up for her valiant effort. Holden turned on the entertainment system and cranked some tunes while he went in for another beer. He asked Paige if she was okay when she just requested a can of coke. Holden asked if she wanted some rye in her coke. Paige again turned him down. He shrugged and went for the drinks.

Holden turned in early because he had to get up for work but the two girls sat on the balcony well into the morning. Holden could occasionally hear them giggling over the music playing in the living room but still managed to sleep over all the noise.

The next day while Holden was hard at work sharing the freak meeting with Kurt on the boardwalk, the girls spend the day downtown leaving no mall unturned. They went to a patio bar for lunch and enjoyed the ocean spray in the warm summer sun. When Holden left work he was walking to the parking garage when he heard the sound of thunder coming up behind him, before he could turn and get out of the way he was tackled by two over hyper sisters both of which were carrying their weight in shopping bags. They looked helplessly at Holden as they begged for a ride home. Holden contemplated if he was going to let the girls in the car with him, Chelsea grabbed him securing his arms behind his back while Paige dove into his pockets to swipe the car keys. She dangled them in the air "you don't have a choice now, Chelsea, should we let him come home with us or should he take the bus?" The timing couldn't have been better, Mike walked behind Paige and ripped the keys out of her hand and tossed them back to Holden. "There ya go man, I suggest the bus for them and their little bags too." He said as he continued walking to his own car.

"HEY, NO FAIR!" Paige yelled at Mike. Mike yelled back "Losing is never fair," then he crawled into his car and drove away. Both Chelsea and Paige started walking towards Holden. "You don't have anyone to help you now," Paige said as they continued to slowly walk towards him. Holden slowly walked backwards towards the car. Once he got up against it, he jumped over the hood and into the car, leaving the passenger side locked. The two girls ran to the car trying to open the door. Holden just sat in the leather seat and pointed and laughed at them. Paige looked around, pulled up her shirt and pressed her tits against the glass. Chelsea laughed and Holden popped the locks too let the two in. Once Chelsea was in the backseat, Paige buckled into the front seat then leaned over and kissed Holden. "I knew you'd let us in." Holden laughed, brought the car to life and headed for home.

Paige and Chelsea filled Holden in on their day; Holden in turn told them what he did all day to the exaggerated yawns from the peanut gallery in the backseat. Holden brushed her off and kept talking in amazingly graphic detail about every piece of paper he printed off, every inane conversation he had, how many coffee's he had and what he had for lunch. Paige was laughing; she knew he was exaggerating the mundaneness of his job for Chelsea's benefit. Finally, after having enough Chelsea interrupted Holden and asked what the plan for dinner was. They asked Chelsea what she wanted to do, she said she was online and saw a cool little dinner theatre she would like to go to. Paige and Holden thought it was an excellent idea but they wondered if they could get tickets. They drove by the restaurant and Paige called them from her cell, luckily they had tickets for the 8 o'clock show which gave them enough time to run home and change.

The dinner theatre wasn't what Chelsea had anticipated. She expected better acting and better food but it wasn't a complete let down, she had a great story and she even managed to order drinks without getting carded.

Although she was three years younger than Paige, Chelsea looked 5 years older. She too had long straight hair but she was a couple of inches taller than Paige and although she was very far from fat she had more mass than Paige and a much bigger tits, which she had no hesitation accentuating. The night ended fairly early with Holden turning in and the girls went back onto the balcony. Paige grabbed her and her sister a drink and they began to talk. Chelsea noticed Paige didn't mix alcohol into her drink nor did she drink all through dinner. Chelsea asked her what was up, she wasn't drinking and she seemed preoccupied. Paige sat in silence; Chelsea sat and waited for her sister's response. Finally Paige swallowed hard and looked Chelsea straight in her eyes. "Chelsea, I think I'm pregnant."

"Whoa!" Chelsea said,. "How do you feel about that? Does Holden know?"

"No, and I'm not sure how I feel about it, I don't know if I'm ready to be a wife let alone a mom."

"Bummer dude, but seriously that is awesome. You'll make a great mom; Holden is great you're done school now, what is your problem?"

"I don't know dude, I'm just worried it's a big step and I don't know how Holden will take it and he hasn't even asked me to marry him…" Chelsea interrupted her. "Seriously, relax, it's not that bad, this is good news. Mom is going to be so happy." "It is good news isn't it?" Paige reiterated.

Chelsea let out a shriek "I'm going to be an aunt!" "Shut up, Holden will hear you." Paige said.

Paige, feeling more energetic and positive about her possible state she called it a night. The following hour, Chelsea tried to watch TV, turning up the volume to drown out the sound of her sister getting nailed in the next room. Holden wasn't sure what inspired Paige but he wasn't about to question it.

The next day the girls went out shopping, this time leaving the previously ransacked malls alone, they concentrated on the downtown core stopping in almost every little shop they passed by. Chelsea, wrapped up in the aunty thing, kept pulling out baby accessories and told Paige all the stuff she was going to buy the baby. She also spent the better part of the day telling Paige why naming the baby after her was the only choice. Paige, sinking into the hype reminded Chelsea she wasn't positive and she would wait a couple of days then get a home test.

Once Holden got home, the girls were waiting for him. They decided they were going to have a BBQ for supper but first they needed to run out and get some things. Chelsea said she was going to miss the outing so she could talk to her boyfriend online. The happy couple ribbed Chelsea for a bit before they left for the store. Holden got down to the parking garage before he realized he forgot his wallet. He took the elevator back up to the apartment and apparently entered very quietly. He overheard Chelsea "Ya, they went to the store. Yes, I got it, yes I'm using it, Okay I'll turn it on, but it has to be fast they won't be long."

Holden was curious about the conversation; he cautiously walked towards the living room where he left his wallet. He heard a humming sound coming from the living room, he peaked around the corner and there was Chelsea completely naked with the webcam positioned on the table to see her entire body. Holden was amazed; she had an incredible muscular body. Her large breasts, which he wanted to see on more than one occasion, were so very firm that they didn't move as she began to fuck herself with her vibrator. A toy apparently her boyfriend bought for her before she went on the trip. Holden sat behind the wall trying to figure out the best way to approach the situation. He had to move fast, the moans from his girlfriend's sister and her internet lover were beginning to arouse him. Finally he just walked in. "Don't mind me," he said as he grabbed his wallet Chelsea struggled to find a blanket to cover up but Holden was gone before she could. She could only hear him yell "Very nice by the way." Embarrassed she cut the session short with her boyfriend and went out to the balcony for a drink. Neither Holden nor Chelsea brought up the subject again.

Thursday night Tamara showed up for ladies night. Tamara began to bug Paige about not drinking. Over the course of the night, Paige, with the prodding of Chelsea, told Tamara her suspicions. The drunk Tamara screamed, stood up on a table "Get me a drink over here I'm drinking for 2!" She jumped off the table and hugged Paige. Paige had to remind them both again not to get excited but they ignored her. The night continued on like that. Paige realized going to the bar sober was painful but she toughed it out for her little sister. Finally last call was announced and it was time to head home, Paige pried the two girls off the dance floor and away from the two prospects that were buying them drinks all night, much to the guys chagrin. Before they parted ways, Paige made Tamara promise not to tell Mike until after she had a chance to tell Holden. Tamara agreed and told Paige she'd be there for her if she needed anything. Paige hugged her, thanked her and they jumped in separate cabs. Paige and Chelsea crawled into their own beds. Paige tried her best to not wake up Holden but it was too late. Holden was curious about the evening so Paige filled him in on everything. She told him about the hot girls at the bar, she began describing in detail one particularly hot girl, she described her hair, her make up, her outfit right down to her shoes. She described it in such detail it was arousing Holden, which was Paige's intent. She slowly slid her hand beneath the covers and below the waist band of his boxers. She grabbed his stiffening cock and began to firmly stroke it. Holden sat back and listened to Paige and visualized the girl. Paige then went on to tell him what she wanted to do to him as she began stroking him faster and harder. Her lips were now against his ears as she spoke. He tried to twist over to fuck her but she refused to let him, she wanted to make him cum her way. She then lied on her back and changed hands so that the hand that just held his cock was now exploring her own pussy. Holden enjoyed the experience. He wanted to do more to aid Paige but it was obvious she had something specific in mind. Her hand was slow but firm moving over his cock. The steady tugs built him up slowly which made the sensation that much greater for him. Paige turned herself on with her story and she was always able to click her mouse just right to get herself off fast. As she was about to make herself cum she slid down the bed so her mouth could take Holden's cock. She moved her hand to the base of his cock as her mouth then resumed the slow steady pace which her hand created. The extra warmth and the moans emitting from Paige pushed Holden over the deep end, he told Paige he was about to cum so he wouldn't surprise her by exploding in her mouth. She didn't pull away, instead she pushed her head down further on his shaft and let him fill her mouth. She simultaneously made herself orgasm. Holden relaxed, the unexpected sexcapades were going to make him sleep well, so he thought. Paige swallowed the massive gooey load, kissed her way up Holden's chest and after using her mouth to clean away as much of the cum as she could, she kissed Holden. Holden, without hesitation kissed her back. She finally pulled away, with a tear in her eye, she told Holden how much she loved him and how she couldn't imagine life without him. Holden wasn't sure what brought on the unexpected sincerity but he reciprocated the sentiment and hugged Paige. She began to cry, which was completely out of character for the normally strong Paige. "What's wrong sweetheart?"

"Holden, I love you."

"I know baby, what's wrong?" Holden asked.

"I think I'm pregnant.

12

Holden didn't move when he heard the news. His eyes widened as he absorbed the information but he remained speechless. Paige looked at Holden for signs of hope that everything was going to be okay. The still shocked Holden met her stare. "What? How'd this happen? What are we going to do?" He asked, still trying to let the news sink in. Paige now fighting back tears, questioned herself whether she should have told Holden until she was sure. She was beginning to regret her decision. Paige paused before answering Holden. "What do you mean what are we going to do? And as far as how'd it happen, I'm pretty sure you were there every time."

"I know but I thought we were protected, what are we going to do?" Holden asked with concern in his voice.

"Nothing is 100%, I don't know what were going to do." Paige replied. Holden trying to let the information sink in, leaned back in the bed putting his hands on his forehead. "FUCK."

"Nice Holden." Paige said as she got up to leave the room.

"Where you going?" He asked.

"In to sleep with Chelsea, I can't be around you right now," her tears began to flow. She needed Holden to be strong for her and his reaction was the exact opposite of what she hoping for.

"Wait, Paige, we need to talk about this to figure something out."

Paige ignored Holden as she firmly closed the door behind her. Holden remained in bed for several seconds as several thoughts ran through his mind. He regretted his initial reaction but it was too late to do anything about it now. He could only try to apologize to Paige and hoped that she understood what he was thinking. Holden got up and being concerned about his girlfriend he neglected to get dressed. Knocking on the door he tried to talk to Paige through the thin door. Finally the door opened but it wasn't Paige behind it, it was a very tired Chelsea. She exited the room and closed the door behind her. She ignored the fact that Holden was naked as she herself was wearing only a T shirt that barely hung below her waist.

"You're an ass." she said to him

"Tell me something I don't know." Holden said hanging his head in shame.

"Look, she knows you love her she is just upset and confused. This has been bothering her for days now and she needed you to be more supportive."

"I know, but that's just it, she has had several days to let it sink in, I just had two minutes. It's a lot to take in ya know?"

"I know, just sleep on it. I'll talk to her to try to calm her down and things will be fine in the morning, I promise." Chelsea said reassuring Holden.

Chelsea then turned to go back into her bedroom but being so tired she stumbled and reached out to Holden for support but missed. She crashed down onto her knees in front of the naked Holden. She reached out for support and her hands landed on his thighs since they were the only thing she could find during her stumbled. Her face thundered into his thigh causing him to let out a small moan. "Fuck me." Chelsea said, startled by her trip. Seconds after the thump, the door opened again, Paige came out to see what was happening. She saw her sisters face buried into Holden's naked waist. "Nice," she said turning and slamming the door locking it behind her. Chelsea, now at eye level with Holden's cock thought to herself, nice indeed but she dared not saying anything. Holden and Chelsea had to laugh at the apparent misunderstanding, very '*Three's Company*' Holden thought. Chelsea climbed to her feet and started to pound on the door in an attempt to explain to Paige the misunderstanding. Paige wasn't in the mood to accept any explanations. Holden ran into his room and put on a pair of shorts before he rejoined Chelsea in trying to explain the situation. Tearfully, Paige finally swung open the door. "Fuck you both, you want him, he's yours!" Then she slammed the door again. Holden could hear her crying in the room, he felt helpless. He wanted to go support his love but he couldn't. He finally told Chelsea she could have the master bedroom, he was going to stay outside Paige's room in hopes that she would be willing to talk.

Chelsea fell asleep in the master bedroom. Holden, with his back to the bedroom door finally heard Paige's sobs stop, several minutes later he too fell asleep. To him it felt like he just closed his eyes when he heard the alarm going off in his bedroom. He scrambled to his feet with the events of the night before still very fresh in his mind. He ran into the room to turn off the alarm, forgetting about Chelsea he dove across the bed to avoid waking anyone. Crashing onto Chelsea, she sprung to life. "What the fuck?" "Oh shit, sorry, I forgot you were in here." Holden said. She rolled over; the blankets fell off her naked body. As Holden struggled to get to his feet, he realized he inadvertently used one of her tits as leverage. As he tried standing he could see her exposed ass, he thought to himself great asses must run in the family. He became guilty when he realized that he was getting hard looking at Paige's sister. He finally rolled off the bed, the entire interaction only took about five seconds but he was happy it was over. He was also glad she was going home that day; she was getting dangerous to be around. Holden showered and got ready for work avoiding the master bedroom at all cost. Before he left the apartment he gently knocked on the spare room. "I love you with all my heart Paige, together we can get through anything." He then left for the office.

All day he couldn't concentrate and it was noticed at work. Mike asked him if everything was alright, Holden took him into his office and explained everything that happened. "That's heavy…so you're going to be a daddy eh?" Mike asked.

"I guess so," Holden reluctantly said

"How do you feel about that?"

"I don't know man, it's weird. I know I love her and I want to be with her and we talked about kids but you know, all our lives hearing those words 'I'm pregnant' has been a very bad thing. It's just hard to wrap my head around the idea that we're grown ups and it's not necessarily a bad thing."

"Grown ups," Mike said laughing, not believing it. "Dude, I'm married and I still don't feel like a grown up." Holden just looked at him in agreement.

During the day Holden tried calling Paige, he also sent several text messages without getting an answer. He couldn't wait for the end of the day. Once he was finally done, he scurried home not sure what to expect.

He got to the apartment, unlocked the door and headed in. He was surprised to see the place empty. He was upset that she wasn't there, he was anxious to talk to her again but he assumed she was out with her sister before it was time to put her on the plane for home. Holden went into the bedroom and changed out of his work attire into something more comfortable. He then went to the fridge to grab a soda; he noticed a note on the kitchen counter. "Holden, I'm sorry about last night, I know nothing happened between my sister and you but I need some time to think, I'm not going to be home for a couple of days. Paige." Holden's heart sunk. He reread the note several times then took a seat on the floor. He pulled his cell phone out of his pocket and called her number. He didn't get an answer so he left a message expressing his concern for her and asked her to call him back. He thought it would be unlikely if she did but he needed to know she was safe. Also he wanted to tell her he was excited to start a family with her but he didn't feel comfortable leaving that as a voice mail. He was worried she might think he was saying that just to win her back.

Over the next few hours he tried his best to not obsess about it, he knew she would call him soon but the harder he tried to put it out of his mind the more he thought about her. Finally he called Tamara to see if she heard from her. She said she hadn't, then sent Mike over to calm Holden down. Holden and Mike sat, watched a roller hockey game on TV and had a couple of beers. Neither spoke much but Holden was appreciative of his friend being there for him in his time of need. Even with Mike there he still couldn't stop worrying about Paige and wondering if she was ok.

A couple of hours passed when Holden's cell rang. It was Tamara, she said that Paige was there, that she was okay and she was going to stay there for a couple of days. Holden thanked her for telling him and for taking care of her. He also asked her to work on Paige to get her to talk to him and also tell her he loved her. Tamara said she'd try her best.

Holden spent the next few days reflecting on his relationship, what his life had become and how much Paige meant to him. Paige did the same, since Sunshine had visited she had been doing that a lot, even more so after she found out she was pregnant. She felt lost and lonely. Her sister reassured her that she was doing the right thing; Paige wasn't so sure she was ready to settle down. She felt too young and wanted to do more things like travel before she became a mother and settled down. She loved Holden; she knew that much, but things were moving way too fast for her. Tamara tried to help her but she knew only Paige could decide what was best for her.

Holden, not wanting to be at home alone obsessing about Paige spent more and more time at the office. His office had a view of the arena so he could watch the team practice and their games as well as the house league teams that used the surface when the pro team wasn't. When there was nothing going on he would just stare at the empty rubber surface and think about his love. It was one of those nights. His MP3 player played music through his laptop, the lights were low in his office and his feet were up on a table beside the window to the arena. He was lost, staring blankly out the window when he heard a knock at the door. Turning in the direction of the door, he saw Paige standing in the doorway with her bags in her hands looking at him. "Mike told me you'd be here, I'm sorry, can I come back now?" she asked sheepishly. Holden scrambled to his feet and ran to the door; Paige dropped her bags and jumped into Holden's strong arms. She began kissing Holden all over his face. "I love you so much, I'm so sorry for over reacting." she said.

"I'm sorry for being an ass, I should have been more supportive, you just caught me off guard," Holden said.

"I know baby, its okay, I love you."

"I love you too." Holden said holding Paige in his arms. All the worry and stress over the past week evaporated in that single moment. He had his love back and he swore he'd never let her go again. Paige too felt relief in Holden's arms. She knew things would be okay as long as she was with him. Holden carried her to his desk, supporting her with one arm; he cleared his desk with the other. She was kissing his neck the entire time. He put her down on the desk as their arms were running all over each other. The passion was like it was their first date. Holden had often fantasized about taking Paige in his office and as he looked up and saw the empty surface down below he had a brilliant idea. He climbed off Paige and grabbed her by the hand. She had tears running down her face. He brought her in close to him, used his index finger to wipe away her tears as he kissed her and told her everything was ok. He led her by the hand into the depths of the arena. It was dark; Holden was using a flashlight to navigate his way around the tunnels of the basement. He finally led her up a ramp that led to the home team's bench. He sat her down on the bench then ran out to his car where he had a bag with their inline skates in the trunk. Before he brought them into Paige, he ran to the announcer/DJ booth and turned on his MP3 player filling the arena with music. He set the lights to the arena on low so there was just enough lighting to see. The dim lights cast shadows all over the empty arena; it spooked Paige until Holden rejoined her. Once he got back, they got their skates on and began slowly skating around the arena. They casually talked about the last week and how much they missed each other while holding each other's hands the entire time. As the song *'Pump It'* by the Black Eyed Peas played, Holden sprinted ahead of Paige to show off his skating skills for her. She clapped and cheered at his antics as he sped around behind her and skated as hard as he could towards her then he put his hands on her shoulders and jumped over her. She wasn't a strong skater and she was worried the force of him hitting her shoulders would knock her over but he barely touched her as he lept over her. She was suitably impressed with his ability. After *'Pump It'* a slower song came on. Holden put his arm around Paige and led her to center arena then spun her around. Almost losing her balance, Holden caught her and gently guided her to the floor. As he kissed her, she tried to dig her heels into the surface but the wheels of her skates just kept rolling away. Instead she used her arms to pull Holden tight against her. She just kept repeating that she loved him over and over again. Holden could feel the intensity in Paige. He was happy she missed him so much. Holden shared Paige's passion. He reached under her shirt and in one fluid movement pulled her shirt and bra off and rolled it up into a pillow for her. She pulled his shirt off, popping some buttons off in the process. Holden stopped to look at his girlfriend. At one point during the week he wasn't sure if he would get to touch her again so he wasn't about to pass up this moment. His hand ran all over her bare skin feeling every inch of her as he took in her soft texture and her warmth. Paige welcomed Holden's tenderness. She started to become very submissive, letting Holden explore her body as if it was the first time. She ate up how he looked at her and how he was touching her. He knelt beside Paige as he unclasped both their skates, first he pulled them off her, and then he took off his own. Once the skates were off Holden stood up and slowly undressed. Paige stayed on the floor topless, not making an effort to take off any of her clothes; she didn't want to miss Holden revealing his well sculpted body. He noticed Paige's eyes burning through him; he took off his clothes as slow and deliberately as possible. When he got down to his tight boxer/briefs he very slowly pulled the elastic band down, first showing Paige his shaved pubic area, then sliding it down his shaft until it slid over his head. His hard cock sprung to life with enough force to slap himself in the stomach. Once his cock was exposed he let his boxers fall to the floor. She reached up to grab the cock she was longing for the past week but Holden moved just out of her reach. Paige let out a cute hmmpft when he moved. Holden just laughed at her. He then crawled on his knees to Paige. He undid her belt, her zipper and pulled off her jeans revealing she wasn't wearing any panties, also revealing she had a freshly shaved 'landing strip'. Holden had never seen her with anything less than a completely bare pussy. He ran his fingers through the course hair. "What do you think?" Paige asked.

"I like it, why the change?"

"I just thought I'd try something new." Paige said blushing. Holden smiled with approval before he leaned in and put his mouth on her hair and gave her a kiss. Then he licked both sides of the patch of hair with his tongue, Paige, again tried digging her heels into the floor for support and this time they held. Holden moved from beside her, crawled over her leg rubbing his penis on her thigh as he did. She felt the piercings graze her skin. She couldn't wait to feel them inside her again. She wanted to scream at the top of her lungs FUCK ME but she restrained herself. Holden gently put his hand on Paige's ear and looked deep into her eyes. "I love you," his voice crackled as he said it. Simultaneously he sunk his cock deep into her. She embraced him tightly; he continued to cup her ear as he gently made love to her. Her fingers dug deeply into his back, leaving long scratch marks as his shaft penetrated her over and over again. Both didn't say a word and their eyes never broke lock. Holden had made love to Paige several times before but never with this shared passion, it was also the longest they've been without sex since they first assumed a physical relationship. Paige's fingers continued to clench Holden's back as he slowly and methodically thrusted into her. Her pussy, starving for attention accepted his cock and formed firmly around his shaft, his piercings tickling her lips with every movement. Everything that was inside them both, the sadness of the past week, the love, the intensity combined to make one big culmination of emotions that released between them at the same time. Holden began to cum without warning; it even caught him by surprise. The sudden commotion inside Paige caught her off guard and caused her to orgasm. They both forced themselves closer to each other. After they were both done, neither moved, Holden again brushed Paige's hair behind her ear. Both looked as if they were tearing up. "Welcome home, I love you." Holden said as Paige grabbed Holden and hugged him tight. She could feel his flaccid cock still inside her, his cum still slowly leaking out of him. "I love you too. Don't ever leave me." She begged

"I won't." He promised.

After several songs played, they released their embrace and got dressed. Holden ensured there was no residue left on the arena; it would be hard to explain why one of his players injured himself slipping in a puddle of his cum.

On the drive back to their apartment Holden asked Paige if she would like to go camping on the weekend. He found several potential sites that he wanted to check out. Paige told him she'd love to so they checked out the

BC campsites online and picked the perfect one and hoped that it would be theirs alone for the weekend.

Saturday morning finally arrived; Holden and Paige packed the BMW with everything they would need for a night of camping before they went to the grocery store for some last minute food ideas. They packed the cooler with meats, buns and wine and then hit the road. The road they took was in the same direction as the one they took for their picnic, accept instead of turning west off the main highway, Holden kept heading north for a couple of more hours. They figured the further away from the city they got, the more likely they would be alone at the camp site.

Paige tried to read the map while Holden navigated from the GPS in his cell phone, when the voice told him to turn he turned. He followed the voice, which eventually led them to their ideal spot. It was a secluded area that the BC foresters made as a condition for their forestry license. It was barely big enough for 2 tents but it had a picnic table, a small beach and an incredible view. The beach they were on had a small fresh water lake that got its water from the melting snow peaks on the neighbouring mountain. They were in a valley, peaks surrounded them accept for an opening to the west. The mountains seemed to part for the pair, giving them a most incredible view of the ocean. They looked down on it like royalty looking down on their kingdom. Paige slowly started to unpack their car while Holden set up the 2 man pup tent with ease. He then told Paige horror stories of when he was young going camping with his family. The tent they used was a large canvass tent that needed at least two people to set up. It had several metal poles that needed to be screwed into each other plus there was a center post that was slightly larger than the others and it was easy to mistake for a corner post. He dreaded setting up that tent. Paige said it was lucky for them the hardware store sold foolproof tents. No doubt, was Holden's response. After the campsite was set up to their liking, Holden started a fire in the designated pit. After the fire was roaring and there was enough wood gathered to keep them warm throughout the night, Paige decided to go take some pictures. She stood by the car too put Holden and the fire in the fore ground and the mountains and beach in the background. She then walked over to the ledge of the mountain and looked down at the ocean, to get several pictures from that angle then turned a 180 degrees too take more pictures of the campsite and the lake making sure to get Holden in as many pictures as possible. She positioned the camera on a log so she could get a picture of herself and Holden with the lake and mountains in the background. The flash went off and they went and sat on the picnic table. Holden was going to turn up the car stereo but Paige asked him to wait, she wanted to sit and listen to 'nature' for awhile. Holden thought that was a good idea so he waited. Both sat in silence for a bit. Despite the higher elevation and the snow capped peaks, the air was warm. After sitting in silence for a bit, Paige jumped up and started taking off her clothes as she walked to the beach. Holden thought she would have learned her lesson from their picnic so he just let her go in. By the time her toes hit the cold mountain lake she was completely naked. She casually walked in and once the lake hit her waist she dove in disappearing under the water. She quickly resurfaced gasping for air; she snapped her hair back causing her long hair to spray water in an arch as her hair flipped over her head. Holden had Paige's camera and he snapped pictures of her entire swim. Paige saw him with the camera so she started posing like a swimsuit model, sans swimsuit. She positioned herself in all kinds of poses then she crawled up the sandy beach and rolled around covering herself with sand as Holden continued taking pictures "work it, work it," was all he kept saying. Paige laughed at Holden. Once she was completely covered in sand she slowly crawled back into the water to clean off. She started swimming around, Holden continued to take pictures of her as she swam. Her hair floated free in the water, her bare ass occasionally peaked out of the watery depths. She then stopped and swam back to Holden until her feet could touch the bottom so she could slowly walk out of the lake; the scene reminded him of the pool scene from *'Fast Times at Ridgemont High.'* Her toes left impressions in the sand as she walked towards the tent. Holden watched her as the water cascaded off her perfect body. She reached into the tent to grab a towel and started drying herself off. Once she was dry she pulled her summer dress out of her bag and pulled it over her head, then took a seat by the fire. Holden saw that she was still shivering so he went to the trunk of the car and pulled out a sleeping blanket and put it over Paige's shoulders. Using one hand she grabbed the blanket and pulled it further around herself. Holden put some hot chocolate in a metal container and let it cook in the fire. He then went to the car and turned up the stereo, he made a CD just for the occasion and it played quietly in the background. Holden joined Paige on the log as they waited for their hot chocolate. He asked her how the water was. She told him that it was much warmer than she had anticipated and teased Holden for being too chicken to join her. Holden assured her that he would take a swim with her later. Paige warmed up quickly once Holden served her some hot chocolate.

The sun was starting to set behind the mountains. Holden went to the trunk and pulled out a rod and reel. Paige asked what he was doing. Holden said he was going to catch them some dinner. Paige laughed at him and watched on as Holden stood as close to the lake as he could. He cast his lure into the lake and sat patiently for quite awhile. A short time later he reeled in his line, looked at Paige and told her it was the spot and that he was going to walk further up the lake. Paige could still see him but barely, he was standing on a log casting his line. As Holden continued to fish, Paige slapped some hamburgers on the fire pit grill. By the time Holden returned admitting defeat, the burgers were done. Paige also slipped into a cotton sweater and jogging pants. Moving to the picnic table; they dressed their burgers and quietly ate. "Mmm I do love fresh fish," Paige teased as she bit in to her hamburger. Holden looked at her, she continued, "what were you going to do with it once you caught it, do you know how to clean a fish or even how to cook one?" she asked. Holden looked back at her as seriously as he could "I didn't think that far ahead, all the movies I've seen on the subject, the guy caught the fish and the woman cleaned it, I just assumed it was one of those girl things."

"You think all girls just know how clean fish?" "Ya, is that wrong?" Holden asked with a smirk, Paige rolled her eye. The sky was getting red and as the sun slowly faded making the night air much cooler. After they finished eating, Holden began cleaning up. Paige stopped him and she undressed again, "Let's go for a swim before it's completely dark." "Are you nuts, it's cold."

"At least we know there aren't any fish in the lake to attack us," she said as she ran into the water. Completely submerged in the water with only her head peaking out, she started teasing Holden relentlessly until he began to take off his clothes. He slowly walked to the water's edge, the small waves licked Holden's toes and he withdrew to the sandy shore. "WIMP!" Paige yelled. Holden decided to approach it like a band aid. He yelled his war cry and charged into the water, tripping as the water reached his knees causing him to crash into the lake. He stumbled to his feet but once the air hit his wet body he figured he was warmer in the water so he dove in and grabbed Paige from under the murky depths. She let out a playful shriek as he grabbed her leg. Paige and Holden splashed each other in the water for a bit, she then swam seductively over to Holden and wrapped her arms around his broad shoulders. He put his hands on her waist as she wrapped her legs around him and they kissed. The sunset was a brilliant orange and red and was now low on the horizon. Paige moved around until Holden was inside her. They watched the sun disappear into the Pacific Ocean below them. Once the sun was gone, only the fire and a crescent moon provided light. The dancing flame cast shadows all over their camp site. Paige refocused on the cock inside her; she was impressed Holden was able to stay so big and hard in the cold water. Holden moved his hands from her waist to her ass. She used her legs to fuck him, they weren't kissing but their mouths were open and very close to each other. They could hear each other's subtle moans as they fucked in the lake. The cold water was starting to take its toll on Holden, his thigh muscles began to cramp so he carried Paige to the beach. Once he was close to the shore, he lied down on his back, his cock never left Paige. She assisted Holden until she was on top of him. Once they were supported by the ground Paige became more aggressive thrusting on top of him. Leaning back she moved her legs so her feet were beside Holden's head. He put his arms on the outside of her legs into a position they never tried before. The trick with that position was all their moves had to be very smooth or he would fall out of her. She leaned back; her back was just about in the water allowing the tiny waves to wash over her shoulders as she fucked Holden. He tilted his head and kissed Paige's ankles as he watched his penis penetrate her, the best thing about this new position he thought was the view. Watching himself penetrate her was increasingly hot in his mind. He became worried he was going to cum before she even started; to slow things down he got Paige to change positions again. She stayed on top but got back on her knees and spun around, Holden shimmied up the beach a bit so Paige wouldn't be as deep in the water. With her back to him she lowered herself on his still hard cock, another view he could watch himself penetrate her. She did all the work, her ass bobbed up and down on his cock; he watched her pussy swallow his length as she fucked him faster and harder. The moonlight silhouetted the mountain range and cast a reflection on the water; Paige watched the reflection as she rode Holden. They were both getting colder but neither was about to stop. Paige spun around, leaned in and kissed Holden. Holden hugged her and easily flipped her onto her back; she clenched her legs tighter around Holden so he wouldn't slip out of her. Once she was on her back, Holden began fucking Paige slowly with increased speed. The waves were slashing against them. Paige's hands ran through Holden's hair covering it with beach sand. Holden was now pounding Paige hard; she loosened her legs from around his hips and put her feet flat on the sand, spreading her legs wide letting Holden penetrate her deeper. Paige put her hands down into the sand digging her fingers in hoping for some resistance but only came up with handfuls of mud. Her eyes broke their gaze with Holden's as they began to roll back into her head. Holden had never seen her do that before but he took it as a good sign. Trying to get his knees firmly in the ground for more leverage he just slipped awkwardly around inside her. The unpredictable movements helped Paige not fall into a rhythm; instead, every thrust penetrated her differently helping her orgasm heighten. With one hard deep thrust Paige let her orgasm release onto Holden. Holden was getting closer himself and hearing her cum, the moans and the extra force she was fucking him back with certainly helped. Paige's orgasm subsided but she knew Holden was yet to release; she then turned her attention on him, scratching his back, moaning, talking dirty and flexing her pussy muscles. Holden was no match for her, the last "oh ya, that's it fuck me hard," was enough to finish him off. Once again he filled her pussy with cum. They shared a momentary embrace, as their adrenaline wore off they began to get much colder. They decided to take another quick dip to wash the sand off them. Hand in hand the dove under the water. Holden, confident the sand was out of all of his crevasses started to walk towards the tent, he looked back at Paige. "You coming honey?"

"Give me a minute, I have sand EVERYWHERE!" she said. Holden left the water, went to the tent grabbed a towel and grabbed Paige a dry one as well. Paige took her time splashing around in the water. Holden watched her, the way the moon lit her up, he thought she looked exquisite. Holden slowly dressed, then stirred up the fire, throwing on a bigger log that he thought should last them the entire night. Paige joined him by the now roaring fire. He offered her another cup of hot chocolate and she gladly accepted it; she held the tin cup with both hands. Holden looked at her small frail fingers intertwined around the cup; they captivated him as he imagined them wrapped around his cock. Refocusing on reality, they exchanged ghost stories and as if on cue, they heard a wolf cry in the distance. Holden took a break in the conversation to clean up the campsite. He put their food in a plastic bag, which they put in a net and hung on the other side of the campsite to prevent any unwelcome visitors. Holden elected not to put the food in the car, just in case the curious bears decided to try and get into it and not only ruin their chance to escape but also damage his pride and joy.

As Holden was securing the food, Paige started making s'mores on the campfire. Holden came back proud of his outdoorsy ability. Paige gave him a s'more for his efforts. After a few more scary stories, they crawled into the tent. Although they both had their own sleeping blankets, they elected to share one. They fell asleep embracing each other.

The next morning Paige was the first to wake, she carefully crawled out of bed so she didn't wake Holden who was sleeping peacefully next to her. She opened the flap to the tent and crawled out, getting dressed outside in the fresh morning air. The fire had died down but did not go out during the night, so she stirred it up and fed it another log. In no time the fire was roaring again. Holden woke and crawled out of the tent, he saw Paige sitting quietly by the fire. The sun was starting to rise, mist was rising from the lake, and he could see the marks in the beach sand from the night before. Paige was wearing a bulky sweater, the arms covered all but her fingertips, and she was hunched over by the fire trying to get warm. Holden watched her for a minute before letting her know he was awake. She turned and smiled and offered him a cup of hot chocolate. Holden told her he would be back for it in a minute. He walked over to the car, on the way over he saw fresh prints in the dirt that he imagined belonged to a bear. He decided not telling Paige would be the best thing. He dug through his glove compartment, found what he was looking for and began to walk back over to Paige. She looked at him and tried to figure out what he had on his mind, he looked unusually focused for just waking up. She held up his hot chocolate again, Holden grabbed it took a sip then told Paige to get ready for a hike; he wanted to walk up the trail to watch the sunrise. Paige thought that was an excellent idea so she changed her socks and put on her running shoes. Since she was getting warmer, she changed from her warm sweat suit into the sundress she was wearing the night before. Holden grabbed her by the hand and they headed up the hill. Holden didn't tell Paige about the fresh bear tracks but kept them in his mind. The trail was very narrow, Holden broke the way but was careful not to let any wayward branches hit Paige in the face, she appreciated his extra effort. Along the way Holden froze, Paige, not paying attention crashed into the back of him causing him to stumble. "What's up?" Paige asked. Holden ushered her in front of him and mimicked her to be quiet. She peaked through some branches and found herself just a couple of feet from a family of deer. The biggest of the bunch, Paige assumed was the male, was so close she could reach out and touch it. Holden put his hand on her back as he tried to see the deer as well. Behind the male was 2 smaller deer complete with the white and black spots on their back. They watched them for as long as they could before Holden suggested they kept moving so they didn't completely miss the sunrise. Paige agreed and with her first step, she broke a twig causing the family to scatter. She looked back at Holden to apologize but he didn't give her the chance. When she looked back at him, her brown eyes were huge with excitement; she had a smile that made her look like a schoolgirl on Christmas eve. She looked excited, hopeful and very pure. He grabbed her and as she opened her mouth to speak, he pulled her into him and kissed her. She could tell by Holden's intensity that she was in for more than just a kiss. He picked her up in his arms, as he did when he guided her through the doorway of their condominium. He carried her only a few feet deeper into the woods when he found a large flat rock. He sat her down, stood up quickly, and undressed. She watched him, laughing at the haste in which he was undressing. Once he was naked, he focused on Paige. He walked over to her and gently pushed her back so she was resting on the palms of her hands. He knelt before his princess and ever so carefully leaned into her knees, using his hands to guide her dress over his head. She looked down at the bulge under her skirt and imagined how she would look pregnant. That thought disappeared quickly when she felt his tongue pressing against her panties and onto her clit. She felt his mouth making her panties hot and wet. He finally started pulling at her underwear; she took the hint and raised her bum off the hard rock so he could free her pussy from their cotton confines. He pulled them down her thighs, over her knees and to her ankles. He then slipped one of her feet out and as he was about to pull them completely off she told him to stop. She wanted them hanging around her ankle so she could find them again when they were done. Holden thought it was a good idea so he left them where they were and went back to work under her dress. His fingers reached around under her thighs, digging deep into her flesh. She was angled awkwardly for him to penetrate her so he settled for kissing and licking her clit and labia. As Holden licked her, Paige closed her eyes but visions of the past few days flashed back in her mind. Trying to not lose the mood she opened her eyes. She looked around the vast forest. She had always loved making love outdoors. She imagined people watching her, the feeling that she was being watched or even filmed was often enough to bring her to orgasm with very little effort from her partner. As she was in the height of her fantasy and Holden buried deep below her dress she heard a twig snap and she saw a shadow move in her peripheral vision. She tried to jump but Holden's grip on her thighs was to tight for her to move. Looking in the direction of the shadow she saw nothing. She then imagined a man hiding in the shadows watching her getting eaten out. In her mind's eye she could see him reaching into his pants and pulling out his long hard cock. He began stroking it to her so she began putting on a show for him. Her moans were loud and exaggerated. Holden didn't know what he was doing different; he assumed she just really enjoyed the fresh air. Her movements and moans kept him motivated to please her. Paige kept looking off into the empty forest, she gently opened her mouth inviting the stranger in. She reached into the air, trying to pull the figure towards her as Holden's tongue still danced deep inside her. She had enough, she could feel her juices running down her leg, she wanted the strangers cock. Her desire was to much for her to control. She tapped Holden on his head; he pulled the dress back and peaked at her over the material. "You knocked?" He asked. She just stood up, not saying a word she was still looking into the shadows as she pulled her dress over her ass then laid on her stomach over the rock. Her legs spread as wide as they could possibly go inviting Holden to move in behind her. Flexing his thighs as they took his weight, he guided his firm cock into her waiting pussy. He barely had time to slide his entire length into her before she started moaning and thrusting her hips. Her clit searched for something to rub against but despite how violent her body moved it came up short every time. She continued to fuck Holden to the pleasure of the imaginary stranger. She reached back and grabbed Holden's hand and pulled it to her mouth causing him to lose balance, thus penetrating her deeper. She started sucking his fingers as she wanted to do to another cock. She didn't understand why she was as horny as she was but at that moment only one cock wasn't enough for her. Making the best of what she had, she sucked his fingers substituting them for the long cock that stayed just out of reach in her imagination. She forced his fingers deep down her throat causing her to gag. Holden didn't know what was possessing Paige, he just knew he wanted to please her. He reached up and grabbed her hair. As he pulled hard on her hair he pushed his cock and fingers deep inside her. She let out a cough and spit out his fingers as she orgasmed. Instantaneously she stood up, Holden could see the stream of her fluids running down the once dry rock. Even though she just had an orgasm she was still very focused, without talking she repositioned him so he was now sitting on the rock. He gladly sat, wondering what she had in store for him. She knelt down onto all fours. She dropped with enough force the dress blew up and was half way up her back exposing her ass to the wilderness and her imaginary friend. With her hands on the forest floor, she used her mouth to take his cock; at first, her outstretched tongue was at the base of his cock then she slid it up his shaft. Once she got to the tip, she used her tongue to scoop up all his precum before sinking her lips around his manhood. She took his length entirely in her mouth; she could feel the head sliding deep down her throat. She kept her eyes open in hopes to get a glimpse of the man in the shadows. Paige had no desire to tease or toy with Holden. She was now using his cock as a tool to satisfy her own needs. She sucked him off methodically to put on a good show. Feeling the eyes burning into her exposed body she reached between her legs and frantically started rubbing her clit. Finally she let Holden's cock fall from her mouth and she took it in her left hand as her right hand abused her own clit. Keeping his member pressed against her cheek she started stroking him, long deliberate strokes making sure Holden could feel every inch being satisfied. Both her hands were moving fast and sporadic, Holden couldn't take much more of it. With her scent still fresh on his lips, he took a lick. He then looked down at Paige, who looked more like Syn as she was caught up in the moment. Her hair was cascading over his legs, his cock was pressed into the flesh of her cheek. The scent, taste, visual and sensation all combined into one massive overload. Holden cam across Paige's cheek, she stroked him faster and harder as she felt him splash against her skin. Her fingers rubbed her pussy harder as she imagined herself in porn, performing for the man in the woods. Her imagination caused her to have yet another orgasm. Upon completion she let out a loud sigh then collapsed onto the forest floor beside the rock which still supported Holden. "Wow, what was that all about?" Holden asked.

"Wow is right, ya, I don't know but it was great wasn't it?" Holden couldn't argue. They stayed where they were for a few more minutes before standing up, Holden cleaned the leaves out of her hair and then looked at the mess he made on her face. Using his finger to clean as much of the cum off her as he could, he then wiped his finger clean on the rock that was still wet with from her orgasm. Getting as much as he could with his finger he pulled off his shirt and finished cleaning her off. Holden elected to hold onto his shirt instead of putting the now soiled garment back on. Paige smiled, not only that he sacrificed his shirt for her but at how great she thought his chest looked in the morning light. Looking over her shoulder, deep into the woods to see if she could catch another glimpse of her voyeur, she found nothing, as she expected. She smiled a bit bigger at her dirty little secret.

Paige and Holden walked another half an hour until they reached a cliff edge facing east. The sun had already risen but the sky still maintained the morning colours of yellow and red and the view was spectacular despite missing the actual sunrise. They could see deep into the valley for miles and miles. Behind them, they could still see the ocean but their private lake was completely hidden from view. Holden grabbed Paige by the hand, he fumbled in his pocked as she looked curiously at him and then he began to speak. "Paige, since I first laid eyes on you, I knew you were special…" "Oh my god." She said cutting Holden off, he just continued.

"This past year has been the most amazing in my life, today is a perfect example. Having you gone the last week made me realize I didn't want to live another second without you." He then took a deep breath, dropped to one knee. "Paige, will you marry me?"

12.5

Paige looked down at the kneeling Holden, her eyes began to swell. Holden jumped to his feet to embrace his girlfriend and potential fiancée. His heart was beating so fast he thought he was going to pass out. He felt Paige's tears against his cheek; he then thought it was odd when he felt her body shaking like she was out right crying. He expected her to be emotional but he didn't expect the response she was showing. He pushed her to arms length so he could see her, he then realized she wasn't crying tears of joy but tears of sadness. The excitement drained out of Holden and his legs began to get weak when Paige looked at him in the eyes. "Sit down, we need to talk." Holden wasn't sure what Paige was about to say but he knew it wasn't going to be good. He sat on the ledge overlooking the valley. Paige sat next to him and grabbed his hand. Their feet dangled several hundred feet above the valley floor and she looked at him through her tear filled eyes. "Holden are you only asking me to marry you because you think I'm pregnant, because I'm not, I found out while I was at Tamara's. I don't know why I was so late, I think it was my new birth control. I know I should have told you that night at the arena. I'm sorry," she said guilt ridden like she was confessing something she did wrong. Holden looked at her, his eyes were now swollen and red as he fought back tears. "Paige, I was surprised when you told me you were pregnant. I was wondering if we, if I, was ready for a baby but I wanted to be with you and there for the baby. I proposed to you because I love you, I can't imagine a second without you, whether you're pregnant or not. We have the rest of our lives to have babies, what I want is the rest of my life with you." Holden's fight to hold back his tears was lost. Paige looked at him; she wiped his tears away, leaving hers on her cheek. Holden repeated himself

"Will you marry me?" Paige paused, looked down at the ground then she raised her eyes sheepishly to Holden's. "Holden, you know I love you…"
"But?" Holden interrupted.

"But…" Paige continued "I can't marry you, not now. I have something to tell you…" She paused, waiting for Holden to say something but he remained speechless. She took a deep breath, "Over the past couple of weeks so many things happened, Mike and Tamara got married, I thought I was going to be a mom, a wife, Mel and Chelsea coming to visit, Holden, I don't know who I am anymore or what I want…everything is moving just too fast. I need time."

"Time? What do you mean?" Holden asked, still completely lost.

"Holden.." Paige began, Squeezing Holden's hands tight. "Holden, I sincerely thought you were going to propose to me on our anniversary, I really thought I was going to be a mother and I really thought I was going to settle down to a house in the suburbs with a white picket fence. Holden, I really wanted it but when none of it came true, I thought back about Mel and I thought about Chelsea. I loved my life as a dancer; don't get me wrong I love my life with you. But, I have to know for sure if I'm ready to settle down. I know I want to be with you, but I'm going home for a few weeks just to clear my head. I booked my tickets, I'm leaving next weekend, and I hope you're not too upset." Holden sat motionless to take in all that Paige just told him. "Holden, I can't ask you to wait, I truly hope you do, I love you, I WILL be back." She said and went to hug Holden, Holden pulled away and began looking into the valley trying to absorb everything. "You can't ask me to wait? How long are you going to be gone for?" Holden asked not wanting to hear the answer he was expecting. "I don't know," was Paige's very somber response. Holden sat, tears freely running down his face. He was thinking about what was said to him. In the last 5 minutes he began to lose everything. He was no longer going to be a father and the love of his life was leaving. Paige did her best to reassure Holden but he wasn't able to hear her. She just kept repeating she loved him and that she'd be back. Holden wanted to believe her, so badly he wanted to believe her. She was convincing, however, he knew the next several weeks were going to be very hard but when they were over, they'd know if they were meant to be together.

They slowly walked off the hill to their campsite, packed up their things and got in the car. The drive back was quiet and Holden tired to put the news out of his mind so he focused on driving. Paige sat quietly turned towards the door, she just stared out the window, crying. Holden occasionally looked over at her, his heart sunk but what could he do, he wasn't pushing her away, he certainly didn't want her to go. He found it hard to console her because it was all her decision. He just focused his attention back on the road and left Paige to herself.

Over the next week he tried to show Paige how much he loved her and subtly tell her he didn't want her to go but he knew ultimately the decision was hers and hers alone. Neither told Mike or Tamara the news but Paige told her family. They tried to talk her out of leaving by reminding her everything she had to lose. Her dad got mad telling her he knew she'd find a way to blow it. Holden thought that was unfair of him to say but he didn't entirely disagree with him. Holden wasn't vein enough to think he was her savior by far, if anything she saved him but he thought that together they had a perfect life and he couldn't understand Paige's willingness to just let it go. They tried to keep living life like nothing was happening but her departure day was looming. Holden had to leave the apartment as Paige packed, since she was flying she was going to leave most of her belongings in the apartment and would send money to have them shipped if she decided not to come back. Holden found it to hard to watch. Paige knew how hard it was for him because it was hard for her. Holden struggled at work, everyone noticed how distracted he was, Mike knew Holden intended on proposing so he asked how the camping trip went. Holden didn't answer. Mike continued trying to figure out what was wrong and Holden just told him he would explain everything later. Mike reluctantly let it go at that.

Friday came around quicker than Holden at hoped; he hoped it wouldn't have come around at all because Saturday was going to take Paige away from him. As Paige was out taking care of some last minute details, Holden assured her he would take care of everything that he could at home while she was gone. Holden decided to make Paige a special dinner of all of her favourites. He even considered drugging the food so she would pass out and miss her flight but he knew that wasn't realistic. Paige came home and found Holden behind the stove; he had chopped up fresh vegetables, fried chicken and cooked sticky rice, all the ingredients to make a very delicious stir-fry. Paige pulled two big bottles of red wine out of a bag, she knew it was going to be a rough night and the wine couldn't hurt. Once dinner was ready Holden popped a CD he made specifically for that evening into his CD player and turned it up. He also put the same play list onto her MP3 player so she could listen to it on the plane if she wanted to. Once he hit play the lyrics *"HEY HEY MOMMA SAID*

THE WAY YOU MOVE GONNA MAKE YOU SWEAT GONNA MAKE YOU GROOVE" rumbled through the surround sound. Paige looked at Holden, she didn't want to cry the entire night although she knew it was going to be hard. Holden remembering the song they first saw each other too was enough to set off her off on her emotional rollercoaster. She didn't move towards Holden, she just looked at him, the love in her eyes ran deep which made her decision to leave even harder for Holden to understand. Holden dished out the sticky rice and covered each plate with a generous portion of the teriyaki stir fry. He carried the plates to the table which he painstakingly set with perfect detail, a fact that wasn't missed by Paige. They quietly ate dinner while songs continued playing. Each one was a sentimental favourite of Holden's. They were songs he would listen to when he was feeling sad or depressed. Half way through dinner "somebody" by Depeche Mode played. Holden put down his chop sticks, walked over to Paige and extended his hand, she smiled the best she could given the circumstances and reached out for his hand while she stood. The two danced for three carefree moments, both forgetting about the problems of the past week and not thinking about the enviable time apart. The words of the song sunk into Paige, by the end of the song tears were streaming down her cheek. Holden apologized and said his intent wasn't to make her upset but to have a reminder of how much he loved her so she would never forget while she was away. She said she loved the CD but didn't need a reminder, she would never forget how much he loves her. Holden wasn't sure what the future had in store for them but it made him feel better to know she really did intend to come back. After the song ended they sat back down and continued eating. Paige drank several glasses of wine, Holden began hoping she'd drink enough she'd sleep though her early morning flight but again he knew that wasn't a realistic option either. When supper was done Holden cleared the dishes and reached into the fridge to get dessert. He pulled out a match, lit the two dishes and brought Paige her crepe suzettes. Paige clapped at the flaming dessert Holden was serving her. "How elegant," Paige said excited. They made idle chit chat as the CD continued to play. The mood was beginning to lighten as Paige made fun of some of Holden's song choices. Holden laughed along with her knowing some were unnecessarily sappy. When dessert was done, Holden again cleared the table. He blew out the candles on the table then they both walked to the couch. Holden turned on the fireplace even though it was already warm in the apartment; he was trying to set a mood. Holden was going to turn off the CD and turn on a movie but Paige stopped him. She snuggled in tightly while wrapping her arms around his, she told him she just wanted to sit and listen with him for a bit. She wasn't ready for a movie. Holden was happy with that. She put her feet up on the couch and curled up into him positioning herself into the fetal position. Holden put his arm around her shoulder. Paige started talking about her trip and how nervous she was about going. She was worried that he would easily replace her and she would be making the biggest mistake of her life. She was scared to leave him she also repeated that she was coming back. Holden didn't say much he just listened to her nervous ramblings. He tried to reassure her the best he could but he didn't do so with confidence, he was too uncertain about their future so he just laid back in the couch holding her. The song "Save Tonight," by Eagle Eye Cherry played. They both stopped listening to the lyrics and squeezed each other as tight as they could. At the same time they leaned forward and took a sip of wine. Falling back into the couch at the same time, Paige let out a sigh as she got comfortable. Holden leaned his head back and closed his eyes listening to the music.

He began to dream that he was fucking Paige, his cock was getting hard, the dream felt very real. He soaked it in as long as he could and he woke up worried he was about to have a wet dream when he saw Paige's head in his lap as she was sucking his cock. She looked back at him, "Good morning," she said then went back to taking his cock in her mouth. "Umm, good morning." he said, he looked at his watch. It was 7 am, he was pissed he fell asleep on their last night together. Paige put extra effort into rubbing him and sucking him. Her hands glided up and down his shaft following the movements of her mouth. Holden cautioned her that he was about to cum, she told him that was okay and to make it good because it had to last him awhile. "What about you?" He asked. She looked at him "I have your anniversary present to hold me over until I get back." She continued to stroke his cock, her grip was firm but gentle as it caressed his penis. Her warm wet touch felt so great, Holden tried to block out the thought it may be the last time he would feel her touch in that manner. Her lips stroked him up and down, he twitched and began to cum. She swallowed as much of it as she could, the rest seeped out of her lips down her chin. Once she was done, she knelt up beside him and used her tongue to clean up the over flowing cum. She looked at Holden, once she did her best to clean out her mouth she kissed Holden, open mouthed, deep and passionate. She straddled his waist as they kissed. Her arms embraced him tightly. She finally stood up and looked at Holden's watch. "I guess I should shower, it's getting late." She undressed in the living room and walked into the bathroom, Holden could hear the water running and couldn't resist, he walked in to brush his teeth but really he wanted to see Paige's wet naked body under the shower faucet. He took his time brushing while watching her silhouette. Holden took a seat on the toilet to be as close to Paige as he could. She climbed out of the shower. As he watched her dry off he knew his time with her was dwindling down to mere hours, if that. Paige didn't mind him in there at all since she didn't want to be alone either. Holden followed Paige into their bedroom as she dressed. Holden fought back tears, Paige too was trying to be strong. Once she was ready Holden grabbed her bags which were full of some of her necessities for a prolonged absence from her home. He carried them down to the car and threw them in the trunk then he hurried to the passenger side to open her door for her. "A gentleman right up to the end." Paige joked. The end, those words haunted Holden but he didn't say anything to her about it. They stopped for a coffee on the way to the airport. For the remainder of the drive they quietly sipped away on their coffees through downtown traffic while the song 'Think of me.' From the *Phantom of the Opera* soundtrack played on the car's speakers. He knew it was one of Paige's favourite songs from the play but he also knew out of all the songs he put on the CD, it has the most meaning.

After Holden parked his car Paige ran and grabbed a luggage cart. Holden loaded it up and pushed it to 'departures.' The line up was long but luckily Paige printed off her boarding pass at home. The baggage drop off line was considerably shorter, short enough that when she was ready she just walked up to the counter. After she had her baggage checked she and Holden walked to security. Holden walked as slow as he possibly to prolong his time with Paige, he couldn't believe she was really leaving. Since he found out he hoped beyond all hopes she would change her mind. She didn't, she stayed strong. It was time for her to go through security. They stopped to look at each other. Holden hugged her and she eagerly hugged him back, finally let her emotions show as she began to cry. Holden felt tears running down his cheek as well but he did his best to keep them under control, he didn't want to have to walk through the busy terminal crying on the way back to his car. As they shared their embrace, the words 'Cause I'm leaving on a jet plane I don't know when I'll be back again' ran through his head. Paige finally pulled herself way from Holden to give him a kiss on the cheek. She then grabbed her carry on and turned towards the security gate.

Just before crossing through the doors she stopped and turned to

Holden one last time. She raised her fingers to her lips and blew Holden a kiss then turned and walked through the doors and she was gone. Holden waited for a minute hoping she would come running back to him, she didn't. Holden was doing his best not to break down and cry in the airport. He turned and headed back to the parking lot. The automatic doors opened wide allowing Holden started walking to his car. When the doors closed behind him he felt a rain drop land on his forehead. He looked up at the sky; the clouds were turning black then opened up in torrential down pour. Holden looked to the ground and walked impassively to his car, ignoring all the other pedestrians that were running for shelter.